CURRENCIES OF AUGUST

Donald Anderson

CKBooks

This is a work of fiction.
Any resemblance to actual persons is pure coincidence

You can contact Donald at
donald.anderson@marist.edu.

Names: Anderson, Donald R. (Donald Robert), 1944-
Title: Currencies of August / Donald Anderson.
Description: New Glarus, WI : CKBooks Publishing, [2016]
Identifiers: LCCN 2016945345 | ISBN 978-0-9832984-5-8 |
ISBN 978-0-9832984-6-5 (ebook)
Subjects: LCSH: Young men--Fiction. | College teachers--Fiction. | May-December romances--Fiction. | Man-woman relationships--Fiction. | Fathers--Death--Fiction. | Dwellings--Remodeling--Fiction. | Poughkeepsie (N.Y.)--Fiction. | LCGFT: Domestic fiction.
Classification: LCC PS3601.N44 C87 2016 (print) | LCC PS3601.N44 (ebook) | DDC 813/.6--dc23

Printed in the USA
CKBooks Publishing
PO Box 214
New Glarus, WI 53574
ckbookspublishing.com
Front cover image by Jill Battaglia
Back cover image by Paula Kelly Design

To all first grade
teachers who
inspire and amaze

INTROIT

The month of August is a muggy paradox, one worth more consideration than it is normally given. Too often we wish it away even as we cling to it. It butts up with weary insistence against the rest of the year; and for those of us—namely *most* of us—who grew up with Septembers of new beginnings, August was the soggy dread of beginning once again. It was in defiance of the movement of time. It hunkered even as we awaited the freshening that came once the beginning had begun. It was school. It was a new neighborhood or town or state. Somewhere into August we would notice, as a kind of haunting, that the sounds of summer had changed. Dawn was quieter. Evenings closed down sooner. Summering birds had already departed, their songs erased from the air. Insects were chirring with the monotony of closure. A dotting of yellow leaves floated free of birches and honeysuckle bushes. The heads of black-eyed Susans were pulling inward to concentrate on the seeding to be done. Goldfinches were already beginning to have group feastings on them. August seemed to be in search of something more presentable, something to rival the respectability of September and October—months of renewed purpose, of vividness, of a different kind of breathing and being and believing. A successful search was not impossible, given the right opportunities. It might take more than slippages of time, but that was somewhere to begin. And then, if you start to experience the belief that August is, finally, something special, you're faced with the daunting question: "Is it love?"

PART ONE

Temporary Quarters

ONE

I first met Nancy Feller, and her graceful command of time, when I was six years old. Even pre-Nancy, I was a pleasant enough kid, able to amuse myself in a way that apparently satisfied my parents during the earliest years of accommodating myself to their settled lives. They were both academics: he, curiously named Alban (like a city with its tail bobbed), was fifty-two at the time of my birth; and she, Ellen, was about a decade younger, though that was a small enough gap compared to what I would eventually be up against. To most who knew him, he was "The Professor." He taught at one of the more stately and established colleges in the area, a campus with vines and congratulatory oaks worthy of estates along the nearby Hudson River. She taught at a community college with boxy buildings and landscaping still in its infancy. They would each spend their evenings, as I remember them, secured in rooms of their own: he in what was in every way a study; she in an upstairs room with one small and insulting window. But she was "the instructor," after all, and he was indeed The Professor. Why she finally left Alban and myself to our own shaky devices shouldn't have been that difficult to understand for anyone living in that chalky environment, but as I would discover, those things we believe we understand at an early age do not always stand the test of discovery.

Well before that departure took place, Nancy Feller came into my life like a well-crafted lesson plan. She was indeed somewhat older than me, about eighteen years to be exact. I was not the first nor will I be the last to be numbingly smitten with his first-grade teacher, but, as I look back, this little boy's crush was designed to be different—designed by what, I am still trying to understand, even as I continue to test the idea that it might be better not to. She was splendid-looking, of course. She had auburn hair, a softly compressed mouth, and eyes that gazed with perfect vulnerability behind whatever kind of glasses she wore then. I didn't much notice the frames—only what was behind them. She was not overwhelmingly tall, but she had stature that was more than her simply outsizing me. As I would tell her years later, Nancy was regal and rough-edged. Her uncertainties were commanding. Her softness was crystalline. It would be a long while before I could put these impressions into language such as that, but the seedlets were planted early and surely.

Helping to build my fascination with her was the artistry of her voice. It was immediate. It was beyond reach. It warmed and chastened. It was curlicued with a young, womanly laughter that seemed never to deny itself and a passion for words that had me praying against silence. It was remarkable. She called me Jeremiah with the gratitude of one reading a favorite line of verse.

Naturally, I told Ellen about her. I doubt I told The Professor—or if I did, it was lost in the black-hole enormity of his mind. As a teacher—as opposed to a professor—Ellen enjoyed hearing about the ways of others in her profession. I suspect she was a good teacher herself, but I had no real way of knowing.

They did meet—Ellen and Nancy—on at least two occasions. "Conferencing" was that opportunity for bringing parent, teacher, and student together to untangle the ways of young people. I was there, on the perimeter of their pleasant interaction, and a mental picture survives of the two of them—from one of the conferences or a composite of the two. Ellen was slight in appearance with close-cropped hair that placed her into an immediate contrast to my teacher. Unlike Nancy, she had a precise voice, as if she were reading recipes aloud to a small gathering. Apparently she heard mostly good things about me because the picture of her tight, well-regulated smile stays with me, even now when other images cloud the picture.

The classroom where the conference took place was one of those in a school built during the Great Depression. It had the feeling of foreverness—although recently the school has been converted to condominiums. It's almost sacrilegious to imagine, and, when I pass by, the thought of entering one of those contrived residences makes my head shake. It still has tall windows that used to be manipulated by a pole with a hook on the end, but the tile half-walls the color of dried leather must be sheetrocked now and without the cool comfort I would feel beneath my small palms as I moved about the room with a first grader's need to command through touching.

Little did the parent at that meeting know that I was falling for Nancy Feller with a mysterious and annoying certainty that could only be ratified by time. Nor would Ellen be around when I first sprang that annoyance upon a very small part of the world. She had left The Professor by the time I was in junior high school. With her penchant for the definitive, she made a clean break from her career, her small colossus of a husband, and from myself. She had never seemed a selfish person while she was still in my life. She had tended to my youthful needs and willingly seemed to be friend as well as mother. She threw a baseball with a slender but accurate arm when we would play catch beneath the sugar maples outside The Professor's study. A location deliberately chosen, I suppose. She would snuggle gratefully with me to watch a video or puzzle about a book. Her occasional laughter was pleasant and yielding.

There was a time, just weeks before she disappeared, when we rode bicycles to the grounds of the Vanderbilt Mansion, one those great estates that had become part of the National Parks Service decades earlier. I had never seen her on a bicycle before; so when a new one appeared next to mine in the outbuilding where it had been stored beside lawn equipment, it was like a special announcement. It was a properly female bike with a bell aching to be sounded. I waited. A change was clearly in the wind, and I knew it would involve me. The bicycles sat side by side for two weeks, seeming to converse about the weather and hidden plans. I didn't touch mine during that waiting period: it would have been an unseen violation, and I took a special pleasure in biding my time—until she came to my room one Sunday morning in July to propose our outing. She was remarkably comfortable as we rode, her bike in the lead. She spoke of the miles of riding she had done as a young woman, speaking back over her shoulder with the confidence of a true cyclist. While I wore a helmet, she declared that she was too old to be using one now, speaking with an edge of fearlessness I had rarely heard in her voice.

The grounds of the mansion were busily peopled, but the estate had the good breeding to feel uncrowded. We stopped at a bench that had just emptied of watchers. It was one of the premier views in the valley: at the top of a steep hill maintained to look like a vertical pasture. Below was the Hudson, partially but provocatively blocked by trees that overlooked railroad tracks, the ones constructed by robber barons to move them efficiently more than a century earlier. There was the occasional sound of an Amtrak moving north or south, signaling its approach to small crossroads that led to the river. On the opposite shore was the ribbon of a freight train. Best was the view of the Catskills in the background, precisely outlined, their time-mocking magic indisputable even then.

On that day, my mother opened up, as if that bench had empowered her in a visionary way. She talked of growing up Italian in a transitional section of the Bronx. Like me, she had been an only child, something distinctly unusual in her culture. Her parents had moved back to Italy shortly after her marriage and were still alive at the time of my birth. For a while, I received cards with strange-looking money folded inside. They and the extended family lived outside of Naples in the vicinity of Sorrento, and she said how she wished to accompany me there, to help me understand why the view of the bay had been so impelling to residents and visitors over the centuries. That was the word: "accompany." That she never took me there when

I was little suggested to me that, for some reason, she never would. There was an untold story.

I loved how she gazed toward the mountains, almost unaware of me at times, before turning back to see if I understood that distant gaze. It was an explorer's look, and I imagined for years that when she left she had gone somewhere far into the west. She rarely spoke Italian, but on this day she said, *La bellezza deve essere più di un'agetto da guardare; deve essere un qualcosa in cui ci puoi entrare*: "You should do more than make beauty an object to stare at; it should be a presence you enter into." For once I can quote her directly. The phrase was so distinct, a declaration to be taken away and recorded. Her voice seemed squeezed around a phantom memory; she took such pleasure in it.

Then, in less than a month, she was gone. It was almost as if she had ridden her bicycle from the Vanderbilt overlook into her own land of renewal. It was The Professor who told me. She had packed her car while I was completing my final day of summer camp, choosing for whatever reason to avoid a farewell scene. She had taken the bicycle, and when I found the empty box of a bike-rack in the trash, it was like uncovering the outer husk of an insect. Overall, it was an incredible and unfathomable bit of self-removal. I had presumed there was little left in my parents' marriage, and I was well aware of the so-called broken homes of several schoolmates. But this was a doozy, for both its suddenness and its distinctly clean edges.

My father brought me into his study that night, the room with cherry-wood cabinetry and the smell of oiled leather and printer ink. He was never a large man, but even then, when I had almost reached adult height, I had yet to feel taller. There was also the carefully groomed beard that had always seemed necessary to his outward defenses and at this moment extended horizontally with the bristly pronouncement of violation. He rarely wore a necktie at home, but on this late afternoon he did. I can pretty well recreate his monologue, delivered in a voice that prided itself on inherited resonance: "Your mother has left us, Jeremiah. She has chosen to no longer be a part of our lives. *Where* she has gone is none of our business, apparently. *Why* she has gone we are also not privileged to know." He paused, gazing at his hands. "Unless, that is, she said something to you. You did have a kind of closeness."

I assured him I knew nothing.

Had I known I would be recalling this years later, when he too was gone, I might have done a better job of absorbing his words and actions. But some things survive better with a touch of inexactness. He concluded his brief announcement by telling me that we, of course, would make do and move ourselves steadily forward. We would "endure." I thought I heard a catch in his glorious voice, but I doubted it.

The next day he shaved off his beard, as if it had never been there. It made him look for, a time, ashen and puckered but ready to move on. And by implication, so would I. There was plenty of room for resentment within me, but our hour at the mansion kept suggesting that her departure was an unspoken gift given by her to me. It almost made sense, and Professor Alban Curtin, through his stewardship of indifference, did in a way help me feel it would be easier to repurpose myself with her clean departure to guide me.

When I began my own uncertain attempt at teaching, I finally began to receive sporadic e-mails from Ellen. They were her first communications in a dozen years. There had been no birthday greetings, no Christmas cards. I had grown used to her complete absence from my life, and hearing from her now was more startling than heartening. How she knew where I was teaching—or *that* I was teaching—was another piece of the puzzle that was her. More than once an e-mail would say she was well and, among other things, grateful for her life. She would sign it with her maiden and married names, "Ellen Scarsella Curtin," but said nothing about where she was, what she was doing, or when we might meet again. I was tempted to ask, but within each of her brief communiqués she urged me not to write back. Her most revealing request may have been that which read "Be content without me. It will serve you by saving you so much."

Whether her new life was a commitment to total self-absorption, I had no way to know. But I accepted her request for a time, as if I was offering a palpable gift to a phantom recipient.

TWO

It would be two full decades after I first sat in her room of low-rise desks before I met Nancy again. I certainly hadn't planned to. She was as reasonably out of my life as the soul of an enthralled first-timer could allow her to be. Our year together had brought me through the fog of first-grade adjustments. I was probably motivated to be a better student than I might have been. Even though I had a pair of academics for parents, I might easily have resisted the obvious task of emulating them. But who can know? I read feverishly in and outside of class, learned my multiplication tables, identified the states and their capitals on blank maps, and generated report cards with warm praises written on them. It barely occurred to me, however, that the conclusion of that first year would have me moving on to someone else, someone less enchanting. By the end of summer, I finally accepted the reality of having to face a new classroom, and I had at least composed a note to hand to my Mrs. Feller when I saw her. It was my first piece of serious writing, a labor of many August evenings as I drafted and redrafted. It was a confession of my feelings about our year together—not a love letter exactly, but a piece of sincere homage little more than twenty words in length—on a piece of unlined construction paper intended to survive through the ages. On it, I had pasted a magazine cutout of a pear, my favorite fruit. Even in my ardent young mind, an apple would have been an overplay of sincerity.

The note was never to be delivered, however, because Nancy Feller was gone. In her classroom was a man, dark-skinned and very tall, and every bit the unfulfillment of expectation. It was the second-grade teacher, Mrs. Holst, who told me that my enchanted lady had left "to become a mother." She said it like she was unsure whether she should tell me, but she did so efficiently, as if she knew the extent of my loss. Later in the day, I tore apart the note and fed it in shreds down a urinal.

And that was that. Nancy Feller would not come back until the tendrils of coincidence began to wind their way into my adult life. It was with some annoyance that I found myself pursuing the same career as my parents—when I had every reason not to. It made me feel cheap and unimaginative at times that I was not only trailing after Ellen and The Professor, but that I was still in the Hudson Valley—at another college at least. As an undergraduate, I had tested other possible paths, ones that might lead me to a career in law or archeology or even business. But the pull was too strong. If teaching was not necessarily in my blood, it *was* in my overall wiring. The idea of teaching as I imagined teaching should be done was like a fanfare in my brain as I trolled my way through graduate school in the Southwest and tucked my doctoral diploma in a drawer, thinking its presence on a wall too much like self-congratulation. I would have taught anywhere, but that fanfare-force brought me back to the land of my childhood, my brittle upbringing, and to Nancy.

It was unreasonable to link Michael Feller on my Freshman Writing roster to the other person I'd known with that last name. It wasn't until Nancy came into my office two-thirds of the way through his—and my—first semester that the tendrils became visible. But there she was. Her hair was nearly the same shade of auburn, and her voice still had the same buoyant serenity; but she no longer wore glasses, a small fact that troubled me then and for a while afterward.

Michael was an interesting classroom presence. He seemed genuinely attentive, wasn't openly tied to any electronic device that I could ever see, but spoke rarely—and usually in the form of short utterances when he did. He was obviously fascinated with a gingery young woman who sat in front of him but not to the point of complete distraction. The problem was that he wouldn't write. He had turned in no work, in spite of accelerating pleas and my unvoiced fear of being inconsequential to one of my very first students. I even asked Willie, the young woman, if they were friends enough for them to work together. She replied, "Not likely," with curt dismissiveness, though she was one of the peevishly outstanding students in that group of nineteen.

It was Nancy who set up the interview after midterm grades were released. It was one of those late-October afternoons in the Hudson Valley that slices into you. It was just after what people call The Peak, an unmeasurable outshoot of time when the turning trees are their most perplexing. Much of the leaf-fall has already taken place, and the ones that remain, with no purpose but to let go, are at their most vivid. They wave slightly, modestly, but with such an articulation of beauty that one almost has to turn away.

After twenty years, her first words after introductions were, "I hope you won't take it too personally that you're the only teacher he's not doing well with."

I didn't know how to prioritize the several new elements of important business. "Given all that, it's difficult not to personalize."

Her smile had changed little over time, except for a few new facial lines to reinforce that look of soft command. "It really isn't all that much," she said. She looked at me with a kind of curiosity, a wideness of pleasant unknowing. "I get the sense you're new to all this." Her eyes gazed around my rather tiny office with its view of a shopping center. Michael, meanwhile, sat comfortably in the chair next to hers. He seemed to have his own kind of unknowing, not as immediately pleasant as his mother's but one that fit his crunched-upon posture like a pillow.

"All what, do we mean?"

"Teaching?"

"On the contrary, Mrs. Feller, I've been around teachers and teaching most of my life. They've taught me everything I know and a whole lot more."

"Things you'd like to forget?" She was dressed in a businesslike outfit of pants, blouse, and navy-blue jacket. She was buttoned securely, but for a moment I had the embarrassing thought that beneath it all were breasts I had sublimated for twenty years. Breasts. I was thinking about her midlife breasts. I felt chagrined and puzzled.

"What is it?"

It was a head-shaking moment. "I started teaching in August, if that's what you were wondering. So, yes, I'm new to this part of things—the meeting-with-a-parent-of-a-student-who-doesn't-wish-to-meet-with-me."

She glanced at Michael. "I thought you said you'd been in to meet with Mr. Curtin."

"*Doctor* Curtin," I corrected.

"My apologies. I didn't mean to slight you." She appeared to take enjoyment. She seemed to know *something*. And she was taking advantage of that something, whatever it was.

"It's silly of me. It's a new little badge I wear. Hopefully I can tuck it in a drawer soon."

"Then let's try calling you 'Professor.'"

"Let's not."

"What then?" We clearly were not talking about Michael.

"We'll find something."

"No need. Michael will start producing for you, I'm sure."

We all paused, even her son, in the middle of the extended pause he had been taking since coming into the office. I looked at him. He had an air that was gloriously restful and satisfying, as if his mother had given birth to an already-answered question—one needing not to be asked again with conscious insistency. But what it was...?

I had been standing since they arrived, my back to a corner formed by the window-wall and a bookcase. The oddness of it finally pushed me into my seat. "Okay, Michael. Let's try it just for fun. Why won't you write for me?"

I had stunned him in some way, but he finally spoke. "Write?"

"You *can* write, can't you?"

I saw his mother frown for the first time. "Michael can write."

"*Plenty*," he added.

"'Plenty,' is it?" I was starting to love him in an envious way.

Nancy beamed with her own detached aura of mother-love. I could have hugged both of them and given thanks for the eddies of emotion that come unexpectedly. I didn't.

"Michael has been writing since he was three," she instructed. "He wrote his first story about a river that became a mandarin orange."

Nor was that startling. "I'll hope to read it sometime."

"I still have it."

Of course she did.

Michael shifted in his seat with the look of having been talked about far too much already. He was handsome in his own peculiar way—handsomer the more one looked at him. But it was like the good looks of a weathered statue—odd in a college freshman. He was wearing a flannel shirt and shorts, even though the weather had become noticeably colder in the days since midterms. He had what appeared to be the end of a harmonica protruding slightly from a shirt pocket, and I could almost imagine him feathering a sea chantey on some bleak but inviting coast. When I would watch him leaving class, he had that look of someone pushing against the edge of a natural limit—even as he appeared most of the time to be following the young woman who rose from the seat in front of him.

I tried addressing him directly again. "'Plenty' would seem to have room for an English composition or two, Michael."

"I suppose."

"What would you like to write about? I'm the teacher. I'm God. We could create an assignment for you and you alone, if you'd like."

"I don't think that would be fair," he replied.

His mother nodded. "I would agree, even if you are God."

My next question, to her, was spontaneous and unguarded. "Do you still teach?"

She grasped her chair arms with strong fingers—stronger than I remembered. "What makes you assume I teach?"

"A lucky guess."

She laughed pleasantly. So did Michael. "Do you have a built-in teacher-detector?" she asked.

"At times."

"Pretty cool," he volunteered. "Mom used to teach. She sells houses and stuff now."

"I taught a long time ago, Michael." She looked at me with her unprotected eyes relishing the moment. "Would you like to see my certificate? I still have it."

"But why the hell would you ever stop?" I was stunned with my own brashness.

She was as well. "Pardon me, Professor?"

"I'm so sorry. My crudeness sometimes gets me in doodoo."

"Doodoo," Michael intoned.

Nancy's eyes had misted ever so slightly, pulling at something from within. "You're a puzzling person, Professor Curtin. Are you always so possessive of your students' parents?"

"Never once." Then suddenly, "Is that what it seems like?"

"Yes. Yes, it does. It's unbecoming." I was certain she had used the same word on occasions a long time ago—a somewhat embroidered word of disapproval. Very schoolmarm. Very appropriate to the graceless situation at hand.

We were rescued by the appearance of my department chair in the open doorway. I realized I should have closed the door for business purposes, that there was probably a protocol about these things. More importantly, I thought of the last few sentences of dialogue drifting into the great, grasping ears of Phyllis Friel. While I was being interviewed by the search committee, her ears had consumed so much of my attention I was certain I had blown my chance to be hired—that and the fact that she knew my father to be an "inestimable" scholar. An adjective of that many syllables had felt like a net of judgment dropping over me and caused a partial plate to peek with wicked accusation from the side of her mouth.

"I beg your pardon, Dr. Curtin." Phyllis said it with an almost scatological downward swoop. "I had no idea you were engaged."

"We were just leaving," Nancy Feller assured her.

"But we haven't settled anything yet"—and I realized that was an especially stupid bottom line to cast before the lady with the ears.

Dr. Friel was decidedly unruffled, and I doubted, in fact, if a ruffle would dare to approach her. "Just a reminder that we have a meeting now." She smiled bleakly. "Excuse my having to interrupt." And she was gone.

Nancy and Michael had stood. She had a hand on the back of Michael's neck, preparing to steer him through the door and into a kind of nobody's land. We *had* accomplished nothing. The mystery of Michael was unsolved. Her pop-up presence in my life was ridiculous but incongruously challenging. And, worst of all for that moment, I had no idea what meeting I was late for, where it was, and whether I even knew about it or had simply forgotten. *A meeting.* It was one of the things about The Academy I had been warned of, and here it announced itself on the same day I tried to convince myself I would in no way be drawn once more into fantasy fixations that had been put to rest with the swallow of a urinal.

THREE

I studied Michael in class for the next two weeks. He continued to sit like a happy gnome, staring over one shoulder or the other of Willie Furman. It was clear he had feelings for her, though, in Michael's case, feelings would prove difficult to categorize. Willie at least got him to communicate, though not with me. Their chatter before and after class was invitingly bumptious (especially on her part), and I would occasionally try to break in on these exchanges as a path to Michael. It never worked. Usually they both shut up.

Willie was not what one would call a beauty, but she was striking in a roughhewn way. She had a kind of military walk and defiantly good posture, and coppery eyes that could put you in your place, even if you didn't know you were being out of place. I admired her voice. It was carefully modulated, becoming dramatic at times—a voice she seemed to enjoy and came from a mouth that was usually embellished by bizarre shades of lipstick. She had interesting hands, and she wrote in her first essay—a piece of autobiography—about the intensity she achieved from learning to play on a parlor organ that had come down from generation to generation in her family. I happily pictured her pumping the slanted foot pedals with combat boots on her feet. She claimed her primary goal in life was to pound a Bach fugue out of what she referred to (in capital letters) as a "GIANT FUCKING WURLITZER," that she might study the organ seriously someday, but for now she was happy to shake a couple of walls. It was one of the few things I liked about teaching so far: that you were able to drop into an occasional composition that felt candid enough to shake your own inner walls. It received an A for both form and content, and her second essay concluded with an original Italian-style sonnet about the flatulence of field mice, having nothing to do with the rest of the piece. Still, it was irresistible, and I included a couple of quatrains about air fresheners in my comments. My versification wasn't nearly as good as hers.

I decided I would try once more to reach Michael through Willie. She looked at me suspiciously when I asked her to stop by my office if she had a chance. There had always been a slice of her that seemed to be contesting even when she was contributing congenially and perceptively to classroom discussion—and even while her essays continued to demonstrate a pleasure in what she was doing. She clearly loved the engagement of ideas and wrote not so much as if she had something to prove as to celebrate a world of discoveries that had glazed into conviction.

She came one afternoon in November, during the quiet week before Thanksgiving. Unlike Michael, who still dressed for summer, she was bundled against gray skies and damp winds that blew up the river. She remained a bundle through our brisk and brief conversation.

"Did I screw up?" she asked without preliminaries.

"Hardly likely," I assured her.

"No. *Very* likely. I can be a major screw-up. Not that you need to know that."

As I watched her, I saw an underlay of sadness I'd not sensed before. For some reason now, she was without the protective layer of brilliance and constructed self-assurance that served her impressively.

"I would agree. I probably didn't need to know that."

"So now you do." She was still standing, folding her arms around her. "I'm bad—as bad as I can be. And it sucks out."

"Sit. I can get us coffee or tea or whatever."

"Vodka?"

I laughed. "Not likely; not even tempting. I don't drink."

"You should. Then you might be a little less weird. Or smoke a bone. Loosen your head strings."

"They're tight, are they?"

"Most likely."

"I appreciate the diagnosis. They may have gotten tighter in the last couple of minutes. Sit, please."

"I don't need to. What's this about?"

"Michael Feller. Your buddy."

"My buddy?" She snickered briefly. "Do you want me to rat him out?"

"Not in the least. I'm just having a hard time reaching him. I was looking for help."

"Why don't you try his mother again?"

"Ah."

"Mike doesn't need help."

"Because he has *you*?"

"Hah."

"We've reduced our conversation to tiny words."

She flapped her arms slightly. "Good deal. And on that note..."

"You're a piece of work, Willie. Do you smoke before you play the organ?"

She had moved toward the door before turning back. "Sometimes. It loosens my strings...and my wings."

"It must be quite an experience."

"Try it. See how it feels."

"I'll let you know."

"You remember that corny stuff about the family parlor organ?"

"Sure do."

"I made it up."

And that was that. Another failure. Perhaps a worse failure. I wondered whether I had crossed some faculty-student line. Had I gotten too personal, even as our words kept shrinking in front of us? There was, I realized, no guide-book for these kinds of situations. The beauty of college teaching, I had supposed in my first weeks, was that it was basically an improvisation. The rules should be grounded in common sense and occasional puffs of inspiration. The learning should be created in moments, rather than predetermined. At least in my field. However, as I stood there I realized I had learned nothing in these two minutes. Why had a student who had done exceptional work for me suddenly taken such an obvious dislike of me? And then...why was she as hard on herself as she was on me.

§

My very first semester in this profession would soon end, and I was provided a token of redemptive encouragement by a senior colleague who believed in the power of the syllabus. Charles Gillis was the type to pop into my cubbyhole of an office for visits. "Chuck" he liked to be called, even by newcomers. An odd choice for one who generally wore a suit and tie. He had taught for more than forty years at this same school, had never married, was on campus from early morning until late evening, and was rumored to sleep in his office on occasion. He liked to think of himself as an institutional founder, though the school had existed for more than a half-century before his arrival. Nonetheless, his nostalgia could be useful in a decidedly boring, monologic way. It gave me a sense of the recent history of the place, its evolution from a primarily male campus to one where 60 percent of the student population was now women. It had proven to be a struggle for him.

"You know," he told me for no apparent reason in early December, "one of the changes I've noticed over the years is there are so many female students. There are more and more all the time. Have you noticed that? And they have gotten taller—the females, that is. I don't know what to make of it. I realize I've lost an inch or so from my more vigorous days—which is enough by itself. And it *will* happen in the mysterious future to you as well."

"I'm sure it will. I'll let you know when the time comes."

He chortled ungracefully. "A young person's joke. I won't be here, of course." His once-blond hair was mostly gray now, but it still gave him an aura of freshness, that and the smooth roundings of his cheeks. They were playground pink at the moment, even as he spoke of his own death.

"In that case, I'll think about you."

"I can't wait."

Why he took any sort of pleasure in these visits to me was a puzzle. He had a large and comfortable office in another wing of the building, two doors from the Dean. Gillis was our eighteenth-century person, though he rarely if ever published in his field and seemed more attracted to conferences about science fiction. He may have been looking for an acolyte when he first pulled me aside at a greet-the-majors event to see if I had any peculiar interests of my own. I assured him that "Speculative Fiction," as he called it, made me intellectually and emotionally woozy—like reading cereal boxes. He wasn't offended but indicated that I might come to an appreciation of it with the right kind of maturation. Perhaps he dropped in on this occasion to see if I was putting forth promising shoots. Or perhaps he was lonely and knew I wouldn't resist his soliloquizing.

"It's not just that they're tall," he went on, "but they keep getting taller. Is it something in the modern diet? With so many of them I end up talking at their chins. Or their breasts." I had learned early on that he was a "boob man." It went beyond covert glances; he also took a confiding pleasure in talking about them.

"The trouble with that," he elucidated, "is where to locate one's eyes. I mean, I know they're in my head, but where to look?"

"I'm a little taller than you," I said consolingly, "so I haven't run into that problem yet."

"You will."

"I'm sure."

From there, he went on to talk about the beauty of a new syllabus. He had already constructed his for the next semester as a way of coping with the frustrations arising from his current courses. "It's not as if I'm so all-fired conscientious that I get things done ahead of time. But I'm a neoclassicist. I need order. And there's nothing more orderly than a virgin syllabus, even if it's one you've used before. Doesn't matter,

Jeremiah. I like that name, by the way. Very prophetic. 'Let the judgment run down as the waters, etc. etc.'"

"I think that was the prophet Amos."

"Whatever. I had a priest when I was quite young who could make the waters run down your pant leg when he recited that. Thrilling stuff."

"Undoubtedly, Chuck." I had actually thought of asking him about my Michael Feller problem—the voice of experience and all that. I now realized I would have to wait for a more inspired source than my senior colleague, who often seemed, as he did on this day, to be awaiting advice from me.

He was about to leave when Willie Furman returned with Michael Feller in tow. She had him by the wrist, her now mittened hand clamped around it like a mossy handcuff. She nodded briskly at Gillis, dismissing his presence as of little consequence, before saying to me in a bell-like voice, "If you think he's a baboon, I'll show you his butt. Whatever makes you happy." I assumed Michael had no idea why he had been commandeered for this appearance, but her off-kilter championing of him at first drew a glow from his face that quickly melted into astonishment as the words sank in. He seemed on the verge of swooning when she spun him around and led him through the doorway. The mingled sound of her work boots and his high-top sneakers made a babble of departure that was strangely pleasant to listen to, particularly since I had been reduced to silence.

It was Gillis who made an analytical attempt at putting the atmospheric furniture back in order. His face had taken on a plaster-like fixity during the invasion. "I don't know if I would consider that insufferably rude or a pinch of high drama, but once, and once only, before I retire, I would be pleased to have that happen in my office."

And that was that: his aura of personal seclusion shadowed him into the hallway.

FOUR

And then Nancy reached out to me again. It was just before finals while I was reflecting on what the whole teaching thing had amounted to so far. I had gone into a profession neatly parroting that of my parents: one of whom had cleanly brushed me from her life and the other who had apparently handed her the brush and made his own work look like the paradise of the self-righteous. I had wished to be anything else. It was a phantom life that stood before me with a Do Not Enter sign through college and even into graduate school.

But there was that incredibly persuasive pull. Always. Edgar Allan Poe had called it "The Perverse," the allowing of one's better judgment to be violated by its opposite. And look what happened to him. I had taught Poe during this first semester in one of my introductory courses because I knew students would be drawn in even if they hated reading, which most of them did. I had been right about him at least. Most of them loved the besotted self-tormentor. They were never quite alert to the way he questioned their own right to think of themselves as the rational Olympians of the animal kingdom, but they read him at least. On the other hand, I got it. I was spitting in the face of all reasonableness—the instructive nature of my past and the clear future of my students. In addition to Michael, who would not write, there were several who would not read, who quite reasonably in their own minds should not be expected to read, who would enter the classroom without a book, a notebook, or anything to set before them and seemed rightly satisfied. How long could my own fascination with the words people recorded stand up to their indifference? And who was to say they were wrong? Could even Alban Curtin withstand this glacial advance? I certainly wasn't going to ask him. I needed a sign, and Nancy possibly knew that. Possibly.

Rather than phoning, e-mailing, or texting, she had sent a brief note sealed inside a lime green envelope and neatly return-addressed. The flap had scallops around the edge, a detail that made any inclination to resist remembered-love curl like a sigh within me. It was like a cumulus cloud had been inserted into the general emptiness of my mailbox. She had perfect handwriting, of course, the work of fingers that apparently still relished the feel of a pen. Someday, I knew, handwriting would be gone altogether, and I would miss what I had actually seen very little of in my short, digital lifetime.

The note was brief and elliptical:

Dear Professor,

It would appear we have both misunderstood Michael. It's no one's fault, but a letdown on our part nonetheless. Perhaps we should talk one more time to see what we can learn from this. My schedule is generally flexible.

Sincerely,
Nancy Feller

She included a phone-number and an e-mail address after her signature.

There was more to contemplate. What was it we had jointly misunderstood? In what way were we joint owners of a letdown? And a letdown of what? Of Michael, certainly, but of ourselves and each other? Lord. Had she always had a cuteness with language that would have been lost on a six-year-old, however precocious he might have thought himself to be? Or was this a recent acquisition she was now trying out on college teachers? And had she said she was in real estate? If so, was this a twisted little pitch to market an idea? And if that was the case, what was the idea?

I spoke to Michael one last time before our final class together. He had had perfect attendance. He had never been late. He continued carrying his notebook and the course reader. He turned the pages when he was supposed to, and he often wrote in the notebook. It was not for me to know *what* he wrote, but he generally eyed what he had entered with nods of pleasure. I suspect that often he drew rather than wrote, and at times before class, he would hand the notebook, opened to a specific page, to Willie in front of him. She seemed to find her own pleasure in it. Meanwhile, she continued to submit quality work and dialogued with me in class as if she valued me on some unknown level. She seemed to enjoy it, her metallic eyes flashing at me with the keenness of a person in charge. If she and Michael had any aftershocks from her baboon rant, they never showed it.

I asked him to stay after class for a minute. Willie looked at me disapprovingly but left the room without him, glancing back from the doorway. He stood before the lectern with the softness he could spin around himself when doing something he hadn't chosen to do, the top of his harmonica peeping above a shirt pocket again. "I thought I would give it one more try," I told him.

"Try?"

"To find out why you're unhappy in here."

"I...I feel happy."

"You *feel* happy or you *are* happy?"

"What?"

"I think there's a distinction, though I'm not sure I can explain it."

"No need. It's all good."

"All?"

He didn't add anything. He stood with much of the serenity I associated with his mother, though I realized I had only seen her once in twenty-some years, for five minutes in a fidgety office. I thought about Michael's father. I knew nothing of him. In fact, I had never imagined him, even when Mrs. Holst had told me Mrs. Feller was going away to become a mother. If I imagined anything at that time, it must have been my version of an immaculate conception, well before I knew the notion had once reached larger proportions. But what would a *Mr.* Feller possibly be like? How much of Michael was actually traceable to him? I stopped wondering. I wouldn't do to Michael what I wouldn't do to myself.

"Never mind," I told him. "You may be way ahead of me. But it doesn't bother you this was all for nothing?"

"This?"

"This course."

He stared calmly at me for several moments—then said "Wrong" with simple conviction and left the room.

§

About the same time as this minor pedagogical upheaval was going on, there was a period of what was called "campus unrest" unfolding in the vicinity of my building. The concept of tenure seemed to provoke constant uneasiness within the academic community and beyond. While I understood its importance to preserving the free-flowing right of faculty members to think and say what they wished, I also understood those who saw it as a path to *not* thinking at all once the tenure gates were secured behind them. It was an issue I hoped I would not have to think about, that I would escape it by magically surviving without it, by fastening myself to an institution where tenure did not exist or by leaving teaching—my solution for many academic puzzles. I would ignore it as long as I could and then reroute myself appropriately, a shift that was still five years away. Until, however, the issue came suddenly closer than I could have imagined.

Barbara Lynn Hynes taught women's studies and could be unconventional in her teaching and campus behavior. Her class sessions were times of excited debate and unrestrained language, as I knew from conducting my own sedate sessions in Classics next to her. I was forced during some of her peak moments to close my door, but usually I knew the pulsations from her classroom could serve as a way of nudging my own students to consciousness. And I admired her immensely. She had taken an interest in me during my first weeks and would ask me, in the corridor, if her class had been too stirring. I would encourage her to keep stirring away and keep me hopeful about my own ability to reach a level of creative agitation approaching hers.

She often walked with me to our office wing, decompressing from her just-completed session and chiding me for shaking my head at her ambling narratives. She was an impelling person with an uncontrolled blaze of red hair, taut cheeks, and large hooped earrings. What I loved most about her, though, was her rich Mississippi accent, where the southern veneer seemed at odds with the bombast of her language. I was stimulated by visits to her office, where the walls were covered in slogans and where she had added touches of paint to overlay the generic sameness faculty offices were supposed to maintain. According to her, "the bigs" had not been amused.

There were many of my colleagues who apparently felt demeaned by her. It was as if she represented a realm of conviction and performance they were incapable of ascending to. That was my guess at least. She *did* intimidate me, but in a way that gave me wisps of buoyancy rather than the belief of some that she was a dooming presence that had entered their stable lives. For others, it was obvious she was too "southern." Even the placid Chuck Gillis referred to her as a hick, and it was clear he couldn't imagine that hair and that accent being wrapped around a worthy mind. Apparently the tenure committee had felt the same way.

Professor Hynes had somehow managed to keep her tenure denial from her students until December. Initially, she refused to say why she had kept the secret, but once the news was out and the students were storming the battlements, she told me she hated a martyr who wasn't willing to be shot at dawn—and she doubted she was. I doubted her doubt. The protests went on for several days, into finals week. The media was called in; students chanted outside administrative offices;

there was an attempt at a general strike defused by many of the tenured faculty and others who threatened their classes with more rigorous exams and automatic failure for those protesting rather than taking their finals. The provost announced a willingness to "review her files," and many realized the phrase meant the issue was dead and properly buried. Barbara Lynn told me at one point that she was embarrassed to be the cause of something that could only end up "lookin' laak peed pants."

I had finally joined with the students and a handful of my colleagues in carrying placards and petitioning for fairness. I may have been nostalgic for long ago times on campuses when protest was commonplace. More, I think, I had developed a strong sense of loyalty to the woman with the streaming red hair whom I could imagine advancing across a battlefield in an oversized French painting. She thanked me, whereas my dean chastised me. He was a withered man at a relatively young age, still trying to grow a moustache that would fit him properly but looked instead like dying sphagnum. He stopped me returning to my office after one of the protests and warned me with chilling conviction that there could be "repercussions." I asked him if that was in the nature of advice or a threat, and he thrust his hands into his pockets as if he was measuring the opportunity to pee his own pants. Education was everywhere.

§

I tried e-mailing Nancy. There was no response for two or three days. Finally, on an afternoon when my head hurt from grading exams, I called her provided number, not knowing if it was a cell or landline, home or office. The voice at the other end was familiar enough. When the answerer intoned a "howdy-doo," it was clear I had reached her at home.

"Is this Michael?"

"Could be."

"Yes. So it could." I heard pleased laughter.

"This is Jeremiah Curtin."

"The teacher?" I could hear Willie Furman's voice asking "Who is it?" in the background.

"The teacher man," he told her.

"Curtin?"

"Sure."

Suddenly, there was a brisk "Let me talk." Presumably she'd taken the phone, but she said nothing at first.

"The inevitable Miss Furman?" I finally asked.

"Certainly."

"Why am I speaking to you?"

"Who'd you want to speak to?" There was a radiant challenge in her voice. The fog in my brain suddenly cleared, and I found myself grateful for her presumption. It had a clanging kind of sexiness.

"I'm not sure that's your business."

"Whose, then?"

"You *are* bad, aren't you?"

"I told you," she challenged. She spoke to Michael, pulling the phone slightly away from her mouth. "My guess is that he doesn't want to talk to either one of us. That leaves Nancy." Interesting. It was all becoming more and more interesting.

"She's not here," I could hear him say. "She's meeting Dad." Then I heard harmonica music, skillful and meditative.

On so many levels, I had entered a home that was not an abstraction but, of course, a place of woven lives and purposes. While modern phoning seemed to be putting an end to communication, this was proving an exception. I would see my students outside of class with their cells to their ears, but they would not see me. They had in their own minds satisfied themselves on the propriety of avoiding one of the most precious of human activities: making eye-contact. I realized I was only a few years older, a longtime owner of mobiles, but there were moments I wanted to jump up and down in front of them—on a sidewalk, in a corridor, crossing a parking lot—and remind them that a few minutes ago we had spoken in the same room about lines they had written or the severe beauty of Laura Wingfield blowing out candles. The disconnect, the segmentation was a threat to me in some way. Be organic, I wanted to tell them. Don't just recognize my existence. Recognize my presence. If they heard, it would be gone in a few steps. It would be flushed away.

But here in the Feller household was something different. Maybe the organic could still be reached through the right wires: mother, father, son, a strangely loyal girlfriend. Eye-contact. Sea chantey music. It made me fretful, and there was nothing more to talk about.

"Is there a message?" Willie asked.

"There's always a message," I said.

"Clever."

"But there's not always a messenger."

I hung up, thumbing the edges of piled exam books, gauging the unspoken and communal texture of them. For just an instant, I wished for each student's forgiveness.

FIVE

"I would like to take you to coffee."

Nancy Feller was standing in the doorway of my apartment. It was a week before Christmas, and on the outside of the door I had hung a large Santa face, which now peered at her companionably. She held a small bell in her hand, which had evidently fallen from him when she knocked.

"Season's greetings." Her cheeks were a beautifully December red.

"How did you know where I live?"

"That will be my secret for now." She gave the bell a shake.

"Would you like to come in?"

She tugged at the top button of her coat. "The request was to take you to coffee."

"I don't drink coffee."

"My god. And someone told me you don't drink."

"Spies are everywhere."

"Yes."

"I generally don't *drink* drink. There are *some* liquids I swallow."

"Well, that will have to do. Get your coat."

It was late afternoon, and the pastel pink and gray of the sky was evaporating quickly. We were on foot, heading to a place she assured me was nearby. My apartment was one of many cobbled out of Rhinebeck houses dating back to the late 1700s, mine being half of the original first floor, complete with a large fireplace and an impressive number of bookshelves. Since moving in, I had only attempted one fire, which had downdrafted smoke in an incompetent, tenderfoot way. I had female companionship to share that inaugural fire, a perky sometime friend from the Registrar's Office. But with her professed dislike of most anything unexpected, we weren't headed toward a relationship in any event. The smoke had merely hastened our realization. The bookshelves were still empty. I had grown up with a love of the physical book, but most of my recent acquisitions had been electronic. One of The Professor's comments about squeezing the published word into a "plastic box the size of an appointment calendar" was demoralizing to contemplate. But I did dust the shelves from time to time to keep their freshly painted look of expectation intact.

Walking beside Nancy Feller gave me the quiet sense of doing a Winter Wonderland routine even though there had been only brief December dustings of snow so far. She wore ladylike boots quite unlike Willie Furman's decisive stompers, yet they still gave Nancy a purposeful stride and seeming pleasure. Or perhaps the pleasure was mine. Our pace synchronized easily and for a time substituted for talking. Rhinebeck, especially in winter, presents itself as a quintessentially perfect village—and it has consciously striven for decades to *be* so. It has an intersection at its center that is buttoned into place by small shops and old restaurants. It has a grid of streets with houses that are asked to conform honorably to the periods in which they were constructed. On this evening, it was seasonally accentuated with wreaths and garlanding. It smelled clean and essential.

"You do drink hot chocolate?" she finally said.

"In moments of misplaced weakness."

"We'll see, then."

We were standing in front of a shop I had not seen before, down one of the side alleys off Market Street. I didn't, in fact, recall turning down the alley, an arc in our short journey that felt like a kind of witchery on Nancy's part. She opened the door and escorted me into a coffee shop not much bigger than my campus office. The walls were brick with an overlay of finely detailed shelving in colors of bluish-gray and pink, very like the night sky we had stepped under just before. The smell was a mixture of coffee beans, chocolate, and pine from candles and bakery objects resting with unpardonable innocence inside a glass case that cut the room in half. Four small tables crowded one corner, each empty at this hour.

"We close in fifteen minutes," the only person in the shop warned us. He was an unreasonably thin man for this place of temptation and he wore tinted sunglasses, though I think that only occurred to me at a later time.

It was cappuccino for Nancy and the hot chocolate for me—and a cannoli apiece. It was she who ordered and paid. A nod of her head finally unfroze me.

"Allow me a moment to come back to reality, Mrs. Feller."

"How interesting. Where exactly were you? And call me Nancy."

"No, thank you. Some other time. This is all very nice of you, but now that I've re-entered and discovered myself staring at a cup of whipped cream, I need to ask what's going on?"

"What do you mean, Professor?"

"And don't call me that, please."

"I'd forgotten. And what shall we call each other?"

"Let's try 'you' for now."

She was eating the pastry with evident satisfaction. "That will have to do then. I do love foods that have no respect for healthy desires. Are you opposed to sweets?"

I watched the proprietor licking his slender fingers, though I hadn't seen him eating. "Look," I finally said, "I don't want to seem disrespectful—or unappreciative—or how about awkward?—but I've seen you once for a few minutes in my office with your son weaving his personalized reality, then I get a note from you—on pale green paper, no less—and I send a couple of e-mails—to which you didn't respond—and then I call your house and end up talking to your son's brass-bottomed girlfriend, and finally you appear at the door of my apartment, which I have no idea how you knew the location of—or even how you got into the building—and then you whisk me into the night like the Salagadoola lady from Cinderella, you steer me into this shop where lips come to smack, you buy me cocoa and a goodie that's staring up at me like a come-hither finger, and I'm flabbergasted into a temporary coma until I finally hear shop bells tingling in my brain. So what's what?"

"I feel like I know you."

"Oh, my god. That?"

"What?" she asked.

"What do you mean 'what'?"

"What do you mean 'What do you mean'?"

"Drink your coffee."

She had lost her aura of genial command and stared at her hands laced around the holiday mug in front of her. It was the look of a sibyl reading tea leaves. Her fingers were trim but athletic, and her nails were coated with forest green patches. It was the first I had noticed them, and I fought to keep myself from smiling.

"Then what did you mean," I asked, "when you said we had both misunderstood Michael?"

"My little green letter." She seemed to be recalling something that had left her forever in spite of my having just mentioned it. The sound was that of a lament. "I wrote it when I realized how delicate expectations can be. I saw you standing there in your office—you were standing, weren't you?"

"I couldn't imagine sitting. Don't ask me why."

"It was like you were hovering above your ideals about teaching and whatever else. You looked suddenly afraid of them. It made you a little snappish." She paused. "But that doesn't matter. It was darling."

"An interesting word."

"You were seeing Michael from the point of view of a teacher's failure. I was seeing him from the point of view of a parent's. But is it a failure that we care so much about an individual who in no way believes that he is a failure? He's not."

"Then why did he totally write me off—so to speak?"

"But we don't know that he did." She paused again, looking fixedly at me. "I need to call you *something*."

"Jeremiah will do."

"Then you will call me Nancy."

"No."

"Why *is* that?"

"No particular reason." She was bemused again. "Are you saying he had his own reason for doing what he was doing—or not doing?"

"Of course he did. A perfectly understandable one."

"Which is...?"

"I have no idea. Do you? Have you ever not done a thing because it was the thing you were supposed to do?"

"Constantly."

"And did you feel the world was watching you because of it?"

"Not usually."

"I think, for Michael, it's a way for him to peer at the world and see if it's interested in him or not. Perhaps, Jeremiah, you were a window he could look out of." She seemed to consider what she had said to see if it made sense to her. Then she added, "And I imagine the reverse might also be true...that once in a rare moment a student is a window a teacher can look out of. Why not? And, besides, cappuccino has a way of making me say whatever might be worth saying whether it is or not. It's the way the vapors reach the brain, I think."

"Vapors."

"Yes, certainly."

The shopkeeper was preparing to close, and he offered to box my untouched cannoli and her half-eaten one. The whipped cream had finally melted into the cup of chocolate and I took a deep swallow of it. "This is actually good," I heard myself remarking.

"See?" She gazed in a way that seemed to be measuring me. "Don't you find it a hopeful sign that teaching hasn't driven you to the bottle? Or are you just too fastidious?"

"If I am, then I should go into raising orchids. So far, teaching is one of the least fastidious things I can imagine doing. On the other hand, I *have* discovered there are those who find it the prime place for bewitching others. Did you?" I asked with more insinuation than I intended.

"Did I what?"

"Did you find teaching to be a time of bewitching others? And if so, why did you give it up?"

She stood. "Perhaps, Jeremiah, we can sort through this further on another occasion."

"You're going?"

"We're being evicted. Didn't you notice?"

"Not a well-planned outing."

"I suppose not. That's the way it is with impulse."

"You may have forgotten I have a place ten-minutes' walk from here."

"Not at all. But I have many things to do."

"Once again, we've gotten nowhere—except for the vapors."

"And where is somewhere?"

"Don't be dismissive. I don't think it suits you."

"My mother used to say there are suits for every occasion."

"All right, then. I'll take her word for it."

We walked back along Market toward her car. Once more she looked pleased with herself. Her hands were deep inside her coat pockets, like those of a teenager, and she inhaled the night air with her nose raised and her mouth slightly open. "I just received my divorce papers. That's somewhere, wouldn't you say?"

"Divorce?"

"You've heard of it?"

"The back side of vows."

"The front side of new worlds. Do you disapprove?

"Does Michael?"

"If I were to think deeply enough about it, I would probably realize it was his idea."

"Michael's?"

"To be precise. A year ago he pointed out that I was miserable and that Marvin—"

"Marvin?" It had begun to snow softly as if the odd angularity of the name had caused a rip in the sky. *Marvin.* It was a name of distorted dreams.

"I didn't name him," she said merrily. "I only married him."

I once again realized my Nancy Feller had a wicked side, that the quickness of her tongue was at times grounded in the ability to cut herself and others into small fancies. Had she always been this way, even while she was drilling addition and subtraction and puffy readings into my mind? Or was this a product of her recent liberation? And what else had she been planting in me twenty years ago? *There* was the nearly blank slate of my trusting brain waiting for her to draw—or doodle—upon it. And for someone who responded to her with his little bud of adoration, what had I let her get away with while she was settling into her marriage with a man named Marvin and apparently conceiving Michael on my time? A strangely irrational jealousy feathered me, much like the snow that was beginning to adhere to our coats and to the darkened shrubbery we passed.

"This is my car," she said, interrupting my flutter of thoughts with a supernatural sense of timing. It was a small car—good on gas, no doubt, but probably not good on slippery roads. Its black paint gave it a hostile readiness, and I could see piles of what looked like real estate stuff on the passenger seat.

"We need to talk again," I told her at last.

"Why?"

"To accomplish."

She clicked the door opener, though we were still on the sidewalk side of the vehicle. "You *do* have a way with words, but it will take time to be certain *which* way."

"Time?"

"What were you hoping to...accomplish?"

"Tonight was your idea, I believe."

"Yes. Yes it was. You don't think it was a good one?"

"Possibly."

"Then, if it *wasn't* a good one, that might be exactly enough. Time, that is. And if it *was*, there may never be enough. Think about that."

"And?"

She shook my hand, then kissed me briefly on the cheek. "Merry Christmas, Jeremiah." She drove from the curb with a splish of tires that sounded weary and relieved. A tinny version of "Silent Night" spilled from one of the holiday speakers back near the center of the village.

SIX

The Professor told me of his cancer on Christmas morning. I had slept at his house the night before, for the first time since I found my apartment that summer. Throughout my four years of graduate school, I rarely came home for visits. He didn't seem to expect them, and I was perfectly busy trying to prove my worthiness to carry his name—though I tried not to let it feel that way. I did spend a month in my old bedroom prior to the apartment, though my father had seemed uncertain how to deal with my sudden presence. While I was there, he offered little in the way of suggestions for my upcoming attempt at teaching—or what he referred to in the face of many doubts as my "career." It was a word super-laden with inevitability at a time when I would have been as happy to think of it as a path to crossing something off a life list.

He had treated himself to a part-time cook over the years I was away, after a long period of eating meals out and making do in his own kitchen. It was Ellen who told me he had had experience as a short-order cook before arriving at his professorship period. It actually troubled me to think of him as having been so face-to-face with the world in an apron and with grease-spots layering him. I felt no love, but I did feel a kind of retroactive uneasiness, as I did about most anything from his early life.

There was a time when I would look for pictures of both parents in their childhood, but I always came up empty. If photos were hidden away in the house, I could not find them. How I wanted reassurance that each of them, and especially my father, had a time that could be called a *youth*—that he had once looked at the world through the eyes of a child and made quiet promises to never grow up. I wanted a photo of him in shorts and a polo shirt, licking at a melting something that would run in fingers down his chin. I wanted to see him with the paraphernalia of playtime. I wished him a small model boat he would have taken between his hands and dropped into any body of water that satisfied his boy's need to sail away from himself. The only known picture of my parents was taken on their wedding day—or so the inscription on the back told me. Otherwise, there was nothing else to indicate it was a day of ceremony. It was in a leather frame turned to the back of a linen closet off the downstairs bathroom. He was in what looked like white muslin pants and a pale golf shirt, like something from the *Gatsby* era. She was in a peasant dress, which revealed the tips of sandals. If they were trying to look casual about what they were undertaking, they had succeeded skillfully. Each wore an expression of neutral acceptance.

The cook, Louisa, was from Goteborg, a throwback to the turn of the twentieth century when Swedes were a common import. She was most likely in her late thirties with hair as lightly colored as damp cotton and a laugh of calm pleasure. She had a daughter of her own and enjoyed envisioning for my benefit how her child would one day become a "budding" (to rhyme with "pudding") teacher of the "yenerations." I cherished her crippled g's and j's, and at times I felt it would be unfortunate for me to disappoint her. And how ridiculously well she cooked. She had found a supplier of venison, proclaiming it was not in the same class as Scandinavian reindeer but would have to do. And there I would be, eating Bambi's mother—as opposed to Rudolph's, thankfully—and experiencing a well-being that came close to gluttony.

My father and I attempted to make these few dinners into our own version of pleasantry. We could have sat at opposite ends of the dining room table like an aging couple of the crumbling gentry, but I found my way to the chair around the corner from his own. He took a single glass of wine with his meal as if it were a duty, and I would compromise my teetotaling to raise a glass with him. There was a beauty to wine in a wineglass, I discovered, and admitted to myself that one day I could imagine dropping this little bastion of control to placate the memories of those who had looked at me with suspicion over the years. Such a little thing so carefully protected.

On Christmas Eve, Louisa roasted a pheasant before going home to her own family. She placed it between us with a flush of accomplishment. "For the two professors," she proclaimed. "I t'ought the men of literature would be pleased vit' a bird that could fly from the pages of a good book—ja?" This bird's flying days were over, of course, but we both seemed to appreciate the lift of her imaginings. My father thanked her with a trace of wistfulness, nodding his head as if he had heard it all before, though it was clear we were being treated to a rare moment of originality.

We talked more than usual that evening. He had put on music that was not quite for the Christmas season but had its own texture of good wishes. Mendelssohn, I think. A breath of Shakespeare. At one point he said to me through the music, "You know, of course, that I have no religion. There has been none in my life since I shook my fist at God on a hill behind the Dartmouth campus. I was nineteen, and I had had enough. I had for years been asking a phantom in the sky to take care of various people and to make the world a calmer place. That obviously hadn't been regarded with any seriousness, and I assumed that fist of defiance would prove conclusively whether I'd been hoaxed or not. I would be struck with lightning or met with indifference. I would be dead or I would be released from superstition. And so I was."

"Just like that?"

"Precisely like that. It was as clear-cut as a blackout. It was efficiency raised to a cosmic level." He seemed buoyed by the idea and carved second helpings of pheasant with meticulous knife strokes, even though his hand had trembled beforehand. "That is not to say, however, that I am unable to be moved by religious impulses, by the hungers of the spirit. I've always had a softness for the great music of the season—Christmas, Easter—and the longing to be transcendent."

His final word stunned me, leaving me little room to consider the implication of what he'd said. "Did you ever wish to undo the blackout?"

His thick eyebrows drew together. "To countermand the order? Most certainly not. Not without—"

"A communiqué?"

He studied me, his pale eyes growing wary for the moment. His face had always had the ability to form into sudden masks, like those of Greek actors: *hypocrites* they were interestingly called, able to convey an unvarying expression to the upper tiers of an amphitheater. And to be replaced by another mask, equally as singular and expressive—equally impenetrable and penetrative. I wondered how often he had looked at his wife in a similar way and how she had met that gaze at this same table. Surely I had been there to see it, but had I only taken a child's thin notice of it?

"And so, Jeremiah, that is an oddly shaped word, wouldn't you say? Spare me all communiqués." He poured his third or fourth glass of wine, an unusual amount for him. "Give me your thoughts on teaching, but spare me your communiqués."

I looked at him with uncertainty. This was territory I was not anxious to explore with him. He was, after all, the master craftsman of the art—or so the commendations and various framed memorabilia in his study had forever signified. There was a picture of him clasping hands with a to-be-disgraced senator that froze in place an enthusiasm I could not imagine residing in him. As many years as I had looked at the photo, it was a perplexity. Two generations of students had professed an admiration and appreciation for him, and there was a brief period when I was quite young that those who had succeeded in significant ways would be entertained around the same table we were sitting at now. They were his acolytes, his bootlickers—something I hoped never to have. I would satisfy myself instead with Michael Feller—my transcendent failure.

"Tell me about your first impressions as you embark on the profession. Tell me what it has meant so far."

"I'm not able to."

"What is that?"

"Give it meaning."

"Do you worry that it has no meaning?"

"Does a first-grade teacher?"

"I'm not sure how that has any earthly thing to do with what I am asking."

I stared squarely at his tired, implacable face. "Did it *never* occur to you that what you were doing was a waste of time?"

He was bewildered by the question at first and then regained his composure. "Only recently." He stood unsteadily and spoke with the gravest articulation: "I had hoped to get out of here without the least acknowledgment of such a question. Ridiculous, of course. Quaintly ridiculous." And he started out. For the first time, I noticed a cane leaning against the china cupboard. I was quite sure he hadn't used it coming into the room earlier. Apparently, it had been positioned there by someone—Louisa—with a "just in case" casualness. He took it now and proceeded into the hallway, then turned back as if about to add to what he had said. He rethought and closed the door behind him, a door that was rarely, if ever, closed.

I looked at the china cupboard, using it as a focal point. It and a sideboard and the table and chairs had come with him into this house. They had belonged to his parents, people I had never known, a result of his having waited so long to reproduce. Most of what I knew about them I had learned from Ellen, who had known them as not only in-laws but also as former theater people who had taken her under their wings when she thought she might act. She was seventeen at the time, and they had ended their professional lives to run classes at a small acting community near Portland, Maine. They had apparently cherished her as the daughter they never had and, according to her, filled her with the conviction that acting honored the glory of risking one's soul combined with the counter-conviction that it was not, finally, worth the risk.

They had prospered from their theater days but had left it when, apparently, Grandfather Curtin caught himself flying too far outside of his planetary sense of self. Perhaps a year before she left, Ellen told me of how he broke down while playing Krapp's Last Tape, lost his lines in a cloud of doubt, felt the character drain out of all ten toes, and felt his own withered self become more transparent than plastic wrap. He had been unable, for the moment, to distinguish the actor from the character or from the tape recorder that was his fellow actor. It was, apparently, a splendid meltdown. From then on, and with the reluctant concurrence of his wife, he would satisfy himself by leading others to such exposures but would not do it himself. He had frozen himself out of his art and developed the talent for keeping himself well-wrapped in the misgivings of others.

Including Ellen, apparently. She claimed to have loved the feel of being oneself in another, but she was bright enough to finally acknowledge the risk. It was when she met their son, the studious Alban, already well-established in university life, that she decided a career in teaching would satisfy her, and eventually him. What attracted her to him, I didn't know. He was, of course, the offspring of those perplexing theater people, and yet he stood aside from them. He would, through his place in The Academy, find a voice that was enduring, while they had been creatures of the ephemeral. It was all too staccato to piece together, like the sound of the cane that had just tapped beyond the darkened dining room door. There would be more time to make sense of it, although much sooner than I thought.

§

When he asked me into his study the next morning—leaving a Post-it on the door to the bathroom I used—I assumed it was to deal with loose ends. Our attempted conversation the previous evening ended as if a bell had gone off, a distant ringing that echoed like an alarm through the rest of the night. There had been no exchange of presents, nor was I sure one had been intended. Still, I had gotten him an old map of his beloved London to add to his framed collection. I brought it with me into that imposing space and saw through the pair of windows behind his desk that Christmas morning had prettied itself, regardless of what had happened the night before. The side yard where I had sported with Ellen was covered in new snow—so perfectly laid down it gave the impression that one should never walk there again, that no tracks should mark it. The room smelled of evergreen, and I noticed one of the windows was slightly open. The oaks of my childhood had been taken down years earlier, replaced by a grove of spruce and cedar. The study air was as refreshed and agreeable as I could ever remember it to be.

He motioned to the chair on the opposite side of the desk from his. "I have lymphoma." Neither of us spoke for several seconds. "It is often treatable, but in this case I doubt it."

My hands were upon the poorly wrapped map that sat upright across my knees. "How do you know?"

"How do I know what?"

"Its...treatability," I croaked quietly.

"I've talked. I've listened. I've read."

"You've talked to doctors?"

"Of course I have, Jeremiah. How else would I know what I know?"

I deservedly felt the shroud of inanity settling over me. Here was a man difficult to talk to under the best of circumstances, and now he was in the process of announcing the likelihood of death. His death.

He read my incapability. "There's no need to talk further about this now."

"When, then?"

"The arch response would obviously be 'Why talk about it at all? Talk is a poor healer.' But let us find another time. It is Christmas, after all."

"In a weak moment, I bought you this map. It's London in the 1660s. Your period."

He reached for it and then set it unopened on his desk. "Thank you for weak moments." After a silent interval, he took the paper off and held it up briefly. "The poorly labeled Restoration. Fires and plagues and beautifully rendered deceits." His eyelids blinked three times. "I didn't think to get you anything. It never occurred to me."

SEVEN

Not only had Nancy Feller shown up unexpectedly at my apartment on her chosen December night, but a few weeks later, on The Epiphany, I also received a visit from Michael and Willie. It was, in fact, an evening of many visitors. I was already providing a place to sleep for a former lady friend, the smoothly promiscuous Sara Sampson. She was using me as a staging area to interview for jobs in Manhattan, taking the Poughkeepsie Metro North each morning and returning at night. We had been on-again and off-again—quite literally—during graduate school. I was infatuated with her sleek arms and envious of her ability to airbrush loyalty with a cool laugh. She was bright and ambitious, certain she had no idea why she was pursuing a degree in literature but that, in the end, it didn't matter. And she liked a "good read." Presumably, I was one of them.

We shared my bed the days she was with me, though she had instructed me, to my relief, that she was not in a mood for what she called hot-humping while she was untangling her latest goals. I offered my couch for use by either one of us, but she wouldn't hear of it. She was happy enough to talk as we lay side by side, and she did plenty of it. She spent part of one night trying to piece together her first orgasm, trying to recall when it had occurred, with whom, and *if,* in fact, it had been a real orgasm. Having grown up in Wyoming, she tried to re-imagine a genuine buckaroo, as she called it—one where you humped yourself blind. For some reason, she was unable to come up with a clear recollection. I felt sorry for her.

I thought it was Sara tapping at the door on that evening of visitors—though she was not the tapping kind. That it was Michael and Willie reorganized my emotional preparation for my houseguest into a scramble of disorientation. At first, I didn't recognize them, they were so outside of where my thoughts had been. But when Willie spoke without greeting, things focused.

"Nancy says you're giving up teaching."

Willie was even more heavily bundled than she had been during her performance in my office. She wore a scarf over her head that looked like a peasant woman's babushka, making her seem twice her age. Michael, of course, stood behind, in her lumbering shadow.

"You don't have that quite right," I told her.

"It's what she *thinks*."

"All right. That may be. Would you like to come in so we can straighten this out?"

"Sure," she said. And Michael repeated the word.

Michael cased the place, while Willie reached into her back pocket to extract an envelope. "It's your Christmas card. A little late but what the hell." It was already unsealed so it was easy enough to remove the card, one cheerily showing Mrs. Claus pounding away at a distorted pipe organ. It was signed "Your students, Mike and Wilhelmina." It was in her handwriting and interesting that she had formalized her own name and familiarized his.

"Touching," I told her. "And most unexpected."

"What the hell?" she repeated.

Actually, Michael wasn't quite casing the apartment. It was more like he was absorbing the idea that a person from a distinctly different context should have any place of his own. His eyes took in the scattered wall posters, the empty bookshelves, and he peered into the bedroom where a slip was thrown over the back of a chair and an open suitcase gaped on the floor. He took special notice of this, staring at it with profound concentration before turning back to the living room. "It's pretty good," he complimented. Willie, meanwhile, had positioned herself cross-legged in the only comfortable chair in the apartment, near the temperamental fireplace, with her back to the window.

"Would you guys like something? Soda? Cider? I think I still have eggnog."

"Nothing," she said brusquely. "We can't stay long. We just want to know why you're running away from teaching."

"As I said, Michael's mother may have misinterpreted something I said. Besides, you two are done with me. What should it matter?" It was a dumb thing to say, and she knew it.

"Horseshit. We aren't done. Not by a long shot."

"I'll keep that in mind. And if I decide to retire in the near future, you'll be the first to know. But now that you're here, how did you find me? Michael's mother?"

"Nancy? No way."

"And yet people keep finding their way to my door."

Michael had positioned himself near her, leaning awkwardly against the fireplace surround. "Got a girlfriend?" he asked.

Willie was startled and put her feet on the floor. "Mike," she said with a choking shout, "what the hell?" It was the third time she had said it.

"Not at present," I told him, trying to calm my voice. "But if you stay around a while, you'll meet a puzzling person from my past. And what about you two? Do you call yourselves a couple?"

"A couple of what?" she asked, as the door opened on what seemed like a missed cue of only a few seconds.

In walked Sara Sampson. She had the frazzled look of a person who had covered a good deal of ground that day but still retained her striking ability to command a moment efficiently. "Why, Jeremiah, honey, I didn't know you had children. I must have missed the telegram. You must introduce us immediately." She pulled a bottle from her purse and held it trophy-like. "But not yet. Not quite yet, boys and girl. I got a job and it's time to celebrate. Our Little Cowgirl Sara is going to be the Belle of Wall Street before you can say whoop-de-doo."

It was Willie, of course, who was unable to hold back her own gentrified Hudson Valley version of whoop-de-doo.

"Why thank you, little one," Sara responded and then peered closer at her. "Why you're not so little after all. Are you one of Jeremiah's fertile fields...or are you with that silent gentleman behind you? Well, doesn't matter. We're all in this celebration together. Care for some Comfort?" She extended the bottle toward Willie, and it was clear Sara had already lowered the amount in the bottle well below its shoulders.

"Got a thin one, Mike?" Willie asked, undeterred by the gush of Manhattanized energy that had just taken over the room.

"Coming up, Will," he told her with unusual assurance.

Sara dropped her purse to the floor with an officious thunk. "Looks like we're ready for a real party." She stared at me. "Jeremiah, you are generally the pooper's pooper, but are you going to drop your headmistress skirtiness for one night and join on in? Or you just goin' to bed?" She stood thoughtfully in front of Willie. "Don't worry, child. We're not lovers or anything. We're only sleeping together for a couple of days. I love your hair by the way. It's the shade of a Guernsey milk cow. Wish I had it."

Both Willie and Michael seemed pleased with the turn of events. He was in the process of smoothing a proficiently rolled joint with his lips and she was finger-combing her hair. I felt myself beginning to suspend all of my instincts for neatening things when the doorbell buzzed. For once, it was someone who had actually waited outside the main door. I had given my address to Barbara Lynn Hynes several weeks before and invited her to stop by over semester break. There she stood with a slight but stunning woman who turned out to be her partner, Emily. Each held a bottle of wine, Barbara Lynn's red and Emily's white, and I felt the blessedness of one who was having all responsibility taken from him. Barbara Lynn knew Willie, of course, from campus groups developed to promote and provoke. They hugged like the oldest of dear friends with a spontaneity I'd not seen in Willie before. And with that, she said something about getting her brother and was out the door after taking a tug off of Michael's joint.

Emily had Botticelli-beauty and a peaceful luster. She wasn't much taller than five feet and she wore glasses that seemed too large for her face, but she emitted a quiet clarity of purpose that played with true harmony off the theatrics of Barbara Lynn Hynes. Even Sara seemed initially hushed by Emily's impeccable radiance and took the wine bottles from each of them like a well-coached hostess. It was something transcendent to watch, and I was still mostly watching.

Willie returned in a matter of minutes with Hamilton from upstairs, who, as these things go, was her half-brother. He was probably a year or two younger than me, a computer guy at IBM in East Fishkill, who had his sister's hair, even if he was already beginning to lose traces of it. He liked jazz, and I would many times hear the encouraging sound of his foot tapping above me. We had been on friendly terms since I moved in, and he seemed to have appointed himself as house impresario, offering help and advice about the place whenever he could. He lived opposite a woman in her eighties or nineties whom I never saw, but for whom delivery people carried up groceries and other necessities several times a week. According to Ham, she had lived there for decades and had been a governess for one of the Roosevelts. The apartment across from me had been empty since I moved in, a situation I thought little about and was grateful for.

Ham had once or twice offered to teach me how to build a fire where the smoke went up the chimney, and he and Willie came in now with kindling and small splits of firewood in their arms. "Hey, Jerry," he said, trying to shake elbows and losing some of the wood as he did. "My naughty sister here was going to drop in on me, but I guess the dropping in is on you now. Hope you don't mind. Got any newspaper?" When I brought some, I was rewarded with the word "Magnificent!"—delivered with Teddy Roosevelt gusto.

The puzzle of Willie and Michael—and Nancy—locating me was apparently solved. The naughty knuckles of coincidence had tapped out another part of its coded messaging.

Like that, I was throwing a party, attended by people who took unexpected pleasure in each other. They were the happy playfellows of non-anticipation, and I lost any reluctance about joining them in this sudden playroom. Sara made a big deal out of my taking a few swigs of Southern Comfort, but I was more interested in revisiting the companionability of marijuana, a friend of my teenage years after Ellen left me to my mysterious musings. I was grateful for it then, for its peaceful nudging, but glad enough to air out my mind by the time I was halfway through college and suddenly serious about making myself useful in some way. Michael took a special satisfaction in sharing the three or four joints he had just now rolled into existence, drawing me into a kind of buddyhood with him. Willie seemed indifferent, showing more interest in Ham's growing attentions to Sara. I watched as he and Sara, changed now from her interview outfit into a Denver Broncos jersey and pajama bottoms, laid the firewood carefully on the barren grate and brought it to life with well-rounded whoops of celebration. Sara put an arm around his shoulders, and they snuggled in front of the fire like longtime fellow campers.

How easy it all seemed, and how easily she made a surprising moment so easily digestible. It was a talent I had once praised her for. And Ham himself had an ease of being captured I would not have imagined in him. He had always seemed too fidgety for any seductions except virtual ones. They talked of many things; they ranged about without any awkwardness caused by changes of direction. She was particularly taken by his description of the housebound lady across the hall from him. Miss Ellie he called her. I could hear Sara profess dreamily at one point how she was taken by the idea of being boxed into a single set of rooms, "like a dried walnut safe in its same old shell. How romantic is that!" This from the woman who had just returned from conquering Manhattan and had real difficulties staying in one place for any amount of dedicated time. "I want to meet her," she said. "I want to know her and give her a sloppy embrace—just so's I don't break any brittle bones."

On the floor near my feet, Willie agreed she'd appreciate an acquaintanceship with a woman who might reach a hundred—a "fucking amplitudinarian" she called her. I had negotiated myself onto the couch between Barbara Lynn and Emily as they passed a bottle of Valpolicella across my legs. Michael was parked on a beanbag near the room's front window, moving his legs with the satisfied conviction of a four-year-old on a park swing. He had selected a Gershwin sampler from my CD rack. As if he had intuited the correct sound for the occasion, he had started it with a look of pleasure. I could feel Willie shift comfortably, and for a time, I imagined the six of us as a tableau of contentedness—until Michael's phone rang with the sound of cathedral chimes.

It was Nancy. That was clear enough, as he waved the phone with the word Mom across the top of the screen. He seemed puzzled at first, until Willie told him, "Well, answer it, dodo."

He extended the phone toward her, across an unreachable distance. "You." He had never seemed the kind to be paranoid, but for the moment he was.

"Listen to you," Willie scolded. "It's your phone. And your mother. What's with you?"

He said, "Hunh," and took the plunge. "Mom?" She was finally in my living room but without absorbing the calmness that had fallen upon the rest of us. "Yeah," he told her, "I'm cool...I didn't say when I'd be back...I did?...You don't have to worry...Where?...I'm at—my teacher's...You know: Professor..." He seemed stumped and then went on after a cue from her. "Yeah, him." I could hear traffic music on the streets of Paris coming from the recording. It was frenetic and celebratory. I experienced, and not for the first time, a wish to be there, after the Great War with my coat collar folded up around my neck, a snug hotel room waiting for me. I took a swig of Emily's wine as it passed me. Barbara Lynn's head had tipped against my shoulder only minutes after telling me that she and Emily had become engaged that afternoon. I wanted to ask who popped the question but hadn't been able to find my way to it without sounding awkward. I would try it again later. I did, however, feel the privilege of having been told, and I was warmed by sharing their happiness.

Suddenly, Michael was handing me the telephone, looking relieved. I had to work at finding the word "Hello," which felt dried out in my throat.

"Do you often party with your students?" the voice asked. It was neither critical nor bemused. It seemed to be trying to commandeer a fact that had a degree of usefulness.

"Good evening, Mrs. Feller."

"Dear God. Names again."

"Yes. And I wouldn't call it partying, exactly. It's more like an unexpected event. Parties need to be thrown."

"I see. And how is Michael doing at this un-thrown event? He sounds a little..."

"He is." I didn't have a liar's fortitude.

"Of course he is. Is he corrupting you?"

I laughed. "Of course he is. But he has excellent taste in music."

"He gets it from his father."

"Marvin?" I spluttered.

"Yes, good old Marvin. He just never spun the right kind of tunes for me."

I considered what she had said but let it pass by. "Willie's here, too. Did you know her half-brother lives upstairs from me?"

"Of course she's there, and yes I knew."

"He showed me how to build a fire. He's a real Boy Scout. Now he's snuggling with my one-time girlfriend." Sara laughed delightedly, and Nancy was silent. Finally I asked, "Want to come join us?"

Her silence was more protracted. "Just take care of Michael. Don't let them drive."

"They'll be fine. I'll make sure they spend the night."

I wasn't sure how that came across, but she said crisply, "You do that," and clicked off.

There are conversations, of course, that will replay themselves indefinitely if you let them. They can be endlessly edited and poked at for their subtexts. Instead of letting that happen, I nudged Barbara Lynn slightly. She was humming to the music and smelled of wine and apple-blossoms. "Do you party with students?"

She enjoyed the question. "I wouldn't have met the lady on your left if I didn't."

"Oh."

"Does that make me the Scarlet Professor? There was a time, I'm told, when such a thing was quite respectable." I waited for her to go on, and she did. "I ask you, is there a *proper* way to meet a nice girl? Is there one beyond reproach?" It was as if she were lecturing slightly without her usual classroom thunder.

"Let's hear it for reproachability," I said with a slurring of the last word. I had been so intent on remaining articulate that I was apparently paying for the effort now. I turned to Emily. "So you were picked up by the reproachable Dr. Hynes."

Emily was only a few degrees levitated, considering the amount of wine she had swallowed. There was a modest church girl air to her when she responded with, "I picked *her* up." She smiled demurely, a melting absolution of a smile that had me palming Willie's head.

"Hey, easy up there, big shot." The redoubtable Willie had remained comfortably parked in front of the three of us on the couch. She had seemed as tame as a golden retriever and I was sorry to have annoyed her. She stood and walked toward the fire. Her leather-solid stride was as soldierly as ever, but her hands were fluttering as if she was shaking them awake.

She *was* an enigma. She had a mental and emotional muscularity always close to the surface of her negotiations with the world. She had a rough beauty that would have been marred by any attempt to make herself more traditionally attractive. Except for her challenging dabs of lipstick, makeup was not a thing for the face, but something to be applied internally to where she protected a shy child of another time. You could feel it in her, in her writing, in the way she pondered over a piece of poetry, creasing her forehead with wonderment, and in her music, I assumed. She was a wondrous young woman who had, for the most part, wrapped herself in barbed wire. I was for, that evening, in the land of the enigmatic, but she was the lead puzzler. She turned back to look at me and proclaimed, "Teachers are a strange bunch who ought to know better...about everything"—before dropping onto the floor next to Sara.

§

By the time the fire imploded to scattered coals, Sara had gone upstairs with Hamilton, while Michael and Willie were pretzeled together on my bed in stoned slumber. Barbara Lynn and Emily had let themselves out quietly. No one, in fact, had said good-bye or good night to anyone else. There was evaporation in every direction. I was gladdened by it. Farewells are usually overplayed by most, as if departure was the ultimate human uncertainty, making it so much more necessary than it needs to be—so much urgency shoved strand by strand into the feared indifference of others. I was glad to be alone with a scuttling cloud of drink and smoke and watching.

I lay down upon the couch and listened to the rhythm of bedsprings from above. Sara—who had been good for me at times. It was Ellen Curtin who had first brought me into layers of living where there were no explanations, and Sara Sampson had been the reinforcing thrust. She had appreciated passion without being packaged by it. She hated sex in movies, on television, on billboards, in magazines. It was all, she said one night just before mounting me, "like stud service for starved imaginations." It was too "prescriptive." It was all right in books, though she claimed to be growing sick of books in general. On that occasion, it didn't feel like an instruction; rather, her rant had seemed to heighten the strains and pleasures of our moment—in a gazebo during a sudden desert thundershower.

In my couch reverie, I thought of lesbian love, envisioning it as probably the purest form of human sexual activity. Why it should seem that way, I didn't know. Maybe it was the cool perfection of Emily, whose last name I hadn't learned and who looked like she didn't need one. She was *that* medieval. She had a crystalline sexiness that suggested an ability to blend totally, to fuse herself into another while never losing the distinction of being herself. She was a high school social worker in one of the rougher districts of the Valley, as if she could walk unscarred through whatever ugliness was tossed before her and give back to that which was trying to take her core innocence from her.

A perfectly designed enigma. Perfection *was* possible, the air around her wanted to say. How perfect to sit between her and her tempestuous lover—soon to be married. With which of them to be the bride? How did that work? Hadn't I wanted to ask them? Surely there would have been no resentment. They were too much at peace, the peace of genuine consequence. And the redoubtable Dr. Hynes soon without a job, dragged from the academy by her violently red hair. It wouldn't matter. She was too important to be waste material. The way Michael seemed to me more and more a smudged manuscript wound within himself. Unto himself. His denial of what I thought I had to offer him was leading me in a direction that didn't seem all that incorrect. Just fanciful. He was there to offer me instruction, though for now, he was a difficult text to parse. He was, for certain, his mother's son. Her voice on the phone was not that of the distressed parent. It was that of a spirit who knew him only too well and would occasionally strain to track the footsteps he left. For me, her voice had taken on additional meanings, and as my reverie climaxed, it was Nancy Feller I wanted to be drawn into—and how perverse was that? How purely beyond normal thought?

EIGHT

I began the spring semester with little of Chuck Gillis' clean-slate enthusiasm. He, of course, accosted me in the mail room with a burst of good feelings. He was a walking daffodil. Not only was he wearing a frightfully green and yellow necktie but he had the exuberance of a flowering specimen that had just sprung to the above-ground world from the papery cage of a bulb. He held a forbiddingly thick copy of Boswell's *Life of Johnson* pulled from his mailbox and was waving it in the air like a pennant.

"He who's tired of a new semester is tired of life," he declared, looking at me to see if I got the connection to one of Dr. Johnson's oft-quoted statements about life in London. I got it, but I didn't feel inclined to show it. It was already apparent based on our brief acquaintanceship that in a matter of weeks he would bemoan the staleness of the classroom, his reluctant students, and his own best plans falling fast asleep behind his lectern. For forty years, I guessed, he had run this cycle of renewal and disappointment as a way to pass through his career as unperceptively as possible. But he was good at it, without a doubt.

Gillis anointed one of my shoulders with the copy of Boswell then softly chirped a first-day greeting to a colleague in Philosophy. Mikhail Jefferson was partly African-American with skin light enough he might have attempted to pass as white a century earlier. In his forties, he was an occasionally frenetic, sonorous speaker and sporadically agreeable to those around him. He taught courses in the Bible and the history of Christianity, and people like Gillis reacted as if they expected to pull a beam of light from him. Like Samuel Johnson, Chuck was a firm churchman, and, in the presence of Jefferson's expertise, seemed comforted by the man who had his hands on the inner workings of belief. When speaking to him, Gillis lowered his voice to that of a librarian.

I had developed a nervous liking of Jefferson. His charisma had students competing, like purchasers of a must-have new product, to register for his courses. His office sessions were like those I had heard about from earlier times: young men and women contesting him and each other with a pitch of intensity one found in no other office in my building—except that of Barbara Lynn Hynes. Phyllis Friel had referred to him as a pied piper, and from her it was difficult to tell whether it was a compliment or a warning. I assumed the latter, though she was so tightly strung it was difficult to be certain of anything with her. But she did cause me to examine my feelings about Mikhail Jefferson more fully, making me wonder, among other things, whether charisma was an overlay or a presence from some deeper source.

Jefferson and I shared a table at a campus snack shop several days after Chuck Gillis' salute to the new semester. He was marking passages in a paperback version of the New Testament while pulling shreds of spinach from a salad with his other hand. It was a neat but disorienting trick, and I attempted to leave him alone. He wouldn't hear of it and put down his yellow marker. It had seemed like an odd application to scripture, even to a heathen like myself,.

"Markin' up de word o' de lord," Jefferson said, sounding deliberately Pentecostal. Then, as if he had sensed my uneasiness, "It makes some people profoundly nervous"—phrased to sound merely professorial. "Sit." I did. "I have students who want to take me to task for using stickers to mark specific pages. When I tell them this book is only black lines on paper, they have been known to give me looks I wouldn't even try to describe. It is one of the benefits of teaching such a text in such a course."

"Playing the devil?"

He laughed a short, precise laugh. "Of course, brother."

"You're serious, aren't you?"

"About being spiritually naughty? And why not?"

"Is that what it is? Naughtiness?"

"Are you never naughty when you teach?"

There were half a dozen students in two groups nearby. The laughter within one group was presumably not directed at our discussion, but I found it an encouragement in its own way. "I'm enjoying your word choice. I'll have to think about it."

When he asked how long I'd been teaching, I refreshed his memory, and he looked at me with a companionable seriousness. "Then I give it to you with all my heart. 'Naughtiness,'" he announced with a pastoral inflection. The others in the room cast startled looks, and he waved his hand like one offering a benediction. "For all of you. Profound naughtiness."

One student with a dab of chocolate on her lip waved back at him. "Thanks, Professor. Every night, on my knees, I will thank you for it."

"Bless you, child," he said and then turned back to me. I enjoyed his ease, even as he leaned in to speak more confidingly. "If there is a God, he—or she—is a very naughty VIP. Vagabond In Power, that is."

"You're that uncertain?"

"About?"

"Things. What you teach."

"Of course. I've never taught *what* to believe—only why it is we do the believing we do, in a backhanded way. What better than the tradition I grew up with? You obviously worry about your teaching. Maybe you need to make more of an effort to find out what you're uncertain about."

"I'd like to think I'm well on my way."

"Good. Look at my last name. Jefferson. An American god. The Sphynx. The man who had no qualms about putting his self-evident penis into Dusky Sally. I may well be descended from him, but I choose not to know. Choosing not to know should be the fourth in the list: life, liberty, the pursuit of happiness, and choosing not to know what I do not fucking wish to know." He sat back and snapped the book in front of him closed. "Sorry if I threw salt on your lunch. I've got a class to prepare." He had slipped into a different persona, as if he'd just finished scolding me for doubting him.

§

I wanted to drive past Nancy Feller's house—Nancy and *Michael* Feller's, that is—later that afternoon. Michael's address was simple enough to find on my list of advisees, though he had never come for an advisement session and he was, I finally learned, no longer in school. The address was also on the famous lime-green envelope which, protectively, I'd slipped into a book. It was a habit, and in this instance, as well as others, I couldn't remember which book in particular.

The beige-colored house was a split-level at the outskirts of Poughkeepsie, on a cul-de-sac that made driving by seem less happenstance than I would have liked—assuming people spent the day staring out of windows. I did, however, make my clean getaway, with the loop at the end giving me a second chance to look quickly at where they lived. For a late-January day with only traces of snow melting along the edge of the driveway, it appeared well tended to, the yard orderly, the house itself snugly self-contained on its elevated piece of ground. Only a string of Christmas lights over the garage door suggested things to be done. Nancy's car was sitting in front of the garage with dark normalcy, and I drove on without being sure where I was going except into the surrounding countryside.

I thought of my one-sided discussion with Mikhail. He had come to my office after his class to ask if I thought him to be a fearful dining-companion. I assured him he had aided my digestion and that I hoped we could talk more. He tossed a piece of chalk up and down in one hand. It was clear he had no idea he was doing it, that it was a classroom prop used to generate his own paths of thinking and he had carried it into the hallway like a disconnected part of himself. I enjoyed the dexterity and his unselfconsciousness about it. There was much more to know about him and his anti-Jeffersonian cynicism, and he too was starting to become another piece in a puzzle that was best labeled as my path to the future.

There were larger patches of snow as I headed east off the Taconic Parkway, but the roads were clean and welcoming. Occasionally, I left the main highways to search other roads where the woods were thicker and the hills of eastern Dutchess County began to present themselves. I could see snowed-in lanes and logging trails off to the sides and houses that moved backward in time, farmhouses from a span of three centuries when this was dairy and fruit-growing country, manned by slaves in many cases before New York outlawed the ownership of humans in the 1820s. Even this Empire State had not been immune—even the builders of this area could not resist the temptation or the ability to be in denial, and two centuries later I thought of Mikhail Jefferson still resonating from that amazing indignity.

There are small hamlets scattered around the rural parts of the valley, as if they had been dropped there by Washington Irving or Fennimore Cooper. Usually they were crossroads where a general store and grange hall or church had been situated. One I discovered was configured differently—a kind of jug handle off a main highway. There were perhaps a dozen houses and what looked like a classic general store with its front porch intact and a grouping of chairs and benches, even in midwinter. Above it was a sign announcing the Quaker Falls Emporium, and as I opened the window of my car, I could hear the stream and narrow falls that had run a mill at one time—now remembered by a blue historical marker. How constant that sound must have been throughout the years during the advent of steam and electricity and the growing circus of modern technology. How indifferent it sounded now, its beauty a given, even with utility taken from it by time. I left the car and approached it, feeling the water's eventual push toward the Hudson River or another place it would know well enough when it got there. Now, ice was bunched up against its banks, but the center of the stream remained unimpeded and fully free to express what drove it.

I walked partway around the jug-handle to where it elbowed its course furthest from the highway and its now muted sounds. Most of the houses were from the late 1800s, the kind that would have had small fields to cultivate and plant modest orchards in. Most had carriage houses or sheds that had evolved into garages at the end of short and rutty driveways—as if asphalt were forbidden here. Most, too, were in good repair, recently painted and comfortable in their hamlet nearness.

Except for one. It looked to be the oldest, but that may have been more a matter of how discarded it appeared. Snow covered any sidewalks and driveway it might have and had crept onto the porch where it would stay unmoved until a decisive thaw. It was a symmetrical structure, with the front door properly centered and sad-looking windows facing the road in an orderly pattern. Bandage-like shades hung at varying heights within the windows, giving off a tattered reminder that someone at some time had tried to close the place from the outside world. Decorative brackets under the roof-line were missing or falling apart. What looked like gutters were punctuated with leafless seedlings and broken branches. Snow melt dripping from the roof rolled over them rather than into the rusted downspouts at each end. A string of sheds ran perpendicular to the road, with one at the nearest end that looked like an enlarged doll's house.And though I wanted to make my way along them, I was wearing the cautious shoes of a teacher rather than those of an explorer. The house gave me the pangs of someone who has returned to a place from his early life to find uselessness and the end of hope. The feeling was similar to that caused by the bicycle rack carton left behind by Ellen. Each was a discarded container that pushed memory away from itself.

"The railroad used to go behind there," a woman's voice said to me. She was walking a small black dog who sniffed its disappointment at finding an interruption to his expectations.

"Railroad?" I asked opaquely.

"They used to come inland in every direction once they left the river. So you didn't know that?" she asked with pleasure. She was round-cheeked, middle-aged, with large sunglasses on since the sun had come out and was glaring off the mush of snow-piles. Her voice had a trumpeting quality, but in a congenial way—like the herald of pleasant announcements.

"No. No, I didn't."

"The little building at the end there—the cabin, I call it—was a barber shop. From what they tell me, people waiting for the train in the morning used to get themselves tidied up—although why they didn't do it at home is way beyond me. Seems wasteful."

"Maybe some just like being pampered," I suggested.

"So we do. I do love getting my toes done. I drive all the way into Pawling to do it. The phrasemaker who came up with 'twinkle toes' must have had me in mind, I like to say. They really do twinkle," she added confidingly. "You wouldn't believe it."

I looked at the house. "No one lives here, I guess."

She had a flair for the obvious—mine, in this case. "Oh no—not for years and years. I moved here fourteen years ago and it looked like this then. A shame."

"Why?"

"Which why is that?"

"Why would anyone abandon it?"

"The local kids think it's haunted, naturally. I couldn't be sure about that. But sometimes the home part of a place just dies out of it, you know. One of my neighbors knew of two men who lived here, and when they—died, or whatever—there may have been no heirs, and things got tangled up in the law like they tend to do—and...I really don't know. I wouldn't make a respectable investigator."

The dog was tugging at her, and while it seemed she could have enjoyed a longer discussion, she yielded to the more forceful will and continued onward with a perky shuffle—not before giving a vague wave with a gloved hand. I thought briefly of her pampered toes before taking one more look at the house and the buildings beside it. As a student of literature, I had been slow to accept the idea that there is a broad range of texts, not all shaped to be a version of a book. I had heard one or two of my own professors argue the idea that films were texts, that magazine ads were texts, that the way people dressed was textual, and

I had been chewing on the idea for several years. But now, facing this infirm house, the concept made sense. It was as palpable as a beaten-up Russian novel—its pages thumbed by those who had lived there—and propelled outward by the numb stare of its windows.

Part of the pleasure of a reading that moves us is sharing it with another. Surely now, I needed someone to talk to.

NINE

"Would you be willing to take a little ride with me?"

"Why little?" Nancy Feller's voice coming through the phone was ripe with curiosity. That was good for starters.

I had not thought about the house in Quaker Falls for several days, trying to move it to a more dependable part of my brain where I sent practicalities to rest in neat folders until I needed them. There, the idea of the house could be flattened and slipped into the folder marked "Ridiculous." But it wouldn't go. It was a picture that kept reprinting itself or a song lyric that kept tumbling the same sound through an inner ear. I pictured Nancy in her sensible tract home with its asphalt driveway and concrete steps even as she took command of her new life as single mother of my ephemeral Michael. She would know the workings of the normal world even more clearly now that she had apparently removed the major abnormality from her life—and she was in real estate—and she had taught first grade, of course—with me in it. She had forever had her hands on how to make things function—with the possible exception of her son.

She had immediately known my telephone voice, though she had only heard it that one night during my unplanned slumber party. Now, nearly a month later, she sounded younger, with motherly concerns brushed out of her voice. Her playfulness was reassuring, given the plan I was about to propose to her.

"'Big' then. As big as you like."

"And when is this ride to take place, Jeremiah?"

"Whenever you'd like. Any afternoon you're free. As the new kid in town, I teach mornings."

"It is afternoon now, isn't it?" It was—a mellow Thursday when winter had fully paused before the final push toward March. It was sunny and puddly.

"It most certainly is. We might have enough time."

"Yes? For what?"

"For a brief journey."

"You'll need my address. I would judge from your tone you're intending to gather me up?"

"Yes. And I know where you live."

"Mmm," she said quietly.

As we drove, I explained the house idea to her, and she was as practical as I hoped she would be. She asked the needed question of how I would pay for it, a subject I had been mulling even as I chided myself about how poorly prepared I was to take on the sheer logistics of such a project. It was not as if I had grown up doing odd jobs for the family. Odd jobs, in The Professor's mind, were for hired people to deal with. I knew what a hammer was and a power drill, but I had sawed through the cord of a circular saw when I was trying to build a miniature log cabin for a middle-school project. I had put the saw and its severed lifeline back into its carrying case and never looked at it again. I assumed it was still sitting untouched in The Professor's basement.

In the Feller living-room, Michael had responded warmly to my announcement that his mother and I were going to look at a "spooky old house." He had been listening to Willie practicing a piece from Bach or Handel on an electronic keyboard, and she had barely looked up from the intricacies of her fingerings. It sounded like a fugue with its own melodic spookiness, and it apparently added to Michael's enthusiasm about what Nancy and I were about to do. He generated a longer sentence than normal, adding his own air-fingerings of the piece Willie was playing. "Sounds like a plan to make hay with." That was a good thing, from what I could gather.

Nancy looked pleased to be a passenger. She had tilted her seat back slightly, and I could imagine her wanting to press her feet against the dashboard if she had been younger. Her auburn hair bobbed girlishly from under a knit hat made with zigzag designs and thin, pendular earpieces that touched the movements of her face like silent punctuation. As we made our way into the country, she gazed from the windows like a person who had not been there before. She had a slight late-winter sniffle and quietly blew her nose from time to time. It seemed a small inconvenience she barely noticed.

"You would think, Jeremiah," she said in the midst of listing the practicalities she wanted me to consider, "that being your age you would have outgrown infatuations with the things that can't be done."

"Is that what you think this is? You haven't even seen the house yet."

"I don't need to. It's in your eyes. They're like a child's seeing a pretty bird and wanting to fly."

"Why did you come, then?"

"I didn't know where we were going. I gather you wanted my advice."

"I do."

"No, you want my advice on a dream you're trying not to wake up from. It's very endearing, like the boy wanting to fly. That's worth my time. Besides, it's a pretty afternoon and a way to shake off cabin fever. Willie, too. Her music can be overpowering when the walls are closing in."

"So I would imagine."

She considered what she had said while she dabbed at her nose. "That's not to say I don't find it wonderful when I'm in the right place for it. She has a gift, a drive, and she pulls so much passion out of what she's playing. I used to think Bach was too churchy. He was preaching through his music. Do you know what I mean, Jeremiah?" She had apparently made my name a part of her vocabulary. It was one less speed-bump in our talk.

"I think so."

"But I do think she's changing that for me. If you find a drawing of Bach, you'll see him with his long, long, long white wig. I would hear it in his music. His wig. Like a judge's."

I nodded. The image was a satisfying one.

"But Willie popped his wig off." She turned to me with a pranking smile. "Did you ever imagine that under his long, long thing, he was totally bald? Though I have no idea if he was or not."

"I'm disappointed to hear it."

She was happily exploring this new image, like the boy wanting to fly. "Wouldn't that be something? Of course, such a wig might have been hiding all kinds of things: sandwiches, rubber bands, a pair of panties—or possibly a contented cockroach." She was quiet, like she was dialed in to a whimsical fugue of her own. "Silliness. You apparently bring it out in me, Jeremiah."

"I'm honored."

She tried to ground herself again. "It's how Willie approaches it. Even on her little plug-in contraption, she attacks with passion. 'Attacks' is the appropriate word, don't you think?"

"I don't know. I've not really heard her. Just that little bit before—when she was working to crack my skull with what she was playing. Pretty intense."

"I suppose. She has very mixed feelings about you. That's plain enough to see and hear. But we need a time to hear her play for real. She's trying to get permission to use the chapel organ on your campus. I'll get you invited if that happens. We're slowing down. We're there?"

"We could just call off this part of our journey, if it makes you apprehensive."

"No. I want to see that light in your eyes again. You need it."

The house looked less forlorn now. Much of the snow was gone, and the splotched metal roof had a look of old, airy relief for having nearly endured another winter. I was more aware of beaten-down bushes—forsythia and honeysuckle (according to Nancy) and what seemed like fruit trees at the edge of a field behind the house, a tree-line at right angles to the sheds I had seen the last time. Further back was a stripe of low hills, still partially snow-covered.

It was growing late in the day, and the sky had the same tones of pink and gray as the early evening walk I had taken with this same woman in Rhinebeck before Christmas. Six weeks had moved by quickly enough since then, and while I had not seen her during that time, I was beginning to feel I knew her better. There had been that brief phone conversation, little to build a deepening knowledge upon. Perhaps it was her passenger playfulness on our way to see this odd piece of property. Perhaps, too, it was the fact that I had known her in a subterranean way for twenty years.

She stretched before the house, twisting her arms skyward after she had gotten out of the car. "Dear, Jeremiah," she said at last after I had prodded her with a "well?" "Is it that you have a special thing for lost causes? Are you announcing that to me here? And why?"

"I hardly know."

"While I hardly know you, it feels like I shouldn't be surprised that you've brought me here."

"Perhaps you shouldn't be."

She looked motherly for a moment. "Is that why you have such an attachment to Michael? He says you and he have started to text and e-mail each other."

I had, and, for the moment, it was like she had detected a deep secret.

"Occasionally. Do you think of him as a lost cause?"

"Not at all. But he must seem that way to you."

"Of course, at one time, when I was falling all over myself not to screw up with him."

"And now?"

"He's written in a language I can't figure out yet, but I'm convinced it's worth the effort."

"Yes," she agreed.

We walked toward the house, up the bluestone flags that led to the porch. Her eyes were lowered, as if trying to maintain a respect for something. "I do mostly rental properties," she said softly. "I deal in places that have no permanence. Temporary quarters. It saddens me if I let it, but it's a living, as they say. But this—I hardly know what to say. It must be almost two centuries old. *That's* permanence, even as beaten up as it is now." Her eyes seemed to water—perhaps her cold or an unanticipated push from the moment. "Oh god," she said suddenly, raising her voice, with adolescent delight, "it has Yankee gutters."

"It has what?"

"Like wooden boxes built in as part of the decorative detail. See?" She pointed upward.

"But how would you know that? You're the queen of suburbia."

"I have a past, Jeremiah." She smiled. "Not *that* kind of past. But I'm a girl from the mountains. The Alleghenies, in fact. My father was a restoration carpenter, and these gutters were a joy to his eyes, especially the ones he had rebuilt. Heavens, he would relish them and mourn when people tore them off their houses and stuck up metal ones. He called it amputation." She paused. "Did you think I grew up on a quarter-acre lot?"

"I...I never thought, period. I have a hard time giving special people back their earlier times."

"Oh? Special people, is it? Am I a special people?"

"You can't imagine."

"He died three years ago—and—and, oh, he was a strong man. He had the hands of a sculptor and a voice to go with them—when he spoke, which wasn't very often. I'm sure Michelangelo thundered that way, except in Italian. *Boom*! *Boom*! And then days without a word. Booming silences. And then the big one." She paused. "I've wondered since, whether too much restoration can kill a person."

We walked around the side of the house to where the sheds and the former barber shop were lined neatly and looking like they had survived time better than the house itself. Driving to Quaker Falls, I had told about what I had seen on my first visit and the bits of information I had gotten from the woman with the dog. I had searched online to verify the story and found a map with one of the many single-track railroad lines going directly past this hamlet. "I love the idea of it.

People stopping in here to get their moustaches trimmed—their derby hats on a hook by the door—and the smell of Vitalis or whatever they rubbed on then."

"Aren't you something," she said.

"Do your Yankee gutters change your mind about this place?"

"Are you hoping to find gold coins buried under one of these trees?" We had walked to the narrow orchard at the rear of the yard. She was certain one was a pear and one an apple, but she was unable to identify a third one. They were, she told me, full of many years of suckers, but they might be pruned back into service. They were already forming buds and they would, if anything, lend a beauty to the property.

"I know, I know," I replied to her. "But there are times when you get these ideas inside of yourself, and...are there still people like your father, do you think?"

She stood in front of me. "Would it matter?"

"But you do think there's *something* to the idea. I can see it in your face. A girl from the Alleghenies can't be that insensitive."

"A girl from the Alleghenies can think it's a lovely and a moronic idea all at the same time. Don't take it personally."

We looked at the rear of the house. It had a stark lack of ornamentation, and the small porch coming off the kitchen was sinking back to earth on one of its outer corners. We stepped upon it carefully to look in through the door's window, where another torn shade let some of the day's last light inside. The kitchen itself had more in it than we would have guessed: an enamel table, what looked like a bandy-legged electric stove, chairs pushed against the walls like a dance of ghosts had been held there recently, and a woodstove showing its backside to our peering eyes.

"What do you think?" I asked.

She sighed. "It's all too personal, Professor. And it's getting dark."

As we got back into the car, I noticed the woman with the dog walking in our direction. I gave her a partial wave, and in my rearview I saw her stop before the house. She pointed out something to the animal with a noticeable smile on her face.

§

What happened when I returned Nancy to her house was beyond anticipation. She had said very little during that drive from Quaker Falls to the suburbs. Though her sniffling had stopped, she held a Kleenex in one hand and occasionally twisted it with the other, and she would rub her chin against it with a slight up and down motion—as if she was trying to conjure a message from the wadded tissue. Her face was without any definable expression except a striking absence from the moment, which I read initially as a strain of anger. When I had stopped the car in front of her garage, she turned and said to me, "Come inside. I think I'm close to figuring it out."

"What about Michael and Willie?"

"It won't matter. It's a large house. And her car is gone. Michael will be at his computer."

In fact, Michael was gone as well. A note he'd left on the kitchen island read, "Will and I are dropping in on dad."

"He misses his father?" I asked, looking at the compelling orderliness of the kitchen. She had taken off her coat and silently asked for my winter vest, which she put on a chair in the adjacent dining room. Bunched together, they looked like a disruptive force in her domestic world.

"'Missing' is the wrong word. I don't think Michael misses things or people. The place where he spends most of his time has no room for that."

"And where is that?"

"His own inner kingdom. But don't ask me where that is. I don't know."

"And do you miss him?" She looked at me blankly. "Michael's father. Marvin. Marriage."

"Why would you ask that?" She took a well-stuffed envelope from a kitchen drawer full of disorganized utensils—her junk-drawer. "These are divorce papers. They should answer those questions."

"No regrets? People have them, I've heard."

"It's nice to be up on these things, isn't it?"

She clearly was not in a mood to talk of any fallout from her divorce, but she did talk a little of Marvin and their twenty-some years together. She spoke of his recently flourishing tax preparation business and reverted from that to when she had first met him as a new hire at a CPA firm while she was getting teacher certification in Albany. They had met through friends, and their first date was at the Saratoga racetrack. "I should have realized then," she commented, "that he was a bad bet. He tore up his losing tickets into such tiny pieces I thought he was going to sprinkle them on his hot dogs. He ate about six of them that day. I never liked his mouth. It was graceless." But she had married him and had Michael for what she called mysterious reasons, did her mom-thing, studied real estate, got her license, and a year ago told Marvin she wished to "undo things," that he might have more fun without her, and he had agreed that, yes, he might. The undoing went efficiently, and he was gone by summer with suggestions that he had entered a new lady into his ledger.

She had poured each of us a glass of pink-tinted wine without asking if I was drinking yet. Her mouth looked anything but graceless as she tasted it with small but repeated sips. "As far as this afternoon goes, I'm afraid I was a little overwhelmed by your imaginary place of retreat. First, it was so quiet there I kept hearing my heart beat. Or it could have been yours. I don't really know. Heartbeats have always been bad omens, Jeremiah. Heartbeats that I notice is what I mean. They're not unhealthy in the least, but they warn. When I was little, I would go into the loft above my father's workshop while he was doing a project somewhere in the area. There were old hay bales from a time long before me, and I would lie on them and listen to my heart in the stillness of all that straw. I would count along with it only until I didn't need to any longer. One time, though, I was drifting in the silence, and I saw a bat hanging from a rafter above me. He was upside down, as they are supposed to be," she noted instructively. "But he was watching me with his full attention. I broke an ankle—this one," she said, pointing at and flexing the foot, "jumping down from the loft. The ladder would have been better, but I was in no mood to think, you see. I was a peculiar child. And I'd forgotten to wear my glasses." She refreshed her wine. "So much for heartbeats."

"I think I understand."

"But that wasn't the most of it...this afternoon. I loved that house, and its little buildings and its trees and bushes that need pruning. But not for you."

"For you, then?"

"Of course. What could you possibly make of yourself there? It would make you into a truly odd character, and you're odd enough as it is."

"Why thank you."

"I'm just being honest. But for me? I don't want it, of course, any more than I want you to have it. But do you know what it made me think of, when we looked in the windows?"

"A place of instruction," I ventured.

She was startled. "How could you know that? How did you mean it?"

"Your face looked like you were realizing something back into existence. That's the only way I can explain it, Nancy."

"But that's exactly it. How beautifully odd you should know *that*. Here's how it was, so listen." She refilled her wineglass. "It reminded me of the final day of my one year of teaching when I was alone in the classroom, and I felt the emptiness of the entire building. I had been packing up, and I was taking things off the walls that my little artists had drawn, and I had no idea what to do with them. And, of course, I could hear my heart beat. I was about to tumble out of my loft." She stopped, and there were tears in her eyes. "God I loved that room and those crappy, priceless drawings—and I never went back."

I don't imagine I will ever need to know which of us took the other into what became a transparency of pure holding. We could have stepped back to watch the two of us together without damaging what we saw, it was so contained and so outside of us. I finally pulled back to speak to her. "I wish you had."

"How could it mean so much so suddenly? They're gone and grown and it means nothing to *them*."

"Don't sound so certain. To some it could have meant everything."

"Aren't you nice?" She kissed each of my cheeks and then my mouth. The softness of it was without any definition. It was what it was, until it became the leading edge of startled passion in both of us. Her eyes finally looked clearly at me. "Come," she said and took my hand. "We can't stay here." She led me down a stairway off the kitchen into what must have been the family room—when they were still a family. Now it seemed a sorting station with boxes and bundles bunched about. "Marvin's things," she said. She lifted a large carton from one of two loveseats and asked me to lie next to her. "We'll scrunch," she said softly but officiously. "I want to be next to you. This will have to do."

How we made love is too complicated to describe, and it might not have happened, I think, if we hadn't spent so much time adjusting and readjusting like two teenagers in the back seat of a Volkswagen. Comfort gave way to frustration which gave way to laughter which gave way to a startled sense of conspiracy which gave way at last to the commands of freed passion. It was quite astonishing— quite beyond astonishing—until we heard the sound of an automobile outside.

TEN

Teaching would be a safe haven for a time. The perplexities of the classroom seemed to have diminished noticeably with Michael off exploring whatever he explored and Willie now lending her challenges to other colleagues. My new cast of students was politely engaged with what I was offering—although engaged might be too strong a word. They were good about attending, though I had no mandatory attendance policy, much to the annoyance of my chair. To my silent embarrassment, I had a dream about Phyllis Friel one night where she scolded me for the laxity of my standards (something she'd merely hinted at in real-life discussions) and then removed her clothing. Her ears had seemed somewhat smaller surrounded by her stringy nakedness, and she was forcefully proud of the exhibitionism which took place in a boiler room somewhere on campus. She didn't have the courtesy to tell me what we were doing there and she quite fortunately faded into another, less vivid dream before she could propose what it was I was supposed to do about the display she was providing. I do recall that she had a sizeable wooden cross between her breasts, and when I saw her at a meeting the day after the dream, I looked for any telltale cord around her neck. I was shamefully relieved when I couldn't detect one.

Nearly a week had gone by since Nancy and I had "christened" the love seat—as she was wont to refer to our moment out of time and beyond the bounds of practicability, particularly if we were even remotely susceptible to repeating what we had done. We spoke the day after the christening by phone to joke about Michael's sudden arrival after being dumped in the driveway by Willie and of our return to the kitchen pretending to discuss that very love seat and her willingness to sell it to me. I doubt he bought it for a moment, but if not, he seemed pleased by his suspicions and talked easily about having met a woman identified to us as Marvin's "new babe" and the embellishments she had helped add to his apartment. Michael volunteered parenthetically that Willie thought she was what Marvin deserved. The meaning was clear enough.

The next few days, Nancy and I both seemed happy to retreat to the ordered safety of e-mails. They were mostly newsy exchanges, although she did give me a history of the love seat, purchased just before her separation from Marvin. The couches had sat in the family room unused during the transition to new lives, and she noted at one point, "I've always heard redecorating is a sure sign of a dying marriage. Does that make me a cliché?" I wrote back with the assurance that she and the love seat were anything but. Mostly it was the chat of two persons apparently trying not to make sense of being overwhelmed. Until her most unnerving e-mail, the last in the series, where she concluded with the casual announcement that I needn't worry about "shotgun circumstances. I still use birth control." It was a stark reminder of contingencies within contingencies, the material educated twenty-six-year-olds should normally be attuned to.

I went for a walk around campus. It was during class time, and the sidewalks were an uncluttered minister to my thoughts. It was a meticulously maintained campus where dandelions, I had been told, were forbidden from enrolling and trained dogs were used to keep Canada geese from pooping up the lawns. While it was a sight I hoped to see, knowing I would be rooting for the geese, the order was a comfort on this day, especially as it looked and felt like winter was about to return once more. I realized e-mailing was basically out of the question from this time forward, if there was to be forward time. I wondered whether her last statement was a cleaning-up piece of business—a you-are-free-to-go-now concession? Was she doing the responsible adult thing? Had she been the *responsible party*—and had her e-mails been keystrokes to the clarification of her own feelings? But that, of course, did not work out plainly. We had been given the gift of mutual seduction. We had allowed ourselves a candled oneness, at least for that short bit of time. And there was all the rest, my conviction (now stronger than ever) that I had loved her on an arguable level since I sat in her classroom as a little boy who drew pictures for her to hang on the walls with all the others, but ones I truly intended for *her*. Even more off-kilter than the gap of our ages now was that phantom reality of long ago—which it would be dishonest to never share with her. It was too very beautiful to keep hidden, a part of the beauty we had created on the christening couch, as small as a wish and as large as its utterance.

I heard geese above me, as if they had been listening and knew me to be one of their unconquerable champions in the middle of being conquered by my own thoughts. Their sounds were unequivocal as they exchanged with each other signals of homes past and homes to come, waiting readily for them. It was their own symphony, their oboe voices squeezed into the sky for my benefit as well as theirs. There was still inside my musings the image of the house in Quaker Falls, waiting for me to embrace another strand of impossibility and climb upon it. I ached for it in almost the same way I ached for Nancy Feller, the person who more than anything seemed able to read the parallel strings of knowledge and stupidity.

And the students who were now beginning to fill the sidewalks, their classes over or about to begin again—the constant cycle of learning and erasing, coming in one door and out another like a Marx Brothers' sketch—capering so artfully. I would build new schools if I could. I would make them places where choice and the desire to be freely moved would be their own parallel strings. There was a dearness to them, these younger brothers and sisters of my temporary partnership. I knew I wouldn't be teaching much longer—perhaps no longer than the current semester. My courses were slotted for all of next year, waiting for me to insert myself into them and give them shape and reason, but

I was having a more and more difficult time imagining it, and without imagination, how could I give belief to all that was so doubtful.

I gradually recognized that Michael Feller was standing near the doorway to my building. He was thinly dressed, as usual, and with his phone was taking pictures of students and faculty in their coming and going.

"Michael," I said. "What brings you back to the circus?"

"Yeah," he responded, slipping the phone into a pants pocket. "People who come back to things are gamey."

"They smell?"

"Sort of."

"I'll remember that. You're waiting for Willie?"

"I came with Mom."

"Mom?"

"My mother."

"Who is...?"

"Looking for you, upstairs. She left me here, just in case."

"And here I am."

"Sure."

"And the pictures?" He squinted at me. "The pictures you were taking?"

"I like the way things move. People on sidewalks. Then holding them still with a picture. You can feel them push against it." For Michael, it was a dissertation honed to perfection. I asked him if he was staying outside, now that he had found me, and he thought he would.

When I got out of the elevator, I could see Nancy standing across from my office wrapped sleekly in a loden-green coat. Her hair was different in a way I couldn't quite define, but she looked younger and looked at me with shyness or coyness or a blending of both. She had an envelope in her hand that she waved at me, and her mouth softened as I drew near to her. "No more e-mails," I announced, unsure of why I had led off with that.

"No more," she said agreeably. "They make my fingers tingle. This is no time for arthritis." She held out the envelope and exhaled slightly. "I've brought you this. Let me show you."

In my office, she removed several pages and laid them on my desk. She had researched the Quaker Falls house, using her real estate savvy and contacts in municipal offices to discover bits of its history, its current status, and a guess at its price. As she concluded her presentation, she touched my nearest forearm and added, "It still makes me sorry to feel that this isn't, as they say in my business, a good 'fit.' Not for you. I can't imagine you could get a mortgage, and the costs of making it even minimally livable would be very dear."

"Dear?"

"That's how they talked in the mountains. They probably still do."

"I truly hope so. Anyhow, it means enough that you went to all this bother to shatter my fantasy."

"Not to shatter it, Professor—only to put a *fragile* label on it." She reached into a coat pocket to pull out a smallish book. "But as long as you're having your obsession, I thought you might like this." It was a brief history of railroads in the area, bound like a small hymnal and stiff in its bindings. It was doubtful it had ever been read, although there was a simple inscription on a flyleaf: "For Mame"—or "For Mama". It was difficult to tell.

"Where did you find this?" I asked.

"I have friends in bookstores. You, sir, aren't the only remaining reader on the planet."

I was struck with a small bolt of awe at the book's existence and her having found it. So much of my recent life had been devoted to older texts and the real-life hungers that made people write about the worlds they lived within, real or imagined. I would resonate with the idea that some of them could believe enough in what they were doing to fancy my reading them years into the future. But this, this little nonliterary book, resonated in its own way. It was someone's passion for weeks or a part of a lifetime.

"It's not very well written. There are typos," she warned me.

"I'll love it better for that. I really will."

"But look," she said, taking the book from me and turning to a page bookmarked with what looked like a piece of paper napkin. "Look at this picture, Jeremiah. It's your fantasy hamlet with a milk train pulling into the station, and the station isn't much bigger than your barber shop."

I stared into the picture, taken in 1886 and impressed onto a post card. It didn't show much else except the surrounding hills. There was one grainy person standing on the platform, a woman from what I could make out. "And there," I said, jabbing the photo, "someone with all of that one long ago moment to be a part of—doing who knows what? But *she* knew. She knew perfectly well. It's crazy how old pictures work against everything else that happens. Call it Michael's Law."

"What?"

"He's shooting the crowds outside."

"Yes." She flipped a few pages that moved with the difficulty of a long, sedentary life. "There are timetables, too. It was fifty-five minutes from Rhinebeck. That's twice what it would take by car now, but it must have been like riding a rocket then, don't you think?"

"Could we go somewhere and talk?"

"I thought we were mostly doing just that."

"Where can we go?"

"I know a place. It's not far."

As we started out, though, we found Michael sitting composedly on the floor of the corridor a few yards from my office. He was flipping through the pictures he had been taking with the look of an artist. "Look at this, Mom." He held the phone up to Nancy. "It's people."

"So I would gather."

"Look at the patterns."

"The...patterns," she faltered.

"People make patterns. They make music. See? Base clef, treble clef."

He drew his finger a couple of times over the small picture, and Nancy gave it her best effort to share his discovery. "Obviously, Michael, you are learning a lot about music."

"Sure."

As they walked toward the elevator together, I felt let down but uncheated. Michael made it unreasonable to feel that way; he continued to redefine significance for me; and, in any event, Nancy's "place" would have had to wait. My own cell vibrated, and I saw I had received two messages: one an invitation to Barbara Lynn and Emily's wedding, the other from Alban Curtin by way of Louisa Sondstrom.

I had been making weekly visits to The Professor since he told me of the disease he was preparing to die from—a process, from what I could see, that felt like a continuation of his years of preparation for a new classroom offering. He was designing a syllabus for non-existence, fascinating me with his approach. I suppose he had always fascinated me but mostly in negative ways. His detachment had left me to my own devices throughout the years of approaching adulthood, but my anger was an effective generator of purpose, even as I found myself walking in his footsteps. I couldn't divert myself from the pull of the scholar's world even as I chastised myself—until, that is, I was able, through some slight of the imagination, to believe I was showing fortitude in the face of what, to others, surely looked like weakness. To be that obvious was an elevation of the spirit. Or so I instructed myself.

Each week I went to him, he was fulfilling his own prediction. He was growing ever thinner, and the veins on his head and arms were becoming more defiant. They were lines on a chalkboard where he was working out his last lesson—perhaps the only improvised lesson of his life. He rarely talked about his condition in any direct way, although he was, as he had always been, skillful with a metaphor.

Louisa let me in after I had perplexed myself by ringing the bell. My wallet contained a key to the front door, and I knew the code for the alarm system. On this day, though, I had mentally locked myself out. Louisa's smile was more compressed than usual, and it was clear his need for her to be there was wearing on her. He ate very little, but her presence remained a benefit to him. Even though he was tended to by a visiting nurse, it was Louisa who mattered. Until recently, she still had the ability to draw a thin line of laughter from him. She would tempt him with Swedish küchen, knowing he was now likely to turn down one of his few indulgences. But for her, the game was still a necessary attention to be paid, and I couldn't esteem her enough for it. She took my hands between hers. They were warm and firm.

"He iss in his bed," she told me. "He did not t'ink you would mind."

I had rarely been in his bedroom. I had even more rarely seen *him* in there, he who had usually seemed to sleep in widely spaced spurts. It was a simple enough room, in contrast to the rich textures of his study. For as long as I could remember, it had been painted a clinical white, now at last too excessively appropriate. The furniture itself was light shades of maple, and there were no books anywhere in the room, not even on the nightstand next to him. There was only a yellow pad and a pencil. The nurse was cleaning something in the adjoining bathroom and had come out when she heard me say "Father" to him. She was tiny, probably less than five feet, a distorted contrast to Louisa, who stood behind me; she had an achingly tight face that looked as if a smile would be an extra chore, but I was struck by the sapphire resonance of her eyes. They matched the one contrasting element in the room—the headband of Vermeer's *Girl with a Pearl Earring* hanging on the wall facing the bed. If the reproduction had been a longtime part of his life, I didn't know, but the face in the portrait had the expression of recent discovery and puzzlement over what to do with it. Her widened eyes were at that equivocal point of neither engaging nor looking away, while her shoulder pointed directly at the viewer like a tool used for portioning realization. Did she remind him of the wife who had freed herself from him, or a place in time where anticipation was making a tactful withdrawal?

The nurse and Louisa soon left us alone.

He was wearing a brown robe of thick flannel, and he had something resembling an ascot tied around his neck. The bedcovers were orderly, and the two pillows behind him were freshly plumped. The only chair was of the metal folding type and had been leaned, shut tight, against the far wall. I stood at the foot of the bed.

"I'm going to hospice," he said without preliminary. His voice was taut but not difficult to hear. "It's a word I have always respected the sound of. It conveys assurance."

"What can I do to help?"

"Oh, this needs no help. I will have all the help I need," he added, contradicting himself. I noticed he had been growing the thin line of a beard around the border of his chin, a faint recollection of the one he had removed after Ellen's departure. Otherwise, he was cleanly shaven and carefully groomed—hair, eyebrows, nails. This personal project, for a man who had grown to detest the affectation of beards, especially in academia, was an unreadable statement. I could feel moisture at the edges of my eyes.

"What do you wish me to know?" I followed up with the hope there was no exasperation in the question.

"Ah," he uttered. "A connection."

"I do hope so."

"Given enough time..." His voice trailed off. "First...Jeremiah...I have a question or two for you."

"Yes. I hope so. I'm glad."

"Don't be. One...will you keep teaching?"

"I doubt it."

"So." It was one of his cherished sounds of dismissal. "Two...will you...regret it?"

"The teaching or the not teaching?"

"I don't know."

"I don't either."

"So." He stared at the Vermeer reproduction over my shoulder. "I thought there might be...three."

"Yes?"

"There aren't." He rested for what felt like a minute, gazing occasionally at me and running fingers along his shadowy beard line. Finally, he took the pad from the night table. "I have a few closing... comments...for you."

"Please. I would like to hear them"

"Point one," he said with no other lead-in and stabbing the pad with a finger. "I don't wish for you to come where I...will be. There is no valuable material there. Point two: there is, as you are...aware, to be no after-activity of any kind." He had made it clear throughout the years that he was no believer in what he referred to as the "death industry." It was, he said, like the "jail industry"—a statement that had startled me more than the preceding one. What did he know about jails? He had, though, taken extravagant satisfaction many times, over the fact that Georgian England pickpockets had worked the crowd watching the hanging of a fellow cutpurse. "I have," he continued, "instructed that any bodily debris—such as ash—be disposed of...haphazardly. And, for your clarification, I will not have 'passed away.'" I knew he hated that softening of such a salient fact. "I will have *died*."

"Point three..." He coughed. "Point three: there will be a...session... with my lawyer on March twenty-second. I will be well out of all this by then. You will be there, even if you have to miss a class. I didn't take the time to check your teaching schedule." His voice was becoming stronger for some reason.

"Point four...Your mother. There is no...need for her...knowledge... of this. If she finds out at some point...so be it."

"Yes, sir."

"Point five." He looked one more time at his notes, then set the pad next to his legs on the bedspread. "There is no point."

ELEVEN

The Professor intended that visit to be the last time I saw him. It didn't turn out that way. I rejected his request and came to his hospice room the day he died. The need to defy was greater than the need to yield, the need to confront greater than the need to disregard, not to defy or confront *him* necessarily. I suppose more than anything, it was the need to defy and confront myself. I wanted one more opportunity to hold my spirit up to his and see if the gulf between could really be that enormous after all. I told Nancy a few days after the visit to his house that I wanted to find a presence in his desire to obliterate himself. I wanted to stand before his careful construction of nothingness and make it mean *something*. It was the same day I tried to convince her that love in need of explanation was blessedly unexplainable. Of course, she challenged me to explain even as she tried to dodge it.

She met me at the Vanderbilt Rose Garden, where she had wished to take me on the day she brought the material on houses and railroads to my office. It was an Italianate garden in an enclosed area of the mansion grounds. In season, she told me, it was a place of reflecting pools and assortments of flowers well beyond roses. Now it was a place of chilled rose branches and scattered leaves and bits of paper along the paths. Great naked oaks stood at a distance outside the walls, brown bunches of last year's leaves clinging to them, indifferent to two huddled people in a chapel-like gazebo at the south end of the garden. The falls of Crum

Elbow Creek passing through the property made coolly garbled sounds in the distance, and the skies themselves had the look of foaming cataracts. We were accompanied by the statue of a woman on a pedestal. She was partly unclothed, wrapped in a gossamer inner garment, and a more opaque stola that she lifted upward with one raised hand. She was gazing downward at the empty pool, which was unable to reflect her at this time of year. One foot was tentatively reaching forward as if she couldn't quite accept the temporary state of things.

"Nice body," Nancy said demurely. "Nice firm breasts. They call her Barefoot Kate. She is waiting to test the waters."

"I see. And what is she supposed to be?"

"My twin sister. But I call her Katherine." She was obviously pleased with herself, and she ran her hand down one of Kate's thighs, before slipping a hand into my arm. "Is this a good place to have the talk you wanted?" she asked.

"It's not as warm as a bar or a chocolate shop, but it's well-aired. And I agree. It's good for testing waters, even if there are none."

"It is, and it's ours for the day. Or what's left of it." Once again, it was midafternoon, giving our time the pinch of concluding business. There was no one place to begin.

"First of all," I told her, "my father is dying."

"I didn't know. I'm sorry."

"It isn't as if you and I have been burning up the air with long, newsy conversations."

"But we *have* been together." She seemed to consider the phrase. "Once or twice. It might have come up."

"I'm sorry. It just didn't."

"I know nothing about your parents."

"My father teaches...taught."

"And that's why you're so conflicted about your own teaching?"

"Conflicted?" She nodded. "Maybe. But that's not on today's agenda."

"I usually find people like you who have agendas also have little intention of sticking to them."

"I'll bet Marvin did."

"Never mind, but yes he did. And your mother?"

"She most definitely has agendas."

"That's not what I meant. I mean, you should tell me about her."

There was an extended silence accompanied by a puzzling sense of doubt. There are times when it is unclear what you feel so very doubtful about, and it looms within like a breath that has been held too long. So I talked about The Professor again, the bedroom conversation, his questions and edicts, and my need at last to directly undermine one last wish. She encouraged me to be with him at hospice.

"Deep down," she urged quietly, "he wants you there. I believe that. Call it intuition, or call me a good reader of inherited stubbornness. I have it myself. When my father was dying, he told me things about myself that I didn't want to hear. My whole life he had trumpeted the sanctity of marriage, and then, at that moment, he told me *I* married Marvin out of thick-headedness—that I got from him, naturally—even though he still loved my mother. And he loved Michael, I'm quite sure." It was quite a performance. She seemed to be summoning up a picture. "But you should go." Her puzzled smile was, in its own way, expressing the beauty of conviction. "And your mother?"

"I can assure you she will not be there." Nancy's face looked strained now, her eyes softly processing the presence of an unknown pain. I ducked within silence again, my thoughts crouching into a compressed and graceless ache. Finally, I blurted "You met her once." I was unable to avoid it, but I saw by the look on Nancy's face that I could not brush past it with a small piece of misdirection. It would have its way with us. "When I was in first grade. Your first grade. It was a PTA night or whatever they call them. She liked you, I'm sure."

She pulled back, and the hand tucked through my arm was removed. "I see. It's good to be liked, isn't it? But, please, let's start this over again."

'Which?"

"Jeremiah, I don't know a great deal about you, but I've already let you unbalance me too many times. You're going to tell me you were a pupil of mine?"

"That's a wonderful word: pupil. I've never thought of myself as a pupil. Is it a word from the Alleghenies?"

"You and your words. You tie tails to them."

"Actually, I would love to be done with them. Do you think it's possible, soul-satisfied wordlessness?" Her face had done a severe masking-over. "And, yes. That was *me* back then. Along with the others who didn't really matter."

"You seem so dangerous, suddenly—so pleasing to yourself." Her voice rose. "Of course they mattered. Every one of them. What is it you're trying to do?"

"I'm trying to prepare you, Nancy, for the fact that I've loved you since I was six. It shouldn't matter, and it should count for everything, but it's going to do what it's going to do."

She stood and put on the gloves she had taken off when we first approached Barefoot Kate. A patch of blush had worked its way up her throat, highlighting the thin lines of her neck. "That's such a dodge, Jeremiah. It's so slick I want to punch you right on your forehead."

"And it matters?"

"Everything matters."

"It's an insurmountable problem that you poured stuff into me at a very young age that's lasted until I could put on my adult self?"

"Yes, I think it is. And I think this version of a conversation has gone far enough, whether what you are telling is true or not." She exhaled. "And what is it, Jeremiah, that we're trying to surmount?"

"Appearances."

"No," she said crisply as if that were the punch to my forehead. "No, Professor, no! You can appear to be whatever you like or *whoever* you like. I'll provide the mirror, but I won't hold it. And I don't have to hear you making your 'words' into schoolroom decorations." She took a deep breath. "And what about your mother now?"

"Now?"

"Where is she? What is she?"

"Who knows? She ran off when I was in my teens. She flew the coop. She left me longing for a new mother." I had tried to sound as facetious as possible. It was another miss.

"You're being ridiculous, just when I imagined being hopeful." She was walking now but turned back while rubbing one glove with the other. "Are you coming?"

"Should I?"

"Don't be a child."

As we left the sleeping garden, it was evident Nancy had regained the purposeful step she had shown in Rhinebeck two months before. Her coat hung below her knees, giving her the sleek stride of someone stalking a piece of ground and claiming ownership of it. Her face had gained a stunning serenity, and whatever color had risen to her throat before had now retreated fully. We moved toward the great, columned autumn retreat built by the son of mammon worshiper Cornelius Vanderbilt, and who, like his super-rich cronies, had been disingenuous enough to call this immense display a cottage. I could see beyond, down a roadway lined with silhouetted maples, the overlook I had bicycled to with Ellen. A few visitors were ending their tour of the mansion, dwarfed under its front portico. They were like gray spittings, the house massively indifferent to their shrunken conclusion. I had had the same feeling the one time I took the tour: that I was, at the end, like a dust ball being swept from floors where people had scarcely lived even in the age of its occupation. As we neared the parking area, after a long, wordless period of time, Nancy finally added to her comment. "Or if you're going to be a child, be less obviously cute about it." She shook my hand, as she had in Rhinebeck.

§

I have heard somewhere that being in a death room during a person's final hours can be a profoundly peaceful time. People speak of a false dawn, a sudden and powerful awakening before the great sleep. The dying person will demonstrate renewed vitality suggesting the crisis has been magically subverted and all of the mournful preparation of the watchers was unnecessary. That wasn't quite the case in the final hours I spent with The Professor, but it was close. I didn't know I would find him in a coma when I arrived; and I suppose, in part, that was why I experienced my own version of tranquil discovery—that and the fact that there were none of the machines and wires Hollywood had caused me to expect. There was only a small piece of breathing apparatus in his nose. The room itself felt more a country inn than a hospital, and the lighting was subdued without being mournful. Antique music like that of a Renaissance banquet was playing.

As importantly, Louisa was there, his only real family for some time. She rose from the chair where she had been looking at a book and patted one of my shoulders. "I knew you would come here." She looked at the figure on the bed. "He may know you even if he cannot tell you so."

"You've been so good to him."

"Only somm of the time."

"That he must know, too." She offered me the book, telling me it was one of his. Even under the soft light, I could make out his name embossed on the cover and binding. It was nothing I recognized and didn't seem to be a scholar's work at all. It was entitled simply *Reconsiderations*, and it was nakedly without a publisher's imprint, like it had given birth to itself. While he had been primarily a critical theorist throughout his career, he had pursued any number of scholarly avenues that seemed worthy of his efforts. Those avenues excluded contemporary literature for the most part, but he had found investigative havens in the Medieval and Elizabethan periods, and to a greater extent in the seventeenth century.

"The dirtier the streets," he once said to me in an offhanded way, "the better I like those who walked there." It was one of his many contradictions—that this person of spotless appearance was attracted to those who wore the accumulated soil of days and weeks on themselves.

"He kept it inside his file cabinet," she told me. "It was in a folder, and he asked me to bring to him. To here. But he already was where he is now. I read a little while I wait. I t'ink maybe it makes me know him a little. Was it a bad t'ing I did?"

"It was perfect. Please keep it, and if you can loan it to me at some point, I would be grateful." She nodded a "ya" and stood indecisively before gathering up the book, her purse, and coat. "I go now. I have the duties at home." It was a reminder of life's rooms, which can sit side-by-side, nest within one another, or have little connection at all except the sound of closing doors.

I didn't know what to say to her. I would see her again, of course. There was much to be done about his house, although I'd been certain since Christmas that he had left instructions with someone on how to deal with those details. He had never said anything to me about it.

With Louisa gone, I had the room to myself except for occasional brief visits from staff people. At first, the music guided my reflections to young Nancy in her hayloft and the grown woman I had challenged with the upside-down-ness of memory. Had the bat in her Alleghany rafters become my inverted view of things? Had the tumbling discussion at Vanderbilt been enough to drive her from me? Had her loft become a rabbit hole? Had her gentle urging that helped bring me to this room been transmuted into her own grounds for reconsiderations? And if so, reconsiderations of what? Had the gift of a railroad book been a reaching out or an indication that there were always timetables for reconsidering? Would the christening of the love seat be its own grounds for reconsiderations—that when passion leaps boundaries, it only makes those boundaries more clearly defined?

And The Professor's reconsiderations—what were they? What was in the book Louisa had been reading? She had been willing enough to leave it with me, but it was hers right then, and it's likely I was unprepared for a work he had written from inside out, the opposite of what he usually did. He should be as I knew him: the dissecting scholar, who cut the works of others into small pieces and quilted them together to satisfy his need for tranquil domination. Or that was how I had grown to think of it. I had read most of his scholarship, not in his house but in libraries where I should have been focusing on other work. But I would, at least, have him in this manner, though I was well aware at an early age about the quest for the father as an all-too-common literary device and the oedipal longing for the mother. There was little I could do about being device-matter to any who cared to look at my own dynamics. Especially Nancy and her hayloft clarity. It was no doubt clear enough that I was hungering for my mother, even though I was not.

There must be frustration for anyone pressed into a pattern, but as I listened to the thin breathing from the bed, I found it became its opposite. It was an opportunity to wage war on coincidence by acknowledging easy judgments and moving through them. I had admired his work and the cool workings of his mind. I was sniffy about critical theory and its detachment from the pain of creation, but I could see how easily he did it, making detachment the gift of an approving god. When I should have been researching for the papers I needed to write, as both an undergraduate and graduate, I repeatedly defied the immediate need in order to push my mind up against his. He appeared almost heroic in his own questing—for what, I could not know. In his writing, he seemed so calmly willing to fail in his drive to detach himself. But he was praised for his efforts. The jackets of his books were tattooed with generous compliments from fellow scholars, and I was pleased for him. And his writing was both meticulous and readable. I could at times almost make sense of what he was saying even though he was reaching down from a realm of critical jargon I found to be like the words of a secret society.

But the book Louisa was reading...what was I prepared to find in that, if I did indeed bring myself to open it at some point? When had he written it? I should at least have looked at the copyright date. Why had I never seen it shelved in a college library? Had he brought it privately into its final form? Is that why he kept it tucked away in a file cabinet so that it would never stand on a shelf? And why had he asked for it now? *Reconsiderations* was a comfortable-sounding title—but not for him. Had he gone against his own granite-smooth grain in writing this? Had he left scratches on the forbidding surface of his life? Why rub against it one last time?

I had fallen asleep when the attending person touched my shoulder to tell me he had died. I had been dreaming my common teacher's dream. I had forgotten to meet with a class for an entire semester and needed to unfreeze myself in front of them, to apologize, and to promise them we would get through all of the material in the two remaining days. The dream students had, of course, been attending faithfully, waiting each period for my non-arrival and leaving, apparently, without complaint or without trying to discover why I had left them untended and untaught for three months. I think, though, they were happy to see me.

His body was still in the bed, his face uncovered. I had never been in a room of death before, and I had avoided funeral homes, drawing support from his own scorn for the way Americans treated the dead. He had left me behind with Ellen when he went to his own mother's funeral in Maine. And when he returned, he had famously said to the two of us, "How grotesquely we make dying a tunnel we imagine our way into through all our living days. Then we make it into a withering thank-you at the last. Let them, if they wish, but leave me out of it." On this day, as I stood by the bed and gazed down at him, I wondered what tunnel he had just passed into. Was it to be confirming darkness, or had he come to a passage for reconsideration?

I could not have imagined the ease with which, at last, I bent over and kissed his forehead before leaving the room to others.

TWELVE

In my very brief time as a teacher, I had been close to experiencing one or two moments of what Barbara Lynn Hynes calls magic. According to her, in the magic class session, students and teacher achieve a relatively unified level where no one is in charge and dialogue of the moment propels itself with unanticipated energy, clarity, and emotion, braiding itself. I assumed in her case this was a common occurrence, given the pulsations I had heard from her classroom during the fall semester. However, she assured me it was quite rare, even for an agitator such as herself who tended to put too heavy a foot on the gas pedal and that if you were lucky enough to experience it at all, you should be grateful and treat it as an anointing from a benevolent being. It was also what kept her looking for a new teaching position after being denied tenure—that and Emily's urging that she continue to do for students what she had done for her: Emily Botticelli (as I continued to think of her), the cherubic public agitator who would be her marriage partner in May, the same day as our commencement. I assumed Barbara Lynn was intending to convey a portion of complex feelings by the timing, but quite possibly that, too, had been a wish of Emily's.

After occasional hints of approaching the magic moment only to see the wave break too early, the high-water day for me came shortly after the death of The Professor. It was as if the two events were connected, that he was affording me the luxury of not feeling his head upon my shoulders if I would but notice. At the least, my bottled up emotions had their part to play and did so with precise accuracy. I felt obligated to teach *Huckleberry Finn* in a course on American literature. It was, Hemingway said, where our literature began, though I had rarely felt I should pay attention to the pronouncements of a man like Papa so given to overdoing and over-saying things. Also, there were the problems of dialect, particularly among the slave characters, and there was the issue of dealing with the word nigger again and again throughout the narrative.

It took three class periods to make our way down the Mississippi, and classroom reactions were what I had anticipated: all the characters talked funny, Huck was a little stupid, Jim was a creature of strange superstitions, Tom Sawyer was repeatedly unlikable, and Twain went on and on. By the time we reached Louisiana, my students seemed like they had been rafting up-river for two weeks. We had come to the point where Huck, knowing Jim has been captured and locked away on a local plantation, decides he should write to Miss Watson back in Missouri, hoping Jim can at least go back to the servitude he has grown up with and Huck can clear his conscience of helping Jim escape in the first place. He feels real good about having written the letter and saving himself from the eternal fires of evangelical Hell, until he realizes he has grown to love Jim during their time on the raft, and he tears up the letter with the astonishing flourish of a line, "All right, then, I'll go to hell."

I had students reading various passages aloud as we worked our way through the text, and in this case Lucia Solis, a young Hispanic woman with an overlaid Bronx accent, who was slightly older than the others, burst suddenly into tears. Lucia uttered "Oh, my God" and closed the book. It was clear this was the first time she had read the scene, that she and many others had not bothered to look at the material outside of class. "He just sent himself to the other place." She had barely spoken during the early weeks of the course, and to call this a breakout moment would be to minimize its genuine drama. Several had begun to sniffle, and as I walked out from behind the lectern, I realized my own eyes were glossing over. I thought to apologize but decided not to: the moment of magic was apparently here. For the rest of the session, there was universal participation. I couldn't acknowledge hands quickly enough, and hands eventually became unnecessary during this fully blossomed conversation. Not everyone called Huck a hero, though many did. For some, he didn't really know what he was doing; he was too ignorant. He was a product of his own age when people thought it was all right to own people, and Huck seemed to think so, too. On and on it went. My eyes had dried, and I asked the others who had cried what had been moved in them. They were not sure, but they were unembarrassed and there was, for a few minutes, a collective understanding—like a light shining upon us from an outer source—and summed up when the young woman who had started it all said to the rest, "He believed that was where he was going—the hell-pit, but his heart was bigger. How could he be anything but a hero?"

By the next class, things were back to normal. Few could be induced to speak, and there was an even greater aura of unpreparedness. Lucia Solis texted to say she couldn't be in class because of family matters. There it was, like an embarrassment erased from the air.

§

With the death of The Professor, my parking lot dismissal by Nancy Feller, and events at the college, I had thought little about Quaker Falls. That was to change when I came home one March afternoon to find Willie Furman and an elderly woman rocking side by side on the front porch of the house. I had sat there a few times in the fall, when the weather was still warm enough, but throughout the winter it had been nothing more than an extended threshold. It was a large, unenclosed area, maintaining the late-Victorian feeling of a time when houses like this held one large family. As Hamilton Graham had pointed out to me, it even had the robin's-egg blue ceiling that was a tradition of its time. It was, he had explained in all seriousness, a way of fooling bugs into thinking it was the sky, though I found myself trying to think like an insect and could make no sense of it.

It was a pleasant day, with the sun still low enough to run its rays onto the porch. The two figures sat there comfortably, like the best of friends, rocking slightly. Willie appeared calmed by the presence of the other woman and smiled as if she were handing out secrets.

"Hey," she greeted me.

"And hey right back."

The other sucked in her cheeks and tipped her head to one side. "I used to hear people discourage the use of that word. 'Hay is for horses,' they would say. 'Hay is for horses.'" Her voice was reedy but pleasant enough, sounding like that of a person learning to speak again. "You're my neighbor from downstairs, aren't you? I've seen you many times from my window. You're always carrying books, and I've seen you drop a few on the sidewalk."

"He's a teacher," Willie told her. "Clumsy when he's not careful."

I ignored her and approached her companion. "I am happy to meet you at last. My name is Jeremiah."

"Yes, I know." She seemed pleased with the confirmation.

"And this, for your information," Willie said indulgently, "is Miss Jewett."

I knew the name from her mailbox—Eleanor Jewett—and I told her so. She mentioned that Ham called her Miss Ellie, and I could do as I wished. I repeated to her how glad I was to meet her, and I was. She was wrapped in a brown shawl that might have given her the look of feeble old age but didn't. Her hands, grasping its edges, still had a semblance of dexterity as she manipulated the garment, and she used them confidently to gesture with. Her face, under a wide-brimmed hat, had few lines, and her eyes communicated a leveling focus. Her mouth had the pucker of self-confidence and the pursed attitude of one who believes the pleasures of life are not over. It was she who told me that Wilhelmina—as she called her—had become her friend over the last several weeks—that Hamilton had brought her over to meet her and they had "hit it off." Willie nodded at that. She clearly enjoyed, in this case, bringing the gift of herself to another. I learned that Miss Jewett had not been out of her apartment since the previous summer, and it was Willie who had coaxed her down the stairs. According to the older woman, "Wilhelmina could make anybody do anything, even if they are afraid of behaving like a damn idiot."

The three of us laughed. Willie was flattered. I loved the quiet pop of "damn" coming from that confident mouth. I asked if I could join them for a time, not wanting to be an interruption but drawn to their little circle. They invited me as if they had been awaiting my arrival. There was no other chair on the porch, so I brought one out from my bedroom, a ladder-back I still associated with Sara Sampson's underthings.

I spent a half hour with my sudden lady friends. I learned from Eleanor Jewett that she had been named after Mrs. Roosevelt, confirmed that she had served as governess for one of the Roosevelt grandchildren (though she coyly refused to name which one), and had spent much of her pre-governess life living in England. She had lived in her current apartment since what she referred to as "The Time of Reagan," and she was sure that president had "shoe-polished his hair, so nobody would notice what an old fool he was." She had a revulsion for cats, particularly ones belonging to older women. I was oddly pleased to hear that, while Willie snorted with quiet satisfaction. It was an unusual bonding point, but it served us well, as if we were sharing a plate of finger sandwiches. She was another older person who guarded her mysteries for whatever gratification they gave her. While she was a good many years older than The Professor, she matched up well with him: her articulation, her well-directed eyes, and her delight in withholding. I wondered if she had written a book.

She had met Michael Feller. She'd found him endearing. She thought Willie might be too much for him but that he would eventually grow into her. I immediately visualized Michael inflating as he stood before the imposing Miss Furman and smiled at his own gratifying achievement. Willie nodded during much of this, rocking with contentment and saying little. The early spring sun had already reddened her cheeks, drawing out faint freckles. In a few weeks, she would look like her more mischievous self. On this afternoon, they added a quiet softness to her face, and she appeared to be under their spell the longer the three of us sat together. It wasn't until well past our being a comfortably settled grouping that she said, "I hear you're buying a house." In her usual frame of mind, it would have sounded like an accusation. For the moment, it had the resonance of a blessing.

Miss Jewett was quick to pick up on the statement. "You will be leaving us? That will be most sad, given that I've just this minute gotten to know you."

I spoke to the older woman. "Don't toss me out of your life yet. It's a small idea that still has a long way to travel."

"That's good," she replied. "I would like to know you a little longer." She paused. "Or possibly not good. You should be doing some settling in by this time in your life. Apartments are fine in their way if they come with a good supply of mothballs. I am one who should know. But there is nothing like a house. Nothing at all. Mostly." She clearly was recalling elements of her earlier life, and I wished I could ply her with whatever would make her share her story.

It was Willie who stopped rocking to say to her, "You must have some doozies." Her friend was understandably puzzled. "Stories," Willie explained.

"Why, of course I do. Would you like to hear a few...doozies?" She wrapped her mouth around the word, reminding me of old news footage showing her first-lady namesake doing something similar.

"You bet," Willie replied.

"Fine, but not today you won't. Lift me up." Both of us stood to help her to her feet. Miss Jewett crossed haltingly to the front railing, and her eyes briefly scanned the street in both directions. She turned to me. "There is nothing like a house, young man...as long as you fill it with love. But I'm sure I don't have to tell you that. You're the teacher."

Willie guided her into the hallway and upward to Eleanor's apartment. I stood in front of my own until I heard the door shut above me. It was like the sound of a wooden trunk being closed, muted but decisive. It made the building feel more comfortably packaged with an actual person—as opposed to a faceless nibbler of walls—who was now added to my life there. And for her to be who and what she was gave the impermanence of an apartment dweller a kind of ballast. It was as if she had descended upon me that day to give the temporary its own life force.

I was putting school materials on the table that served as both desk and dining surface when there was a quiet knock. I could hear Willie's "Hey" as she tested the knob. The door popped open with a suddenness that stunned even the unflappable person staring in at me.

"Oops!"

"It's a becoming sound," I told her. "I never thought I would hear it coming from you. I assume you'd like to come in."

"I assume so." She had recovered herself nicely and came toward the table where I was still removing books from the cloth grocery bag that served as my briefcase. "Books," she declared. "How come there aren't any others in this place? Do you have something against books?"

"Why, no, not at all. But too many books make the time being look too permanent, and, as you have suggested, I may move on one of these days."

"To a house in the boondocks." It was not a question.

"Yes. Or maybe."

"Typical. Yes and maybe." Her freckles seemed to have darkened in the last several minutes.

"I like your friend—your Miss Jewett. I should thank you."

"For what?"

"For springing her from her cell. I'm embarrassed to be just now meeting her."

"You should be."

"What's it like in there—in her apartment?"

Willie pressed her lips together. "It's her. Nothing has moved from one place to another in a hundred years. That's what it feels like. Pictures. Lots of pictures. And books. She's not afraid of books."

"I see. Do you want something to drink—soda? water?"

"No, thanks. But what a guy. Anyway, I have to be going."

"Was there some reason you broke in here?"

She looked at the fireplace where she had settled that night with her half-brother and Sara Sampson. “I just wanted to see what you thought about her—Eleanor.”

“She’s splendid. I’m happy to know she’s not afraid of books.”

“And I wanted to say...you know...about your dad.”

Willie was the imp of the unexpected, but this one outdid her. I instinctively moved away from her, noticing the door was still open and not knowing whether to close it or not. I left it as it was.

“You know, Willie, some people have ‘dads,’ and some have... whatever else. But I thank you. That was very nice.”

“Well....” She moved toward the doorway.

“By the way, that’s where my books are: in his house. I’ll be dealing with them soon.”

“Oh.” She paused. “You won’t live there?”

“No.”

“You’ll still move to the boonies?”

“Can’t say.”

“You’re a strange guy.”

“I guess.”

She looked peculiarly vulnerable as she started out and brushed painfully against the doorframe.

“You never talk about your parents, Willie. Maybe sometime?”

“I would imagine not. They’re not that interesting.”

“You’re worse than our friend upstairs.”

“I told you.” She rubbed her shoulder and darted off.

THIRTEEN

On the same day Nancy Feller and I finally agreed to rendezvous at the campus chapel, there was a department meeting that could have been scripted by Lewis Carroll or Ken Kesey. I had not heard from her in almost two weeks when I received her e-mail asking to meet at two o'clock. While we had supposedly sworn off e-mailing, the slippage of so much time gave it a practicality. It was a puzzling request given the location. I considered a counteroffer, but I had stored up so much to say since our last awkward meeting at the Rose Garden that I agreed to the appointment. And, as it turned out, anticipation of this off-kilter rendezvous was undoubtedly intensified by an off-kilter performance in front of my departmental colleagues.

Seven of us were there for the noon meeting. We were a department of ten; however, two were at one of the many other meetings going on across campus during this Wednesday free slot, and one was seeing a gynecologist—information I didn't feel the need to know but our chair clearly took pleasure in announcing. Phyllis Friel loved the urgency of a meeting, insisted that such sessions start on time (a "prompt curtain" was how she referred to it), and I could picture her waving a baton during these sessions if she could have slipped one into her act. She taught dramatic literature and some theater but didn't seem to know of any playwrights prior to Neil Simon. It didn't matter: her convictions about the lack of value in other periods served her cozily. Chuck Gillis liked meetings even more than she did. They were a tidy field for probing and extended discussions that hopefully, in his apparent estimation, led nowhere. He had told me after one meeting that the phrase "move the question" was as tasteful as a bowel movement. The others on this day were Mitchell Schreiber, who taught Milton and Dryden with gloomy gusto and thought Alban Curtin was one of the supreme academic minds of the last half-century; Rachel VanNoys, an advanced composition specialist who proclaimed her American ancestors had helped Peter Stuyvesant plant his orchard and polish his wooden leg; Richard Woo (Victorian and Post-Colonial); Edwina Sharpe, who specialized in the history of the novel but, like me, couldn't get her students to read them.

Friel, Gillis, and Schreiber were what some referred to as The Triumvirate. They were not only the veterans of the department but would also seek the support of each other to do what Woo referred to as "vile deeds" involving tenure, promotion, and curricular proposals. Rarely would any one of them act alone, but when they were on the same page, they could be formidable. Richard doubted he would have gotten tenure without his Chinese ancestry, and usually he sat at meetings without saying anything, spending his time instead drawing quite good caricatures of the rest of us for his own entertainment. He was usually at a far corner of the conference table where his artwork escaped the eyes of others, but he was often pleased to share his results with me as a colleague who still seemed immune to the influence of The Triumvirate. My favorite caricature was the one of Dr. Friel, taking extraordinary advantage of her outsized ears where a group of sparrows was setting up housekeeping. I tried chiding myself for enjoying the sketch quite so much, but my response was another indication that I clearly was not cut out to be an academic.

On this particular day, we had a guest. Mikhail Jefferson had requested an appearance before the department to propose his Bible course be retitled "Bible as Literature" to serve both Philosophy and English requirements. It seemed a reasonable request to me, one that would not encroach directly on any of my colleagues, and I anticipated an unusually brief meeting that would free me to think about the woman waiting in the chapel. It was a correct assumption but for the wrong reasons.

Jefferson was greeted with smiles by everyone except Schreiber and the stony-faced Woo, who was actually a good campus friend of our guest. They were said to be the two best competitors on the racquetball court and had bonded from the intensity of it. Surface stoicism was Woo's way with people, so that when he did release a rare smile, it was like the sun had suddenly pushed its way above The Great Wall. It was delicious for its rarity, but none of us in the conference room were to be shown it on this day. Schreiber, on the other hand, looked poised for vileness, whether he was backed by Friel and Gillis or not. He had already unwrapped a sandwich. It was, I had learned, a practice of his to tap the contents of a brown bag during meetings. Normally he would wait until a meeting was well under way to begin chewing. Today, there was an ominous lack of delay.

Edwina Sharpe was official note taker for department meetings this semester, and her laptop was slanted directly toward Dr. Friel at the head of the table. Edwina seemed a sexless person with four children, a contradiction deserving little consideration but worth a passing thought during the drone of meetings. She was pleasant to everyone in a way that suggested it was a mask for darker secrets, and her laugh could be disarming: an unoiled roll of sound that made her hands curl. She was already typing even as the meeting was called to order by the tapping of Phyllis' pen.

"Since there is no old business," she said, "except the matter of a stricter dishonesty policy brought up by Rachel at the last meeting—which will keep, since God knows it's a wearying business—we'll move immediately to the proposal brought by Professor Jefferson." Rachel VanNoys was clearly not persuaded by her chair's edict and dropped a heavy breath onto the printed agenda sheet, which slid to the floor between her feet. According to Woo, plagiarism was an issue she had been trying to give a greater urgency to for several years, but my department had long ago come to the conclusion that if one was truly inventive in crafting assignments, dishonesty would be cut off at the neck. At first, it had looked like a sign of enlightenment on the part of my older colleagues. As the year went by, it appeared to be a well-crafted form of laziness. I had felt sorry for Rachel on a number of occasions. She did teach composition rather than literature and was, therefore, a lesser sort to the minds of The Triumvirate. On the other hand, her students liked her, even when she taught rigorous rounds of grammar lessons. They would quake before her quizzes on the rules of long ago, but they gradually became her Grammar Warriors, crusaders for writing that wouldn't buckle at the knees—which *she* was doing now, as she retrieved the agenda from beneath her chair with fingers that didn't want to cooperate.

Jefferson looked at me. He had heard about my department, and now, before things had even begun to move forward, he had come face to face with it. He had pre-distributed a carefully worked-out rationale and syllabus for his proposed course but now looked like he'd just as soon retrieve them from the hands of my colleagues. The discussion proceeded.

Chuck Gillis shaped himself into the role of Mikhail's advocate, since the outsider was the Bible-guy, after all. "I've looked carefully at this," Gillis said, fingering the proposal. "I'm impressed by the quality of your rhetoric and the clarity of your thought. It's no easy task to craft a piece that will be tossed into the ovens of your enemy." He laughed, the chair laughed, and Schreiber laughed as he folded a piece of plastic wrap. It was a well-coordinated sound. Edwina tried to laugh but coughed instead. Woo began sketching, and Rachel held the document with both hands, like a child with a book. "Not that we're your enemy," Gillis continued. "I'm impressed by the collegiality of wanting to involve our majors in *the* great work of western civilization—which, as *we* realize, hardly any of *them* know like we did."

Dr. Schreiber had extracted an apple from his lunch bag. It was not a pleasure to watch his teeth slice their way into the uncut fruit, but he held off the moment. He had been chair of the faculty on two occasions and he had not-so-subtle ways of being in command even when a meeting was being run by another. He steadied the apple by its stem, making sure it would keep its place on the tabletop while he spoke. I quite unexpectedly remembered him dining at my father's table many years ago without benefit of apple or lunch bag, but with considerably less hair and cufflinks that looked like the faces of gargoyles. "There can be a challenge in how one seeks to define literature. It is something we grapple with repeatedly in this department. We had a very idealistic colleague who wanted to define the cinema as literature. It provided an eye-opening exercise in terminology." He hesitated. "I'm quite certain he found an institution that was less precise about the borders of our field."

"He was a touchy person," Dr. Friel interposed. "That comes from being in the wrong field." She nodded at Jefferson. "But we haven't even let you begin to speak yet. Please proceed."

Dr. Jefferson was showing the look on his face that I had seen in the lunch shop when he smoothly eviscerated the drafter of the Declaration of Independence. "No. You proceed. Unless I am mistaken, your minds seem to be made up without hearing from me."

"Not at all," the chair assured him. She looked at Gillis. "You weren't suggesting an immediate dismissal of the proposal, were you?"

"Not in the least. This is the Holy Bible we're talking about, even if it falls outside the realm of what we might consider to be traditional literature and what we are equipped to teach."

Rachel VanNoy's fingers twitched. She usually refrained from discussions except those relevant to her field. "Isn't that why Mikhail is here? Isn't he the equipment we're lacking?"

"'Equipment' is an interesting way to put it, Rachel," Schreiber corrected. "I don't think I'm ready to accept the term no matter how well equipped he is." There was a telling pause, and I thought I heard a low chortle from Woo at his corner of the table. "I hope I haven't offended anyone," the unflappable speaker added. He had bypassed the apple for now and was taking a cup of yogurt and plastic spoon from his bag. I had seen this act before. Usually, he would have difficulty peeling off the foil cover from the top and would pass it to someone else for assistance. This time, it was Edwina. "Would you help me open this, dear?" She took the container wordlessly. It was quite a show so far, and I could feel myself getting ready to do something stupid.

Jefferson's face had now attained the stoicism of steely observation. He looked at the chair, waiting. Phyllis Friel smiled at him but was clearly uncertain how to proceed. She tapped her pen quietly. At some point she had tucked her hair behind one of her ears, making it look like a lid without a container. "Would you say the Bible is teachable, the way, I would imagine, *Moby Dick* is, though I've never thought to teach it myself? I leave that for heavy book people like Edwina. Yes, teachable is the word, I think."

Edwina had a slightly pillowy figure and it was possible she had just heard herself referred to as a *heavy* book-person. She scowled and thrust the opened yogurt container. "Here, Mitchell. Eat." I took a decidedly deep breath. He dropped a hand onto the table, and the plastic spoon accidently flew past Chuck Gillis's shoulder. "And yes, of course, it's teachable," she said. "If you don't think it's the word of God, if you think that's too plebeian for the likes of us, it was at least written by people who wanted to share their own struggling spirits with others. And it has menacing whales, too."

"Whoa," I heard myself saying, with the enthusiasm of a teenager seeing an undressed woman for the first time. I doubt it was all that loud, but it elicited a look of recognition from Richard who extended his thumb slightly. Meanwhile, Edwina had won my eternal respect. I had thought of her as the departmental toady, quietly trying to get along by agreeing with everyone else on most issues. She was now my Mother Courage, and Phyllis looked at both of us as if we had hatched this little demonstration together. "She's right on the button," I explained.

"To coin a cliché," Phyllis instructed. "You, Jeremiah, are a lover of clichés."

"Why, thank you. Better a lover than a eunuch." I said it cordially enough, and I had little idea how I meant it or for whom, but it had stirred things up another degree or two.

"All right, let's bring things back to order." It was Schreiber, who had gotten his spoon back from Chuck and was about to stir the yogurt when Edwina and I had started our mini-rampage. He finally began the stirring, bringing blueberries to the surface with practiced strokes. "Jeremiah, I don't think this is the way to behave in front of a guest. Your father had a better sense of hospitality."

"My father is dead. Let him be."

He was softly distressed once again, and a glob of yogurt spilled onto the apple, giving it an appearance of frosted embarrassment. "Yes. Yes he is. We'll not talk about that any longer."

The session was ended by Jefferson. He creased his proposal along a neat line in the center. "You may have heard the teachable little narrative about Samson in the Old Testament: 'And he took his staff in his hand, and chose him five smooth stones out of the brook, and put them in a shepherd's bag. And his sling was in his hand, as he drew near to the Philistine." It was spoken with the resonance of a gospel preacher, and he thanked us then for an enlightening experience, adding, "I will withdraw."

The meeting was adjourned.

FOURTEEN

The campus chapel was of modern design, of blond-colored wood, and without the stained glass and stonework of more traditional structures. Nancy was sitting in the front pew. Her head was tilted back as she listened to organ music coming from a nearby room and remained that way until I reached where she sat.

"So that's what this is about," I said, glancing in the direction of the music. "Willie, I assume?"

"Yes. You may assume." My sudden appearance had not startled her; in fact, she stood, took my head in her two hands, and kissed me fully on the mouth.

"All right. Completely memorable. If it weren't just for the sacred sounds in the distance, I would guess you asked me here to bless our iniquity. How have you been?"

"In heat."

"Nancy!"

"I've had a peculiar desire to be with you. Willie was a cover, though. I had promised her I would bring you to hear her play."

"In which case, I and the entire firmament will be your accomplices."

"Good. That is a satisfaction. Now sit." She had dropped onto the pew and pulled me after her by a tug on the sleeve.

"Actually," I said, "I can't think of a reason wrong with our being here."

"See?"

"Except—"

She raised a hand. "No exceptions. Let's just say I have come to celebrate you and the proud nest of butterflies you've put in my belly. What better place than a place of worship?"

"But why all of a sudden?"

"It's not at all sudden. There have been butterflies since the time we met with Michael in your office. It seemed proper to ignore them. Now it seems improper, that's all."

"And then?"

"We made love. Or have you forgotten?"

"And you don't feel guilty about it?"

"Not at all. Wicked."

"Which is a kind of guilt."

"More a kind of amazement, I think."

I stood and walked a few feet away from her, trying to recognize the organ music. It rang with power, and I could picture Willie hammering the keyboards. "Point number two—although I don't remember if there was point number one—I've loved you for almost twenty years."

She laughed slightly. "Oh, good heavens, Jeremiah. That again?"

"Yes, that again."

"You're lovely, but I don't believe it for a minute, even though I've spent the last two weeks trying to take the idea seriously."

"Then don't. It will be your loss." I began to grasp for arguments. "Nancy, I actually *did* hang around after school so I could hold the goddamn door when you left."

"I don't remember that."

"Of course not. And this from a kid who was supposed to be exceptionally well-bred but wasn't."

"I don't doubt that. But what makes you—made you—so different from any other first grader? Don't you suppose dozens of broody little boys did things like that for me?"

"Broody? God I hate proving love to someone."

"Yes, so I've heard," she said. "It's like proving time. You've tried this sort of thing often?"

I thought of the scene in the withered rose garden. "No, as a matter of fact. You are my first attempt. What would you like me to do?"

She smiled at me with a gentle smirk. "Prove it."

"Nancy, dammit!" I looked at her. She was beautifully self-possessed, her eyes rich with curiosity. "You're enjoying this, aren't you?"

"It's more entertaining than I would have thought."

"All right. Let's take a break." I paced briefly. "Let's talk about something else. Let me tell you about the meeting I just disgraced myself at."

"If you'd like. I have the afternoon free...even for disgraceful behavior."

I gave a brief version of what had happened while music continued with muffled exuberance in the distance. I asked her at one point what she thought it might be. It was a Bach fugue, she said with conviction—the "Little" one with nothing little about it. She spoke of counterpoint, where two musical lines contest each other while blending together, a term she had learned from Willie Furman and seemed pleased to share with me. She repeated it several times with the motherly satisfaction of passing on knowledge.

"How," she asked at one point, "can the human mind do that—make that out of nothing?" She also seemed pleased with the dynamics of the department meeting as I itemized them for her, and she summarized my outburst as a celebration.

"Celebration of what?" I asked her. "Stupidity?"

"Of growing up," she suggested. "But you will have to decide that for yourself." I thought of her patting me on the head, but the picture faded. "All right, then. Go on with your show-and-tell about first grade."

"Are you sure?"

"I already said I was."

"We never got that far."

"Well, now we have."

"What do you remember from back then?"

"Practically nothing. A few feelings is all."

"How many kids did you have named Jeremiah, eh?"

"None that I can remember. Not a one."

"How pitiful. All right, then. Let's talk about your hair."

"My hair?"

"It was wonderful. The color of a new penny."

"And now it's like an old one."

"Yes...no!" I sat on the pew behind her and leaned forward. "Stop it, will you?"

"I colored it, you know."

I sat back. "I don't want to hear about it. I don't care."

"Please continue."

"You're a difficult house to play to."

"Are we playing house?"

"Would you like to?"

"Would you?"

"I would like to tell you about your goddamn hair."

"Very pretty chapel language."

"I'm having a bad day. Would you please let me get on with this? It may well be my only chance." She smiled back at me. "The way it fell about your shoulders. It was longer then."

"Apparently."

"Yes, apparently. It was a source of endless fascination to me. It was like spun metal. I would imagine it to be the hair of ancient queens, passed on to you for safekeeping in an age of fewer and fewer queenships. It was royal or dynastic or something. But even to my six-year-old's mind, it was vulnerable, too. Or it made you vulnerable. Then. I felt like you were ridiculously out of place in a room full of runny noses and missing teeth and piping voices. I wanted to make it up to you—fervently...if I may be allowed the word. I wanted to justify your right to rule."

"To rule you?"

"The works. The whole fucking universe."

The organ music stopped abruptly, as if my words had pulled a plug from its socket. The silence took a few moments to gather itself. Then Nancy looked back at me. “Do you think we’ll make love again?” There couldn’t have been a more effective way to shut down my diatribe. “I thought it might be worth knowing. Not that we need to do it here.”

“Why Miss Nancy!”

She suddenly rose and walked up onto the altar area, which seemed to provide her with a new resonance as she spoke down to me. “Do you think—do you really think—that you’re the first little boy who has wanted to run off with his first-grade teacher? Even in the middle of your beautiful ardors, Jeremiah, I know you know that.”

“Fine, and I thank you for keeping me from floating clear out of sight. I talked to a stuffed cat back then. I used to tell him about you. He thought you might be too sensible to believe a six-year-old’s passions.”

She peered down at me as the music began again, this time a softer piece. “A stuffed cat, was it?”

“Stuffed with dreams and pieces of cloth.”

“With a name?”

“I don’t remember.”

“Do you know what I remember about you, Jeremiah Curtin?”

“Please don’t bother yourself, Nancy.”

“What if I said ‘Nothing. Not a thing?’”

“You’re being perverse. It can’t possibly be true. I was brilliant.”

“You were six and without teeth.”

“I may still have had them. I walked late, I’m told.”

She squinted slyly at me. “Really. Do you know what that means?”

“Tell me.”

“It means you walked late.”

I paused. “You don’t remember anyone from then?”

“I remember one little boy who tried to swallow a hard-boiled egg and threw up on the principal’s shoes. That wasn’t you, was it?”

“I never throw up—only once when I was eight, after Chicken a la King.”

“I have no idea what the principal was doing there.” She came down a step. "Would it disappoint you so much that your love was possibly unrequited?"

"I busted my ass for you. For you, I turned myself into a prodigy. You wrote on my report card that I was 'heartwarming.'"

"Well, there you are. Maybe I *was* taken by you. Maybe I—" She looked suddenly at the back of the chapel. "Michael...what a nice surprise."

He looked pleased at the discovery. He was wearing a baseball cap that he removed quickly and waved at his mother. "You came to hear Will?"

"Among other things," she told him, coming down from the altar. "You look like you need a trip to the barber." His hair was extending outward in a variety of directions. "I haven't been paying enough attention."

He flinched briefly and then smiled at me. "Howdy, Prof. C."

Before I could reply, Nancy had an announcement to make. "Have I told you, Michael, that this very present-day professor was a student of mine...or so he tells me?"

"Oh, yeah?" He looked at me cartoonishly. "She flunk you or anything?"

"No, Michael. And I doubt she would remember. She was too busy ignoring me. "

"That's almost cool. I gotta go. Will's waiting for me."

We both watched him as he waved with his back to us and disappeared into the side room. "And to think," I told her, "when you left school to have him, I practically had a seven-year-old's breakdown."

Nancy looked distracted. "Yes?" The organ music stopped momentarily, in mid-piece.

"It was in second grade with Mrs. Holst. A nice lady, but she had fingers like cocktail franks and breath like a cocker spaniel."

"I remember her."

"Fine. We're making progress. Without you in the building, I thought I'd been dropped under a bridge. I cursed you for being pregnant. Maybe that's why Michael is what he is."

"And what is that?" she asked testily.

"I honestly don't know. Something special, I would imagine. A curse to curses."

"Good for you." She moved to stand in front of me. "You know, I do worry about you."

"Oh?"

"Odd as it might seem, Jeremiah, I worry that it really isn't me you're so apparently and strangely taken by. It's peculiar enough under any circumstances, our...difference. But this thing of yours...don't you worry?"

"Yes, but don't you." As I kissed her, she looked at me with softening eyes before she let them close. The music had begun again, and I pulled back to look at her. "Do you think they know?"

"I doubt it. But they might. On the other hand, Jeremiah, there's so little for them to know."

"Then, let's give them more."

§

We made love at my apartment, giving up the pleasures of an undersized couch for a bed. Before leaving the chapel, we had stopped briefly to see Willie and Michael. She was wearing one of her vivid lipsticks, this time something the color of engine rust. Her hair was held by a bandanna, and she wore an unorthodox organist's outfit of sweatshirt, shorts, and hiking boots. Her intensity was encompassing, and she acknowledged our presence with a brief nod of the head and compressed smile. On the way out, Nancy modified her previous statement. "I think maybe she *does* know."

"Oh, come on, Nancy. How could she?"

"Sometimes women just do."

"Don't give me that women-just-do nonsense. There's plenty you haven't known about me."

"We'll see."

It was a night to explore each other with our hands and legs and mouths. We passed on preliminaries. While Nancy undressed with an ease and lack of shyness that was unexpected for a one-time schoolmarm, she insisted on removing my clothing piece by piece, as if she were detailing a project. She folded each article neatly, making it more and more natural to watch her. Her skin had a smoothness I had not imagined or desired, except at that moment when she stood unselfconsciously in front of me. What hadn't been important now became a garment drawing me in, and I would spend our time learning it in careful detail. I entered her as if we had not made love before, more like that one other time had been a borrowed dream and this was the wakened reality. She made love quietly, except for a low humming that would turn to gusts of breath during a series of climaxes. It was after the last of these that she finally spoke. "Now, at least, I can leave this world knowing what *that* feels like. Good job." Her face was stretched between a smile and a look of total absence. She had traveled somewhere far from me.

"Do you mean—?"

She touched my cheek with a hand. "No questions for now. You never know when we will have time for that, but not while the bells are still ringing."

She requested Dvorak's *New World* symphony off-handedly, as if every lover she knew would have it. I didn't. The Professor's passion for classical music had sent me in other directions. "I don't suppose you'd like to hear the Benny Goodman band thumping for your pleasure."

"Thank you, my beautiful prodigy, but now that I think about it, I'm completely thumped out. Silence will do after all."

And silence it would have been were it not for the voice of Sara Sampson inflecting in the hallway and trailing her up the stairs. She was with Hamilton, and she had clearly captured the conversation in a way all too familiar. I could hear her shriek something about being goosed in the subway, until the words were garbled as they moved upward. She sounded pleased to be sharing the information with him and anyone else; and if the subway encounter had been a disturbing one, it wasn't apparent in her tone of delivery.

"Interesting voice," Nancy said, rolling closer. "She sounds like a broody leghorn."

"Leghorn?"

"Chicken."

There are moments when what to tell and what not to tell become fairly simple. If Sara were to come tapping on my door for a cup of sugar or a pliable ear or decide to crawl into bed with us (not beyond her realm of possibility), it would on one level be prudent and honest to give the woman lying next to me a heads-up. On the other hand, this was a better moment to again fight the eerily coincidental and hope for the best. As far as I knew, Sara had not been in our building since January when she slipped off with my neighbor for the first time. She had an instinct for bad timing, an extra sense that allowed her too often to shake the grip of normalcy when it was clinging with unusual desperation. It was, to my almost embarrassed satisfaction, as if Nancy and I had been practicing this since I was six years old and we had finally proven me to have been a young genius.

"Sorry about the *New World*," I said to her. "I actually know it and I like it, but, as you know, I'm quite limited."

"I couldn't possibly say that," she purred. "Not any longer. I'll buy you a copy. It makes me think of wide prairies and puffy skies."

"Me?"

"More like me, at this moment." Her eyes had a sincerity I could not remember in another human being—except, perhaps, my first-grade teacher. They were a fusion of passion and doubt, so deeply dark I felt they were looking past me at an image I was unable to see. She had become the visionary all at once, and I felt myself becoming the older of the two of us.

"Way back in that time we mustn't talk about," I told her, "I had this mystical fascination with your glasses."

"Them, too?" she asked with milky resignation.

"They were added markers of your vulnerability."

"I see."

"When you came to my office with Michael, I right away wished you still wore them."

"You knew who I was?"

"Like a bulletin in my brain."

She sat up slightly, looking about the room and listening to the sounds of two people arguing in the apartment above us. Her voice steadied around the muted disturbance. "When I decided to leave Marvin, I got contacts. I thought it would be one way to shorten distances between myself and the rest of the world."

"Yes, that makes sense, I guess. But I did like them. You looked to me—back then—like you'd just started wearing them. It made me sad and hungry to tell you how good you looked in them. I was sure you would never believe it unless I told you."

"You did have a case, didn't you?"

"Yes. Your hair made me want to serve you, and your glasses made me want to protect you."

"And that was love?" she said with a sigh.

"Of course. Or maybe it was somewhere between serving and protecting. I don't know."

"But it was love?"

"Completely."

"Oh, dear." She glanced at the ceiling. Something had fallen, and Sara's overtightened laughter told me she was either delighting in a tantrum or establishing control through disorder that would eventually bring Ham into a state of submission. I had been in both positions on too many occasions. Nancy got out of bed and looked at me, reinforcing her nakedness with a lifting of her arms from her sides. "It looks all right?" she asked simply.

"Looks and feels. And tastes."

"I'll grade that satisfactory."

"Much too low. I'm grading on the curve."

"All right, then." She began dressing, telling me she wasn't ready to spend the night yet, that she still had a home and son to manage, and if Willie *did* suspect, she wasn't about to send out announcements.

"That's her brother upstairs," I said. "Or her half-brother, I guess."

"I'm well aware," she said with a smile. "Their mother is something special, I gather. Willie refers to her as a hotshot lawyer."

"It figures."

"Her father isn't talked about."

"It's an epidemic."

"You've mentioned your father."

"That he was dying."

"Yes. I guess that's right." She was dressed by this time and beginning to look anxious about being there. "I read his obituary. How impressive he was. How challenging he must have been. I've thought many times how to tell you I'm so very sorry, but I couldn't decide how that would play with you. You're so guarded, like a keeper of unsettling news." Outer realities had gathered about her, and her kiss landed thoughtfully upon my mouth. "I believe, actually, that she has a crush on you."

"Who are we talking about, Miss Nancy?"

"Willie. She said you wrote her some poems last semester."

"One piece of verse—hardly a poem—at the end of a composition where she had provided one of her own. Pretty clever, as I recall. How did she describe this exchange of poems?"

"She didn't. She called it a *factoid*."

"I can assure you, I don't inspire crushes, especially with female storm troopers."

"How do you know?"

"I believe I would know. I'm a reader."

She looked at me with a degree of condescension. "I doubt it."

It came to me that I was still naked, and I reached for a pair of running shorts hanging on the knob of the closet. "Doubt it, then."

"They're not going to tell you, Jeremiah. It wouldn't be a crush anymore."

"What, then?"

"Love—elementary variety."

"That would tickle you, wouldn't it?"

"What's that?" She tugged the shorts to waist-level with motherly nonchalance.

"Michael Feller has the hots for a distinctly complicated young woman who has a thing for me who retains his own child-born love for a former teacher who turns out to be the mother of that very same Michael. You might call it an elliptical crush."

"I might call it nothing, Jeremiah, and leave it at that." She moistened her lips with her tongue. "Do you suppose she sat in class wondering if you were descended from ancient kings?"

"I don't suppose that at all."

"Let's leave it at that." She moved toward the door and took keys from her coat pocket. She jingled them softly. "I wish Christmas was coming again."

"And why is that?"

"I might decide not to knock on your door this time. Michael calls it a do-over."

"It would turn out the same. I really believe that."

She opened the door just before Sara Sampson came thundering down the stairs. Her abrupt halt was finely timed, and she peered into the apartment. "Why Jeremiah, you old honey bear. Nice shorts. Did I give them to you?" She then moved on through the front door with mirthful balloons floating behind her.

I shrugged at Nancy. "It seems we'll never run out of things to talk about. That's one worry out of the way."

For that evening, though, we had evidently run out. I could smell her in the bedroom when I returned to it, the scent of unguardedness, sexual fragrances that made the bed itself breathe to me as I stood next to it. It was to be a while before it would breathe that way again.

FIFTEEN

My contest with the powers of coincidence were again challenged soon enough when I attended the reading of The Professor's will—though it would take months to discover the extent of it all. Nancy and I were apparently in another of those awkward-silence periods. For two people sporadically trying to let the improbable constructs of our attraction seal us together, we were, I guess, too observant of the rules of resistance to go very far off the deep end. The chemistry was obvious. The fingers of intimacy were strong and pliable, at least when we were driven by the need to know only what we should not have needed to know. We had experienced the possibility of controlling our shared inner world, but the outer world had its own necessities as I was willing to admit once again...at least while our shared silence worked its way between us.

It was becoming more difficult to imagine structured sensibility as a worthwhile goal. My place of work, and my place within it, had already done its best to warn me off. My need to know if there was another way to conduct the business of living was intensified by my desire to love the person I was in love with. Still, so much was prescribed. Civilization had the certainty of the ages backstopping it. It had all the smugness of dead people stacked in watchful layers to keep the living in line, and it pissed me off. I knew one never really shakes off the past and that the past can offer graceful opportunities to the present—in the form of first-grade teachers or a poem by Yeats—but it could pull them away with a jerk of its own learned insecurities and terrors and awkwardness. Like a magician's cape. Fhoop! And there you were again, back in the zone of silence.

The will had its debut not in a law office, but in The Professor's study. We were a small group. Louisa was there, obviously as a beneficiary. Whatever else happened, her being present gave the proceedings a living touch, and I wished a heathen's blessing upon Alban Curtin for his thinking of her. As she sat on one of the dining-room chairs carried across the hall for the occasion, she held the book she had been reading in the hospice room. I had tried to stop myself from wondering about it, assuming it would familiarize itself in my mind with all of the other things I had no knowledge of.

Two representatives from his university were there: the Provost and the Chief Financial Officer. They sat like undertakers—their sobriety like coolant they had taken for the occasion. Their voices sounded worm-eaten and brittle; their shoes had a high polish, reflecting the twisted glare of the fixture at the center of the ceiling. That light had frightened me as a child. While the only artificial light in the room usually came from a statuesque lamp on the desk, the metallic contortions of the ceiling fixture had felt like they were designed to strangle all brightness. I looked up at the unusual sight of the four lighted bulbs overhead, startled out of their long sleep of uselessness by the hand of the lawyer, apparently. They were on when I arrived as the last of the group, and I knew Louisa would not have thought to create such a contrasting atmosphere for a room that had outflanked change for so long.

The person at The Professor's desk introduced herself as Joanna Wexler. She was a handsome woman, well into her fifties by my guess, with reddish-brown hair pulled decisively back from her face, and during our brief session, her mouth and eyes created the fixed expression of a tranquil insider. She spoke in a calm, throaty voice, and began without preliminary.

"Dr. Curtin asked me to sit in his chair for this gathering. I trust none of you will mind that," she interjected, looking directly at me. "He was quite specific about what you will see, hear, and learn today. As you all undoubtedly know, he was a man of specifics." Louisa's head nodded affectionately. "We spent many hours together—over several years, actually—working on these specifics. Well before he knew he was seriously ill, he was working on a range of details. It was, in many ways, a charming angle from which to view him." It was an odd statement, though delivered with little shift of tone and only a small compression of her lips. It felt like a personal announcement inserted into an occasion I had assumed would be effectively depersonalized. If she was announcing that there had been something more than a lawyer-client relationship between them, she was doing so from the very seat of power. She did look well-fitted to his chair. I had not seen this woman before, nor had I heard of her. The envelope announcing the reading indicated her practice was a private one without partners. "It is not really all that unusual to plan so far ahead. Many do it. However, Dr. Curtin, I think it would be safe to say, went about it as if he were preparing for a Broadway opening some years in the future. Perhaps his family's background in the theater had something to do with it, though that was not a specific he chose to share with me. At the same time, he did permit me the opportunity I am taking now. He suggested a few simple preliminary reflections would not be out of place and might serve the occasion well. I hope you agree."

The four of us looked at her noncommittally. We were on the receiving end of a brief lecture, and like first-day students, we were not inclined to question the flow of her satisfied feelings at the opening of a semester. Still, the tone of voice and the masked fixity of her face had not altered. If she was shape-shifting, she was doing it out of sight, perhaps where the former occupant of the desk chair might be able to see it. I imagined the ghost of Hamlet's father urging uncompromising loyalty from beneath the stage floor.

She went on. "He was very insistent that this reading of his will take place on March twenty-second. I am not able to offer up a reason. Does it have a literary significance? Perhaps. I am, however, not educated enough to know what it might be." She looked directly at me. "Possibly you, the next Dr. Curtin, will find the answer. I would be interested to know." She waited for a reply, and when there was none, she went on. "The room is set the way he wished it. The chairs are arranged as he had planned, and the lighting is as he desired it to be. He revised these details on a number of occasions, and he also wished me to convey that knowledge to you. That seemed one of his more insistent requests. It was as if he wanted you to be aware of his rough drafts. I believe he even used that phrase at one point or another. He wanted us to begin precisely at four o'clock in the afternoon. I notice that the sun is coming in behind me. That's an interesting detail, but he could not have known what the weather would be like unless he had a very fine almanac indeed." It was an opportunity to raise her voice, but she didn't. The effect of the sunlight offsetting the murk of the overhead fixture grew increasingly transfixing. The lawyer was haloed, and the yard beyond where I had tossed a softball with Ellen was a shadowland of evergreens by contrast. Magic or accident, fate or happenstance, it was a stunning piece of staging.

The actual reading of the will came almost as an anticlimax. For the most part, it wasn't a reading at all, but a précis of the bequests, once again in keeping with my father's instructions. The university was left the house we were sitting in to use as it saw fit, to sell or retrofit to some other purpose. In addition, $500,000 was donated to the institution to endow a chair of Theoretical Studies, and his manuscripts were left to the Special Collections section of the university's library. The two representatives in attendance nodded administratively with no expressions of surprise. Louisa Sondstrom—presumably his final revision to the will—was given $25,000, the dining room furniture, and her pick of any items from the kitchen. Her head dropped with a pulsation of disbelief, and she looked at me to gauge my reaction. I smiled my approval, and she quietly shared the one Swedish phrase she had taught me: *Tack så mycket*, her gentle thank you.

For me, Joanna Wexler read rather than summarized, her voice pitching slightly and her fingers holding the document in front of her fidgeting on the reverse side of the page.

To my son Jeremiah, who makes the business of growth a fairly burdensome undertaking, I leave you my desk chair and my books to do with as you wish. Your love of the written word has become a source of doubt for you. While that may seem unfortunate to some, it is only unfortunate if you blame love for its own disappearance. It is no trick of nature. It is a normal transformation of certainty into that which tests it. As my friend Voltaire instructed, "Doubt is an uncomfortable condition, but certainty is a ridiculous one." Now, that having been said, I move on to the matter of your financial legacy. You will receive $999,998 in one sum or at intervals of your choosing. I could have afforded to include the other two dollars, but I did not wish to overburden you with a round number that has much more significance than it deserves. It is not my intention to free you from the obligation to do good work. I hope only that this will allow you an opportunity to discover what that work might entail. My confidence in you is not absolute—nor should it be. However, I do leave you an accompanying word of hope, that you will treat with honesty your passions and your denials of them.

Best wishes, Alban Curtin.

The light spill behind the lawyer had lowered to the point where reader, chair, and desk were almost entirely washed out in the expanding blur of sunset. The university benefactors nodded at me agreeably and rose to shake my hand, and Louisa, waiting her turn, wrapped her efficient arms around my waist.

I could make out the shape of the lawyer coming toward us. She moved with a merry stride now, and, as Louisa stepped back, told me how my father had gone back and forth on whether to shave one or two dollars from the tidy million. "One week it would be a dollar; the next it would be two. It was one of his most difficult decisions in this entire process. He finally decided, I believe, that two was a less obvious figure.

Shoddier is the word I recall him using. Quite a person," she concluded.

"Yes, he was," I agreed.

"Oh," she said with a sudden return to the desk. "He did leave one other thing he wanted me to give you." She pulled a sheet of paper from a manila envelope with words handwritten across the top. In the center of the page was a computer-generated question mark, in a double circle like a bull's-eye, or a peephole, with the field surrounding the symbol rising from light to dark like an early dawn.

The assembled stared at it fixedly, except for the lawyer, who read from the envelope, "For my wife Ellen, should she ever care to provide an answer." Ms. Wexler followed with a clarifying revelation that Alban and Ellen Curtin had never divorced. Since he never talked about his runaway wife after the day she left, nor did I speak of her in front of him, there was no way this interesting bit of information could have been known to me. And, of course, the runaway had not bothered to describe their situation to me in her skeletal e-mails. It had not been difficult to assume the legal end of their marriage, and this new fact—coupled with the envelope and its piece of paper now entrusted to my care—was another culmination on this day of revelations. It was beginning to feel like a storage closet had been opened after years of avoidance and what came tumbling out was nowhere near the end of whatever was jammed within. His inflated question mark looked obvious enough centered on its otherwise blank page: "Why did you do what you did?" or a version of that. Its obviousness, however, was so unlike him it felt like a head fake. What had their feelings for each other been like even in the better days of their marriage, when they were, among other things, bringing me into their lives? Looking at the envelope, there was a suggestion of an actual attachment that had caused the pain of trying to forget the unforgettable.

As I stood there with the others, and watched the darkening of the space outside his window, the possibility of his loving her and their loving each other proposed itself. The question mark may have been his own repressed pain in manuscript form, and it was suddenly desolating to think of the years of relative silence he and I had passed together and apart. Nancy had read his obituary. It had not occurred to me to even look for it in the days after his death. What had it revealed about him, and how had it referred to Ellen, who, unknown to me, was still his wife on the day he died?

The lawyer standing before me interrupted my reverie. "I trust you will come to see me soon to work out the details." She handed me her card, which had an embossed podium to one side of the printed information. "Your father thought I might also be able to offer good counsel should the need arise."

"You were close?" I asked.

She smiled. I realized the two university men had left in silence, adding to the hollowness of my question. Louisa Sondstrom stood uncomfortably near the dining room chair she had brought in. Her hand stroked one of the carved arms as if it were that of a child. "We'll leave such things to the forbidden planet of the lawyer-client privilege. However, as you know, closeness was not a word he would have used easily."

I nodded. "And?"

She retreated to the desk to put her materials into a cloth bag with a woven Indian design, rather than a briefcase. I gave a nod of approval for her quietly twitting the sobriety of her profession as, I suppose, my own tackier version of a book-bag was intended to do. "Let me think about this. When you come to see me, we can talk further about him if you'd like. The paths may be tricky."

"Let me think about it, too. Whatever it is I'm thinking about."

She was pleased. "As well put as I could have done." She extended a hand and inventoried me with a small up-and-down nod of her head. Then she was gone.

Louisa waited for me to acknowledge her. I noticed for the first time that she was outfitted in a beige jacket and skirt that complemented the cottony highlights of her hair. She was also wearing a very light shade of lipstick—the only time I had seen her with any kind of makeup.

"You look very nice," I told her.

"*Tack*," she said, floundering modestly.

"I am so happy he remembered you. You were, I think, very good for him."

"He was always kind to me."

"I'm glad to hear it."

She considered her words briefly. "It is sad you and...he...were not closer."

"Did you ever wonder, Louisa, what it might be like to believe you shouldn't know something—a story, maybe—and when people start telling you that story, the knowing gets even worse?"

"I tell my daughter to listen to everyt'ing with quiet ears. It's vat my mother used to tell me, but a young person does not understand yet." She held out the hand with my father's book in it. "I vanted you to have this book I stole from the professor."

"It wasn't stealing."

"I did not ask him."

"Louisa, it feels like he wanted you to have it." She placed the book on the desk. "Do you know what a wizard is?"

"Yah. Harry Potter. The Sorcerer and the Apprentice. Mickey Mouse and the vater buckets."

"Think of us as his pair of mice—Mickey and Minnie. I think. I don't know for sure. He has me doing a lot of guessing lately. Pretty good for a person who is no longer here."

"Vizards maybe don't ever die, do you t'ink? In Sweden, ve haf a story of Elf-könig, ver special humans get elf powers after death."

I laughed. "It's hard to picture. He wasn't tall, but tall enough, Louisa. I suppose even he could be brought down to size."

"Yah, maybe." Her face went from grateful to tearful in a disarming instant. She apologized and handed me the book as her eyes bubbled with emotion. She pulled a handkerchief from the inside of her jacket and flapped it like a sign of surrender before blowing into it.

"Louisa?" I asked.

"Nothing," she said, recovering. "I yust feel sad for you. I feel sad for the all-alone."

"But I'm not," I tried to assure her.

She bunched the handkerchief in her hand. "Yah. I hope so. It's yust a feeling I get. I get feelings that stick at me. I felt it on Christmas Eve in the other room. It vas a meal I cook for the all-alone."

I pictured that night: her roasted pheasant with its garnishes, his music, our wine, the attempt at candor, his sudden departure from the room, his parents' furniture soon to be Louisa's. I walked silently with her to that room, taking her arm through mine, and opened the mahogany door into it. We gazed at the formality of the interior, its best-room polish visible even in the retreating daylight. The smell of lemon oil unfolded itself.

"He usually ate over there," she said, looking back toward the study. "For Christmas Eve, he told me, 'Louisa, t'row open the doors.' He was yolly. Is that the word?"

"Coming from you, it is. Will all of this fit in your house?"

"Yah. I find a way. I told him it was the most beautiful furniture. I loved cleaning it. I never thought..." And she stopped. She seemed on the verge of tears again. "I go now." She took one of my hands between both of hers and patted like she was preparing pastry dough. There was earnest affection in her eyes. Whether for me or the man who had been my father, it didn't actually matter. It entered me with a flutter of comfort. As I walked her to the driveway, she made an unexpected comment about Joanna Wexler. "The lawyer lady," she ventured, "is a halfway red fox." Again, it was evident how protective Louisa had felt of my father.

"Why do you say that?"—and I wanted to add "Which half?"

She shrugged. "I only say dat. I don't know so much." With that, she told me we would see each other again and hoped I would be made happy by what I had learned that afternoon. It was nearly dark now, and it was only after she had backed from the driveway and gotten partway down the street that she remembered to put her headlights on.

The house was dark as well, except for the muddied light from the ceiling fixture in the study. I put on the desk lamp and turned off the overhead before settling into the chair that was another of the strange bequests of the will. I hadn't sat in it since I was quite young, when, a few times, I would steal into this inner sanctum. It was any little boy's piece of playacting, I imagine, but in my case, I was enacting only part of the script handed down to me. I was not pretending to be him as much as to order him about. It was no oedipal desire to eliminate him but instead to make him bow to my commands as my imagination placed him in the chair across from me and gave him simple instructions—one of which was that he explain himself to me. When the chair would swivel, the noises it made were responses from a compliant subject; it would groan the other side of the dialogue.

I didn't know if I would even keep the chair. It still had its authoritative, leathery look with broad-headed upholsterer's tacks that dotted it like brass military buttons. I had noticed by the light of the desk lamp that the leather was cracked and darkly oiled where I imagined his head tipping backward over so many years to puzzle out an idea or rest from the crash of thoughts. Most likely, such a piece of furniture would not work in another context. It would look absurd in my microscopic office at school, the one I would probably abandon at the end of the semester. It would not sit companionably with the multipurpose Formica-topped table in my apartment, the apartment I was growing increasingly anxious to leave. The house in Quaker Falls, should that idea surface again, was a place for rockers or Windsor chairs rather than professorial desk chairs.

The house in Quaker Falls: the idea *had* just surfaced again along with the recollection that in addition to this chair, I had been given a roomful of books and the near underbelly of a million dollars. There were so many threads to pull at, threads of motivation, implication, actuality, and consequence. Some of it was so obvious I found it totally resistible. I was, for one thing, financially independent to a point—that point being centered upon how I wanted to live and define the task of living. He seemed to be angling for that in the comments read aloud by Joanna Wexler with her own command of the situation and her own pieces of the puzzle. Why had she seemed so pleased with the way things had unfolded, and what was it about her that made the kindly Louisa Sondstrom doubt her? What had been the lawyer's relationship with my father, and what did it actually matter if they had screwed around—to use a term he would never have used himself? I was, for no reason, entitled to deny him some pleasure, some ease from the buried pain—the one-sheeted question mark—of his recent years. But why did their sexual relations, if there were any, feel like a conspiracy? And against whom? And why was I conspiring with the squeaks of his chair to put them in a place that should be none of my business—and might, in fact, be totally wrong? Was the very chair I was sitting in a part of a plan by the Elf-king and his consort to make me independently foolish? He had said that he wished me to do good work. What, I would have asked him, would that entail?—and he would have replied that only I had any way of knowing—and he would be right. The Elf-king would as soon trick me into a discovery of the good, but I must also do so passionately—an interestingly tall order—from elfin texts.

And the book...Louisa had left it on the desk, neatly aligned with the edge of the blotter. Had she read it? Part of it? All of it? Or had she felt it at last to be a violation? Yet she had seemed to be reading with considerable concentration in the room where he died. Was I ready to break into it and bring it into the opening that was me? It was what I did for a living. It was what I had always loved about the literary process: the raw unexpectedness and brief feeling of being known by another. Would the author be able to provide that, and would I allow him to test his other self—if that's what it was—against me? And why did what he had put into writing arouse more curiosity in me than had his life? His own living details?

I picked up the book and held it in the palm of my hand, a few inches above the surface of the desk, trying to weigh its contents through the texture of its cover. It felt peculiarly light for a hardcover work, like a pamphlet, like its insides were feathered. That was enough. The Elf-king had had a remarkably effective day already, and I was unprepared to go further with him right then. I set the book on top of the envelope containing the targeted question mark and stared for a minute or two at the trail of light spilled into the hallway by the desk lamp. Finally, I gathered up the little two-item pile, switched off the light, closed the door to the study, and let myself out of the soundless house.

SIXTEEN

It was, actually, another book that diverted my attention from The Professor's. I defiantly put his on one of the empty bookshelves of my apartment, where it stood alone like a piece of statuary. I did not deny its presence, but its isolated existence made it less threatening to me, no more a source of curiosity than any other decorative object...for the present. I had moved the desk chair with the help of Richard Woo's pickup truck, but I still had a month to think what to do with the study full of books while the university decided about the house.

Richard didn't seem like the pickup-truck kind of guy. He was meticulous in his clothing, incapable, presumably, of wearing jeans to work. He did have his killer reputation with racket sports, but I never spotted him wearing any type of athletic shoe when he was going about his academic business. When we carried the chair from my father's study, it left a hole in the room that was nearly audible—an uneasy exhalation that even Richard seemed to recognize. We placed it without a word into the bed of the truck, laying it immodestly on its backside.

The ride to Rhinebeck revealed one of the unknown dimensions of my colleague. He was, it emerged quickly, a devotee of bluegrass music or almost anything with a banjo.

"The more pluckin' the better," he proclaimed as he put a Flatt and Scruggs CD into his player, sounding like Sara Sampson while looking like an Asian scientist. I was about to discover the thing about banjo music, aside from filling the ears with bubble wrap, is the way it makes the landscape spin by faster than normal and punctuates talking with easeful pops and prickles.

He confessed he'd been wanting to compare notes with me since the fateful department meeting. His fingers tapped on the steering wheel as he savored with complete satisfaction how the session turned out. "It was," he said, "without a doubt the most fun I've had in one of those departmental steam baths in the ten years I've been here. And Jefferson told me he'd never enjoyed rejection this much since his second wife came out." Richard and Mikhail were, of course, best buddies, and it was pleasant to be let into their circle for at least the length of a ride to Rhinebeck. "He agreed with me, by the way, that we can't let you leave teaching."

That was unanticipated, especially with a mandolin accompaniment. "Who said I was leaving?"

"Let's call it general knowledge." He nodded to the music. The taut lines of his face revealed the quiet curvatures of a smile. "You're wondering what the offshoot of hard-hearted Maoists is doing with mountain tunes."

"There is wondering that can bring happiness," I said.

"So there is. Actually, bluegrass isn't all that different from traditional Chinese music. It's just friskier. It's hard to imagine sucking a jug and getting laid to what I heard in my grandparents' house."

He had done his graduate work in Chapel Hill, he told me, and would slip out from under his study of the Victorians by driving with friends to festival weekends, particularly the MerleFest in Wilkesboro. He was a fan of moonshine in moderation, which to him meant two or three jars with a lot of ice. It was the legal stuff, though he had promised himself a pilgrimage to a genuine still with revenuers in pursuit. "I'll take you along," he added.

"I'm on."

"When I watched you in the meeting," he reverted partway, "I felt like I was catching the tail-end of a mountain jamboree. You made me feel re-e-al good, bro."

"I'm glad to hear it, I guess."

"Don't guess! You even got Edwina going."

"I think it was the other way around."

"Doesn't matter. Not at all. It was a fine collaboration, and I haven't seen her so jazzed up since—ever."

"She was impressive."

"You both were, which is why you're an idiot to leave teaching and a slacker to boot." He said it seriously but softened it with another prim smile. He alerted me to the fact that the CD was now pumping out "Foggy Mountain Breakdown," which had the joyous abandon of a high-speed getaway.

After we had gotten the desk chair into my apartment, I offered to buy him a beer. He declined and asked if I'd walk with him instead to a bookstore near the center of the village. His daughter's fourth birthday was approaching, and the pressure was suddenly upon him to not "screw up things." He smiled with angular resignation. "My wife has this idea that I let *her* do all the heavy lifting when it comes to pleasing others. I don't know where she gets that from," he said with wistful irony. "Maybe I *am* too Victorian: let Nanny worry about the little ones. But I do want to understand the metrics of their growing." I had met his wife, Sharon, at the school's Christmas party, and she struck me as a formidable presence in the life of her taciturn husband. She was Jewish, a Barnard grad, a tough New Yorker with a punchy sense of humor and delicious laugh. Even at that party, I had been lifted to a singular level by their mix-and-match marriage. There were inviting stories everywhere.

As we walked, he spoke again about life in our department. "There are the smuggoes, as I call them, the ones who think they have it all in place and all figured out. But they're eventually going to start drooling or dying." He stopped abruptly in the middle of the sidewalk and put a hand on my arm. "Sorry about that. I wasn't thinking about your father. I should have been."

"It's fine. I wonder how his department feels about his being gone after...forever. I didn't really know any of them...at least as I got older. He kept them in their own world."

"I met him a couple of times. At conferences. Formidable. Complex. I read his obituaries. Wide-ranging, to say the least."

I had finally downloaded the piece on The Professor from the Poughkeepsie newspaper. There had been no mention of his marriage or of me, but it did indicate what I hadn't known before—that he had briefly directed off-Broadway and had worked for a time at a Wall Street brokerage house. How the newspaper knew what I did not was another of those insane parts of trying to understand him. Richard's hand still rested on my arm. "Don't be so obvious about him. Teach!"

"'Foggy Mountain' anyone?"

"You have the gift. It doesn't matter where you got it from."

"And does it ever get any easier?"

"No." He was emphatic. "Especially when the big boys—and you will have noticed they're almost all 'the boys'—when they shit on us rather than listen to us. I know that goes on everywhere, but this is supposed to be a seat of *enlightenment*." He wrenched the word, wringing it with his mouth. "And an academic department. Ours, for example, is a bunch of bugs in a mason jar. Trapped together." He stared at the sidewalk. "When I was in the haze of undergraduate fantasies, I imagined seriously pleasant chats with colleagues, levitated by glasses of sherry." He sighed. "Yeah, well..."

"And?"

"I don't know."

We walked silently the rest of the way. Tulips were clustered in planter boxes, and the village looked as becomingly prepared for springtime as it had for the Christmas season. It had that ability, as if unseen stagehands were always in well-masked wing space to shift sets with precise timing. By moments, it had a way of being too perfect, if one thought about it.

The bookstore itself was upstairs over a restaurant and run by transplants from New York City who tended to it as part of a step-down retirement: two gentlemen who intermixed new books with old and smiled on customers as if they knew where the dirty volumes were hidden. Richard looked about, seemingly unable to focus, scratched his hair a number of times, shrugged and asked, "Any suggestions?"

"You're asking the bachelor?"

"I should be better at this. I still imagine reading with my children, but they want to play games on anything with a screen. I keep telling myself that when they're older, I'll read them Alice or Pooh. I'm willing to wait them out, but I'm not entirely hopeful."

And then I saw the book. It was so familiar I took a step backward. *Riff and Raggles*. I had read it in Nancy's class. While this was a new imprint, the cover had changed very little. A dark-furred dog stared at a white cat, its expression partway between a temptation to bite and a desire to make nice, and the cat looking back with indifference, her posture resembling that of *The Girl with the Pearl Earring*. The background color was as I remembered it, faded sage. To feel the pages respond with crispness to my fingers was almost anachronistic. They had no business being untouched.

Richard finally had a focus. "What's that one?" he asked.

"A book I knew as a kid. I didn't know little people still read it."

He took it from me and held it up as if he expected something to fall from it. "Can I blame you if she doesn't like it?"

"Be my guest."

Later that day, after Richard had made his purchase and was gone, I went back to the store, convinced there had been more than one copy of *Riff and Raggles*. I'd been puzzling for the rest of the afternoon over which was Riff and which was Raggles, but that wasn't the primary reason for returning. It was a calling, and I had the added possibility of a second book I could either read or avoid—another candidate for the special bookshelf. When I assured one of the gentlemen that I had seen two copies earlier, he assured me I had not. He gave a most sympathetic smile, clearly the type of man who did not like dealing out disappointment. But I could see his brain rolling tumblers of titles with that frightening catalog-capacity bookshop people have. "Wait," he said as I turned to leave. "Come over here. Let's have a look." I followed him to the Used section, and his discovery of the book was almost instantaneous. He apologized for the book's condition. The front cover had been scotch-taped back in place—many years ago judging by the discoloration of the tape. "Someone must have been very fond of this book," he said. "Perhaps that's why I kept it in our holdings. It has meaning."

"I'm sure it does," I told him.

"I could order you a contemporary copy if you don't mind waiting a few days."

"I wouldn't think of it. When I look at the tape, I'll think of these nice minutes you and I spent."

His face was alive with pleasure, and I could picture him in his own special chair marking in pencil the resonant passages of a book he had selected from a knee-high pile next to him.

§

I called Nancy later that night.

"Would you like to have a pleasant argument?"

"I've been thinking about you," she responded.

"Does that surprise you?"

"I've been trying not to."

"That never works," I suggested. "It's as impractical as stifling a sneeze."

"Yes, I know that, but I thought it would be good to find out if I might have gotten better at it. There must be certain qualities one gains with age. That, apparently, isn't one of them." She took a breath. "How are you, Jeremiah, and what is it you wanted to argue about?"

"*Riff and Raggles*."

I had devoted a quiet ten minutes to reading and rereading my new book when I returned to the apartment, poring over it as I would *The Tempest*. Its illustrations were eerily familiar, and that child's sense of delight in knowing what was coming next rose like a giggle. That my copy had been repeatedly held by another child or other children made it a shared experience—like the moments Richard Woo hoped for—but those children who had worn the cover off and taped it back on again were the father and mother of me at that moment.

When I was done reading it, I sat in The Professor's chair with the book on my lap. The chair was temporarily near the door to the hallway; as I sat, I could hear the voices of Eleanor Jewett and Hamilton Graham on the landing above. I could understand little of what was being said, except the rumble of his favorite phrase: "Magnificent, Miss Ellie!" While there was an immediate impulse to join them at the top of the stairs, there was a much stronger need to hear Nancy's voice.

"I will say this," Nancy responded. "If you would like to engage in pleasant disagreements, I would prefer to do it in person. I would like to see your face so I will know how much it is you're making up."

"Fair enough. Can you come now?"

"I can." And she clicked off.

While I waited, I thought about the name Ham Graham and the process of naming in general. Hamilton Graham had robustness, decisiveness, Founding Father resonance, and I couldn't imagine why he had ever allowed it to be shortened. "Ham Graham" sounded like an odd snack, and the possibilities for snideness seemed too many to imagine. I had tried very hard since I met him to think of him as a person with one name, like Bono. But he actually didn't mind the shortened version, from what I could tell. He often appeared to appreciate it—a bell of honor to sound before the world. Thankfully, very few until then had tried calling me Jerry, except a nice man in the history department, who not only used that corrupted version but also called me "kid" at times.

Ham had become a source of fascination for me lately—name or no name. There was, of course, the matter of Sara Sampson and my sympathy for what she must be doing to him. If she and I had been a strange couple in so many ways, they were agonizingly stranger. The look of puzzlement he'd begun wearing lately had become a fixity of his—he who, when I first knew him, had the eagerness of a man brimming with helpful ideas and a pleasant way of never forcing them. He would still use his Bull Moose outbursts to punctuate conversations, but they lacked the conviction of the autumn months, and I felt like the changes of seasons had left him behind, standing uncertainly. Sara could do that to a person, but I knew it was probably too late to help him through this challenge. I wondered what she called him.

Then, too, there was the growing sense that I knew him from another place or another time, that he had passed through my life before. If I had had this feeling when we first met, I undoubtedly would have asked him. Perhaps he was just that kind of person who had a "reminding" quality, that he is the double of one or hundreds. There was his half-sister, of course, but he seemed nothing like Willie. He was a thin slice of her, meticulously, keenly pleasant (at least until recently), while she was a hammer thrower of coiled and rangy emotions and more vibrant physically and facially. Perhaps it was nothing more than their having a share of the same mother.

Nancy tapped on my window, one you could step through to get onto the front porch. It had a mischievous sound, the clicking of her fingernails. She was outlined by the streetlamp behind her and the porch light to her side, giving her the look of a cross-lit performer. Her eyes were shadowed and beautiful.

She had brought a small cake with her that she handed to me. "I made this the day after our last time together. I froze it on the odd chance that I might see you again." We kissed and held the cake between us. It gave off the last of its freezer breath, a nurturing contrast to the warmth of our mouths. She noticed the chair when I set the cake on it. "Your father's?"

"Yes."

She touched it with two fingers, swiveling it away from us. "Is it friendly?"

"Aren't you something! It might be if you sat in it."

"I don't think so. And what is this? Have I hurt it?" She saw the book underneath the cake and slid it out from under.

"Don't you recognize it?"

"No. Should I?"

I took it and held it in front of her. "*Riff and Raggles.*"

She looked at it with abstract curiosity. "That's what you said on the phone. And is this what we're going to have our latest upset about?"

"But pleasant. We can disagree pleasantly or not disagree at all."

She took the book back and thumbed the pages before returning it to me. "I'd rather not disagree. And who was that lady who bought you your shorts?"

"Ah...Sara, a one-time annoyance of my more youthful days. I mentioned her over the phone when you called to check on Michael that time. She's dating the guy upstairs—Willie's brother—or half-brother."

"Yes, I know. And why did she buy you shorts and call you... whatever she called you?"

"I don't recall."

"It doesn't matter. It was my own younger self coming out. I will assume my midlife dignity again and put her back in her place. Tell me about this book."

"You taught it to me."

"When?"

"What do you mean 'when'? You honestly don't recognize it?"

She smiled, thickly indulgent and picked up the cake. "Why don't I cut a piece of this for you and you can tell me all about it?"

"Your irony is very sexy."

"That will have to do. Who knows where paths might lead."

She took the cake into the kitchenette, tried several drawers until she found a knife and two forks, then extracted a plate from the dish-drainer in the sink. "There are others in the cupboard," I instructed.

"We'll share." She completed the task with practiced ease and led me to the couch. "Sit, and tell me about your book."

We made love first. There were shades to be pulled and lights to be dimmed, and the book and plate found places on the floor before we did a full-sized version of our first time in her basement. She turned me on my back and remained upright while she lowered herself onto me, claiming it was important she stay on the lookout for intruders. It was also, she said, her first time "driving the bus," which took time to decode. The passion was rapid and explosive, and I finally put my hand over her mouth to keep several startling disclosures to ourselves. The exhaustion was exhilarating, mutating into whooshes of breath and a crescendo of laughter.

"All right, Professor, let's get to your book."

That would happen later. For a time we explored each other's face, tracing the lines that shaped them, testing lips, fingering ears, and brushing the contours of eyes. There was no faraway look this time—no other planet to come back from. Her immediacy was powerful, linking time to the totality of the present. There were no leakages of past or future, until I finally felt the striped pain of scratch-marks on my sides. I congratulated her, and she was clearly pleased with herself, even as she tended to me with the dampened corner of a hand towel.

"You don't own a washcloth?" she asked.

"Sorry."

"I'm the one who should be sorry. But I promise to make it up to you."

"Please do."

We finally dressed and ate bites of the cake with tentative fingers at first until there was a transfer of passion to sugar and chocolate.

"All right," she said at last, " now tell me about your book."

"You honestly don't remember it? A neurotic dog and a goody-goody cat...and a world without fleas?"

"Go on." She was licking chocolate icing from an index finger.

"And this line, 'I am happy when I love'...said by a cat to a dog next to a stream with a sky full of unrestrained butterflies. Look." I showed her the illustration in vivid patches of blue, red, and gold. The butterflies were fluttering like confetti. "Who knows what else you were dumping into my head back then."

"Do you think you were brainwashed?"

"No—or rather, why? Do you think I was?"

"Not any more than I may have been these past few weeks."

"Pardon me?"

"Oh, come, my darling Jeremiah. Here's this freshly hatched divorce case who found herself coming onto the great seat of learning just a matter of months ago to see the puzzling young teacher of her rather oddly motivated son, who happened to be trying his hardest to flunk out of college and make this newly self-sufficient mother feel like she's somehow dropped him on his head." She was walking about the room now, doing a kind of visual inventory and occasionally picking up small objects for inspection. "Even though she knows it's his right to be as odd as he would like to be, she somehow knows she is using that son to show her competence and not his. But she assumes it will be good for him on some level—that other peoples' practicalities...even meddling mothers'...should never be ignored—no matter how impractical they are. Are you following me so far?"

She had by this time taken *Reconsiderations* from its shelf without looking at it. "You see, while she's tried, she's done very little since the divorce except sort out the insides of things—cupboards and whatever else. And what happens?" She froze, staring fixedly at me. "She finally decides it is time to help her son—and herself—sort through the messes people leave out there in the world of events. So, she comes to his campus to be the good mother, hopefully seeking more for Michael than for herself. And what happens? Her son's professor follows her home one day—in a manner of speaking—to announce that he has loved her since he was toothless—an announcement she understandably tries to ignore. Can you believe her insensitivity? Can you imagine the practicalities involved? She is, as has been indicated, a practical woman, after all. So, for practically no reason, she begins to fall in love with him."

"Really?" I was mesmerized by her performance, but I wasn't about to let the last part go by unnoted.

"But not right away, mind you. I wasn't that impractical." She hesitated. "And you, of course, dragged me to that seductive wreck of a house in the country, and you got me looking for books on old railroads. *Old railroads*? Can you imagine that?"

I stood and approached her. "You have been storing a good deal, haven't you?"

She snuffled. "Of course I have. You've got me full of...stuff! And, of course, I remember your ridiculous *Riff and Raggles*. I used to read it to Michael. You weren't my only brainwashing victim." I tried to reach out for her, but she stepped back. "Not yet." She put The Professor's book on the mantelpiece, unaware, it seemed, that it had ever been in her hand. "Are you surprised this whole thing makes me wonder?" She ran a hand along one of my shoulders. "And then, by the way, here is this lovely, firm flesh after two decades of soggy bread."

"A shocking idea, Miss Nancy."

"There. See what I mean? All the bad things I end up doing lately. A month ago I would have flossed and brushed my teeth twice before I came here. Today, I took a swig of Pepsi instead. From a bottle. So who's brainwashing who?"

"Whom."

"No grammar. Not from you, and not now. Probably not any time, as a matter of fact. And I'm sorry I gored your skin." She paused, unwinding at last. "But not *that* much."

"I heal quickly."

"And you'll have lovely little scars."

"Yes."

"I have to go soon. My fairy godmother will throw fruit at me."

"I don't mind if you tell Michael."

"At some point. But he'll tell his father. That's the way he is. He shares things. But it's none of Marvin's business. Not yet. There may come a point when I will make it his business."

"Will he start flinging ledger books at me?"

"Marvin is schooled in indifference. It was a year ago he moved me from the asset to the liability side. I could envy him if I let myself."

I looked at the yielding command of her eyes, still as unsettling as they had been in the tiny moment when I first tried to read them. "You're beginning to remember, aren't you?"

"Damn you, Jeremiah, damn you and your grade-school pinheadedness." It was the first time I had heard her swear. "Why is memory so important to you?"

"Because that's what I was. Pinheaded to a fault. And I can see why you wouldn't want to remember."

"No, you wouldn't. You wouldn't because you can't."

"So we'll play in the dark. We'll love darkly. Isn't that what it is anyhow? And we'll forget the rest. We'll dump it. We'll blow it out of the water."

"And how will we do that?"

Strangely, I thought of Michael. I saw him with his cell phone taking pictures of people patterning their business as if primarily for his need to discover still beauty in action. His delight in the capture of unintended design fit him like a quiet satisfaction of hunger. "I wish I knew. Your son will teach us. He will divert us into a new way of looking at things."

"Oh?"

"What the hell. I'll be so busy trying to figure out if I'm his archrival or his buddy or phantom brother or substitute daddy or unsuccessful teacher that I won't have any choice but to try to understand him. That should clean out a whole roomful of notions."

She considered the idea. "When Michael was four, he scared the life out of me by climbing the birch tree at the front of our house—the one that broke his arm a few years later. When I got him down and got my face straightened out, he told me he'd done it to tickle God's feet. I've never forgotten."

"You shouldn't."

"You see. it's important for mothers to remember...not for teachers."

"Except when they're being taught."

"Oh? To know how we came to know? Is that it?"

"Yes, I think so."

"And now that we know what we know, Jeremiah—and now that we know how we know—do we know anything?"

"It seems like we know we love each other."

She put on her coat. "Let's let that idea breathe for a while. And for once we can leave on a pleasant note. This way I won't have to waste the time baking for you tomorrow."

"Fair enough."

SEVENTEEN

When I was alone and the intensity of the apartment had worked its way into undusted corners, I saw the book on the mantelpiece where Nancy had placed it, moving it from one part of the room to another as an act of levitation she seemed unaware of. Its blue covers had fit without impression into her hand, at rest there as she unpacked the feelings stored within her. But I was glad she'd held it, possibly making it less radioactive for the next person to touch it. Already, I had developed a faith in her touch and its ability to ground time and set it carefully in its place. I was sure she had done no less now. That she had spoken of loving, even in the midst of her impressive diatribe, was a point of information I had not expected. It was a slippage, I supposed, but no less important than the fact that it had been said. Had she said it while her nails were slicing into my skin, I'm not sure I would have found it as genuine. Orgasms can speak in tongues, and they can play about a wishful ear like a windstorm passing out to sea before leaving the debris of disbelief.

The cover of *Reconsiderations* gave it the look of an enlarged exam book. It was the same shade of powdery blue that had soullessly invited generations of undergraduates to fill those blank innards. Had he replicated the color deliberately or subconsciously or for no reason at all? Perhaps they matched the eyes of a high-school sweetheart or the body paint of a Ford Taurus. Or no reason at all. I had come to the point where everything about him was beginning to matter, after years of thinking nothing about him need matter all that much. I was becoming hyper-analytical, an attribute I had warned myself about during my college and graduate years and during this experimental year of teaching. I realized, too, at that moment, that I was again avoiding the book, that the task of opening its cover and looking within still awaited me.

I discovered there was no copyright page, no front matter at all except for the title page. His name sat below the single-word title, unadorned, a simple "Alban Curtin," with no academic embellishments. The font size of the name was significantly smaller than the title, a whisper of self-identification that made his *Reconsiderations* seem a bashful offering to whomever it was intended for. Finally, it was time to turn its pages. The evening had strengthened me. I had, after all, confronted the knotted world of *Riff and Raggles* with a brave assist from the woman who was evidently becoming a partner to my fixations—or had at least indicated her susceptibility. On this day, I had been jazzed by "Foggy Mountain Breakdown," clawed by a former schoolmarm, and cured of fleas by a fictional dog and cat. I had also learned that Michael Feller had tickled the feet of God. Powerful stuff.

As I flipped the pages with my thumb, it seemed the entire work was dialogue. I was so caught off guard I thumbed it a second and a third time. I could see an occasional stage direction but there were no prose passages at all—no exposition, no helpings of traditional discourse. It was divided into sections, preceded by subtitles. The first, in bold print, read, "**Literature is above all a form of dementia.**" There were two characters named Marty and Maud, sitting at a kitchen table, in pj's, and eating pistachio nuts. Right away, the author created the feeling theirs was a regular occurrence:

MARTY

(splitting a nut with his thumbnail)

What will it be tonight, old trot?

MAUD

Something tasteful. I want culture. I want to inhale it and sneeze it right back at you.

MARTY

(patting her hand)

What a wonder of absorption you are. You can't ever get enough, can you?

MAUD

And don't you forget it, buster.

MARTY

As you know, I have a tin ear for even the best and worst of music and no stomach for anything I can't imagine drawing or painting or sculpting. Since I have no creative abilities in those areas, I am at the mercy of my stomach. So let's say phooey on that, Maud. Let's do literature.

MAUD

Well, why not? Let's make a night of it.

They seemed engaging enough, and I was happy to play along with them. If The Professor was treating himself to an evening of anti-intellectualism, he could count me in, and I experienced yet another wish that we had been able to do something similar in person. It was Maud herself, in what the writer described as a "husky voice, like the sound of a papal bull" (the author had not been partial to punning, so I didn't know what to do with this), who rolled out the dementia concept with playful assists from Marty who occasionally disagreed only to be agreeable. It was a kitchen-table rendezvous after all. Maud spoke of writers as avoiders, who puffed forward their creations to keep their hands clean and their spirits unwrinkled. She chided them as the children of indifference who sought acclamation for their weaknesses.

Writers, according to Maud, were clever addicts, able to hide their dementia within neat margins. And on she went. While I still hungered for a context—a time and situation for this piece of writing—the text by itself had its own comforts.

Other sections unfolded through the increasingly absurdist dialogue of the couple at their table. They talked of things like who really wrote the plays of Shakespeare, though I never heard The Professor enter into the authorship controversy and imagined him viewing it as a settled question. Marty, however, thought otherwise. "If you bow before the academy like a bony dog, they will not only believe anything, they will make it scriptural. Those professors are a wily bunch because they are inherently lazy and oh so needy."

They talked about politics and the carnival of distraction it provided for a passive public. They talked of fashion and food and theater (admitting to each other that that's where they were at that moment, being staged with their pistachios), tennis (my father's only known physical outlet), Lewis Carroll, and the stock market. Carroll was a "mathematical vagabond who turned numbers into naughty girls." The stock market was clearly a field the author had studied with his own analytical thoroughness and parsed it into a degree of personal wealth even a big-time academic could not have amassed from his profession alone. He had made his time on Wall Street into his own golden goose, and Maud rose to her own level of ribaldry by describing the stock market as "the barnyard fowl that shits fair-weather funds for those with their fingers up the right place."

I read their discussion of marijuana with an almost peeping interest, especially when Marty noted that prisons inhaled those individuals who had the dangerous inkling that confinement was bad for the soul. During this particular meditation, Marty and Maud shared a long pipe, looking something like the clay puffers of Dutch burghers. They referred to theirs as an Amsterdamnable buzz, and I wondered if my father had puffed his own way through these dialogues. He grew even buzzier as his characters worked toward the conclusion. It was a pleasant and occasionally bewildering miscellany of topics and pronouncements.

Marshmallows, for example, were what a person should chew if there is a desire to know what *The Nutcracker Suite* would feel like on the tongue. More than once I laughed aloud and wondered again about Louisa, the room at hospice, *Riff and Raggles*, Richard Woo's four-year-old, Nancy's nineteen-year-old, Willie Furman, Baroque counterpoint, Huck Finn and Pap, Canada geese above the Hudson, the settled lawns of the campus, Barbara Lynn, and "Emily Botticelli." Marriage. It was an expanding flow of people and images, induced alchemically by the frowsy couple at the kitchen table spelling out their chronicle of needs and mistakes, damage and beauty, commitment and indifference—all aired through their unmistakable love of each other. Whether he had intended it or not, he had captured the truth of their oneness.

It all flowed quickly. Clearly he had grown more confident in what he was doing, whatever its purpose. The dialogue had an increasingly crisp edge and momentum, and my laughter came more and more easily, like that of a delighted first grader during story time. Suddenly, though, the gates of the artist slammed shut, as if the journey had been a setup, and here I was at the center of a labyrinth. The final section was headed with Dantean starkness: ENTER HERE IF YOU SEEK TO LOSE YOUR SON. I closed the book, set it next to the one with the dog-and-cat cover, and fell asleep on the couch where my skin had been ribboned. That entry would need to wait.

PART TWO

Homesteading

ONE

I haven't been around money all that much in my twenty-seven years. Or I should say I haven't been around cash all that much. I grew up in a large, well-furnished house in a presentable Hudson Valley neighborhood. Our street itself was a double row of the "best kinds" of older homes, well-maintained reminders of the early twentieth century, when the area had been developed by bankers and store owners who had not made it all the way to the top yet but could feel the trajectory in their backsides. It had been all-white then and remained pretty much so now. As a child, I thought little about money, in spite of my surroundings. I was bookish and yardish, an anomalous kid who didn't nag about getting things. There was a weekly allowance, usually left on my bed-pillow by Ellen. When she departed from her husband and me, I began doing small jobs—at the neighborhood library where the son of Professor Curtin was a welcome fixture and, for a time, at a weekly newspaper where I never got to write in spite of numerous hints in that direction. College was paid for as part of a reciprocal arrangement with The Professor's university, and I earned pocket money as a busboy in a Lebanese restaurant where I unintentionally spoke with a slight accent for a couple of hours at a time and developed an almost obsessive fondness for varieties of hummus. Graduate school was paid for by grants, research assistantships, and enough tutoring to buy Sara Sampson a mug of beer when her nerves were on edge and I was the chosen comforter. And now, my teacher's pay went twice monthly by electronic forces into a checking account. Tapping an ATM was the way cash finally found its way into my wallet, but it never felt that I had earned it—not in the same way plates dirtied with baba ghanoush had translated into real currency with no feeling of detachment.

Even three weeks after the reading of the will, I was still not thinking much about money. It was, I suppose, a new luxury to not acknowledge the obviousness of what was mine for the taking. At the same time, I wasn't ready. Money in a large amount represented another unknown. I thought of Alfie Doolittle in *Pygmalion* ruing the loss of his beggarly contentment at the hands of an iniquitous providence, money delivering him into the hands of middle-class respectability—although for me it wasn't that exactly. I was middle class enough to begin with, and I had a healthy skepticism about packaged morality. But the unknown was the unknown: a tonic in some cases, a dissembler in others. *Which* was to be *which* could still be put off a little longer. Presumably, no one knew, outside of those who had been in The Professor's study that day. My colleagues increasingly knew about books and a chair and no doubt assumed there was an element of money involved. That would do for now. And most fortunately Nancy Feller didn't know. I wanted us to stay, however briefly, where this intrusion couldn't touch us yet. There were enough forces already, mostly having to do with the dimensions of the playfield we would or could set for ourselves. Were we to confine ourselves to being lovers—a pleasant enough confinement, rich with discoveries we both admitted to—or would we soon consider how to thread our intimacies into a larger, self-protective world? Most importantly, I didn't feel like I could face an inheritance until I faced the last section of *Reconsiderations*, which had been reshelved with *Riff and Raggles*. It was my plan to keep them both at a safe distance for now and let decision take a grade-school nap.

This protective bubble was finally popped by Willie Furman. In another of her dashes from seeing Eleanor Jewett, she proclaimed breezily to an otherwise empty front porch, "I hear someone is a millionaire." I was in one of the rockers, committed to thinking about nothing, a stack of ungraded papers on the floor next to me. She didn't bother to turn around but skipped down the steps with a backward wave of her hand.

It was time to see the lawyer.

I had received two texts from Joanna Wexler's secretary proposing meeting times. I had let them pass into electronic limbo, sure I could hold out a little longer. That time was past. Her office was in a squatty structure just south of Poughkeepsie, near malls and auto dealerships, looking like it had been lifted from Ellen's old campus and dropped haphazardly into this location. I had e-mailed the secretary to ask if four o'clock would fit into her schedule. Ms. Wexler was there on the dot, waiting at the door of her inner office.

"How excellent to see you again, Jeremiah," she said compellingly. "I was afraid you were trying to scrub me out of your life. Not a good idea." The secretary, a man of middle age, gave the undercutting half-smile of one who knew too much. He was, of course, not what one expected in a legal secretary, given his gender, his age, and the fact that he wore his hair in a short ponytail. He reminded me of guys that drove parcel delivery trucks, although he did appear to be wearing long pants.

"I'll make a note of that."

She led me into an office, much like mine, with a view of traffic and three fast-food restaurants across the way. She had an apparent fondness for large and jungly floor plants, and I thought about the amount of oxygen they were giving off, even as I came to the immediate point of my visit. "One of my students congratulated me on being a millionaire yesterday."

"You should be pleased."

"Why should I be pleased that a confidence has been broken—one between you and me."

She paused to consider. "Did you say she was one of your former students?"

"That's not what I said."

"It was my daughter, I assume."

I sat, muttered "shit," and stared at her. "Willie?" The resemblance of their coloring was now more obvious.

"Her version of Wilhelmina."

"She told me her mother was a hotshot lawyer."

"I would imagine."

"But why did you share my business with her?"

"Because she's obviously a fan of yours, and she and I have long had issues of trust. I thought giving her a small secret to hold would be good for her, and it was not like I was alerting her to a disgraceful disease you have. Apparently she dropped the ball. Are you all right, Jeremiah? You look like your head is about to fall off. "

I had a brief impulse to leave the office without responding. I did, during the fall semester, walk out on one class after realizing that only two or three extremely quiet people were prepared to discuss the day's reading—something by D.H. Lawrence, puzzling stuff that demanded the active clutter of minds. I'm not the grand-gesture type as a rule, but in this case it worked remarkably well. I received a handwritten note from three of the unprepared, apologizing and asking me not to take it personally. I also received a text from one of the invariably prepared—a hyper-reticent chemistry major with straight As, assuring me everything would be fine in the future. I admired her assuredness, and, coming from her, I chose not to doubt her. And she was right. The next class was naughty and energetic, with the kind of gendered disagreements the wayward Lawrence would have found satisfying.

The lawyer stared at me as I lifted my head into a more combat-ready position. She seemed to have altered slightly since I saw her in the falsifying light of The Professor's study. She looked older, and there was a subtle sag to her lower lip that made it possible to imagine a cigarette there.

"My life is full enough with surprises," I told her, "without adding any more, Ms. Wexler."

"Call me Joanna." I knew that was coming.

"I doubt it."

"What is it you're angry about, Jeremiah? That I'm a hotshot?

Which I'm not. That my daughter, who generally dislikes me, thinks you're a legitimate hotshot? That you're somewhat rich as the result of no effort on your part? That you can become a social freeloader? That I knew your father?"

"Knew *how* exactly?"

"Why is that of any importance?"

"And the guy who lives upstairs?"

"Who's cohabiting with your former girlfriend?" She considered. "An interesting word, don't you think?"

"You *are* well informed, aren't you?"

"It's what I do." She was leaning against the front of the desk, her slender legs crossed at the ankles. The cloth bag with the Navaho design was slumped on its side just behind her. In the work of teaching, it was disagreement ending nowhere that served me best. It was the friction and not the outcome that mattered. In her case, as I looked at her, it was clear outcomes were everything.

"Is producing a daughter who's angry with the world also what you do?"

"I *did* produce her. I didn't raise her." She said it with chilling precision, her words separated with crisp exactness, like elements in a quadratic equation.

"What the fuck," I shouted stupidly. She didn't blink. "Is anybody doing what they're supposed to be doing anymore?"

"And what is that?"

"Committing themselves, making what they do at least have the appearance of being valued. Instead there's this mesh of vague promises and chance happenings—like we're waiting for an event that we don't necessarily care about so long as we have our waiting to occupy us. We make a business of it. And your daughter: she's talented, smart, and gutsy. She's full of promise, and you can't even get along with her as two fairly bright adults? Forget she's your daughter. Forget you did whatever you did after she was born. Admire her for what she is."

"Birth is no miracle, in spite of what some may think. The miracle happens when we come to the point of acknowledging the fact."

"A heartwarming thought."

She was apparently unmoved. "Would you like to talk about your money now?"

"Why on earth did he spend all that time with you cooking up this one-dollar or two-dollar load of horseshit? What pleasure did he get from that? What pleasure did either of you get from that? Or from each other, for that matter?"

"Do you think I'm going to tell you? Do you think your pouty harangue is all that effective?"

"And why does she accuse herself of being bad?"

"Who is that?"

"Your daughter."

She smiled unkindly. "We are bouncing about quite a lot, aren't we?" She turned toward the window and looked at the pulsations of traffic. It was nearing the Hudson Valley version of rush hour, and the choke of vehicles seemed to soften her. "I should imagine she's terribly fond of you. Too bad."

"And which bounce is this?"

"Your Willie, although I understand you have a slightly older girlfriend."

"Which would annoy you more?"

"Neither one, Jeremiah. I am merely one of life's interested observers."

"You're charming when you withhold. Remind me to tell you sometime of a diamondback rattlesnake I spent a few minutes with in the Arizona mountains. He or she was beautiful and mysterious with interesting eyes, but with a surprising ability to accept me for what I was. Most importantly, he or she—I didn't bother to check—was extremely noncommittal. That must be what cold blood has to offer. Alas, my time with that bedazzling snake was rather too brief, but that's how those kinds of things are. As far as your daughter goes, she is in love with music and has a refreshingly pleasant relationship with the son of the older woman whom I never thought of as my girlfriend, but she might be convinced to accept the term if I bought her an ice cream sundae. And, may I add, between you and your daughter, this little sector of what Manhattanites wrongly refer to as Upstate is becoming a storehouse of information about me, my family, my recent inheritance, and those who are potentially close to me." Not being given to speechmaking normally, I took a breath. "Would you like to talk about my mother?"

"No. No, I wouldn't. But if you'd care to, I would be pleased to hear more about your snake at some future time. I believe I knew him."

"It would be a delight." I was finally running down and needed to leave. "Maybe we can schedule a second attempt at this."

She nodded efficiently. "Yes." She circled the room and opened the door to the outer office. "I have another appointment. Bartlett, my secretary, seems to have left for the day. Raised voices make him nervous, something to do with his time in prison, I would imagine. But I will have him contact you to set up a time." I feared the coming of another probing handshake from her, but it was not to be on this day. I let myself out, thinking about Bartlett's name and background and how smoothly she shaped the creases of her face. It was the face of Snow White's stepmother, questioning the mirror before her with the silken assurance of an inquisitioner while betraying how vulnerable she was to betrayal itself. I could imagine her strength being held together with hidden patches and a great need to overcome—to overcome *what* was merely another in the mysteries I found floating about me. Again, there was the tangle of parent and offspring—my father, her daughter, Joanna at an intersection of those who would pull the cords of responsibility and indifference. She had grown in my mind to be a construct of each pull. It was a way to understand Willie more deeply, but as far as The Professor went, it was still impossible to know if he was the lawyer's collaborator, her mentor, or a by-product of what she represented.

Perhaps Bartlett was also emblematic. Joanna seemed to be looking for a reaction when she mentioned his time in prison, but whether she was trying to unsettle or earn admiration was another uncertainty. Had she become his benefactor? Was she using him to make a statement? Had they had a lawyer-prisoner relationship, and, if so, had it continued when he came out? Or, again, none of the above in another section of this wickedly non-standardized test to which I was presenting small, dotted guesses.

At home, I took *Reconsiderations* from where it nestled with my first-grade reader. I had bought a six-pack of Belgian beer, put one in the freezer, and searched for half a joint that had been left behind by Michael after the unplanned January party. I found it at last in a mugful of pens and pencils on the Formica table-desk and set it next to the mug—a relic of Ellen I had taken from home when I went away to college. It then followed me to graduate school and to this apartment. The mug was rose-colored with yellow blobs of fruit that looked like swollen toes. I had never drunk from it but had early committed it to its present use. Now, though, with the contents emptied on the table, it seemed the moment.

There was an errand to do first. A package had been left on the front porch, addressed to Hamilton Graham from Sara Sampson. A knock on his door brought no response until the door behind me opened and he stood within the surprisingly bright lights coming from Eleanor Jewett's apartment.

"Mailman," I announced, holding out the package.

"Ah, my rejection bundle from our mutual friend. Magnificent." He had apparently been expecting it and tucked it under one arm after shaking it briefly. "They must have rung, but I was having a lively time with our friend here."

"Is that the clumsy professor?" a voice from inside called. For a person of her age, the tone was more resonant than it had been during our meeting on the porch. "He must not be allowed to get away."

Ham led me into a room that was the way his half-sister had described it: books, pictures, and the feeling that little had moved in decades. Yet it was anything but a mausoleum for memories. She was no Miss Havisham, desiccating into forgetfulness. She and her guest had, in fact, been watching something on a flat-screen television, and while the room did contain an extraordinary number of pictures, a large percentage were from recent years. Many were of politicians, including several of Barack Obama and Hillary Clinton, often arranged to make them look like they were talking to each other. Unsurprising was the large number of photos depicting Franklin Roosevelt and Mrs. Roosevelt mostly covering one wall that served as her personal gallery. Her Democratic loyalties were there for the world to see, even if the world never came to take a look.

She was seated in an upholstered armchair and was holding a remote. When I was well into the room, she clicked it, freezing a black-and-white image on the screen. She rubbed a handkerchief across her lips and smiled her welcome. "We were watching old stuff," she instructed. She had taken an aperitif glass from a six-sided table next to her and sipped tranquilly.

"Not quite the whole story," Ham corrected. He shook the package again before dropping it onto a settee angled slightly toward Eleanor's chair, the two pieces forming a viewing area.

She stared fixedly at the package. "Is that from your bronco girl?"

He sighed. He was still in office clothes, in a suit-jacket but with the necktie loosened, giving him the look of a man just in from the grind. "Only some items to return."

"Sorry," I told him, trying to settle any feelings of guilt.

"You were an unspoken warning," he confessed to me. "Nobody's fault. She just has this talent for making risk feel like dessert."

"Yes, I know."

Eleanor set the glass back on the table with the delicacy of an artist. "Women can be such scoundrels, though most people apply the term to naughty men. I'm a feminist, you see. I apply the term equally to rogues of either gender. But I am sorry, too, Hamilton. She did make your face grow as long as a beagle's in the last month."

His expression appeared to grow even longer after she said this until he carefully removed the remote from her lap.

"So, that's enough of *that*! We were devoting our attentions to subject matter of much more value and interest." He gestured with the device. "See that beautiful being frozen in place on the screen? That's none other than the lady of the house here." He nodded in her direction, and I stared at the image of a young woman with decidedly 1940s or

1950s hair-styling and costuming, who was receiving the attentions of a soldier with cap in hand. His eyes were wide with ardor for the slim woman standing before him, and he looked like he was about to go onto one knee.

I turned to her. "You do have a past."

She nodded. "Indeed I do. But so will you. So will anyone who stays around long enough to make others think about such things."

"You were quite beautiful."

"Aren't you disgraceful, Jeremiah. And now?" she asked coyly.

"Now, you are merely stunning."

She nodded again. "I suppose that will have to do."

"And what did you—your character—say to the man who is about to pass out from sheer desire for you?"

"Let's find out." She took the remote back from Hamilton and clicked the suspended scene back to life at the moment where she would tell the soldier that his request for marriage was lovely but simply impossible. Hostilities were over, she told him, and it was time to put impulse back in its place.

I was stunned. "Eleanor," I protested as if I had known her forever. "I can't believe you did that to this poor guy."

"Of course, Jeremiah, I didn't do it. The person who wrote the words did it." She dabbed her lips again. "Not that I wouldn't have said the same exact thing. He was rather pompous. Although I have to confess, I did have feelings for Cameron, the actor. I could have gone for him. In fact, I did." She smacked her lips with perfect assurance.

"Why, you wily thing." Ham's face had shortened considerably. "And is this the night you spill the proverbial beans? My sister will be sorry to have missed it."

Eleanor was undeterred. "She knows enough as it is. But she will have her day, I'm sure." She ejected the disc, turned off the television, and asked Hamilton to refresh her glass with a "pinch more" Cointreau. She focused on the film part of her life for this evening, letting me know that it was the man across the hall who had forced the secret from her after seeing the film on an old-time movie channel and bringing his discovery to her for a confrontation of facts and a confession. His ability to identify her from more than sixty years ago was a feat to be admired, and she had apparently admired it enough to own up to that particular part of her life. Now she sat ennobled by it. She looked every bit like a faded film queen, though, as we learned, she had never been one. She had had a relatively brief career doing secondary roles as part of a stock company for a British studio.

"I was," she said, "a creature of the parallel plot." She puckered. "Well-placed for intrigues and complications, don't you know?" There had been a dozen or so such films before she grew homesick for America, returning during the Eisenhower years. "He struck me as a general who had missed too many naps," she commented, "but he grew on me. He was Republican, but I always liked the confident sound of his name."

She showed little reluctance in retelling how she had lived during her days in England, a communal arrangement where relationships fluctuated like the shifting of roles from one film to another. Several actors and actresses shared a house—and each other—in the Surrey countryside where she said, "the sinning was easy." She spoke of how it had all come about: "It wasn't as if anyone said to the rest of us, 'Let us go and take up a life of casual debauchery.'" She took notable pleasure in the last word, articulating as if it were an incantation. "There was no script, so to speak. That's what made it quite extraordinary. I'd never experienced anything like it, and my guess is I am not likely to do so again." She gave a partial wink, as if her eyelid had stuck to the eyeball. "You see, there are so many ways to experience closeness. This one, as I say, didn't come with a script. It didn't need to."

Her only reluctance that evening was admitting she had DVDs of all her films that had remained in print into the twenty-first century. "It is so opposite to letting go of the past, but it's so convenient; and after all is said, why shouldn't I?" She admitted to having her own personal festival about once a year and promised to invite me to her next one.

When I asked about her life among the Roosevelts, she closed down the conversation, except to say, "What people don't know..." She wasn't able to add the rest of the sentence, and Ham and I knew it was time to go.

In the doorway to his apartment, with Sara's package under his arm, he broke an extended silence. "Our Miss Ellie made it all sound so easy. Could it have been, or has she simply forgotten?"

"Why would she want to? And, by the way, I met your mother today."

"Counselor Wexler?"

"The same. She was my father's lawyer."

"So I understand."

"Were they...a couple?"

"Could be. Can't be sure." He seemed anxious to tuck himself into the apartment with his package. "She was a student of his, I think she told me. You know how those things go."

When I returned downstairs, I discovered the beer in the freezer had frozen solid. I opened one of those at room temperature and sat down to the remainder of *Reconsiderations*.

ENTER HERE IF YOU SEEK TO LOSE YOUR SON

MARTY

(Now in a nightgown and pointed nightcap)

Well, my dear, it's been quite a night, hasn't it?

MAUD

Yes, quite stimulating, Marty. I feel years older.

MARTY

(Wiping his forehead)

I had begun to worry, you know. You were growing remarkably youthful. I was afraid you were going keep lessening until you vanished altogether.

MAUD

Yes, that's always a possibility, but don't you worry your pointy old

head tonight. That nightcap, by the way…it gives you a decidedly unrestrained dignity. What will become of me if you poke right through the top?

MARTY

We seem to have much on our minds, but, as they say, too much is never enough. I do believe we have proven that any number of times.

MAUD

Of course we have. By the way, did you check on the lad while you were changing before?

MARTY

Changing how, my dear?

MAUD

Well, you're always changing. It's quite something. But in this case I was referring to your evening wear.

MARTY

It's actually close to morning, so evening wear won't do.

MAUD

I see.

MARTY

And, yes, he was there, but it was difficult to see if he was ours or not. The light was pointing in the wrong direction.

MAUD

That would explain it. So there is no need to explain.

MARTY

But I do believe he was moving his lips.

MAUD

Gas?

MARTY

Undoubtedly.

MAUD

And did he mention his name?

MARTY

Actually no. No, he didn't. And what is his name, my blessing?

MAUD

(Pondering)

Now there's a perfectly good question, but a perfect waste of time, you'll have to admit. You know, Marty, it has quite slipped my mind.

MARTY

There.

(As an accusation)

Is it true you were bred unleavened?

MAUD

Flatly.

MARTY

I'm told he limped.

MAUD

Only on one leg and then only in the beginning.

MARTY

(Somewhat thunderstruck)

But that's it. That's his name!

MAUD

What? What?

MARTY

Gen…

MAUD

—eral.

MARTY

No, no. Gen—

MAUD

—ital.

MARTY

Gen…

MAUD

—isis. Genesis!!

MARTY

What's that, pray?

MAUD

The lad.

MARTY

Oh, well it's a nice old-fashioned name, don't you think, Maudie?

MAUD

It's no wonder we keep forgetting.

MARTY

(Humbled)

Actually, I don't think I ever knew.

MAUD

That could be. You originally wanted to call him—what was it, Marty?

MARTY

Fred.

MAUD

Fred. Yes, I suppose so. Did you know a person named Fred?

MARTY

No.

MAUD

Sad, isn't it?

MARTY

(Suddenly, with eagerness)

Only a titmouse.

MAUD

That's better.

MARTY

And my paramecium.

MAUD

Better still.

MARTY

But I inhaled him.

MAUD

Which is carrying intimacy a little too far, don't you think?

MARTY

That is precisely what the archbishop thought. How extraordinary for you to say that.

MAUD

Fatigue will do that to you, and I'm famished.

MARTY

We should send out.

MAUD

The lad?

MARTY

(Reflectively)

A possibility.

MAUD

In this state, I am incapable.

MARTY

Not at all. You're perfectly capable. You can cape with the best. You can caper…on Cape May…holding a capon.

MAUD

May I?

MARTY

Capably. Most capably, Maudie. You know, I think the lad had a thought last month.

(A toilet flushes elsewhere in the house.)

MAUD

Oh?

MARTY

Something about patience, as I recall.

MAUD

How interesting.

MARTY

He had just found a mushroom growing on his nose.

MAUD

Remarkable.

MARTY

Still, he was impatient at the last. He had a revoltingly urgent need to find out if it was a toadstool.

MAUD

(The toilet flushes again.)

That is perfectly understandable and potentially adorable.

MARTY

(With a distant look)

Do toads put their feet up, actually?

MAUD

Only when they can't tell a fly from a zipper. Or when they're dead.

MARTY

Yes, I knew that.

MAUD

Of course, darling. You know everything. It's what makes you a sterling father.

MARTY

Yes, sterling. "Sterling" is a splendid word, isn't it?

MAUD

(Peering offstage)

I believe the sun is rising.

MARTY

Did you say son?

MAUD

I said no such thing.

MARTY

(Standing and crossing to her)

All right then. Just as well.

(Kissing her on the cheek)

Good night, my dear. Let me know when you're back down this way any time in the future.

MAUD

I might do that.

(She exits, leaving him holding his nightcap like a security blanket, twisting it slowly back and forth as the lights fade.)

My head had begun to throb. I tend to be impatient with those claiming headaches since I almost never get them. I had just received a chiding message on patience and impatience which simply added to my anger at being seized by such a weakness. The lad...presumably that was me, the patient kid who had accepted his mother's abdication and his father's calm compliance, the stuff of mushrooms and toadstools. If I read the fucking thing correctly. The Elf-king had struck again from an unknown seat of sorcery. He had made sure there were pathways enough to befuddle anyone who had the misfortune to read this closing dialogue—this nasty declaration of new games after the bizarre pleasantries leading up to it. Here were hints of illegitimacy, conspiracy, and cruelty in this final guesser's maze. It was catnip for anyone who loved piecing together the inner workings of a text; it was also a warning against exactly that, a reason to leave it all behind. It was a shameful performance but irresistible in its own lowly way. It was a puzzle apparently beyond solution, but tantalizing and motivating...and I was pissed off enough to go with both the push and the pull.

TWO

One of the dangerously good things about literature—derived, no doubt, from its being a form of dementia—is when you feel the author is writing to you, even across large separations of time and space. It is a realization that each of us comes to if we've experienced the seduction of a text and, as such, is not all that important to say. But it comes with a danger. We can so lose ourselves in a work that we do lose ourselves to ourselves. There is, too, that more subtle danger of thinking a text is meant for us when it is not. I had that experience in an undergraduate creative writing class while I was infatuated with a classmate who I was sure must be infatuated with me as well. With each piece of poetry she read aloud, I became more convinced her feelings were intended for me—composed as they were with such longing that they had to be messages for my benefit, even though we had barely spoken except through glances that brushed quickly past one another. It didn't matter until, that is, I realized she was pregnant, her other-directed belly growing more defiantly as a corrective to my weekly misreadings. I did write a sonnet for her that I intended to read aloud at the end of the semester, but it, of course, was an act of silliness. She was out of class that day, having a sonogram.

I didn't tell Nancy Feller about that Art of Poetry experience—she would have been entirely the wrong person—but I did rant to her about Marty and Maud's descent into hell and the need I had to assume it was all about me, him, and a woman who refused to be identified but could serve satisfactorily as my fictional mother, for now.

"Is it a form of narcissism, do you think? You have been known to personalize things when you'd have been better off not to." She said it quietly but with the firmness of a scolding. We were in her home office, a small cubby off her living room that had once been a side porch, enclosed and winterized in the midyears of her time with Marvin. She was seated with her back to a rolltop desk, a classic that had been given to her by a relative in the Alleghenies and seemed to take up half the floor space, but it fascinated me with the orderliness of its pigeonholes. They were as well-arranged as her words and her efficient delivery of them.

I was standing by the room's single window, looking at the covered pool in the side yard. "The thing is, he used unworthy puns about toads and mushrooms." She looked at me patiently. "Do you use that pool now that you-know-who is gone?"

"I might."

"In fact, as far as I know, all puns struck him as unworthy." I looked outward again. "I've never dealt with a pool."

"Michael mastered the upkeep routine years ago. Much better than you-know-who."

"Marvin."

"Yes, Marvin."

§

I had spoken to her at length about the house in Quaker Falls, and she had made several phone calls after my convincing her I had figured out how to deal with finances if the price was reasonable. As expected, the property was part of an estate in the care of assorted cousins, second cousins, and other shirt-tailers who knew little about the most recent occupants. No doubt, the basic systems like electric, water, and heat would need replacement or upgrading, and who knew what the house was like structurally? Nancy had an inspector who could render an opinion for me. It would all take time, but she had received permission for us to look at the insides if we were still interested. I was.

"I'm telling you, Nancy, what it offers is starting to become clearer."

"Would you like to explain it?"

"I can't yet. It's a feeling. It's in my brain, but it's on the right side where it can spoil itself a little longer with not having to explain itself. It's like love."

"How nice that you've been able to practice for this." Her sarcasm was cushioned by her concern. "Does this mean, at least, that you will continue to teach?"

It was a reasonable question, even though she was still annoyed with my suggestion that a house—or a home—could serve as an alternative to a career. It was clear in her field of vision that was not how things were done.

"Don't know yet."

Nancy frowned. "There are times I'm still not sure what to make of you."

"Make of me what you will—and when you will."

"A challenge."

I could feel Willie's presence before I knew she and Michael were in the house. She had, over the months, become especially good at foreshadowing herself. I could feel the air compress and the living room start from its afternoon nap. She was dressed, however, like a milkmaid with a crinkly sundress polka-dotted like her nose. I could hear Michael outside calling after her, but her entrance told me she was ready for a one-on-one.

"I have a bone to pick with you," I told her. It was the best I could come up with.

"People say the stupidest things," she replied, reading my thoughts. "What kind of bone, and what's the picking for? And why would anyone want to pick a bone in the first place?"

"You betrayed private business of mine."

"I betrayed it to you. So what's the big deal?" She seemed quite certain of what I was talking about.

"The big deal is..."

"I'll bet you've been talking to my mother."

Nancy had stood. "Would you like me to leave you two?"

"She still doesn't know?" Willie asked, nodding toward her.

"And would you like to betray my secrets to somebody *besides* me? Here's your chance."

Michael had come into the house by then, carrying a pizza box and a two-liter container of root beer that dropped from his hand as he tried to extend it to me like a greeting. "Have you told Michael?" I asked Willie.

"Jesus, it's your stuff. *Nobody* knows."

Nancy had frozen in place, and Michael had secured the bottle with his feet. "Anyone want a slice?" he asked, extending the unopened box.

"Then you have my blessing, Willie. Fire away."

"'Blessing,' bullshit." Her sullenness made me wish for a pair of milk pails to hand her, as the unusual slump of her shoulders worked to dispel the last of my anger with her.

I could see the cool determination of Joanna Wexler leave her standing disarmed and unfocused. "It's okay. I don't know why I haven't been able to speak about it, so you've done me a favor."

"No," she responded simply, leaving it unclear where she was directing the word.

"Jeremiah?" Nancy was showing a depth of concern I'd not seen in her before, and my instinct was to put an arm around her. I spoke instead.

"I've been known to play denial games, so it's confession time. When I was a kid, I refused to acknowledge Santa, but I clung steadfastly to the legend of the Tooth Fairy, even though I never got a dime out of her. I was selective. I thought fairies made more sense than fat elves. And the whole coming down the chimney defied all fireplace logic. Recently, I inherited a large sum of money."

"Hah," Willie sputtered. She took a slice of pizza from the box Michael had placed on an ottoman, creased it down the middle and took a decisively large bite. Michael seemed torn between watching her and watching me while nudging the root beer bottle into a vertical position with toes extending from a sandal.

"Which is what this young lady and I have been doing our little snit dance about. She learned about it from her mother the lawyer, who provided the information as a trust exercise."

"Bullshit," she said through strings of mozzarella.

"*Which,* the more I think about it, she fulfilled admirably. You can't, as you say, really spill the beans to someone who owns the beans—namely me. I own a lot of beans, Nancy, though I've been trying my best not to remember it. Willie's one piece of sniping on my deserted front porch was just the goose I needed to start lurching my way to the end of denial. So, my fine freckled friend, I apologize to you, although I have any number of questions I'd like to ask at some point about your mother, your brother, my father, and whoever else comes across my radar. And, Michael, I don't know how you got that bottle to stand at attention with two toes, but I am mightily impressed. On top of that, Nancy, I should have been more forthcoming while you were worrying about how I was going to manage the purchase of a run-down house on a fugitive teacher's salary."

Nancy was still silent, and Michael was staring with admiration at the bottle beside him. Willie, on the other hand, spoke quite plainly. "You quit and you suck." She took another bite.

Nancy had finally moved from her office into the living room. "My God, Jeremiah, you do have issues"

"All right. Thanks for that. And, Michael, would you like to say your piece?"

"I think we should go see it." He had finally lifted the bottle from the floor and was carefully removing the cap.

"See what?"

"The house—the one you and Mom have been talking about for weeks."

"We have?" Nancy asked.

"Well...you have, at least." He took a swallow from the bottle and passed it to Willie.

"I have?"

"You've been like a crazy lady, Nancy," Willie assured her. "No offense intended."

"None taken, I'm sure." For once, Nancy Feller looked genuinely puzzled. "I've been that ...whatever?"

"Mom," Michael told her, "ever since you and him went to see the house, you've been talking about it like...it...was this big new thing in your life."

Willie eyed her. "You've been talking about 'this old wreck of a house' like you were going to invite it to dinner."

Nancy spasmed into laughter, one of the least ladylike sounds I'd ever heard come from her. "Well aren't I something? All right, Michael, and did you think we should go see it now?"

"Now." One little word sent us on our way.

§

Nancy insisted on driving. It was the first time I'd been a passenger of hers, and it felt like a family outing. She had begun to chatter, and I was happy to listen and serve as unneeded navigator while Michael and Willie ate pizza in the back. He bounced the box on his knees.

"I've driven this route over and over again in my mind, but if you want to fuss about my ending up in Schenectady, you have my permission. I do wonder how it will look now in April. It was so forlorn the only time I saw it. But we get to see what any bulbs have been doing. And you have to love the idea of bulbs. They come to life whether anyone is there to see them or not. They're not like a tree falling in the woods. Daffodils make a sound, but it's a sound for the eyes. How's that for an idea, Professor? We stick them in the ground, and I'm sure they're grateful, but they can't possibly care afterward if anyone's there to see them or not. My mother has planted masses of daffodils and jonquils throughout her life. She calls them her announcers. They tell the good news of spring. She gave up on tulips because of the deer. I've pretty much given up, too. I think you'd like her, although what she'd think of you I couldn't be sure. She's a *real* Allegheny girl. Her father, my grandfather, ran a sawmill. When she was a teenager he would threaten to tie her to a log, like in melodramas—is that what you call them?—if she was bad. *He* was a character. He was against public dancing. It was against his religion. But he would dance in the kitchen with me standing on his feet. My mother thinks Michael will be one of the first earthlings to land on Mars."

There was a "Hunh?" from the back.

"Your grandmother," she said into the rearview mirror. "You've heard her say that. She says you're so out of this world you might as well make a name for yourself."

"She talks to water," he murmured approvingly to Willie. Nancy nodded, turning into Quaker Falls and going slowly past its country store. "We're here?" he asked suddenly. He was out of the car in a moment, awkwardly handing the pizza box back to Willie.

The yard *did* have a variety of daffodils, hyacinths, and crocuses. Nancy pointed to where the tulips, sure enough, had been chewed to spiral stumps by deer. One side of the yard was lined with forsythias in full blossom, indifferent to their years of neglect. The lawn had already awoken to the point where it readily showed how far it had submitted to nature free of human attention. Wild onions, as Nancy identified them, were growing in scattered clumps, and there were countless dandelions, their bold beauty making me think sadly of my weed-free campus. The younger members of the party were busily trying to look inside the shaded windows, tapping on the diagonal pitch of the cellar-door opening, discovering in some weeds a mailbox and newspaper tube still on a wooden post that had at one time fulfilled their duties by the side of the road, cast aside vessels of delivery. Nancy and I were drawn to the rear of the yard where the solemnity of wintering fruit trees had exploded into distinct sets of blossoms. She acquainted me with two apples and a pear as if they were distant ancestors. But she stepped back when we came to a fourth tree next to the dollhouse structure. Its mass of light pink blossoms were larger than those of the other trees, and she suddenly moved forward to thrust her nose into one of the flowers.

"Oh, Jeremiah," she exclaimed, almost as a cry of pain, "I know what it is! Smell it." It was not like I expected my sense of smell to identify this exotic-looking blossom, but putting my nose to it did take me to a place of rich potency with an antique aroma suddenly released from centuries of entrapment. It was a heavy odor, impatient with its own inner urging for expression—so different from the quiet coyness of pear blossoms. I have often thought a keen sense of smell is what differentiates great writers from those of the second tier. If this tree were to describe itself in words, it would have immediately thrust itself into the canon of the remarkable.

"What?" I asked her.

"It's quince," she said, grounding me again. "My grandmother had a small orchard of these. She would say terrible things about people who thought they were good-for-nothing—inedible and ugly fruits, they would say. She would speak of such people as being pretty much the same thing. After all, she was married to the man who threatened to run my mother through a sawmill and make boards from her." She was laughing at some or all of what she had said, her eyes joyous with memory and discovery.

"Quince. You're sure."

"I couldn't be any more sure, Jeremiah. She would make wine from them, the only supposed stimulant my grandfather would drink. He had this idea it was *the* actual fruit tree from the Garden of Eden. I don't know where he got such a notion and why he liked sipping forbidden fruit juice, if he was right, but he was very, very selective in his likes and dislikes and had no trouble justifying them, whether his facts were right or not. My grandmother also made jams and what she called conserves from them. My mother still attempts it every now and then." Nancy tugged at the end of a branch. "You've struck golden fruit here. If only my grandmother was still alive."

Michael had wandered in our direction. "Will went to the store to check it out. I've been looking at the sheds. You can't see much. They're all locked. I bet there's all kinds of stuff inside them," he speculated and then shifted his focus. "Mom, you look like you've been doing bong hits."

"She's been inhaling trees," I told him.

Nancy and I presented a jumbled version of what she knew and I had learned about the quince tree and its place in Michael's ancestral pages. He was fascinated by the information and, like his mother, stroked the tips of several branches before putting his nose to one of the blossoms.

"Ultra far," he remarked, and I thought that would do it, his comment a word longer than normal already. However, on this rare occasion, he was stirred to explain himself. "Trees. They give off messages, don't you think? They tell you whether you should listen to things or cover your ears. And here is this one, right in your yard, you know? It wants you to come here and make him look good again. He's got all these... what're they called, Mom?" he asked, poking at a cluster of shiny, small branches in several of the quince's eye-level crotches.

"Suckers," she reminded.

"And they don't really suck, but the tree doesn't want them there if it wants to make good fruit. Right?" Nancy nodded. "I guess they do look sucky but not very." Then he added suddenly, "Don't you think he should buy the house, Mom? It's been here by itself, you know? It needs to get warmed up again."

Willie was back with a piece of beef jerky in one hand and a peculiar look on her face. "Who's getting warmed up? If it's anybody I know, count me out."

"Your friend Michael wants me to bring this place back to life," I told her. "Is that the idea?" I asked him.

"Sure." He stared at Willie. "You look spooky."

"Nah. It's the store. It's packed with cans and boxes of everything, and people who look like they were going to spit on the floor. And they call it an emporium. What the hell is that supposed to mean? But it's okay." She turned to me. "You're going to fall for this old place?"

"I might," I told her, and her face puckered. "It's going to need loving."

"I'll bet."

"You don't think she deserves it?"

"Huh. Why are houses always women?"

"Because they give birth?" I suggested.

"Crapola." Willie had had enough. "Can we go now? I have to see the old lady upstairs from you. She'll probably think you're doing a jolly good thing. She's always yammering about houses."

Michael had been reading something on his cell, and before we got to the car, he told me to look up quince. "It would make a pretty good essay, dude." He smiled his most winsome smile, and while I had never wished to be "duded" by anyone, in this case I wasn't sorry.

THREE

That night I *did* explore the quince. In the past, doing research had combined elements of frustration and safety. There were dead ends, but even those did little to increase any risk level involved. You simply went on until you satisfied yourself that you had come to a satisfactory conclusion or to no conclusion at all. Few, if anyone, knew when you screwed up; they only saw the finished product. It was a form of disappearing ink. I had already produced several so-called scholarly pieces of no real consequence, and I knew that if I left teaching, I would probably continue to research what interested me. For now, my researches involved the ancients and their fruits. I had heard The Professor chiding the idea of online research and that people like me rarely got their hands dirty opening real books in real libraries or wearing white gloves to touch real manuscripts in real archives. I had done plenty of each, but there was an incredible comfort in sitting at your own desk and bringing information to fingers that were neither dirty nor gloved.

We had scattered from Nancy's driveway. Willie was apparently heading to Rhinebeck, and I was hiding out for the evening in the quiet of my campus office with only occasional sounds from faraway parts of the building. I had cranked open the window, and I could hear the sound of peepers coming from the campus pond that served as an ice-skating rink in the winter. The sound they made—like that of steroidal crickets—was one of the comfort foods of spring.

The return trip from Quaker Falls to the suburbs had been problematic. Willie had grumbled to herself most of the way, like she was casting spells. Michael was locked into his phone, and Nancy kept glancing over at me like I was about to do something erratic. In spite of her ecstasies about the breath of a blossoming tree and the fulfilled expectation of spring flowers, I couldn't tell how she actually felt about the house, inheritance or no inheritance, and Michael's resurrectionist enthusiasm or not.

But he'd been right; his girlfriend did look spooky. Before going to her car, she had issued a muttered statement about what sounded like "fancy women," leaving the three of us without any understanding of what had apparently bothered her about the house and anything else. I thought of her tromping up the stairs to Eleanor Jewett's apartment and wondered whether that fascinating old woman might be privileged to hear Willie's secret hauntings. Nancy provided one of her late-autumn handshakes and urged me "to think about it." About buying the house, I gathered. Michael walked to the forsythias in their yard, as if he needed to tell them secrets of his own. He had kicked off his sandals and was approaching them in bare feet, the end of some private pilgrimage.

In my office, I learned that the quince had a long history: that it may have had more importance to the Greeks than the apple, and it may have looked down on its smooth-skinned cousin as an unworthy successor. The quince was associated with love inducer Aphrodite and, consequently, with fertility, and it might, in fact, have been the congratulatory goodie given by Paris *to* Aphrodite when he judged her to be hotter than Hera and Athena and kick-started the Trojan War. Some theorized, like Nancy's grandfather, that the quince was the actual party pooper for Adam and Eve, which gives it an impressive track record based on just these two instances of roiling up human destiny.

I thought again of the smell of the blossoms earlier in the day, their invitational power suggesting the possibility of danger, and I wondered if that was what the ancients based their quince-lore upon, not the fruit itself but the pungency that preceded it, attracting more than necessary insects to its inner mysteries. It stood in its own corner of that abandoned yard, year after year, secure before the indifference of humans, armed with the ability to awaken the unsuspecting to the force of forgotten discoveries. Is it that the ancients, ancient even to themselves, could smell within a single blossom the ultimate goal of time...to lose itself? New England colonists, I learned, were obsessive about planting a quince at one corner of their vegetable gardens, where it wouldn't shade what was growing there, but would serve as an anchor to the passing seasons and to the repeated rhythms of cultivation that took place before it. I thought of my own lack of knowledge about gardening, a sure inducement to make me start one, planted like temporary parishioners of the guardian quince. I would be guided by it into a clearer knowledge of how time enfolded itself.

The tapping of a key on my door brought me out of my ponderer's fog and back to the starkness of the cubicle and the shaking out of immediate minutes—though I had the briefest thought of Poe's raven. The office doors in that building had vertical glass inserts, which some seeking privacy covered with posters, academic regalia, or whatever. I had left mine naked to the world of the corridor, and I was startled to see the face of Phyllis Friel looking from an angle in at me, as if putting her whole body on the same plane would be too intrusive. Instead of a raven, I thought of the dream in the boiler room and the cross between her sad breasts,as she waved a handful of keys.

She was the third of The Triumvirate to visit in recent days. Chuck Gillis's appearances were never a real surprise. He still seemed to enjoy the intermixture of our generations, still talked about modern students as if they had been genetically altered, and still gave the impression he was looking to me for a clue about the evolution of his own life and career. Mitchell Schreiber had been more of a surprise. He dropped by one midday with his lunch bag in hand as if he was ready to share his cup of yogurt with me, but he merely held the bag on his lap while he talked about his recent divorce and the process of dating at his age. He confessed to being understandably rusty at the techniques of approach and seduction, and I listened to him with uneasy sympathy until he asked me if *I* was "getting any." The crinkle of a grin with which he had bolstered the question left me digging for excuses to leave my office. He pushed ahead, without pretending to wait for an answer, confessing to how the sensibilities dulled after thirty-five years of sharing a bathroom with the same woman. He was convinced there were new and unexplained mores to sharpen him up again, and he did, at last, wait to hear what they might be. I finally concocted an appointment to get my oil changed, and I watched him with some pity as he shuffled down the corridor ahead of me, the brown bag swinging from one hand like a symbol of untasted pleasures. And now Phyllis Friel, wearing a wintry coat though it was a mild April night.

She let herself in, smiling the look of an apologetic invader and saying, "I hope you're not doing anything too important." Schreiber had, I think, led off with the same declaration.

"Is this our powwow?" I asked. The term referred to a meeting she had promised throughout my year there—a chance to assess my progress. It had not happened.

"Oh no. Certainly not. Powwows are not drop-in events." Then she added with brisk puzzlement, "Did I mention a powwow?"

"You said we might have one."

"That's possible. We might. Powwows, I've said, serve as refreshments in the long academic year." I couldn't imagine how. "I merely saw your light, and I've been thinking about your father. I knew and respected him."

"It seems there was a lot of that." I was tempted to say "except me," but I was puzzling over how she could have seen my light from her own office on the floor beneath me in the valley of the dean's most trusted or feared cohorts.

"He was a fine man. He organized a consortium of local colleges many decades ago. It has since gone with the wind, as they say. I had dinner at your house many times when you were quite small."

"And here I am now, all grown up. But I don't remember you."

"I looked different then. I had longer hair." She grew wistful. "At times, it's difficult to think of his being...no longer with us. It marks all of us who've given our lives to the profession. Not to you, of course, though he was your preceptor."

"Yes. I suppose he was." It was an unusual word.

"Though you mark us, too." She was swinging her keyring around an index finger.

"And how is that?"

"I'd rather not say."

I eyed her. "No, Phyllis. I get the feeling you'd very much like to say."

"That's as it may be." She had dropped the keys and was retrieving them from the chair next to her. "Let me just say, don't give up on teaching. Think of him."

"My father? I expect he would be just as glad."

"That's not what he told me."

"When?"

"That hardly matters."

It obviously had to have been in the months leading up to his death, perhaps during the late fall. Had he and Phyllis had their own powwow, and was I the subject of it or a smaller item? Her dismissiveness of the timing only heightened its importance to her holding onto it—hers to enjoy for whatever satisfaction it gave her as well as the satisfaction it gave me to see her surrounding it with her spidery nonchalance.

"Right you are," I responded at last. "And was that why you dropped in now?"

"No one wants their life choices questioned. You'll develop an understanding of that at some point. But you will have to let me know soon."

"I'm not sure I agree with your first statement. Or else, I say from my limited experience, our life choices become posts for dogs. But I will let you know soon."

She looked unsettled and buttoned her coat with the awkward movements of one hand. Her fingers looked challenged by the early stages of arthritis, and as she moved silently away, I could see age dropping onto her like a crumpled sheet. If she had come to rally me for the benefit of Alban Curtin and her own needs, she was making a poor show of it. She could be putting a great deal more pressure on me about coming to a decision, but was she doing a favor for me or for herself? Was it that she and the other two members of The Triumvirate clung together out of their own fear of uselessness, or *was* I too young know what they knew all too well? Was I folding time like a napkin for my own convenience, and should I expect anything more from myself? Or was I still able to see that nothing was all that inevitable except the shutdown of our senses? Youth and age. That old, old contest. Was it still another of the unavoidable things of living? If so, why was I in an undefined form of love with a woman a generation beyond me?

I took an evening walk across campus, choosing a longer than necessary route to my parking lot. I hadn't done anything like this since February, and it was a reminder of how preoccupation can overpower the best of pleasures. As much as I could find reasons not to, there were reasons to embrace the staging of this soft and peeper-orchestrated night. There was the sub-sensual feeling of students preparing for their final weeks, and the lighted windows of the library spoke of fulfilled purpose. Many of The Professor's books would be housed there soon, carted away from where they had wrapped part of his private world to a library of a more modest scope than the university libraries he knew. I would look for them when they were shelved, wondering if they would be noted in some way with the insertion of a special label or the decision of a librarian to leave his "Ex Libris Alban Curtin" sticker pasted to the inside of the front covers. I had been advised that some of the books would go through the oddly named process of remaindering, sent to other places—"disappeared" the way people are in societies where they present a danger. They would end up with online used book companies, small bookstores like the one in Rhinebeck, or they would be trashed—disappeared, though they presented no danger to anyone except myself.

I could smell outdoor grilling coming from the townhouses across from my office building. A few students were sitting on steps, drinking beer openly, happily over the age of twenty-one, seniors counting the days until graduation, but, for the moment, unworried about the alternate world out there. I had felt much the same thing just a few years ago—five to be exact—and I was still waiting for the alternative to define itself. For the moment, though, it was not a worry as much as a puzzle. One of many. Nancy Feller and I had gone from green note paper to being lovers in the course of this second semester. Our first time, on the love seat, had been on Groundhog Day—or so I realized sometime later and kept thinking to tell her. I would say something about how starkly we had seen each other's shadow, and she would try to stay unamused. Though, in the ten weeks since, it wasn't as if we were conducting a torrid affair. In fact, when I had used the word once, she insisted it was not at all an affair, since neither of us was married. I assured her she was wrong. We looked it up in a paperback dictionary, and she was immensely displeased that the definition said nothing about the betrayal of marriage partners. She blamed the dictionary.

I sat on a bench near the pond and took out my phone. There were a few lazy mosquitoes and a couple of throaty bullfrogs playing bass for the peepers. Nearby lilacs had begun to open, and I thought of Whitman's poem on the death of Lincoln, the air scented with profound loss. Not for the first time this day, the sense of smell now startled me, but this time with a perfume of wondering.

Nancy answered my call with sleep in her voice but brightened as I told her of the checkered history of quinces. She saluted their place in colonial gardens, calling it a "tribute to the wisdom of our founders" and then added that the women of the time must have had much to do with it. She confessed to having been asleep in front of the television without the least recollection of what she had been watching.

"Your voice is even better with sleep in it," I suggested, and I reminded her we had not yet spent the night together or woken together. I could feel her moving to an upright position. "Are your feet firmly on the floor now?"

"Yes, as a matter of fact. I think better that way." She hesitated before going on. "There are many things we haven't done. Not yet. Does that make you unhappy?"

"It makes me fidgety."

"Yes, you do fidget, don't you?"

"It keeps me young."

"Yes."

"Sorry. Stupidly put."

"Yes, again. Jeremiah, today has been instructive, don't you think? And worrisome. Your mossy house in the country doesn't look too bad surrounded by daffodils and its poor-man's orchard in the back. But why do you really want it? What is it you think it will bring you?"

"A starting point?"

"But for what? What is it you would be starting to do?"

"Nancy, when you're there, you seem to see what I see."

"But I see it with older eyes. I see it looking backward. I see parts of where I've been—parts that have—or had—meaning to me. This connects to nothing in your life."

"If you'd like to consider yourself nothing, then you can make that argument. Suit yourself. I do begin to believe it's a place I've been, but not in the same way you're describing."

I could hear her moving about, and the clink of what sounded like a wineglass. "Jeremiah, you weren't expecting me to move there, were you? And what is that noise in the background?"

"College amphibians. I am outside on campus. By the pond. The peepers are warning me to be very careful here."

"About?"

"I've honestly never thought about carrying you off to my crumbling house—'mossy,' did you call it?"

"Jeremiah, you haven't even stood inside that house yet. You haven't dealt with the inspector who may tell you to forget about it, and I am glad you haven't asked me to pack my bags and go with you."

"But I might when the time is right, now that you mention it."

"Stop it. I turn forty-five in two weeks."

"That's so unimportant. I've never thought about your birthday. We'll celebrate."

"We most certainly will not. Don't you see how detached from so many things you are?"

I left the bench by the pond and moved slowly toward my car. "I actually called to see how you might define 'being in love,' since you did such a good job with defining 'affair.' But I'm gathering that would not be such a good idea."

"Actually, it's a terrible idea. We'll talk tomorrow or possibly on my birthday. Would either of those do?"

"Get me the key to the house and I'll stop fidgeting. At least for now."

"You've got a deal, buster."

FOUR

A few students had heard I was not coming back the next year. While I was still listed on the schedule of courses for the Fall semester, I hedged enough about those offerings that they began to suspect I was planning the unkind act of disappearance. Lucia Solis, the young woman who had lost her composure over Huck Finn's casting himself into Hell, was the most vocal, treating my presumed departure as an act of betrayal. She wasn't nearly as snide as, say, Willie Furman had been, but she was better equipped to make me shrink in the face of my own uncertain needs. She came to my office to talk of how she had struggled with the help of an opportunity program to finish her education while raising a young daughter. She told me she had one year to go and she had no intention of finishing up without my being on campus. I assured her the presence or absence of one person would do nothing to undermine a person of her talent, who had shown her ability to handle hardships, and that her daughter would not let her do anything but succeed.

She was exasperated with me, an emotion I'd faced with a number of women recently. "Oh, I know all that," she protested. "Do you think I am stupid?"

"My point exactly."

"Hah, the crafty professor." Her dark eyes were wide with the passion of combat. "But there can come a time when the crafty professor makes sense, you know? Not now, but in class...you make us wonder."

"About?"

"Not all of us, but some of us. I talk with them. They like that we get to wonder about more than how to get a fucking A." She said the word with a mouth so rounded, it emerged not as a bomb but as a bonbon. Even network censors would have bowed to this use of the f-word. "Sorry," she added.

"Don't be, and I thank you. You've given me something to think about."

"That sounds like a cop-out. A load of bull. My daughter could smell that one." She was carrying a purse the size of a saddlebag and switched it decisively from one shoulder to the other. "So, are you going to be here for my last year or aren't you?"

"You, Lucia, are the kind of person I would like to tell straight out. You have made the decision harder. I can tell you that, at least."

"Good. You've probably had it too easy anyhow. I hope, you know, you don't think I was trying to be rude. It just came out that way."

"You did famously. There's a book I'd like you to have." I looked at the bookshelves hoping one of the few dozen books there would be appropriate for a bribe. It wasn't that I felt guilty exactly, but I wanted her to leave knowing she'd accomplished something. I saw Washington Irving's *Sketch Book* and was relieved to hand it to her. "Here, it's yours to keep. He came from the city, too, and he liked making fun of teachers. After exams, read 'The Legend of Sleepy Hollow.'"

"That's the Ichabod-guy."

"You've read it?"

"No, but I will now."

"When she gets older, you can read it to your daughter. What's her name?"

"Sophia."

"That means *wisdom*."

"I know. That's why I did it." Her eyes widened again, and she left, dropping the book into the shoulder bag.

§

It was time to see Joanna Wexler again, but I did not want to see her at her office. She agreed to meet me at an Italian restaurant in Highland, a village across the river from Poughkeepsie. She had suggested it, and I liked the idea of crossing the Hudson to where it felt different in another one of those indefinable ways. From the Mid-Hudson Bridge, I could see walkers on the railroad bridge built in the 1800s and abandoned in the 1970s after a fire made it unusable. It had been a major feeder for goods from the west that would work their way through the network of Dutchess County lines, like the one that had gone through Quaker Falls. Local citizens fought for decades to save the derelict bridge from demolition, finally succeeded, and brought about the creation of the longest park of its kind in the world. Each time I walked or jogged it, I was moved by the human capacity for establishing seemingly ridiculous goals and making them a source of celebration.

Lawyer Wexler looked amply professional in a summery suit, but she also looked less determined to control the room than she had in her office. She was seated on a barstool, sipping a brownish concoction with red cherries in it. She offered to buy me a drink, but I told her I'd be happy enough with one of the cherries. That pleased her, and she dropped it into my mouth with the delicacy of a mother bird. She took the drink and, without asking a waitress, led the way to a corner of the dining area where no tables were occupied. The restaurant was uncrowded to begin with, but she had clearly honored my request for a quiet conversation. The owner knew her and tended to our menu needs personally, assuring me that food from tentacles was good for both the body and the brain. It was something Ellen had tried to convince me of when I was quite small—the "brain" part, at least—but that had not been enough to get me eating anything dotted with suction cups. On this day, with Joanna Wexler, I became unexpectedly daring, and well into the meal, I started questioning her with the brave assurance of one who has conquered octopus salad and found it good.

"Who is Willie's father?"

"Marcus Furman." She fielded the question calmly, gazing with the apparent satisfaction of being asked to confide. She dabbed her lips with a napkin and folded it into a cone in front of her. "You've heard of him?"

"From somewhere."

"He was a baseball player. He played in the big leagues for two years before tearing up his shoulder. He was never the same."

"And why won't she talk about him?"

"He managed get to caught shooting things into his body. It's unlikely the stuff would have saved his career anyhow. He was blown out. When Wilhelmina was old enough to understand, at about age twelve, she decided she didn't want to spend any more time with him. That's when she begged her way back into my life."

"Which you excluded her from in the first place."

"So you might choose to say. Marcus wanted her and I didn't want him. There was a neatness."

"My God."

"He could well afford to raise her. He hired a nanny, whom I would presume was available for screwing, but I don't know that for a fact. Nor do I care. However, he was enchanted with the idea of a daughter, for a time. He used to call her Pepper Blossom, but don't tell her I said so."

"It fits."

"If you mess up in big-time sports, they still have to pay you—so long as your contract is a tight one. And I was new to my career. No hotshot then."

"So he traded her back to you."

"He was suddenly terrified by the idea of a teenage daughter sprouting under his watch. She knew he'd gone cold on her, but I think it was messing with his body that really sealed the deal for her. She can be quite a Puritan, in case you haven't discovered."

"Not the word I would have chosen, but I get your point. She can be fierce in her judgments. "

"Yes, she can. And to give him the benefit of the doubt, I guess he was also coming to the point where he was deciding to grow up. He was a few years younger than me—about seven to be exact—and you know how those things go."

"Why would you say *that*?"

"Nothing in particular. It's just that mixing generations can cause as many problems as mixing races. It's got its own cultural baggage."

"You were about twenty years younger than my father?"

"About." Her confiding glow began to slip, and she became more guarded.

"You were his student?"

"Did your father tell you that?"

"Someone else did. And were you lovers?"

"Why would you want to go there again?"

"Is Hamilton his son?"

She was stunned and started to stand, and then sat decisively again. "Where did you get that one from? And why are you trying to write your own Perry Mason script?" I had never heard of Perry Mason, but it was no time for secondary matters. I was enjoying the sensation of pressing her. "His last name is Graham, you may have noticed."

"A technicality, easily manipulated by clever people."

"Yes, no doubt. It's a fascinating theory, and I could almost wish to see how you arrived at it. But wishes cause clutter."

"He lost a son."

"And what would make you say that? You did outlive him, after all."

"I wouldn't bet on that."

She peered at me with what looked like disappointment. "Such a fearful thing to say."

"He also caused my mother to jump ship."

"Not in the least. She caused herself to jump."

"You seem quite sure about that."

"It is, as they say, a considered conclusion after much discussion. Now, would you like to sign these papers or would you rather donate to a worthy cause, thus freeing yourself of your own unworthiness?" She laughed in an accusatory way, her eyes narrowing into tight pencil marks, like strikethroughs on a manuscript.

It began to feel like a seduction without any desire for consummation. Fine. I wasn't ready to give up yet, and it seemed as if she didn't want me to. However, we had gone as far as we were going to get to on this day. I signed the papers that released the bequest to my bank. As I did, she added quietly, "I'm glad his tools have found a good home."

"Tools?"

"Books and what-not." She offered a guarded smile. "Be of good cheer." It was as if she were feeding me another cherry.

FIVE

The end of the academic year was approaching quickly, along with Nancy's birthday and the very real possibility of making a decision about the house. I had told Phyllis Friel I was not coming back. It seemed the cleanest thing to do, and she had been more than reasonably patient with me, whatever her motivations. As much as I had wanted to demonize her throughout the year—trying to see her brittle rectitude as a sign of what was wrong with education in general—I had been softened by her understandable need to make her waning career mean something. In a way, her desire for me to fulfill the legacy of my father was as understandable as her desire to not have her own accomplishments questioned—thin as they were.

We held our official powwow at last in her office with its theater posters and clutter that reminded me of the kitchen cleanup area of my one-time Lebanese restaurant job. That the mismatched piles and stacks were a comfort to her seemed self-evident. They sat like barricades at both ends of her desk and in front of lower bookshelves, serving no practical purpose—making the remains of her academic world as unreachable as she was. Phyllis wished she could tell me the door would always be open if I chose to return, but she reminded me that was not how things worked in academia. I assured her I understood fully. She gave me a bony embrace and then held me at arm's distance as though I could not possibly comprehend her sense of loss. I thanked her again for her fairness on my behalf. As she followed me from her office, she strode with her characteristic angle of walking mechanically into the wind. She asked if I would be at commencement, and I promised I would. That seemed to be a satisfaction to both of us, at least.

Nancy had finally obtained the keys to the house and sheds and asked her chosen inspector to meet us there. She assured me that she wouldn't be going inside the house for reasons she didn't explain. While she refused to go any further in questioning my enigmatic convictions about owning this house, she made it clear that I had a higher calling in life than homesteading.

"Pioneers," she noted, "should have a covered wagon. You've got a rusty Toyota." I told her I was thinking about getting a truck, which produced one of her puffier forms of laughter. Nonetheless, she had followed through on her promises, and her choice of an inspector was an indication she had thought much about who would be the ideal messenger of the realities I would need to confront. That he had initials for a name added greatly to my susceptibility.

P.Q. Jessup had a real ponytail, as compared to Joanna Wexler's neatly trimmed Bartlett, who was on my list of questions for our next meeting over octopus. P.Q. had the stained smile of a longtime smoker and chewer and was missing bits of individual teeth. He was cadaverously wiry and loose-jointed, good qualities for a person who spent his life crawling around eerie parts of houses looking for bad things. But he was pleasant, not the officious doomsayer Nancy realized I wouldn't be persuaded by. He came with his wife, who sat in the passenger seat of his van while he did his mysterious probing. He introduced us by calling her the boss, the woman who kept him from jumping the rails as often as he had before she came into his life. She called him her project and appeared to take real pleasure in his talents—clucking coded messages when he came into her range of vision, their own language of twisted syllables and whistling noises that were perfectly sensible to them. Nancy and Mrs. P.Q. were on familiar terms, and she spent much of the time leaning into the window of the van to talk with her.

It was May Day, the point of mid-spring that stimulates with the soft, sketchy beauty of leaves partially open, before the sudden, smothering assertiveness of trees and bushes with their full foliage. In grammar school, two years after my abandonment by Nancy Feller, it was Miss Finnegan who guided us through the process of creating a May basket from construction paper and filling it with flowers whose cutout petals were built around pipe cleaners. I brought it to Ellen.

Bird songs were playing on a variety of voices this day in Quaker Falls. One in particular was doing a warbling solo of impressive volume, at first, rolling it around like he was cranking up before releasing its full power. I looked at where the song was coming from, atop a forsythia whose yellow flowers were beginning to drop, but I could see nothing. P.Q. informed me it was a house wren, "about the size of my thumb but with a speaker system to be proud of. *He'll* pop you out of bed in the morning. You got to admire a bugger like that." I agreed. At one side of a living room window, a female cardinal, with her small allotment of red feathers, was hopping on a bush with cascades of white flowers that Nancy identified as Andromeda. I knew the Greek legend of a virgin daughter sacrificed to a sea monster, but how she came to give her name to this glorious shrub was still another of those things I would need to look up.

While I inspected the outbuildings, P.Q. climbed his ladder, looking at the two chimneys, poking at Nancy's Yankee gutters, and testing the condition of the metal roof. I unlocked the three connected sheds that looked like prehistoric motels, each containing an assortment of older hand tools, a push mower, something like a very early tractor, and plenty of junk. As my eyes adjusted, it become evident that one of the three had housed horses, while the second had held whatever those animals pulled. The third had been used for poultry, with nesting boxes and containers for grain. When I announced to Nancy that I might get chickens, she waved and leaned into P.Q.'s wife again. The one-time barbershop at the end was entirely empty, prepared by somebody for its second coming. Bolt holes in the floor indicated where a piece of equipment may have been and what I guessed was a mouse nest in one corner showed the holes had been put to good use. Already I was feeling a sense of ownership, and that included my mice.

When I was finally inside the house, I'd come home at last. Mikhail Jefferson had told me some time before about his first trip to England and his visit on a weekday to a small London church dating back hundreds of years and his softly breaking into sobs while sitting in its emptiness. For him, it had been unexplainable. He was a total stranger to structure, city, and nation—it was no pilgrimage, a happenstance pause from a conference he was attending. "But there I was," he told me, "home." He compared it to an epiphany or chakra, whose light will strike for an unsought reason and one must leave it at that.

No sobs, however, while I stood in the front hallway, the kitchen I had seen through windows now straight ahead of me, the living room on my right, the dining room opposite to it, and stairs leading upward from me. Rather than choosing a direction, I stood listening to the sounds of tapping and scraping in the basement where the interior inspection was beginning. The house smelled as I imagined it would, its mustiness releasing itself in startled breaths from wallpaper and flaking paint. I felt welcomed by it, one of many contrarian sensations meeting me this day. I started my personal inspection upstairs, discovering its large hall, three bedrooms (the rearmost with its wide-board floor bowing downward in the middle), shallow closets, and no bathroom. The view from the back bedroom was toward the line of fruit trees and to the field and hillside behind them. That was where I would sleep.

P.Q. was in the living room when I came down, pulling a section of black stovepipe from where it entered the wall and shining a flashlight into the opening. "Nice stove," he said without looking back. "It better be. It's your only source of heat, except the old clunker in the kitchen."

"You mean there's no..."

"Furnace? Never was one as far as I can judge. They kept warm the old-fashioned way—if they kept warm at all."

It was another item for the list he was accumulating: the need for a new electric panel and rewiring, a well-pump that looked pretty shot—"but you can't be sure until you prime it and shoot some juice into it"—

the need for new windows or storm windows at the least, the lack of insulation, and on and on.

"No signs of termites, though. That's a good thing—and pretty surprising, come to think of it. But there's a fair amount of dry rot, especially on these old floors." He poked at one of the pine planks I was standing on, digging up a jumble of wood fibers. He didn't sugarcoat anything but eventually concluded the inspection by saying, "Well, I kinda like it—if you're the type that can stand a pant-load of work." He judged the house had been built in two phases: the rear part, an original cabin, in the late 1700s, and the front part forty or fifty years later. And I had thought I was a perceptive reader.

As we walked to his van, he said he'd try to get the formal report to me within a week—"Before the place falls down," he added with the wink of an anorexic Santa. Then, as if for Nancy's benefit, he told us that, all in all, "the bones were good." He pointed to the roofline: "Straight as a string. Shows how well built it was...is."

I thanked him and shook his gnarly hand and, finally unable to resist any longer, asked what P.Q. stood for. His wife was pleased and said to Nancy, "I always say what's the good of going around with letters for a name if you never tell what's behind them?" She looked at him. "Well, Sweet Potato?"

"'Peter Quince,'" he proclaimed. "My pops was a reader of Shakespeare."

"So was mine," I added.

When they were gone, Nancy and I walked toward the rear of the property. She took my hand. "Will you change your mind?" she asked.

"Is that why you wouldn't come inside? You were afraid I might go into a swoon?"

"I didn't want to see you hurt." There was added pressure from the hand holding mine. "You survived?"

"I want to buy it."

"Oh."

"You're that disappointed?"

"It's my practical side going off the air, telling the rest of me to have a time at the controls. I can't really be sure how that's going to go." I turned her to me and held her. She felt smaller as she crowded inward. We kissed, a questioning, probing kiss, before she pushed a step back. "Who, by the way, is Peter Quince?"

"A character in *A Midsummer Night's Dream*, like your friends told us: a happy lowlife who worked with his hands and thought like a professor. He was undoubtedly a building inspector of his own time. P.Q.'s father must have been as prophetic as mine."

She looked at me sternly. "Why do you have to know so much, and, more importantly, why is everything quince all of a sudden?"

We started moving toward the meadow behind the property. It was early enough in the season that the walking was easy, and Nancy was wearing a version of sensible shoes. "I know stuff that only a few anointed people think is very important—and I can't say I disagree with them. You, on the other hand, are the belle of the Alleghenies, who's always showing me how little I know about anything else. I'm quite limited, as you may have noticed."

"There have been signs, but they give me hope."

"Of...?"

"Enriching you. Is that a good word?"

"Yes. It makes me hungry. As far as the quince business goes, it only adds to my hunch that something important is going on here—maybe not a cure for cancer, but important for us."

"You'll have me believing that by and by." She was back to her full size again and was walking with the conviction of a defensive line coach. "Have you ever noticed all the times you'll learn a thing totally new and fascinating, and then you keep hearing about it like it's more than a coincidence. My grandfather's orchard has taken on an afterlife."

"For weeks—months—I've been trying to figure out if there's a difference between coincidence and fate. Is there a boundary between them—or do we change the names to suit the purposes?"

"Haven't people always done that?"

"No doubt. But I've had so much of it lately, I feel this compulsion to settle on one or the other. Fate *sounds* better. I guess."

"Still, the other sounds like you've at least got a chance." She slipped a hand into mine.

We had crossed part of the meadow, a distance of a hundred yards, and an unnaturally flat strip suggested where the milk train had run a century and more before as it made its way into the hamlet. Nature had taken back much of it, though traces of crushed stone were still visible beneath the spring growth and the spread of smallish yellow-and-white flowers. After we reached the far side of the meadow, jumping one small stream, we climbed the low hillside I had seen from the rear bedroom of the house. It was an easy climb, up a gradual slope dotted with scrubby evergreens and fragrant bushes that Nancy identified as wild roses, almost in full bloom. She introduced me to spindly but colorful trees conveniently called redbuds—though they were more pinkish than red, more painfully provocative than stunning. We finally turned to look back at the house after being as scrupulous as Orpheus and Eurydice about keeping our eyes pointed to the crest of the hill. We roped our arms around each other as we surveyed the hamlet, a patchwork of rooftops visible through the early foliage of oaks and maples, and the steeple of a church pointing from the north end of Quaker Falls. We could see the blossoms of the trees at the back boundary of what was soon to be my property and the house tucked behind them—its imperfections scrubbed by distance, and, like discoverers, we nodded in unison.

We made love there on a soft spot of ground chosen for us by larger forces. With the air of the hilltop moving around us, there was the feeling of cooling transport, all heatedness deep within. It was only after we stood again to find the view before us, softened even further by the dying of the afternoon, that Nancy asked, "Do you think anyone could hear us?" The shadows from the trees at our backs had begun to stretch down the hillside, taking our own shadows with them into the nearest edge of meadow grass and cupping the view of where we had climbed. The house across the way, on the other hand, had been brightened by the departing sun, its old, old windows shining up at us. The bedroom window I had looked from was lighted with complicity.

"If they did," I told her, "they will write it off as ghosts of the

Mohicans celebrating a remarkably successful planting season." I pointed. "See how beautiful."

"It's my New World Symphony. Even if we didn't do what we just... did, I would be happy the lonely old house has been looked at the way we are doing now. How long do you think it has been?"

"I can't imagine."

As we walked back to the hamlet, Nancy informed me of two things: Quaker Falls may have been a stop on the Underground Railroad for runaway slaves, and she still had no intention of playing house here in spite of having just tumbled her mind on the hilltop behind us. I nodded the second part past me and asked her instead how she had found out about the Underground Railroad. She replied simply that she had been doing her own investigations.

I called her later that night to tell her where I wanted to take her for her birthday and to invite her to attend a lesbian wedding with me. She fielded both requests with what, for her, was supernatural aplomb. She also informed me that she had talked to P.Q., who indicated his inspection report would have no surprises, but it would have a good many cautionary conclusions. I could probably close on the property by the end of May.

Two days after the phone call, we celebrated Nancy's forty-fifth in Manhattan at a Middle Eastern restaurant—sandwiched by a round-trip train journey on the Hudson Line—and feeling immodestly public. She declared an instant love of hummus, judging it to be the tongue kiss of the bean world. It was pleasant to consider.

SIX

Commencement approached rapidly. I tried to keep myself unemotional in the face of it. I knew I was vulnerable to the sound of "Pomp and Circumstance," and I caught myself several times glancing at the academic regalia hanging in a corner of my office. It was the first time I would wear the ominously named doctoral hood, and, as far as I knew, it would be my last. I kept telling myself not to get too puffed up over the whole thing, but I could be susceptible to certain traditions—especially ones that involved conferring genuine wishes for success to others. I recalled how The Professor would return home late on commencement afternoons with the look of a man who had slain a lion with his own hands—victorious but just then feeling the aftereffects of a great vulnerability. His consumption of alcohol would increase markedly on this one day of the year, and I would hear him scolding himself with crisp articulations of righteousness on the following morning.

Any sullenness among my students had vanished, absorbed by the stress of exams or the approach of life outside the secure space they were leaving.

One student did tell me he understood why I would want to leave: "You're still young, I guess. Why would you want to get burned at the stake when you could be setting fires of your own?" His logic was beyond me, but he said it with such conviction, I couldn't deny the possibility there might be a potential truth there, and I was grateful he had sought to say anything at all.

There were colleagues who still sounded suspicious or resentful of my decision. Chuck Gillis called it a funny action to be taking and, citing his Dr. Johnson, asked if I had kicked the stone to see if it was real. Richard Woo was disappointed that his urgings had resulted in "the defeat of hope," but he thanked me that his daughter had taken to *Riff and Raggles*, gave me a bluegrass CD, and told me he was willing to talk trucks. Jefferson was interested to hear about the Underground Railroad. He was pissed at me but let me know he was pretty good with power tools.

My most interesting valedictory came from Edwina Sharpe, who thanked me again for our spontaneous collaboration at the department meeting and offered me one of her daughters as a sex-slave when she ripened. Edwina and I had developed a degree of friendship in the final months of the semester, lunching occasionally in each other's offices, attending campus events together, and sharing gossip when the opportunity presented itself. It was she who told me that Rachel VanNoys had finally had it out with Phyllis Friel for her failure to take Rachel seriously. To emphasize she would appreciate a change of doctrine, she plunked onto the chair's desk one of Phyllis' early articles on dramaturgy with several plagiarized passages highlighted in traitorous yellow. Rachel claimed the discovery had been pure luck, brought to her attention by one of Phyllis' students doing research on the subject, a student who needed to be sure he could believe his own eyes. Poor Phyllis had written on such arcane subjects it was likely she thought her misdeed would never be discovered. As Edwina noted, the fact that it was so narrow had necessarily made it more likely the two articles would eventually come face-to-face, and here was the proof. I thanked her for the offer of her daughter and promised to get back to her in a few years.

It snowed on Commencement Day. Snow in May was ultra-unusual in the lower Hudson Valley, but there it was, arriving with sunup: large wet flakes that would melt away in a matter of hours if people just waited it out. But the administration went into war room mode, concerned about many more things than my meteorological reading skills: parents, dignitaries, and special arrangements. They couldn't or wouldn't delay the ceremony but instead moved it from a soggy stadium to the gymnasium. I was in my office, in regalia, when word arrived that the faculty was disinvited from the event due to lack of space. I was sitting in my single visitor's chair—the one on which Nancy had reintroduced herself to my life—when the speaker system used only for emergency alerts started piping Jeremiah Clarke's "Trumpet Voluntary." With "Pomp and Circumstance," it is *the* tingler of processionals, and here I sat, being tingled into going nowhere. It's not that I felt sorry for myself, but it did seem a kind of payback for abandoning academic life. Happily, I was broken in upon by Barbara Lynn Hynes who carried her gown over one arm and told me I looked like a fallen angel posing for a dismissal shoot.

"If they had waited two hours...," I started to tell her.

"Impossible, my darlin' friend. Not on my wedding day. I do have my priorities."

"I quite agree. By this afternoon, I promise clear skies."

"There are seniors all over campus, crying their eyes out—male and female. A genuine unisexual outpouring. They don't know what to think. Sad, sad, sad." Her red hair was dripping, and she gave it a shake like an Irish setter. "Sorry if I sprayed you. I had to see some of the kids and tell them to be of good cheer." For whatever reason—perhaps the splash of snow upon her—the curvature of her drawl had slackened for the morning.

"I'm glad. It wouldn't have occurred to me. This might be your last graduation, too."

"No...no, it won't. I'll find something. Emily has been pumping résumés into the mail on a daily basis."

"She's amazing."

"Yes, she is."

"This is a terrible question to ask on your nuptial day, but do you ever worry about being good enough for her?"

"All the time. Why wouldn't I?"

"I'm bringing a guest today."

"So I understand."

"That's right. Our Willie will be there, too."

"Correct."

"She...the lady...will be a little...older...than me."

"And that's a big deal?" Her smile was targeted with warm purpose.

"What was your coming out like?"

"I never did. I always was what I am. Basically."

"Seriously?"

"One day when I was looking for my baseball, a leetle voice went off that said I would find a nice, efficient—and hot-looking—girl to help me do these kinds of things. I was never very orderly."

"But you grew up in the south."

"During Reagan, the Bushes, and the 'phobes? Yeah, I know. Did I think they were going to lynch me?"

"But you knew it wouldn't be easy."

"It wasn't that bad. You see, I really *was* waiting for my dream girl. I wasn't sneaking inside of just any girl's panties." She took a deep breath. "In fact, it happened only a few times before Em—nothing serious—more informational than anything." She nonchalantly tried to finger-comb her hair and then looked at her watch. "I'm a mess needing serious beautification. But I'm glad you're bringing your special person. It will be good for Willie, and it might keep you from looking with too much lust at my new bride."

"Have I been that obvious?"

"Perfectly. But totally understandable. You should see her undressed."

"My heart couldn't stand it. And, by the way, I love your love for each other. It seems so calm."

"One of us is good at calm. One isn't."

"And for the hell of it, what did you mean about Willie?"

"She still needs to loosen up her head some. But she will. See you at the show."

§

The wedding took place at a small wooden church in the northwestern part of the county, near Tivoli and close to where Eleanor Roosevelt had lived with her grandmother after the death of her parents. The church itself was on a low knoll that provided those standing at its doors an unobstructed view of the Catskills. The sun had cleaned up the day by the time of the ceremony, adding to the beauty of the setting and making me feel like an accomplished forecaster. Cows were grazing in a pasture that was fenced to within a few feet of one side of the church. It was the setting for a classic musical.

Nancy was unusually self-composed during the drive there, in a dress of powder blue that made her look conspicuously lovely. For the first time since I'd known her, she was wearing a hat, wide-brimmed and grayish. She had confessed her lack of knowledge about what to wear to a gay wedding and added she'd had sense enough not to ask me. She had driven, claiming her car looked less apologetic than my Corolla. She had offered to bring Willie with us, but Ms. Furman had waved her off with explanations about other errands along the way. Michael had been included in the invitation to Willie. While he indicated this one might be different, he claimed a general disinterest in weddings.

There were about fifty guests in attendance. Several were obviously Barbara Lynn's students, including a late-arriving Willie Furman who was wearing her milkmaid's dress and carrying a handful of daisies in what looked like an old-fashioned milk bottle—coming across as the last best hope for innocence. The only faculty person I knew from school was Mikhail Jefferson, who sat with us. He had chosen a white linen shirt and beachcomber pants for the occasion. I remembered Richard Woo telling me that Jefferson's wife had left their marriage for another woman, and it was like he had dressed to celebrate his liberation, no matter how much he cared about Barbara Lynn Hynes. He had been one of her fiercest defenders during the tenure protests, on the front lines with the more militant students. When it caused the provost to request his removal from the Campus Committee on Equality, he had complied by opening his letter of resignation with the greeting "Dear Simon Legree." Months later, I had put my arms around his muscular body when he told me.

The nuptial couple came into the church to guitar music—the contribution of two students—moving down the aisle together to kiss all who were there. They were dressed identically, in ivory chiffon that produced a remarkable contrast to Barbara Lynn's still-untamed russet hair and gave Emily the air of ethereal poise nothing would give to the woman she was marrying. The ceremony was conducted by a woman wearing what resembled an Indian sari over a white turtleneck and pants of the same color. She actually had little to do—not even the "I now pronounce you." Mostly they recited bits of poetry for each other and the rest of us—Sappho, Christina Rossetti, Elizabeth Barrett Browning, Joni Mitchell—and spoke of how their love had come to be, personalizing it with simple, unrehearsed testimony. One guitar accompanied Emily in singing Mama Cass's "Dream a Little Dream" with a voice sweetly resonant and hungry. It was Botticelli put to music. By the time they exchanged vows—each saying "I grant you all that I am"—Nancy was crying contentedly into a handkerchief. Even Willie, a few rows in front of us, had put her head on a shoulder of the girl next to her. As testimony, the lowing of cows came through open windows.

The reception was right there, on that same rise of ground where we were able to watch the mountains purpling across the river. There were no tables, only muslin cloths on the ground where we sat in random groups eating from paper plates. It was like being positioned for an Andrew Wyeth painting, and Nancy joked about how she would have to be helped to a standing position later. She had been captivated by the ceremony and the newlyweds and, while we were still inside, had pulled them into her arms like the dearest of friends. She talked of it when we had settled onto the lawn.

"I suppose I've never knowingly hugged a gay person before, so I'm probably going to make too much about how moving it all was. With Marvin and me, it was like the marriage of two pieces of office equipment. Who knew it could be like this?"

"Should I confess to being knocked out by Emily?"

"Who wouldn't be? She's so perfect, I could eat her with a spoon."

"An Allegheny metaphor, I gather? But what about you, Nancy? Would you be devastated by my telling you how beautiful you are?"

She considered for a time, staring at the Catskills. "What a lovely thing to say...and even if it were partly true, how long do you think that will last?" Her smile was self-satisfied.

Jefferson had been working the crowd like a new groom, mingling with students and at one point scooping Barbara Lynn with a hug that lifted her from the ground and forced a lustful version of a rebel yell from her. As that resonated, Willie joined us after a time with her friends. "Tell me about your snake."

"Ah, your mother again. What else did she tell you?"

"Nothing," she said, dropping onto the cloth. "She said you played snake charmer in the desert."

"Jeremiah?" Nancy questioned.

"Nothing. I made it into a bigger deal than it really was because I was showing off for our friend's mother." I gave it the best shorthand version I could. "I was climbing in the Catalina Mountains by myself, about this time of year—hot as blazes out there—and this diamondback was enjoying some shade time under an overhang, so I sat down maybe ten feet away, and we had this terrific stare-off. One of the most peaceful moments in my life."

Willie was disappointed. "That's it? Nothing more? You really are a strange one."

"Sometimes, Willie, it's just a matter of choosing the right moment. And I don't regret being a little snippy with...do you call her Joanna?"

"Only to annoy her."

"And how often is that?" Nancy asked.

"Not nearly enough. She said she'd like to meet you."

Nancy nodded graciously. "How very nice. I'm sure there will come a time."

Willie was comfortably settled by now, eating the end piece of a six-foot hero. "I knew you guys were going out."

"*Going out*?" Nancy replied.

"Or whatever you call it."

"We don't call *it* anything."

Barbara Lynn and Emily had finally made their way to us and crouched to create a group embrace. Small white flowers were woven into Emily's hair and one stem popped free into Willie's hand. Their happiness was so invasive it seemed like the tension would lift, until Barbara Lynn said to Nancy and me, "Not so bad, is it? Almost like bein' in love."

It was said with a congratulatory vigor that popped Willie to her feet. She was holding the hero and the sprig of flowers. "See? I knew stuff was going on."

For a few moments, Barbara Lynn took on the persona of professor, giving her white gown a brief off-kilter look. "The 'stuff' that's going on, Wilhelmina, is the stuff of people being free of what some most unfortunately call stuff. And if ah have to explain that to a person with your very large and gifted spirit, then you can take out your pipe and—" She broke instantly into her whole-bodied laughter and became the newlywed again, kissing Willie on the forehead. "Well, you know."

"Yeah, I get you." But Willie remained sullen, unaffected by the reestablishment of bridal mirth. "You two look good, by the way. I hope you love a long time."

It was Emily who ran a hand along one of Willie's arms. "Thank you. We'll give it every chance."

After Willie had gone back to her friends, the four of us sat for a time, watching small birds scalloping designs in the air above the fields. When I pointed, it was Emily who identified them as barn swallows, the sun glinting off her glasses. A small cluster of cows were staring at us through a nearby fence, their mouths doing that dopey form of sideways chewing, their eyes serene like a stoner's. Guitar sounds were coming from near the church, and two students working as waiters brought plastic glasses of champagne. Barbara Lynn took a sip of hers before she spoke of having "put on mah Superman outfit for Willie. Hope ah didn't come on too strong."

Emily took her hand. "I love how she's always working things out.

That's where her stuff comes from. She'll never take much for granted, but I imagine she may also have a hard time taking things for what they are."

Barbara Lynn reached a hand around Emily's neck and exclaimed "Isn't she amazin'?" before placing a long, wistful kiss on her mouth. It was a moment of fulfilling joy that Nancy and I both looked at with pleasure, little tempted to turn our heads.

When the kiss had concluded, Nancy asked with her own form of frank wondering, "Will you have children?"

"Glad you asked," Barbara Lynn replied, projecting the tone of a carnival barker. "We talked about that last night—not for the first time—and it feels more and more like we will. Whether we'll adopt or go halfway natural, we'll have to see. But God ah want babies with Em."

"Barbie, I thought you were going to have my little mulatto baby." Mikhail Jefferson was standing just behind us, shading his eyes from the sun with one hand and carrying a champagne bottle in the other.

"Sit down, you naughty man." They were well-coordinated sparring partners, and the ease of their freedoms spilled over the rest of us. We sat quietly, listening to cow music, drinking wine, watching sweeps of color behind the mountains, and feeling the comfort of one another freed from the need to talk. It was the same chemistry I had felt with Barbara and Emily in my apartment.

Students began passing by before drifting to their cars, Willie included. A trace of sadness was still in her eyes, but her farewells were delivered softly. Emily's parents had been sitting on the porch of the church and came at last to share the moment. Her father had steely twists of hair and the hands of a mechanic—and such a fondness for his daughter it made him speak with shy undertones. Her mother had much of Emily's easy grace and looked to be the same age as Nancy. When the newlyweds rose to kiss them, the four cried softly, creating a covering layer of quiet. I squeezed one of Nancy's hands and held it until the group above us broke apart, the parents moving to the parking area. Barbara Lynn had never mentioned her own family to me. She was without them on this day when it was clear she had been taken in by another one. I heard Jefferson utter what sounded like "very fine" as the bridal pair wandered arm in arm to where the guitarists and a few students remained. Their white dresses were tinted pink by the late sunlight.

I asked Mikhail about the missing Hynes family, and he shook his head. "It wasn't so much her sexuality as her unwillingness to be like them in other ways." His words were slurred but teacherly. "She hated Confederate flags. She called them banners of amnesia. From an early age. I asked her years ago where her 'personal enlightenment' came from"—he created quotation marks with his fingers—"and she called it the act of being obvious. She claims a siren inside her went off while she was watching *Gone With the Wind* as a girl. She told her parents she wanted to grow up to be a mammy with a butt big enough to flatten stupid people."

"It sounds like her," I said.

"Amazing," Nancy added in a husky voice. "Will she find another job?"

Mikhail's face lit up. "That woman will definitely find another position. She never got Mammy's butt, thank God, but people like that have got to be where they can make the rest of us see the obvious—which, I might add, most spend a whole lot of human capital trying to hold under water."

It was Nancy who finished the thought. "Because, Professor, we don't ever want to admit that we can't see everything...or we allow others to do it for us."

On the way home, we talked of several things. I confessed that I had given my notice to the college, surprised that it hadn't come up during the afternoon. She seemed unaffected by the news, claiming she had made a similarly premature decision, and why shouldn't I have the opportunity to follow in her own thoughtless footsteps? She assumed Willie was beating herself up over me for what she used to think was adolescent lust but now thought was something entirely different, and maybe I should resign myself to the idea that she wasn't going to sleep with me. Nancy looked to see my reaction, but from what I could tell, she didn't see any. She thought Barbara Lynn and Emily would make remarkable parents since they could make up their own rules about who, if anyone, was head of the household. I agreed. Then, apparently to contradict herself, she thought love was probably wasted on ideal couples since they were in another zone of being altogether. Again, I had no idea what *that* meant. She thought Jefferson was scary smart, full of secrets, and probably from a different part of the universe. Like her son. I assured her that she was correct. She was still feeling amused, and uplifted, by the slightly drunken waiter who had come over to us at the end to see if I wanted more champagne—and would I like another glass for my mother? She called it the guy's own personal tutorial for the two of us.

She agreed, nonetheless, to lie down with me in my apartment to commit the act of being obvious. I offered no objection.

SEVEN

With the end of school, I could focus at last on being a bum—albeit a bum with an overstuffed bank account. By early June, I would own a third-world house that had been abandoned for more than a decade, one without electricity or running water, no way to flush a toilet, but with two workable wood stoves that were of no use at this time of year. Of course, this was all part of the game, roughing it for two or three days with enough money in the bank to fund an African village for a decade.

The process of resurrecting the house was clear enough: have an electrician in on the day of closing, have a person to fix the well the next day and hope for the best, rent a dumpster, start cleaning out what didn't need to be there, replace window panes with cracks in them, figure out what to do about screens, etc. I asked Michael to camp out with me when the time arrived, and he came with a sleeping bag and his harmonica.

Until then, there was time to digest other things. I thought of my students—who were no longer my students—scattered to wherever they spent their summers or wherever they would spend the beginnings of their adult lives, and I felt what homesickness must feel like, even though in a physical sense I was about to go home. I missed them. I wanted to hear from them—from many of them, at least. I was unsettled by the feeling, one I couldn't have expected, although one Nancy had thought I was likely to come up against. She described how she dreamed about her one classroom for years afterward, although she assured me she didn't dream about individual people, and once again I refused to believe her. She described the room as a feeling rather than a place, and that made sense to me after teaching in an assortment of rooms during my one year.

I asked Richard Woo whether my feeling was one teachers felt each year, but he laughed and called me a schmuck. We were looking at used trucks together, and he insisted that for him the end of each year was simply clicking off the lights, but with people like me—the *dwellers*, he called them—the lights never went out; ergo schmuck. Coming from him, it was a chunky piece of Yiddish handed to me via chopsticks. He didn't think dwelling was a bad thing necessarily, but he was glad it hadn't happened to him and added that maybe I was a poor bastard who feared he'd just made a lousy life choice.

That was Richard, but he actually *was* supportive in helping me decide on a truck. He insisted I get one without too many gadgets and tittilaters, but one that could go through any kind of weather and wouldn't look like it had been violated when I banged it up with the crap I'd be carrying.

"And be forewarned," he added, "you are going to be prey to anyone who thinks you have nothing better to do than help them move. Nice if it's a damsel in distress but otherwise a pain in the ass. Work up a good list of excuses." When I reminded him he had been kind enough to help me with The Professor's chair, he was dismissive. "I thought it was a chance to guilt you into staying and helping get the department in shape. But you *are* a schmuck." My Toyota had been traded in, and my sole means of transportation now was an orange but slightly dinged-up Dodge Dakota. I was energized by its Badlands name.

Eleanor Jewett was on the front porch when I got out of the truck for the first time. Her lead question was whether I was moving. She nodded her head when I told her I was and patted the seat of the rocker next to hers. She was wearing lightweight slacks that showed the thinness of her legs as she pushed against the wooden floor. She had been reading a book and set it on the table between us. I could see the title *Women in*

Love, the novel by my classroom friend D.H. Lawrence that nearly got him thrown out of England for its antiwar sentiments. There would, it seemed, always be so much to talk about with Miss Jewett, and I realized I would need to keep finding my way back to her. She told me, "It has been a comfort having my young professor so near at hand. And I do like your truck. That is yours, I trust." I assured her it was. "Quite a color. It looks nutritious."

"I'm glad you think so.'

"I'm fond of trucks. I shall be sorry to see you go."

"Another empty apartment," I said. "It will just be you two on the second floor."

"Oh, I'm sure yours will be rented very quickly. This a such a fine location."

"But the one across from me?"

She straightened her back. "You don't know about that? My, I'm surprised. For a young man who is so well informed."

"Mostly about unimportant things."

She was unimpressed. "So you say. Perhaps a statement like that works with your lady friends."

"I'll try it." She rocked quietly, closing her eyes. "Well?"

"What was that, young man?"

"The apartment." We were seated in front of it, and, turning my head, I could see daylight dropping onto its empty floors with the exception of a tool box in the center of the living room.

She blinked several times. "It's a curious story, but they make the best kind, especially when they remind us of how easy it is for people to get their heads caught in delusions." I waited as she gathered what she wanted to say and then proceeded with fixed commitment to her course. "Her husband died in there. Mr. Clemmons. He dropped where he was, trying to move a radiator. She thinks he's in there to this day."

"Pardon me?"

"Not in the real sense, of course. She saw the body removed. She supervised, in fact—quite volubly. I could hear her from upstairs. But for her, the important part of him is still there. His spirit. His ghost.

I've never trusted myself to ask her straight out. I might say what would sound disrespectful. I'm not tolerant of nonsense."

"And you think spirits are nonsense?"

"I certainly do." She leaned toward me, confidingly. "Not that I don't believe in *the* Spirit." She sounded the article as *thee.* "That's a different thing altogether. Spirits make us small and...fanciful. *The* Spirit makes us larger because it doesn't care two hoots about us as individuals."

"Define spirit."

"Not today, my young professor. I might end up on the floor like Walter Clemmons." She was pleased with herself and licked her lips. "You, of course, would like to know what a person my age thinks about what happens next, but I'm not going to tell you. It's a habit of mine, for people I care about. Not telling, that is. But the end result is that she keeps the apartment empty for whatever it provides her. For two years now. And, I'll tell you, she's a woman who would take a lollipop from a baby. She likes the feeling of a check in her hand."

"I've noticed." My landlady had treated me with cool detachment throughout my ten months in her building. During the few times she actually stood in the apartment, she would gaze with eyes that took dissatisfied inventory, disappointed, I guessed, by the way I had accumulated little for her visual benefit.

It was clear Miss Jewett wanted to stand, and I helped her to her feet. She left her hands in mine for several seconds. "We have such interesting conversations."

"Yes, we do. I hope I can bring you to my new place."

"I doubt it. However, it's an idea worth careful keeping."

"Here's your book," I said, handing it to her. "It's a favorite of mine."

"Is that a fact? I've read it ever so many times. Your friend Wilhelmina gave it to me, although it wasn't really a gift. She thought it would be a book about women loving *each other*, not women and men. She didn't finish it, though I hope someday she might. She is, as we once said, a hard nut to crack. Very fine-looking, but hard to crack."

I helped her to her apartment, though she insisted she had become a stronger climber recently. There was still the impression, as I looked at her, of so much more to discover, and I had wasted much of the year making her into the shriveled old woman at the head of the stairs. Once again, I was leaving behind that which was probably impossible to know—but not finally so.

I talked to Ham that night. He knocked on my door as he arrived home, like he had gotten a covert signal from Miss Jewett advising him that she had let out one of the building's most impressive secrets. He did look like a man on a follow-up mission, his jaw clenched and his eyes less than friendly. I invited him in, and we stood behind the rear of the couch. I had already filled a few cartons that stood next to the fireplace.

"That's right," he said, loosening somewhat. "You're moving."

"You knew that."

"Of course I did. It was an icebreaker. I'm not happy with you."

"So I gather. Something about your sister?"

"Something about me. She'll take care of herself just fine."

"And?"

"What is this about thinking I'm your father's bastard?"

I tried to sound breezy. "So you *do* talk to your mother."

"We have regular appointments."

"And do you have regular appointments with your father?"

He was caught off guard and crossed to the hearth where he had first gotten to know Sara Sampson. "I never knew my father. He died before I got to."

"Oh Jesus, Hamilton. I'm really not sure I want to go any further with this, and your angry face at the door is probably what I deserve. I wish I could get rid of this need to know stuff, as your sister might put it. At least tell me that you know where he's buried, that you've been to see the site, and you have some idea what he did for a living—before this whole thing grinds us into a parody of ourselves."

He stood with his back to the mantelpiece. "There are times I've wanted to tell you how annoying you can be with your academic detachment arising from the rewards of being an intellectual snoop. It's what you get paid for, although I'm told you're not getting paid for anything these days. Will you go off to your country shack and teach yourself how to be ignorant?"

"I might."

"There you are—the off-putting young Doctor Curtin who can charm his way into the hearts of many. A parody of himself. I liked you at first. You seemed like a pleasant neighbor. You were quiet."

"I shared my girlfriend."

"She said you would never make it as a passionate human being." He seemed to take special pleasure in repeating Sara.

"And what did she tell you—about you? She's the connoisseur of capsule write-offs."

"That doesn't matter. What's done is done. My mother agrees that you possess certain qualities that would make you more attractive to older women than younger—that someone her age could go for you if she were a few years younger."

"A few years?" I asked.

"She knows you have a thing for older women."

"The idea is repulsive, in spite of my old-lady *qualities*—not that I mean to insult your mother. I'm past that."

"She can't be insulted."

"That's your conclusion after all these years?"

"It is. But now that we've both dealt neatly with her, let me also add that I *did* have suspicions you were balling my sister. I'm past those. I'm quite sure she sees you for what you are."

"Would you care to elaborate?"

"Classroom horseshit! 'Would you care to elaborate?' No, I really wouldn't. And I'm glad you'll be on your way...by June first?" he asked hopefully.

"Not one day later."

He looked at me with the focused dislike of a person who wasn't sure where his anger was coming from and that it put him off-balance. It wasn't from a fondness for his mother or concern for his half-sister or resentment at being dumped by my ex-girlfriend. None seemed likely. He gathered himself and walked to me. "I get the feeling you have no idea what you're really looking for, Jeremiah. If you ever figure it out, you just might discover you've been looking in the wrong place." And for quite some time, that was the last I saw of the man who called himself Ham Graham.

EIGHT

Moving day was not one but several. It began right after closing, the Tuesday after Memorial Day. I made use of a colleague in the college's paralegal program, not wanting to deal with Joanna Wexler—who was, after all, not my lawyer and according to her son, would just as soon see me fall on my face if I wasn't tempted to lower myself on top of her. Nancy was at the closing, though she was technically not my realtor, nor did I actually have one. She was, however, my guardian of terminology, nodding me through it, and my lawyer-colleague seemed happy to have an accomplice. The sellers were represented by a lawyer who was related in a distant way to the house's last occupants. He showed little interest in talking about them but did indicate through the pursed mouth of a guidance counselor that they had been a father and son, each a veteran of a different war, who jointly found Quaker Falls an adequate location for what he called "their demons." There was no mention of wives, mothers, or anyone else, only that they kept chickens, as if that should have been their combined epitaph.

Those who said they would help kept their promises: Richard, Mikhail, even Barbara Lynn and Emily. The latter were a scraping and painting team: Barbara attacking chipped window frames and Emily coating them with precise brushstrokes. Michael was there throughout the first week, sleeping on the living room floor, waking early to discover new skills in wallpaper removal, spackling, repointing brickwork, and whatever attracted his interest—which was most anything. His special fixation was the stairway to the second floor, which had sadly been tiled over with vinyl asbestos squares. One of many earnest decisions from the past that we spent much of our time undoing. Michael was convinced the removal of the tiles would reveal woodwork worthy of his efforts, and he was partly right. He didn't uncover walnut or mahogany but rather a poor man's pine that he attacked with an assortment of sanders from Nancy's basement—working with cool intensity and a bandana over his nose and mouth. On the day he applied his first coat of stain, he was like a devoted novitiate restoring a religious artifact, a process I had watched with quiet awe at a mission in the Arizona desert. When he had stained the bottom step, he stood back to judge the full rise of what he had accomplished.

He found it to be good and asked for a beer. I had a six-pack of Guinness, a housewarming gift from Jefferson, chilled in a refrigerator that was running merrily with restored electricity animating its insides. Michael looked at the bottle suspiciously before twisting the cap and sniffing. I took a sip and handed it back to him. He chugged half the bottle.

"What's the verdict?" I asked.

"Verdict?"

"Stout. What do you think of it?"

"Like molasses."

"Molasses. Yeah, I can see that. Sorry."

"No, it's okay. I like molasses. A little like drinking a cookie. I just don't like beer that much."

"So, when you asked for one...?"

"This one's okay."

"How do you know, if you don't...?"

"I don't have to...know. Not when I do." It was classic Michael. To emphasize the fact, he took another decisive pull from the bottle.

During the first week, Nancy and Willie were absent. Nancy claimed she was busy with work; Willie offered no explanation. Female relief did arrive, however, in the unexpected form of Louisa Sondstrom.

She knocked on the screen door as Michael was adding a second coat of stain to the stairs, and he came close to tumbling over backward. I was in the dining room tacking a piece of sheet metal over one of the rotted floorboards. When I saw her, I felt my fairy godmother had booked a flight from Poughkeepsie. I put my arms awkwardly around her, a hammer in one hand and a bunch of nails in the other. She had gotten my location from "the lawyer lady" and hoped she had been right to do so. How the lawyer lady had my location was another indication of how well-wired she was, but in this case, I finally owed one to Joanna Wexler.

Louisa had intuited without magic powers that the kitchen would be in a disgraceful condition, and she was ready to do what she could. First, though, she needed to ask who the handsome young man with the paintbrush was. Her dimpled smile nearly pulled Michael headfirst down the stairs, and he wisely parked himself on the next dry step.

"Michael," I told her, "is a future candidate for Elf-king, and I hope when the time comes, you will cater the coronation." I explained Louisa's place in my life to him, and Michael nodded agreeably. It looked like he had an immediate fixation on her and her natural ability to embrace a situation. I took her throughout the first floor, trying to read each nod of her head, but finding a general sense of approval in her demeanor. The kitchen was, of course, another matter. It was the staging area for the interior work of the house; paint cans, trays, buckets, and tools were on the metal–topped table that had come with the house. She admitted it was beyond her at this point, so I took her into the yard.

"Yah, this I like," she said. "It is full of colors and bees. Bees are good. You can tell anyt'ing you vant to the bees." I didn't tell her many of the bees were living inside one of the walls of the kitchen, and you could smell their honeycombs when the sun struck that wall. "You need a vife soon to help you with everyt'ing, yah?"

I asked about life since The Professor, and she assured me she was busy—her voice sounding a little edgy—and she was about to help out at his house in its new incarnation as an accommodation for visitors to the University. It was good to hear his home had quickly become purposeful, rather than sitting as an uncompleted thought. I was certain he would be pleased.

She asked if I had read his book, as if the question had been rolling inside her since she had finally entrusted it back to my care.

"Yes," I told her. "It took a while, but I finally read all of it."

She looked intently at me. "It's like a puzzle, yah?"

"I think, Louisa, he was working out several puzzles at once. I don't suppose you have any idea when he wrote it?"

She didn't, though she did think it might have made him feel younger. "But people can do that any time of their life, don't you think?"

I agreed, and told her I hoped she would come when the kitchen was ready for respectful attention. She promised and told me to get a power mower, something she had enjoyed learning to use. Another item for the list.

§

Michael and I were talking on the back porch, near sunset, when Nancy finally made her appearance, at the beginning of what turned out to be a night of high-propulsion events. Michael had played his harmonica for a time, making its lonely strains sound ready to curl into one of our laps. Now, he had a Guinness in one hand and a joint in the other. I was speaking with him about his ability to keep his mother lovingly baffled.

"She thinks of you—*I* think—as her only-begotten wish ranger—son of ancient, low-calorie dreams." He didn't know what I meant, nor did I. I had taken a couple of hits of his smoke, and words had begun to be sounds as much as meanings. "That's a nice position to occupy. I could almost envy you. Almost, mind you. My current position with regard to your mother is a little fancier than yours. I'm avoidable—outrageously avoidable. Like this week. Which makes me occasionally tempting, I guess. And often ridiculous. Like this mumbly old house with the floors that cough when you walk on them. What could be better for keeping people light on their feet?" Michael's own feet did a brief two-step in front of him. "I understand your father isn't too light on *his* since you dropped out of school."

"He thinks I'm going to end up s-shoveling s-shit. He swears a lot better than he used to."

"Good for him. You've done him favors he may never realize. I did the cowardly thing, I confess. I waited for mine to die before I rejected what I still believe were his wishes." Michael took a long draw, watching the glowing tip with studied fascination and holding the smoke in his lungs for several seconds. "One of these days, I'm hoping your mother might not only visit us, but also consent to finally spend a night in this place—once we've got beds and whatnot. That doesn't give you the heebie-jeebies, I hope. You have no doubts that she and I are more than just friends." His contented nod caused him to spill a little of the stout onto his lap. "Want a paper towel?—although I doubt we could find one at this point—and not that it would do any good if I did. Sponging water out of cloth is like trying to explain things to Nancy...to your mother. I gather her idea of roughing it is going a day-and-a-half without a shower. She's so well-scrubbed I..." I tried to straighten myself up. "Sorry, old boy. This is awkward. Sons shouldn't be exposed to such details about their mothers. But Nancy wouldn't be Nancy if she weren't handy with a bar of soap. Which is good. I wouldn't have her any other way. So to speak."

My ramblings were interrupted by a car horn outside. We both jumped at a sound that seemed deliberately aimed at piercing our fog. I looked out at the road from the darkened safety of the hallway. I could see the outline of the reinstalled mailbox but little else except headlights.

"That can't be your mother," I said back to him. "She wouldn't honk unless she was under ten feet of water. If then." Nonetheless, Nancy came into focus. "It's your mother, all right—but she's talking to some honcho in a mega big SUV." That got Michael's attention, and he put out the joint with his lips—a carnival stunt I would never have tried—before slipping it into a pocket of his shorts. How I knew it was Marvin is one of those divine bulletins I'll never understand.

"Your father doesn't have a long smear of a moustache, does he?" Michael's eyes had widened considerably. "That's *him*?" Michael nodded. "Some guess. So what the hell is he doing here? Is somebody going to start yelling through a bullhorn that they've got the house surrounded?"

Nancy came up the walk wearing white jeans and a cotton shirt, looking crisply sexy. She kissed me on the cheek. "He said it was finally time to meet you. He's parking his car. Hello, Michael. You've wet your pants."

I was developing deep cracks in the small buzz I'd had before and turned on the porch light. "Meet me? Why does he need to meet me? I don't need to meet him—and we *are* talking about Marvin, aren't we?"

"Jeremiah, get yourself under control. He happened to be passing by and noticed my car."

"*Happened* to be—in a hamlet on the outskirts of Podunk?"

"That's what he said."

"From everything you've ever told me, Marvin Feller never *just happens*. He may be the one peculiar thing in a random universe that doesn't *just happen*."

"My, but you're deliciously helter-skelter—and not of your own choosing for once. We'll just have to see what happens, won't we?"

"There's no need to enjoy this so much, Nancy. And how long does it take to park a car? Is he painting stripes first, or what?"

"I'm sure I don't know. Michael, see where you father is."

Michael had drifted into the living room and was hovering near the woodstove. "Me?"

"You remember what he looks like, don't you?"

"Dad?"

She took her son by the arm and led him back to the hallway. "Jeremiah, please teach Michael what a good maker of jokes I've become since I met you—though I know you've sworn off teaching." She pushed Michael softly onto the porch. "Just look out front and see what happened." As Michael wandered into the yard, Nancy led me into the dining room and kissed me warmly on the mouth. "Hello there." She looked at the dim outlines of the room. "So this is your Walden, is it?"

"Where the hell is he?"

"I don't know."

"He said he was coming in to meet me?"

"That's what he said."

Michael appeared on the other side of the screen door. "H-he's not there."

"Not there?" Nancy asked.

"There's no car."

"Possibly he changed his mind but not likely."

"Or maybe he went for reinforcements," I ventured. "Does he have friends with baseball bats?"

"He's no mind-changer. Not that I ever saw. But it's been awhile. Jeremiah, why is there a piece of metal on the floor?"

"Why not?" I asked as she tapped at the crude patch with the toe of her shoe. "It's an early American custom—a sign of hospitality."

"I see. It's in worse shape than I thought. Michael, I have a message for you."

"As you very well know, Nancy, I bought this place to give it hope. Houses have souls just like grade-school teachers."

She ignored me and spoke to Michael through the screen. "Willie called to say you left something at her house. Your marijuana, I assume. I reminded her how to get here."

"Great," I muttered. "A gathering of troops."

"Do you need more metal for the floor?" she asked casually, still enjoying the moment.

"Where the hell is your husband?"

"Ex-husband."

"Ex."

"As in ex-professor moving into an ex-house with ex-floors with the help of an ex-student. Speaking of which, Jeremiah, where has my son disappeared to? To change his pants? Michael?" she called.

"With his organ-proud girlfriend on her way and his father lurking in the woods, he's probably hiding in one of the sheds."

"Apparently. I'd forgotten Marvin can be sneaky."

"Is that how he got you to jump into his bed all those years ago? Did he use guerilla tactics while he was waving his calculator in the air?" I turned to Michael, who was once again on the other side of the screen. "Any sign of the enemy yet?" He shook his head wearily, just as a babble of voices came from the road.

Two figures strutted up the sidewalk, arm in arm, and into the light of the porch where moths were creating aerial patterns. Marvin was tall and angular with a surprisingly loud voice. He was wearing dark pants and a short-sleeved shirt with epaulets that gave him a desiccated trooper look. It took a few seconds to recognize the person beside him as the lady who had been walking her dog the first time I saw the property. Without her winter coat, she looked cheery and plump, with an excess of lipstick that had been freshly applied. Her hair was the color of Nancy's but shorter and tightly curled.

Marvin greeted his son with a slight punch to the shoulder, telling him, "You've wet your pants, son."

As Marvin stepped inside, he nodded at Nancy, stepped on a metal patch in the hallway, and called me "Jerry."

"Jeremiah."

"Nice finish to your floor. And good job, Nancy. As names go, his has some real altitude. Nice to latch on to a willing lad with a good long one." That produced a manic laugh from his companion. "And this is Mary Jane Otto. She loves my jokes—eats them up like cashews, right, devil woman?" She laughed again but with more of an effort at control. Marvin turned to her. "This is my family and their new protector, is that right, Jeremy?"

"Pardon me?" I shot back.

"Oh, we've met," she assured him. "Many months ago. We had a pleasant talk, though it wasn't very nice out, as I recall."

"You *did* tell me," Marvin conceded to Mary Jane. "And I understand, Jeremy, you have no job or any intention of getting one?"

Nancy corrected him forcefully. "That isn't what I said, Marvin. I said he was able to drop out for a time because of an inheritance. It's an experiment." It had never occurred to me that I could be the subject of

Marvin's conversations with his former wife and present companion. They all seemed better prepared for this encounter than I was.

"Drop out," he repeated. "So he can advise Mike on his way to the unemployment line? It's good, son—where are you anyhow?" Michael's face appeared in the doorway again, with a moth halo behind him. "I was saying it's good you found a qualified teacher. Qualifications are everything."

"I see," Nancy countered. "And Mary Jane, it isn't clear what your qualifications are for enriching Marvin's life except for your very nice sense of humor."

Mary Jane was flummoxed and picked at one of her ringlets of hair. "I don't get."

"You might tell us how you came to know each other."

"That's not important," Marvin intervened.

Mary Jane was undeterred. "We met through the newspaper."

"You were an ad?" Nancy pursued.

"No. Marv was. He was a four-liner. I could tell there was something right away. Presence, you know?" She turned to him. "Do you remember how it went?"

"Not important," he whispered brusquely.

"I memorized it. Twice."

"Most definitely not important."

"I didn't think people used newspapers anymore." It was all I could offer. I invited them to inspect the house, my initial panic wilting before the actual presence of Mary Jane and Marvin, but with only two interior lights that worked, we remained bunched in the hallway. Mary Jane seemed pleased with my arrival in Quaker Falls and chattered on about the importance of getting to know neighbors, about how she had hoped some decent person would move to this house, and how interesting it was that I was almost a relative of Marvin's. She thought we should have a picnic at her place soon so I could meet more of the neighbors along with her dog Steverino though we had already met, actually. She thought Nancy looked cute in her little white pants. And an amazing coincidence like her "making time" with Marvin just three houses away from me and

Michael and Nancy deserved champagne toasts well before New Year, and she would see to it in the very near future. She was entertaining in her own way, good-hearted and without any of the subtler concerns about how people impacted each other except to provide potions of good feeling.

It's difficult to guess how many more talking points Mary Jane could have strung together for the helpless wonder of the rest of us—even Marvin, apparently. Willie's arrival spared our having to find out. She had a look of fixed determination as she came up the sidewalk, which she directed almost immediately at Marvin. "Well, if it isn't Mister Marvin Michael's Father Feller, everyone—the man who loves me to bits."

Marvin snapped quickly out of his Mary Jane-induced haze. "So now we've got the killer angel here, too." He asked me, "Did you get a permit?"

Willie and he had clearly done this kind of sparring before, and she replied, "If I'd known you were in this neighborhood, I would have called rabies control."

"We're just having a neighborly meeting, Wilhelm," he told her, toeing the piece of metal in the hallway just as Nancy had done earlier. "I would think in a house like this, where you might end up flat on your back in the basement, it's good to have responsive neighbors a shout away. And if you want response, I can tell you all, that's Mary Jane."

On cue, Mary Jane extended her hand to Willie. "I'm Mary Jane Otto. And I just figured out you're Michael's...you know."

Willie ignored the hand, growing sullen. "Yes, we've met."

Mary Jane brightened. "That's right. At Marvin's sweet little apartment. We've done wonders with it—and in it—haven't we, Marv?"

Willie turned to me, her eyes growing dangerous, but said only, "I came to get Mike. Can you spare him for a night, or does he have to sign a time sheet?"

It didn't take more than a minute for Michael to gather a few things and they were gone. The Marvin-Mary Jane spell was broken, and she promised once again to arrange a picnic as she led him down the sidewalk. Independence Day at the latest, she clarified. When they had started around the arc of road to the brightly lit house I now knew was Mary Jane Otto's, Nancy and I both exhaled and held hands like school kids who had escaped fearful punishment.

"Of all the gin joints in all the towns..."I recited briefly. Nancy put fingers to my lips and asked me to follow her to the car.

"You're leaving too?"

"I can't stay. But I brought something for you."

"You *can't* stay or *won't*?"

"Both."

"I realize I can't offer you a bed..."

"It's finally a chance for you to be here by yourself. It's important."

"There are gremlins down the road."

"Who will be busy tormenting each other—although I can't imagine..."Her voice trailed off, the decrescendo of a former wife constructing pictures of her former husband. She opened the car's back door. "Here, help me with this." It was a folded up piece of furniture on its side, impossible to identify. Nonetheless, she asked, "Don't you love it?" It was heavy, and when we had set it on one of the bluestone slabs of the sidewalk, I asked if she had loaded it herself. She was mildly indignant. "I may be old, but I'm not weak. And it is, for your information, a Morris chair, named after one of your literature people, I believe."

I ran my hands along the flat, wide, oaken arms. We raised the frame of the back, which had been lying face forward on the seat, into an upright position. She brought two cushions from the trunk, put them in place and positioned herself in the chair with queenly pleasure. "It's amazing," I told her. "Obviously designed to be transported in undersized foreign cars, even though I do know a guy with a truck. Me, for example."

"It's been in my family for more than a century, but I've had it tucked away in the basement. You might have noticed it when we were down there, but we got distracted, as I remember. It was a favorite of my father's. He wouldn't have known what to make of you—but where you live—that would have suited him just fine. Anyhow, it never felt right for my house."

"And you're giving it to me?"

"As Willie would say, sometimes you can be such a moron. Of course, I am. I used to think about saving it for Michael, but what are the odds of his getting a place any time in the next decade? Besides, he'll get to use it here."

"He's been an indescribable help."

She stood. "I hope that's a good thing."

"You know it is."

"Let's move this into the living room."

After we had pushed some tools aside to put it next to the woodstove, she pressed me into the seat and dropped onto my lap long enough to kiss my eyes and forehead. Then, she stood and said, "I would imagine two clever people could put a chair this size to good use." When I reached to pull her back down, she stepped away. "Not tonight. My god, there aren't even shades on the windows."

"Do you suppose the folks down the road draw the blinds? I may have to take a walk."

"Not with me you won't. Come and protect me," she suggested, moving through the door.

As I held the car door for her, I asked her whether pieces of furniture could have ghosts.

"Why, of course, Jerry," she replied, "even first-rate ghosts have to sit every now and then. All that floating leads to heavenly exhaustion."

When she was gone, I turned out the room's only table lamp where it sat on the floor before returning to the chair. The cushions had sewn-in buttons patterned upon them, and I could feel my back adjusting to their cool presence. And it was true: this was my first night alone in my house of whimsy. I could barely make out Michael's harmonica on the woodstove, the instrument that had comforted our first few nights in the house. Now there was no intermediary except my own thoughts and night noises. I heard bird songs I didn't recognize, hootings I assumed to be those of an owl, and a more melodic warble I would hope to identify at some point. I could smell skunk and thought of Michael pointing to where they dug for grubs in the yard that was not yet a lawn. I thought of how Louisa had been able to do nothing during her brief visit, and yet how her being there had provided a feeling of things being lifted to a more ordered level of accomplishment. A mower: I had begun to think of how long The Professor's money would last and had made a couple of half-hearted attempts at projecting how much I would need to live on and for how many years, but I knew the numbers didn't make sense yet. I knew that I didn't know enough.

If this was an experiment, many of its rules were yet to be defined—and where it was all to lead was a question not to be posed until more of the picture had begun to fill in. I wondered, as I had for several days, whether this examination of alternatives was a form of cheating. And, even so, was I building a life here or, as Eleanor Jewett might say, a delusion? It was not a place to bring a bride or raise a family—not at least in the skewed life I saw myself creating. But could I actually love a woman and a house without bringing them together at some point? I was well aware of living in a time where expectations about relationships changed every day, where married couples went back to live with parents, and committed couples lived in houses or apartments next to each other, where I could imagine them knocking on each other's door for a cup of sugar and pinch of carnal extract. And what was I to make of this gesture at pioneering where improbability settled comfortably three houses away from me, chasing after me like a jovial fury? Marvin, no less, planted like an aluminum Christmas tree in the middle of my imagined prairie. I knew I was dancing with time to begin with—this attempt to insert the work of long forgotten hands into my new life. To take on an abandoned house was, I knew, an act of renewal, yet it was, at the same time, an accessory of my own abandonment. But of what? That was the question the night noises seemed to be pestering themselves about. In this empty pocket of improbability, what was I being asked to fill it with?

NINE

As June moved rapidly along (in the manner of chore time), I realized I had been missing the gossip from campus, although I assumed that would not last for long. Like any workplace, I imagine, part of the engine that makes it vibrate is what we hear about those we have come to know or even those we haven't. A campus, however, is a place where the end product is supposedly people who have been nurtured by other people, though there are those like Richard Woo who question this, preferring to think of it as a place where layers of administrators do as much as possible to avoid the messes caused by people being people. According to this theory, the employees in the classroom serve not to benefit students but to justify the expanding numbers of those who never see a classroom and see the faculty as field hands cultivating students as cash crops coaxed out of overworked soil. I tried not to ally myself with the latter position since it was so obvious, but the more I listened to the networks of incidents that came through gossip of colleagues and students, the more I grew to believe the cynics were right.

The most newsy items were delivered to me by Chuck Gillis as I was cleaning out my office on the first day of summer. It was my only time on campus in the month since commencement. My regalia had slipped off the hanger where I had put it after the snow cancellation and lay like Peter Pan's shadow in a corner. It lay there like a sign of how new life had pretty much taken me over. The house restoration was progressing with daily pulsations of toiling and stepping back to see the end result of particular tasks. It was a new form of entertainment for me, that sense of "I just did that" and the belief that the blood of the place was beginning to flow again. I had gotten a mower with enough "balls," as Mikhail Jefferson put it, to confront the weeds and seedlings coming from the one-time lawn. After double-mowing the first time, learning the new art of not stalling, I brought a chair from the kitchen and sat with a visual fulfillment I couldn't connect to any earlier experience. It was intensely momentary, and the yard itself suggested it would never feel better that it did then. It lay fully satisfied and coherent, like Walt Whitman proclaiming the pleasures of masturbation to no one but himself.

Michael still helped out regularly. We put a cot for him in one of the upstairs rooms, and we created a bed in the rear bedroom for myself—a new mattress upon a heavy metal frame we found disassembled in one of the sheds. He started digging a garden as soon as the mowed lawn indicated where one had existed years before. His endurance and skill were both remarkable, and he built a six-foot deer fence around his piece of ground with precise carpentry skills for the framing and the gates. Nancy joined him on planting day, and he patiently endured her coaching on location and spacing. Willie came a few times and complained about the wobbling of the house's one toilet. I assured her a new bathroom floor was high on the to-do list, but I was already learning that thinking the work could be completed during the summer was a poor estimate on my part. I did enjoy Willie's taunting, even as it rose momentarily above a solemnity the house, or something, brought out in her. Nancy still refused to stay over in Quaker Falls, but she would bring breakfast for Michael and me and then leave for work. She and I had yet to spend a full night together.

Going back to campus felt, then, like an act of abandonment and violation with so much to be done and the rhythm of recent weeks being discarded even for a few hours. But I did wish to know how I would feel there and that surprising discovery of wanting to know what had been going on in my absence. Chuck Gillis helped. He was boyish in both his urgent need to speak and the shorts and Notre Dame T-shirt he was wearing. I imagined putting a whistle around his neck and turning him loose in a playground.

"Well, greetings to you, Jeremiah," he proclaimed from the door of my office. "Packing is such sweet sorrow, isn't it?" I agreed there was something to what he said, clumsy as it was. "I'll be doing this myself in a matter of years. I don't quite know how to prepare myself, but you have the advantage of owning so little."

"I could put my past in one little knapsack," I told him, "but the one I want to use has no bottom."

He looked at me quizzically and then patted me on the shoulder. "I'll have to give that some thought. Meanwhile, I thought you might be interested to know I had a ridiculously slight heart attack and we have a new chair." He seemed equally pleased about both.

"So I gather you're doing fine?"

"I should have called it an episode, but I don't want people thinking I don't treat it with some respect. It's got me walking and eating sunflower seeds. It's like managing the Yankees. Did you ever notice how much seed-chewing goes on in dugouts? When I was a kid, they were sneaking cigarettes."

I admitted I had noticed the sunflower phenomenon. "And item two?"

"Ah, that one. Phyllis is out and Rachel is in—at least on an interim basis. We haven't had a chance to vote yet with everyone scattered for the summer. Quite odd, actually. One day I'm talking to Professor Friel about how to fill the hole you've created—" he looked at me with mild accusation—"and two days later she tells me she's had enough. She's tired of leading the ranks of the spoiled, or words to that effect, and she is even considering a departure from teaching. All very sudden." The temporary youthfulness had drained from his face, replaced by the same lines that appeared when he discussed an unsuccessful course.

"People do run out of gas, I imagine."

"Not Phyllis. She's as gassy as they come. Not to sound crude. She's loved being chair. She saw it as a mission designed for her."

"So you think there's a story?"

"Story?"

"Something she's not telling you?"

"And to have a writing person in charge of the department. That must make Phyllis feel like she's thrown us on the rocks. Nothing against Rachel, mind you. It's just the way she thinks. Not that I would disagree with her to any extent. That's why we've gotten along so well for so long. Of course, I might consider throwing my hat in the ring at long last, but now I have my health to think about." Undoubtedly he did, but it was peculiar to me that a person with so many years in the department had never desired to head it. I wondered what his excuses in the past had been. "Yes, there must be a story. There always is. I wondered if you knew anything."

"Me?"

"A long shot, I know. But you at least did a good job of getting along with the people around here. And she knew your father." That again. "And people know things."

So they did, but I was in no way tempted to say what I knew about the discovery of her academic dishonesty, particularly to this tepid man who was so practiced at reconstructing the fact that he wasn't very good at what he did and leagued himself with people like Phyllis Friel who could keep his cloud afloat. It wasn't for me to pull him out of the sky. He might hear about it at some point, but I doubted he would believe it. I did, however, feel like my departure *had* become a form of abandonment, at least as far as Chuck Gillis was concerned.

After I had loaded the few boxes of books and papers into the truck, I checked my mailbox next to the building's administrative offices. One of the dean's secretaries, an older woman with a smoker's voice, was distributing the day's mail. While most of my colleagues were afraid of her, she had been a kindly buddy to me throughout the year, a guardian of my sapling status. It was, I think, Richard who told me that if Mary Milligan liked you, you were assured a far easier street than if she didn't, when she could dish out misery with Dickensian efficiency. She called me "stranger" on this occasion, and her hands shook with a nicotine flutter. I had occasionally tried joking with her about her addiction to cigarettes, but she would wave a perky middle finger at me if no one was watching. She did it so gracefully I once told her she could go on a talent show for bird-flipping, and she readily took it as a compliment. On this day, she wasn't in a mood for banter but told me simply that whatever was driving me away from teaching must be a helluva lot worse than standing in the cold to get a couple of drags from her Newports. "You probably need a spanking," she added.

"You're the person to do it."

"Yes, I am. And there's a lot of stuff going on around here that you're going to be sorry to miss out on."

"So I've heard. It's good they've got you to keep things running."

"Yeah. We'll see how that goes. But check in from time to time and I'll try to keep you up-to-date." She was extracting whatever was in my box and removing the tag with my name on it. She handed the collection to me with steely complacency. "As my mother used to say, don't be a stranger, or I won't call you stranger again."

This final trip to my mailbox produced more than Mary Milligan's taut dismissal. One of my other recurring dreams was about a forgotten mailbox in a location that changes from dream to dream but had in the last year taken up residence in other parts of the campus: a dormitory, the student center, even the gym. Its contents would be unchecked for weeks or months at a time, pleasantly protected by my own lack of concern. *Why* I had two boxes was never the necessary question, nor would I wonder who would know to send anything to me there. But finally, there would be a dreamy nudge to check the box at last, that there might be something of great importance in it that had, of course, been waiting for me. It was a *let it be known* moment without fanfare. Usually, I would only find outdated flyers or similar stuffings of campus life. This day was somewhat like the final fulfillment of that fixed idea, except in this case, the second mailbox was located within the first. There was plenty of junk, a couple of publishers' sample books, an auto-signed birthday card from the college's president, and, encased in it all, two stamped envelopes—each with totally unfamiliar handwriting.

I had the intuition that I should go to a special place to read the letters, but none occurred to me. And which to open first? During my year of grading handwritten exams, I had developed the habit of beginning with one or two having the best handwriting—that legibility might reflect a more orderly mind and get me off to a more generous start. Often that was the case, and so here, as I stood in the mail room, I chose the writing that was formed like the edges of pansy blossoms, distinct and gracefully shaped and fashionable. It was from Eleanor Jewett, a succinctly delivered message:

> Dear Professor Jeremiah,
>
> I asked Hamilton for your new address, but he happened not to know it. Therefore, I am writing you at the college, where I hope they will know how to get this to you. I think about your new home when I have the time and find myself creating pictures of it. It has been many years since I have had a pleasure ride, particularly in a <u>TRUCK</u>. If you find the time, I hope you might be able to take me to see it. If not, perhaps you would be kind enough to send me a picture.
>
> Your declining new friend,

She signed it with her full name, Eleanor Annabel Jewett and underscored it with a curving pen stroke. She had mentioned having a thing about pickups the first time she saw it, and apparently she wasn't kidding. In a postscript, she added her phone number and commented that her hours were not as pleasant with me out of the house, but that my apartment was now occupied by what appeared to be a polite Indian couple, though she had not met them formally yet.

Eleanor's note gladdened me. Being missed by her (and to be told so with relative forthrightness) had a well-toned sparkle that shone outside the envelope even after I had slipped the piece of paper back inside. I thought of Nancy's note on green paper in November and the pleasant puzzlement it had caused in me. I *still* puzzled over her and her capacity for dancing in close before spinning away and her ability to manage the fierce shell of our feelings without chipping it—or allowing me to. I thought of Eleanor's long-ago free-love household and the management *that* must have required. Or was it simply that it had managed itself, like an organism allowed to live without any obligation to consequence? How did that kind of intimacy survive in a person decades later? Was it the same as the sudden recollection of a single lover, something I had not yet experienced except as the imaginings of a schoolboy? Was it a diffusion of love and an enlargement of it or a dilution or phantom composition of memory? Yes, I very much wanted to see her again. I wanted to know what her heart had seen and felt before death once again dropped the curtain of irretrievability.

After tucking my Miss Jewett's note into a shirt pocket, I walked before opening the second envelope. I had looked at the handwriting again, and it was so nondescript its compressed strokes seemed to have been milled with the paper they sat upon. The letters were small and blocky, unhesitant but reserved. I knew them from another time that would not open itself to me. The postmark was New York City, but there was no return address. The stamp was upside down, and the realization it was from Ellen finally came crashing upon me. I took a heavy breath as I reached the Dakota. The tailgate was still down from loading the things from my office, and I sat there as a place of unfinished business, my feet dangling above the heated asphalt of this solstice day.

I had received none of her darting e-mails in months, a fact I hadn't realized until this moment—like failing to notice a pain that has subsided. The handwriting on the envelope had become clear to me now, my recollection as a child that the gracelessness of Ellen's writing should seem out of place in a woman of artful language, who spoke with words that smiled and made music. She had told me it was a service she had developed for her students, to make her written comments easier for them to read, to appear to them as judgmental without being accusatory. She had also spoken of the habit from her girlhood of standing postage stamps on their heads as a sign of special feelings about a recipient—a visual version of head over heels I recalled her saying. It was, presumably, an invitation now to open the envelope that had been sealed with unusual feelings.

There were others in the parking lot. The dean got out of his BMW and nodded coolly at me. His personal secretary, leaving her car at the other end of the lot, greeted me with a slight wave. Undoubtedly, they had been having a nooner. Their dalliance was common knowledge—and so commonplace-seeming that I had never thought of the rush of their hormones as anything more than a staff meeting with exercise. It was a relief to *imagine* them for the moment as I tapped the envelope on my knee. They each had spouses who accompanied them dutifully to school events, who may or may not have known that anything was afoot but gave off the impression it would hardly matter if they did. I wondered if the dean's pale moustache was a token to the secretary of bristling noontime gratitude. I wondered, too, where they went.

At last, I opened the letter. It was brief, almost telegram-like, with even borders and block handwriting. It was undated, so I looked at the postmark once again. June 1.

DEAR JEREMIAH,

AS YOU MIGHT RECALL, I DISLIKE SURPRISES, BUT HOW WOULD A WORD FROM ME BE ANYTHING LESS THAN A SURPRISE AFTER SO MUCH TIME. YOUR BIRTHDAYS COMING IN JUST A FEW DAYS. I WILL BE PASSING THROUGH THE VALLEY AND I THOUGHT IT MIGHT BE AN OPPORTUNITY, ON THAT DAY, TO LOOK AT EACH OTHER AGAIN. NOON AT POETS' WALK WOULD BE FINE FOR YOU AND ME, I THINK. IF YOU CAN'T BE THERE, I WILL UNDERSTAND.

ELLEN SCARSELLA CURTIN

I had, of course, been too late receiving the letter to respond to the request, but here I was again trying to decipher the ways of parents, as well as myself, and wondering how I would have responded if I had received it in time. Why at Poets' Walk—a site I had essentially forgotten existed? Near the bridge to Kingston. She and I had been there once, when I was about eight and had written my first poem in bald little couplets. She had always said we would go back, but we never did, and my skills as a poet never got much better.

It was Emily who heard me utter the word "Fuck" as I continued to sit on the tailgate. She laughed with pleasant complicity, and I wondered if my legs had been swinging like a thwarted boy's. *Emily Botticelli.* I must have heard her real last name at some point, but if I had, it continued to be brushed aside by my own ethereal conception of her.

"Fuck," she told me declaratively, forming the word with lips playfully puckered, like Lucia Solis had in my office the day she came to rant at me, letting it hang in the air for several beats. "It is one of the fine products of our language, don't you think? My belief is that it is so satisfying to say because it's so satisfying to do. You see? Even when we say it with frustration we feel the satisfaction. I'm naturally sorry you feel that way, but I'm glad you treated yourself to saying it." She looked a younger version of beautiful on this day, her hair in a pair of ponytails coming from beneath a baseball cap—looking to be on the verge of puberty and wise in the ways of being ageless. Her glasses made her wider-eyed than ever. "I don't generally swear myself, but if I did, that would be at the top of my list." She paused, morphing into the kind-hearted social worker. "Want to tell me about it?"

"Why are you on campus? Aren't you supposed to be patrolling the mean streets?"

"I work for a school system, remember? No meanness except from prickly principals and poopy parents." She giggled softly. "Say that quickly three times."

"I'd rather hear it from you."

She eased herself onto the tailgate next to me and tugged on the bill of her baseball cap. "Whoo," she confessed, "that's not as easy as it used to be. My father had a pickup that would make this look like a toy, and I could float like a feather onto it."

"Don't be making fun of my truck, friend. Guys and their trucks are nothing to mess with."

"I'm well aware, dude." She was in high spirits, her words popping playfully out of her. As I had realized before, it would be wrong to desire

Emily Botticelli and wrong not to. Here at our own sudden tailgating party, I wished I had a beer to open for her. "I was here looking for you-know-who," she informed, her spirits descending suddenly. "The deadline for moving out is a week away."

"I'm also well-aware." I pointed to the cartons behind us.

"So you are. And is that why you're dropping f-bombs off the back of your truck?"

"Nope. Nothing easier. I'm packed and done and left my key on the desk like I was checking out of a cheap hotel. My office looked like The Land of No Regret when I shut the door."

"She's been trying for a month to bring herself here, and her office is like a mad scientist's. She said she'd be here, but she said it with so much—whatever—I doubted it. She's turned off her cell so I can't scold her. She's brooding someplace."

"It made no sense—her tenure denial—unless you can crawl inside the tiny minds of the uptrodden."

"It's a disgrace," she said simply, rubbing her hands on her jeans and sighing sadly.

"You may fight my fights any time you wish. But how is all the rest?"

"Marriage?" She may have been the most gifted person I have ever known for cutting through the imprecision of my words, especially when I tried shaping them into a question. I assumed that would have been a valuable asset in a partner even though she made it seem like a form of mind reading.

"Marriage."

She looked wistfully toward the building we had both just come from. "Sometimes being *one* is like being one-and-a-half. It's always amazing, but it gets a little tippy. I mean, here's this person I used to look at from a classroom chair made out of plastic who now kisses me awake each morning like she had never felt she could teach me anything. She's always saying 'Teach me,' and when I ask her what, she says it should be whatever I want. How beautiful is that? As if..." and she paused. "Except the last week or so when it's been like she could barely see me. Not that she was angry with me, but that she had expected me to vanish. I don't know why." She stared at the building and pulled her shoulders inward. "Whew," she muttered. "They make sausages in there—just like Congress. We create these unorganized organizations like colleges and school districts and legislatures to grind out what can't even be digested. What's the point?" She looked directly at me. "You know, Jeremiah, if I can't make anything better than a turdy-looking sausage, I'll be really disappointed in myself and a big chunk of existence. How's that for solipsism syndrome?" I nodded, not willing to admit I didn't know the expression. "Maybe I *would* vanish."

But there she was, making turds feel like quince blossoms—an alchemical thing she was able to do with her voice. I told her so, and I told her about the letter I was still holding in my hand. She knew nothing about my parents except that my father had been a big-time academic.

I asked suddenly, "Do you think it's possible to miss something you never had? Him, I mean?"

"Probably. I get aches when I don't even know what I'm aching for—longings, you know? Maybe there are people we will never meet or places we will never see and don't even know exist that whisper inside us and make us lonely for a second. Maybe all of us are doing it all the time. We're all feeling a hunger for each other that we only know as a breath that snags for the smallest length of time. Maybe we all need each other but we're too messed up to know it." Naturally, I wanted to take her narrow hands in mine and feel them against my face. That need was clear enough. Had we not been sitting on the tailgate of a truck in a potholed parking lot, I might have. "So what will you do, Jeremiah, about your mother?"

"I don't know. There's a kind of freedom, I keep discovering, in not knowing. But I realize that's a tune that can frost your insides if it goes around too many times. I know you're going to say that I should try to find Ellen since she's reached out."

She looked at me with her softly gray eyes before lowering herself from the tailgate. "Well, of course you should. What the hell's the matter with you? And I won't be your friend any more if you don't."

"Yes, that would be a loss."

"Do you know what I like about your house?" she asked serenely.

"Tell me."

"It's full of snags."

"Snags again."

"When we were there, my breath kept catching, like I was telling you before. It's full of snags, like the whole world is watching itself through a keyhole—and your house is *it*. It's a funny thing to say about a house, I guess. But that's what it was. I just figured it out." She smiled with childlike simplicity. "I'm very proud of myself."

"Can I love you for another half-minute?"

"Why shouldn't you?" She wiped her hands on her jeans again. "We'll have to come for a sleepover someday."

"You'll have to find your grumpy wife first. Is a wife what she is?"

"It's what we both are. Good, isn't it? Though we don't use the word. It has a bad history. '*The wife*.'" She voiced the italics and air-fingered the quotation marks. "The words of jailers." She patted the back of my hand. "But I'll find her and drag her by the nose," she said and floated toward her car before turning. "You do your own finding."

TEN

Mary Jane Otto came by with Steverino a few days later to announce she was throwing her promised party on the Fourth. She said it was to be a day of national pride as well as chance to meet the neighborhood. The dog's name came as part of her bouncy greeting, but Steverino didn't seem to like me all that much, perhaps recalling the cold and slushy day we had first met. He sniffed at me through the screen door with displeased snorts until Mary Jane tucked him under an arm. I had been thinking of Sara Sampson's one-time pronouncement that there were certain dogs who ought to be squashed like stinkbugs, and it was as if Mary Jane had read my thoughts.

I invited her in to show her my latest project, the creation of a study in one of the upstairs bedrooms. I had ripped out cheap wall-to-wall carpeting to expose the wide pine boards beneath, brought in P.Q. Jessup with a monster of a power sander, and polyurethaned the floor myself under Michael Feller's yogic guidance. As well as being an entertaining inspector with Shakespearean colorations, P.Q. was also a classic handyman—able to do most anything to a house and armed with an array of tools that made him both highly valuable and formidable. On this day, he was jacking up the back porch to level it, and I looked forward to introducing him to Mary Jane. I had found a beaten-up campaign desk for my study and had put The Professor's chair behind it, where it seemed large enough to eat the shaky-looking piece of furniture—but they were paired for now and would have to work things out. The dog growled in the direction of the chair as if he knew. I had purchased two assemble-it-yourself bookcases which now contained the contents of my campus office, the book on railroads in Duchess County, *Reconsiderations* with the one-page question mark tucked inside it, and my copy of *Riff and Raggles.* Mary Jane spotted the latter with a shriek of delight, which caused Steverino to pee slightly from under her arm and onto the floor—its first new distress mark.

"Oh, Jerry, I know this book! I can't believe you have it—and you a big-time professor."

"*Former* professor—and nothing big-time about it."

In her excitement, she squeezed the dog a little harder but nothing seemed to come out. "Sure. Of course. Marvin says you're a dropping—or dropsy—or whatever the word was." To all appearances, she seemed bright enough, but she had moments when a desired word would curl up like a potato bug. It was a kind of multisyllable brain fart that was entertaining enough to sound like a personal strength of hers.

"Drop-out," I suggested.

She had the book in her hand and had set Steverino on the floor so she could finger the pages. He sniffed at his own micro-puddle with whiskery satisfaction. "Yes," she concluded with a projectile sigh, "it's just as I remember it—every little picture in its place."

"I personally think the book has a curse on it."

She looked at me with suspicion. "Oh, no. Certainly not. It has happiness and...pearls. Yes, pearls! Wise pearls." She pointed at a phrase in the book and declaimed it in a deeper voice, "Love makes the cream rise to the top." The dog and cat were eyeing a milk bottle with soulful anticipation and obvious signs that they were agreeable about sharing its contents. "That's a pearl. My mother said 'Pearls are the osprey of reading.'" If this was a malapropism, it was initially untranslatable, although I later guessed it stood for "offspring." It wasn't clear, of course, whether it was hers or her mother's. She waved the book in the air. "Can I borrow this?"

"Perhaps you can share it with Marvin."

"Well, of course. One can only have so much nooky, can't one?" She pulled a tissue from somewhere in her clothing and dabbed up her dog's slight error without comment. Then she and Steverino followed me down the stairs and through the kitchen, the dog shaking a paw or two when he hit a dry-rotted floorboard—his annoyance being my satisfaction. Mary Jane took to P.Q. as I knew she would and was rapturous in praising the smell of newly sawed wood. "It's God's pixie dust for the nose." She was taken, too, by the bandanna he had around his head—though she called it a scruff, I believe—and claimed it made him look like a genius, by which I assumed she meant genie.

Her language seemed to be developing more leaks, but P.Q. welcomed her to his project like any other difficult-to-identify hand tool. She burbled over his being a man of initials, asked him what they stood for, and seemed satisfied with his telling her his name was the short form of P.D.Q.

She walked back and forth on his newly leveled porch with its inter-patching of new boards and old, while the dog tried to burrow his way beneath it. "It makes me feel like the great Katharine Hepburn," she announced. "I will now recite lines from *The African's Queen*." It seemed fortunate, at first, that she couldn't recall any until she pushed forward a roller coaster version of Hepburn's question to Humphrey Bogart: "My dear P.D.Q, what *is* your name?" Her laughter seemed to reach the hillside where Nancy and I had made our own indiscreet sounds. "And what a drawstring body you have," she remarked to P.Q. without apparent lasciviousness. "You could squeeze out sawdust with your own barren hands. But I must be going. I can't keep two gentlemen from their pointed rounds." The dog looked at her approvingly before grinding out a miniature yawn that had the sound of balsa wood being torn apart by hand.

When Mary Jane and the dog had left, P.Q. told me I'd better watch out for older women and then went back to conclude his project. I wandered further into the yard, pleasing myself with the idea that the kinds of tasks he was doing had the simple grace of being finite, however complicated they were or however many skills they required.

They *did* come with conclusions, and they *did* come with the promise of what-was-once vs. what-is-now. Before and after. I was grateful for my unartful but growing ability to do things with my hands, to cause the work I did to stay with me. It was all so different from what I had been trained to do, where efforts evaporated with thought—and the loss of that thought—within the minds of those who never stayed in place.

The yard had been mine for a month only, but already it had a welcoming familiarity I was waiting to feel within the house itself. Michael and I had pruned the fruit trees and cleaned out flower beds, but the only real modification had been his vegetable garden with its six-foot fence. When he came to the house, it was the first thing he would look at, and as the seedlings began to define themselves as plants, he would rub his hands together and look in my general direction for my own confirmation of what the process meant.

It was good to see these moments of satisfaction, even as it became more apparent that something was bothering him. Michael had always been a creature of quiet ways, but lately those ways had taken on a burnishing of sadness or repression rather than the stillness of his spirit. He was smoking less pot—at least with me—but what was probably a good thing under most circumstances, seemed a readable marker in his case. I told him more than once that he looked troubled, but he denied it, dismissing it as the heat of summer, which he had never particularly liked. Still, he kept working on the house and yard, two or three days a week, appearing to find ongoing pleasures in the skills he was expressing. I asked Nancy if he and Willie were having troubles, and she thought not, that they still seemed close in a huddling sort of way, and she suspected he was beginning to wonder about what the next step in his life should be. She noted that Willie, too, was in a lull—that she had apparently stopped practicing the organ, stopped visiting Eleanor Jewett, and was talking about having a go at the Peace Corps. It was like the opening of the house in Quaker Falls had replicated the unearthing of King Tut's tomb, releasing pent-up spirits that could be construed as communications from a neglected afterworld.

Nancy herself was as supportive and practical as ever and hinted about a time when we would share the bed in the room whose floor held it like a cupped hand. I also discovered she most decidedly had a thing about chairs. The day after Mary Jane's visit, Nancy brought me two repainted Adirondacks to put under the apple tree, now that many of its lower branches had been removed. We faced them toward the westward hill of our passionate conquest, watching as the sun set over it. It was a view to be looked at again and again, she said, and it was good how little distances could step toward us with arms outstretched and give us butterflies. She said it with one hand in mine and the other holding a glass of wine. Occasionally, an undersized apple would fall near us, and she eased my immediate sense of loss by assuring me fruit trees pruned themselves throughout the growing season to prepare for a stronger harvest. It seemed yet another metaphor worth applying to puzzling questions, but I couldn't find a decent application right then with the sun fully behind the hillside, the meadow before it alive with the sweep of birds, and the air around us softly intimate. Until, that is, she told me about her drink with Marvin, a piece of information that fell out of our dialogue like a glossy insert from a newspaper

"Drink?"

"Two actually." She had the look and sound of pleasant clarification that made it clear she had nothing to hide and was glad enough to share it. She took a sip of wine as if to underscore her announcement. "Tom Collinses." She pointed to pinkish-white wisps in the sky before us. "Mare's tails," she noted. "A sign of rain tomorrow.

"Thanks for the information."

"Which, exactly?"

"Whichever you wish. Did you have him over?"

She was quietly indignant. "Certainly not. We met at a bar."

"A bar?"

"That's where people meet for drinks."

"What kind of bar?"

"Does it matter?" I waited. "It was a perfectly nice bar in an Italian restaurant—a place we used to go for dinner in our frisky days."

"Frisky?"

"Wrong word. Marvin was never what you would call frisky... until recently."

"According to Mary Jane, they have nooky."

"Would that be like what we have?"

"In no way!" She laughed, pleased with everything so far, including her ex-husband's nooky. "And who asked whom to this Italian restaurant?"

"I invited him, of course. The idea of inviting me would never have occurred to him."

"And why would either of you think of inviting the other for drinks? And what is a Tom Collins, by the way?"

"It's a drink invented by someone named..."

"Tom Collins. Of course. I believe he played second base for the old Philadelphia Athletics."

"Why not? Was he good at squeezing lemons?"

"I believe he squeezed rubber balls. So your Marvin cocktail is lemon and...?"

"It's like a playful medley of lemonade, soda, and gin," she said, sounding like a television pitchwoman.

"Gin," I repeated, trying not to sound like a nineteenth century temperance peddler. If, however, there was one spirit that had gotten too much bad press over the centuries—from Hogarth's lithographs of Gin Lane to Eliza Doolittle's mother who sucked it down like mother's milk—it was gin. Just the monosyllabic snottiness of the word made it difficult for me, the inexperienced drinker, to keep from framing it into a bottle with a skull and crossbones on it. Especially with Marvin in the picture. "And the reason for the invitation? To your taxman?"

She set her wineglass on the ground. "Our little encounter a couple of weeks ago—if that's what it was—with the playmates from down the road. If there's going to be an attempt at a Disney community in Quaker Falls that will apparently include Marvin and myself—not to mention Michael and his girlfriend—although who ever knows with her...I thought it might be good if the grownups hammered out a few understandings."

"Grownups."

"In age only. I wouldn't presume to seat you at the children's table."

"So long as my feet touch the floor."

"You are my lover, after all." Indeed I was, and there she was speaking it to the twilight. "We can say that word, can't we?"

"Any time you wish." A brownish rabbit was moving slowly near the edge of the yard, nibbling along with the conversation, listening in while maintaining a look of casual indifference. Nancy noticed it as well, pointing without saying anything. We nodded in unison, the motion of the animal virtually suspended in the web of shared sight. "And did you reach some understandings with the other grownup?"

"Marvin got pretty...disoriented...pretty quickly. It's hard to know how much he will have remembered. Apparently life with Bo Peep—what's her name?

"Mary Jane Otto."

"That's right. She seems to have weakened my poor Marvin." She sighed lugubriously and took my hand again. "He agreed—I think—to behave like a good neighbor and not like a former husband. He admitted he had followed me for the last mile that night. He knew a little bit of our relationship, which was drawing me to the eastern part of the county. He had asked Michael a few leading questions, and Michael is not one to lie. That he would be honking at me three doors away from what's-her-name..."

"Mary Jane. Comfortable-sounding, isn't it?"

"Perhaps. In his accountant's mind, it was an alignment too good to close the books on right then. Thus, the pleasant visit of that night."

"Certainly."

"He thinks you might actually be a good influence on Michael, even though he suspects you were a rotten one initially. He still can't believe Michael left school for what he told him was a higher calling. I've never heard him use words like that—though I can feel him thinking it. Saying it to Marvin is a higher calling in its own right. His horrible moustache twitched when he told me."

"It is horrible, isn't it?"

"Keep in mind, only I am allowed to say it, Jeremiah. I expect better from you."

We sat silently for a time. Raggedy shapes that Nancy identified as bats were making erratic patterns over the meadow, charred hunks of paper drafting into the gray sky. Fireflies were lighting and dimming beneath them. The view I had claimed as my own over the past month was creating another version of itself, another wrinkling of the slow-passing season and time of day. With help from the woman who called me her lover, *place* was teaching me how it is never really a fixed point as much as a heartbeat that goes on steadily but with its own needed fluctuations. I began to understand Michael's belief that a still picture moved with its own internal dynamic if you can be loose-visioned enough.

She slapped a mosquito, saying, "I draw insects, so you are probably safe."

I stood. "You think I'm going to let you be the sacrificial meal?"

"I know. But sit for two more minutes." She pulled me back into place. "We can count my welts later. I want to tell you something."

"Sounds spooky."

"Only a reality check. I may be in the early stages of menopause."

"So? Is it fatal?"

"No, Jeremiah, but it's terminal. In our golden months when we found our ages—at times—to be less and less noticeable to each other—"

"As they still are."

"Not true. How could it be? There will be times when it is as noticeable as our noses."

"I've barely talked about your nose. I've spent too much time on your hair and your eyes. You have a brilliant nose."

"Brilliant."

"Not like Rudolph."

"It doesn't matter *what* it's like, and you're back into one of your let's-pretend-everything's-as-fine-as-whiskers moods simply because I'm trying to be honest with you—and remind you that what you and

I may want and what our bodies might want are two entirely different things." She caught herself and smiled. "Sometimes." She finally stood and scratched two or three spots where she had been bitten. And she was right. She had served as a mosquito magnet, leaving me untouched. "Who knows?" she added as casually as she could. "I may be years away from that dreaded change of life. It may be your fault entirely...mussing up my hormones after so many years of hearing them napping and thinking it's better that way."

As we walked to her car, I was happy to change to another subject, telling her I was bringing my new nonagenarian girlfriend to see the house in two days. The note from Eleanor Jewett, I was happy to refer to. The other...not yet.

"I will look forward to meeting your Miss Jewett at some point," Nancy said. "There was a period when Willie talked of little but her."

"And now?"

"She talks about very little, period." She looked down the road. "I see Marvin's car is already in its place. Is she that exciting?"

"Maybe she puts mysterious potions into his gin."

"He doesn't actually like gin. He drank it as a favor to me, as far as I can guess. But you're right, my darling, it's a peculiar force that deposited him three doors from your place of retreat. As they say, you can't make this kind of thing up."

"I would hate to think so."

"For a time I thought I had to protect you from all coincidences, you seem so fascinated by them. Now, I think all coincidence should be ignored."

"Can I quote you?"

"Or have its diaper changed. It feels so immature right now. Big events are being hidden inside quirks of timing, and I don't like it as much as I would like to."

"Wow!" I exhaled. It was a new type of language for her. "I gather you're not going to Mary Jane's Fourth of July weenie roast."

"Not a chance. I might get a hot flash." She kissed me on the mouth for several seconds. "I do cherish you, my puzzle. I do, for the most part, love what we're attempting, in spite of all weenies everywhere. And I thank you for sharing your own special sunset with me." She scratched an arm dutifully and left me with the suddenness of remembered pain.

ELEVEN

Before I picked up Eleanor Jewett for her excursion into the countryside, I dug out one of my Ellen e-mails, the one urging me to be content without knowledge of her and, of course, to not write back. I finally had cable in a house that had obviously never known the feel of a computer on one of its surfaces, and I sat within the back-straightening contours of The Professor's chair as I dusted the keyboard with my fingers. In the fall, I had established an electronic folder for her e-mails—four in all—and labeled it simply "Mystery Woman." The other messages had briefly wished me well on my new career; encouraged me to admit it to others, particularly students, when I didn't have an answer to something; and urged me, by way of reinforcement, to be decisive about uncertainty. That last statement had sounded so much like Ellen's abandoned husband that I wondered for a time if he was channeling himself through a digitally constructed identity of her in order to—what? I couldn't grant him that much cleverness or manipulative power—at least until I read through *Reconsiderations*. Now that I had seen a note in her own handwriting, I could put that possibility to rest, although no further e-mails had come from her after his death.

When I finally ignored her instructions and used her fourth as a possible springboard back to her, I felt the surge of frustration that it had to be like this—that I/we were having to use these tentative and uncertain filaments of communication after having been boxed in by silence for so long. I had already learned that short puffs of silence were usually things to cherish—but long silence became a frozen locker difficult to escape from—human unease being what it is.

The e-mail itself was simple enough:

Ellen/Mother
I would like to think that our meeting at Poets' Walk would have happened if I had checked my mail on campus in a timelier manner. However, as I might be able to tell you, there are reasons for that as, I would like to think, there are for anything else.
Jeremiah

How does one try to sound to one's mother after the hollow of fourteen years has finally produced a small sound: relieved, grateful, perplexed, disgraced? I reread the words several times before sending them, trying to parse its inner workings the way I would have a Holy Sonnet by John Donne. Finally, I charged myself with amateur foolishness and hit send. It would travel to somewhere or nowhere. For now, that would have to serve for decisive action.

Before closing the computer, I noticed the words "Sara Sampson" gracing the inbox. I was actually happy to see the name, one I had learned to manage with reasonable confidence over the last year. It was a fresh presence after the overcooked note to my mother. The topic line contained the brisk fanfare "News!!!!!" Sara loved the exclamation point, calling it in our early days a period with pecker power. A parade of five was not unusual for her. However, the news itself deserved more:

My dear departed Jeremiah,
I've moved back to Arizona, where new opportunities await. It is the land of enchantment after all!! Not only am I going to finally get a doctorate, but I'm getting a doc as well. I'm going to be married to a yummy anthropologist who actually washes his hands. It's all very sudden and unexpected, but you know me!!!? If you run into Hamilton, you might be the perfect person to tell him

my good news. He will probably say I left him under puzzling circumstances. But you know me! When it rains here, I will think of you.
Your Sara

In the first place, Sara Sampson had never wanted to learn that New Mexico was The Land of Enchantment. It suited her purposes to apply it to any state she was in, apparently, though Arizona was a reasonable second choice. The rest of it was also vintage Sara, overstated and under-explained. No indication of what had taken her away from Manhattan. The anthro professor? Or was he an unintended consequence of what brought her there? Was anthropology to be her new field? She had completed her Masters in English and proclaimed she was finished. She felt that literature people were the goofiest collection of oddballs she could ever imagine meeting, and why would anyone think they could leave a footprint on the moon teaching what she called "sourball" poetry? How long had she been gone (a few months?) and how long had she known this guy with the clean hands, whatever that was intended to imply? She couldn't mean me: I washed with the best of them and still do even as a manual laborer—but it was an interesting piece of information. Hamilton? I wasn't sure I wanted to tell him anything except to satisfy the clearly perverse desire to see how he would react and whether he would define "puzzling circumstances." And finally, "When it rains here, I will think of you"—which sounded like a perfect example of sourball sentiments. It was her way of saying, I suppose, that she wouldn't be thinking of me much at all in the Sonoran desert—although there was the flipside recollection of the gazebo in the rain where she proclaimed the perfectly ordinary brilliance of orgasm. Would she like to continue remembering that and wanting to share it as a side-note she kept in a mental drawer even clean hands couldn't open?

As a juxtaposition, I enjoyed her telling me and the Sara-esque way she chose to do so. It unsprang my brain from the corkscrew effort of writing to Ellen. For a moment, it made me fond of Sara's ability to bolt from one temporary post to the next. It brought back pictures of the way she and I would make an event of any Arizona rain, running into it if we could to throw open our mouths and spread our hands to the sudden refreshment of the skies. The gazebo had been one of the few times of coming in from the rain. But Sara married? I wouldn't bet the house on it.

§

I had promised Eleanor Jewett I would pick her up promptly at one in the afternoon. She was waiting for me on the front porch where she had sat with Willie Furman nearly four months earlier. The windows of my former apartment were behind her, and I looked briefly to see shapes moving about behind scrim-like curtains. The nice Indian couple. Eleanor sat with her hands holding a cane between her knees, an accessory I'd not seen her use before, but the light tan raincoat—almost like an old-fashioned duster—suggested a woman ready for a summer outing. When I asked her about the cane, she said quite simply that it was the result of too many lies. I let that go for the moment while I helped her down the steps and into the Dakota—after she assured me twice that she was perfectly capable of going on what she called her mission. When I asked how she felt climbing into a pickup, she tapped the cane softly against my hip and urged me to give her a gentlemanly shove: "And do it like you mean it." Once inside, she sat as purposefully as a gentrified Southern woman, though she objected with righteous clarity to being bound in by a seat belt. I wasn't going to argue with "Miss Daisy."

As we left Rhinebeck, she was quiet at first, seeming pleased that the planned adventure was actually happening—until she asked about two CDs on the seat between us. When I explained what they were, she nodded happily and said, "Do you mean to say this farm vehicle makes its own music? Strike up the band." I explained that the "band" consisted of either Flatt and Scruggs or the soundtrack from *Showboat*. "Flatt and Scruggs," she said with ongoing decisiveness. "Sounds like good horse liniment. Put it on." I played it softly at first, watching her head moving in time to the picking and thinking of how Richard Woo would feel about the growing reach of his influence.

The journey, which I had been apprehensive about, turned out to be a geriatric joyride. I'd had little idea of what we would talk about, except to explain the passing sights and prepare for what she was about to see in Quaker Falls. None of that was necessary. She pretty much duplicated my initial exposure to bluegrass music filling the cab of a pickup truck, making us into a festival on wheels. The day was hot, and she complimented me on how the air conditioning kept the windows closed and sealed the sound in around us. As had I, she asked for repetitions of certain tracks and told me at one point, with the strained lift of her voice, that she was reminded of the pubs of Western Ireland and the high spirits of the Irish people "when they were tuned to the right notes—as they most often were." When I reached at one point to lower the volume, she placed her cool fingers over my hand and guided it back to the steering wheel. As had Nancy, during our first ride into the country, she pointed to direct my eyes toward things that caught her attention. The only object she asked about specifically was the shaft of a nineteenth century limekiln on one of the back roads I had chosen for her. Standing with its courses of stone still fixed in place, it had the look of prehistoric purpose on its rubbly patch of ground that adjoined a 1950s ranch house. According to my passenger, when we stopped briefly, the kiln looked like a chimney rising from a nether world—or, as she put it, "the devil's stovepipe. Even old Satan needs a chance to blow off steam. Or *especially*, I would think." She was immeasurably charmed by both the discovery and her interpretation of it, twice clapping her hands together as we left.

There was a calico cat sitting on my porch when we got to the house, which I recognized as one of several from the hamlet who found it a good place to watch the hushed world of Quaker Falls. They had welcomed me without any snide undertones, and I repaid their kindness by sharing occasional bits of meals with them—especially this one. I recalled my passenger's professed dislike of cats, but she seemed undeterred as we approached the house—until it chose her cane to rub up against, and she was quick to note that "they are drawn to those who have no respect for them. They can't help themselves." She appeared to be walking with more difficulty than she had earlier, and by the time I had her seated on the Morris chair and gotten her a glass of water, I finally demanded she tell me what had happened.

"I kicked a door," she said simply, before going on. "It's a reprehensible thing to do at any age, but for a person who forgets that she has turned into a stick-figure, it's utterly stupid." As to *why* she had been kicking a door, she reverted to her earlier statement about lies, adding that it wasn't a kick worth description: "When you can only lift your feet three inches off the floor, it's not very impressive. But it was impressive enough."

She wouldn't go beyond that, into whatever had triggered the response, but she assured me she had consulted expert help. "The new woman in your apartment is a physical therapist with very kind hands. She assured me I had done nothing permanent—although *permanent* is a word that often makes me laugh at this point of the game. Aspirin would be nice," she suggested. "I do like this setting, and I hope you'll eventually get to show me the rest of the house."

I brought her the aspirin, and the act of swallowing the pills seemed to make her feel almost immediately comfortable. The room had become more livable in the past week with a Boston rocker and couch I had bought at a cut-rate price from P.Q., who had an old barn full of collectibles. The floor was still beaten up, but a cheap area rug covered the area in front of the wood stove where sheets of metal remained over the dry-rotted areas, creating a percussive hiccup to feet crossing it. I had retrieved the map of early London that had been my Christmas present to The Professor, and it now hung over the couch. A TV tray along the wall by the door held my CD player.

Eleanor sat back in the chair before saying to a phantom figure standing behind me, "You know, I've told some whoppers in my day." I dragged the rocker to a spot several feet in front of her and leaned forward. She was grateful for the response, which allowed her a playful attempt at dusting it aside. "Oh, my young confessor, and you think I am going to share choice sins with you?" She formed a zigzag line of challenge with her lips.

"I think you are going to tell me whatever it is that you *want* to tell me. But there is *something* that wants to come out. You *may* have wished for a ride into the country, and you may actually be enjoying it, and you *may* have discovered a liking for banjo music, and you may have tried to cripple yourself for exercise, but you do have *something* that wants to come out. For God's sake, Eleanor—I can call you Eleanor?"

She nodded with her head angled expectantly. "I believe you already have, at some point."

"I could feel it in the note you sent me. It had a fastidious urgency—very ladylike and all that, but urgency. Either you're about to die or something's wanting to peck its way out of you."

"I see," she replied. "If that's to be the way it is, you need to do two things. You need to switch chairs with me. Rockers are much more conducive to disclosure. And you may bring me a small glass of Cointreau." I looked at her blankly. "How rude of me. Wilhelmina told me you don't imbibe."

"She exaggerates."

She lowered her head again as if looking at me over the tops of eyeglasses. "Then tea will do."

I helped her to the rocker before going to the kitchen. I had no teakettle, so I boiled water in a saucepan and pulled a mug from the sink. Of the four electric burners on the stove top, only one was still working—a reminder of another item on my to-do list: finding replacement coils and learning how to install them.

When I brought the tea, I adjusted Eleanor's chair so she could use the top of the woodstove as a side table, leaving our two chairs at an inelegant but appropriately oblique angle. There was the feeling that one of us was about to conduct class, but who it was remained undetermined. She looked at the mug with pleasant disapproval but held it between her hands after she had taken her first taste, nodding at me.

"I lied about the Roosevelts," she began simply. I tried to recall why that should be a meaningful statement, but I was blanking. "I believe I mentioned I was governess to one of the grandchildren." She peered at me, once again looking over nonexistent glasses. "I wasn't." She paused. "It was a satisfying idea because I *did* respect what the name stood for, even though my father thought Franklin was the antichrist. More likely *because* he thought so. My father was a terrible individual. Or so I have always tried to believe. Believing it took energy but was probably worth it in the end." Her eyes seemed to be looking at me for help. I, of course, thought of The Professor, but I had never applied *terrible* as an adjective, even in my angriest years. He was too symmetrically chiseled—too graceful in his own remoteness. I waited for her to regain the thread of recollection; finally she spoke the word "there" and raised her head decisively. "Are our lives only a chain of reactions? Do we act only because we react? I've wondered that much of my life. I wasn't even named after Mrs. Roosevelt. That was a coincidence."

"Do you want to say more about your father?"

"He was an individual—or should I say a non-individual—who thought the Almighty gave him his undivided attention. Let that be enough. Except to say that my mother was simple and good enough to believe him. And let *that* be enough as well." She rested herself momentarily, moving the warm mug in circles on her knee. "So I decided it was better to not be good and see if I could get away with it." Once again she halted, this time taking a tight breath. "And I did."

"Your time in England?"

She handed me the tea, and I put it on the shelf-like arm of the Morris chair that had come to me with cup and glass rings from generations of Nancy Feller's ancestors who had sat where I was sitting now, especially her own father, apparently. Dead fathers were everywhere. I had jokingly scolded Nancy for giving me such a well-mapped piece of furniture, and she challenged me to refinish it if I didn't want to be reminded of all those others.

"*That* I did not make up—although I might have even if I hadn't lived it."

"You made films and ..."

"And made my fellow actors? Is that how your generation would put it?"

"If I were impolite enough. But your face tells me I'm doing all right and to just be quiet." The irises of her eyes had taken on a lavender translucency, a faraway gathering of insights being tasted once more. I had seen it in Nancy's eyes, and it was clear there are things ages share with a perfect indelibility, a faultless comprehension of one another.

"All I have to let you know that might be of any value for you is that the idea of telling people how and where to share their deepest selves ridicules the making of the entire universe. And put that on top of our thinking this...universe...would cease to exist without us. How is that for being feeble-minded?" Her voice had become a dry croak, but she spoke with an actor's resonance as she went forward. "You may wish to know if any in that house loved one more than they did others. And I would have to say I don't know. And I don't care. Someone there said to me it was like trying to determine whether one wisp of fog is more beautiful than another. And we did. We lived in a fog. But it was a fog in which you could see things more clearly than in normal light. It had a virtue beyond morality. That's all I can say." She licked her lips. "Now please hand me that awful thing of tea."

That, of course, wasn't all she could or would say. She spoke more of the Roosevelt issue, claiming it was not so much a fantasy as commitment to a storyboard that suited her creative needs—that beyond the multiplicities of her British years she had entered into a role that was singularly spinsterish and American, appearing to be quintessentially proper and grounded. She was unclear about why she gave up her film career, and I could have imagined she concocted that too were it not for what I had seen in her apartment. She said she had lived for several decades doing various hospital jobs and drawing income from a well-funded artist she had known in London. She referred to it as being "kept at a distance," saying it with an attempted chuckle that lapsed into flattened memory. It was, she said with some wistfulness, another of the fruits of being bad. I told her that her young friend Willie had also spoken of badness as a kind of destiny for her and asked if they had ever talked about it. She looked at me through slitted eyes. "We've talked of a good many things—although not so many of them in recent weeks." Her eyes closed.

"Have you learned her secret?"

Eleanor's eyes popped open, widened into moons of confusion. "Secret?"

"Not the deep dark kind, but what makes her her? What makes her what she is?"

"And what is that?" she questioned guardedly.

"What makes her angry for one thing?"

"Angry?"

"Her own brilliance makes her angry. She seems to hate it."

She drank the rest of the tea and said nothing. Once again, I felt edged up against things I could sense without any clarity—like the wisps of Eleanor's free-love fog. I had assumed her to be a bit player in the drama of the last many months, a woman off the curio shelf of women who had been like the moving pieces of a puzzle: Nancy, Ellen, Sara, Louisa, Emily and Barbara Lynn, Willie and her mother, even skewed figures like Phyllis Friel and Mary Jane Otto. There were times they seemed to be seated at a long table with placards before them containing not only their names but an unreadable line of text beneath. They were a panel of experts about a topic that had not yet been announced, and I sat before them, solo, in a straight-backed chair, waiting for a beginning. Now the one-time lady upstairs, the silent sentry of my comings and goings, had come to the table to join this sorority of puzzlers. An unlit sign above them saying "Let the Explanation Begin" would flash briefly and then go out. Finally, Eleanor Jewett reached for her cane and said, "Show me the rest of your special retreat, and then take me home."

As we walked from room to room, I warned her about the floorboards and explained the slices of metal patchwork. She took my elbow at times, something she'd not done before, steering me as much as being guided. There was an upright piano in the dining room, one of those troublesome objects that transfer from owner to owner like a signature. Only Michael had been curious enough to lift the cover once to punch two or three notes from its stained keyboard. My guest, however, not only pushed the cover back but began with one hand playing what I recognized as the opening melody of The Moonlight Sonata's slow movement, repeating it several times, the tips of her fingers stroking the keys with pure self-indulgence. She looked entranced by it, even as she finally pronounced the instrument badly out of tune.

"Like myself," she added. I had thought to give the piano to anyone who could benefit from it, but I now knew I mustn't. She had broken into its long sleep and wakened it to the new exhalations of the house.

She was perplexed by the kitchen—not its general disarray as much as its connection to her own past, and she struggled to locate it in her memory. "It may be my parents', but it's been far too long, and I've taken great pains to erase it as a place that ever was. Or it may have been the kitchen we all shared in England—if only I could put voices to it. Or it may be nowhere. Kitchens are terrible reminders," she added.

"So I've heard."

She ran a hand along the top of the room's other stove, an oversized coal-and-wood burner in front of the rear wall, feeling the lids where pots would have sat, her palm pausing roughly on one as if gauging the amount of heat it held. She shook her head at an unspoken thought and pushed open the door onto the porch.

"Yes, this will do," she told me as she ran her eyes about the yard. "I worry about the rest, but this, I can see, is what brought you here."

"What is your worry?" I asked, helping her from the porch.

"That you are a professor trying to make yourself into a...what is that horrid German word?" She searched for it while I watched a red-bellied bird swooping low along the grass to catch an insect. Bluebird, possibly. "A hausfrau!" she finally said with pleasant distaste. "I fear being put away back in Rhinebeck with a picture of you on your hands and knees cleaning your front step with a scrub brush."

We both nodded in agreement, and I tried once again to find out how she had injured herself, but even the levity of the moment had not loosened whatever it was she was guarding. "Does it have anything to do with your neighbor across the hall?" I asked with a stab of finality. The sudden compression of her mouth told me I had at least come close.

The ride back was mostly done in silence. She did note that there had been a pickup truck at the house in Surrey, that it was painted something "very dark," not garishly orange like this, and she had loved riding in the back of it, especially with others. She ignored my suggestion that we play the CD again, and it wasn't until we were a mile from the village that she said, as if off-topic, "I like that chimney poking out of the ground. It's the craftiest thing I've seen in years." Crafty, indeed. "What was it you called it?"

"Limekiln."

"Yes. A vent for dark secrets," she said with evident satisfaction.

After I had returned my Miss Jewett to her apartment, I knocked softly on Hamilton Graham's door so she would not hear, but there was no response.

TWELVE

I asked Mikhail Jefferson if he wanted to do the July Fourth thing at Mary Jane Otto's with me. The last I'd seen him, he'd been complaining about a too quiet summer, spells of indefinable loneliness, and the loose threads of a book he was working on. I thought a dose of Mary Jane would lift him out of his torpor and make normalcy a good thing again, but he turned me down, claiming the Fourth depressed him. His explanation was both reasonable and neurotic. Memorial Day was the perfect holiday—the parades were smaller, the summer opened up before you like it did when you were a kid, while the nation's birthday poked the brain with thoughts of September.

"I know it's two months away," he admitted, "but the extra voltage is there, like it or not. Besides, our popgun approach to the business of being created free and equal makes me want to give our Uncle Sam a colon deal with oversized firecrackers. And, bro', in case you want an example closer to home, let me fill you in on Rachel."

"VanNoys?" I asked.

"The very same. Better known as your former chair."

"She was only appointed days ago."

"Exactly. And she has now been dis-appointed." What I learned from Woo was that Rachel had become increasingly frustrated with the way the administration was prepping the faculty to handle a team of outside evaluators during the summer and fall, telling the teaching staff what to say and what not to say while in contact with the visitors. As a first-year person, I had had no direct involvement with these preparations, but I remember a corridor discussion about "good words" and "bad words," and Rachel's pronouncement that the Spaceship Orwell had landed on our campus. She had apparently channeled her astonishment into a piece of Swiftian prose entitled "A Mideast Proposal" and sent it to one of the primary journals of college teaching where it was published and then went viral. The Mideast slant, as Mikhail explained it, was a depiction of outcome-crazy administrators as Ayatollahs, while the academic-freedom-loving professoriate had to strap word bombs to special vests with the school mascot on them. Once the publication reached our dean, Rachel was back to being a teacher of composition. "She was run through the disposal," Mikhail commented, "and who knows what else they'll find to do to her? Tenure or no tenure, she's vulnerable. So leave me out of any freedom toots."

Just as well Jefferson didn't come, even though Mary Jane's small gathering was actually tame by contrast to what would happen later that night. It was her, the dog, Marvin, me, and four somewhat remarkable neighbors who acted as if they had been guilted into attending. Mary Jane introduced me as a "dropout from teaching everyone will most certainly grow to like, even if he is unemployed." Her assurance of my worthiness came from the fact that she too had dropped out from teaching fourth grade many years ago and managed to maintain her respectability—no doubt, I assured myself, through the series of men she either married or diddled, like Marvin. "Five weeks I taught that last time," she declaimed with a barbecue fork waving in the air. "And jeez, I was good. I could make magic." The word startled me; it was both bridge and rebuff. "But I called a kid a name. She was a boogery little blankety-blank-know-it-all-paste-for-brains brat. And I was supposed to warm up to that?" The others waited patiently for her to answer her own question. "If I could have paddled her, I might have made it. I guess the same thing was true with some of the men in my life. You know?" No one quite did, not even Marvin.

For Mary Jane, however, the true rave of the afternoon was the "white hots" she had had shipped to her by someone in her hometown of Batavia. Western New York, she informed us, was the only place in all of mainland America where you could get them—and she doubted Hawaii and Alaska would be any more forthcoming for those in search of this delicacy. "I've been all over this country," she informed the group at her picnic table, "coast to coast, and the white weenie disappears like a terrible sin once you get a hundred miles from Buffalo. Isn't that right, Marverino?" He seemed not to know one way or the other and devoted much of his time to a cocktail shaker that was the endless fount of what he called Pickled Independence, his concoction created especially for the day. I recalled Nancy's description of Marvin trying to handle more than one Tom Collins, but on this afternoon, he seemed to be driving himself to a personal best while maintaining enough sobriety to manage the grill—particularly the white hots.

"Nice black stripes," Mary Jane would tell him. "No wiener is worth a bun if you haven't scorched in stripes—make it into the backside of an old-time cotton-picker." It was my moment of gladness that Jefferson had refused to come.

The white hot dogs were good and Steverino ate several; Mary Jane's potato salad was good; her baked beans were good, though she admitted they were from a can and were the dog's favorite brand; her molded cherry Jell-O with red, white, and blue mini-marshmallows was runny but good. The only thing not all that good was Marvin's Independence drink, and I nursed a single paper cup of it during the few hours I was there. Marvin seemed to lose count fairly easily for a tax guy, and he believed me when I insisted I was on at least my third helping of his liberation juice. I spent time considering how Mary Jane might have colored the red and blue marshmallows, listened to Steverino's prolonged and staccato farting, and tried to prove a winning new neighbor to the others there.

A mother and daughter who lived next to Mary Jane, two houses from me, seemed not to know what to make of colorless hot dogs but made up for it with large helpings of potato salad, flavored, as we were told, by secret ingredients, like a Kentucky Fried coating. They both appeared to be in their forties, problematic for a parent-and-child, and I had a difficult time telling which was which until I settled on the mother being the one with the bandanna around her hair and pewter earrings that stretched her lobes into the shape of inflated lima beans. I didn't learn her name that afternoon since she asked me to call her "Moms." The daughter, Allegra, spoke with the breathy wonderment of a young nun, though her eyes looked as if she needed sleep. They seemed nice enough, especially for people who would try to bring the police down on me a few weeks later.

The other twosome was an older couple who had what Oscar Wilde called the "perfectly scandalous" tendency to flirt with each other after fifty years of marriage. He called her Squirrel; she called him Bobo; and they held hands much of the time. Their house, on the other side of Mary Jane's, had been the station master's in the hamlet's railroad days, and he offered to show me the model train set-up in his basement—designed to look as things were back then. Bill and Lucille. On a day of national celebration, I would have placed them at the top of the birthday cake.

I explored Mary Jane's yard with the flatulent Steverino at my heels ready to bring me to task should I disturb his domain in any suspicious way. The yard was dotted with his poop, little haloes of darker green grass feeding from them. It was a large yard, larger than mine, with a fenced-in patch of sweet corn at the back. The plants were to the top of the fence already, and I thought of the adage "waist-high by the Fourth of July." I wanted to open the gate and move among the half-dozen rows, but I chose instead to walk around the perimeter of the patch, reaching in from time to time to stroke the emerging leaves and tassels between my thumb and fingers: textures as decidedly different as sighs and small kisses.

It was at the very back that I noticed two or three shapes jarringly out of place. I thought to reach over to weed them out when I realized they were cannabis plants camouflaged by the corn. I had known a few pot growers in Arizona, and the five-pronged leaves waved at me with the familiarity of distant relatives.

"What, ho, Steverino," I said to the dog. "Your mistress has an interesting hobby." He looked at me with a mixture of anger and puzzlement, wagging his tail with uncertain strokes. "No wonder she was making up new words the other day." I wondered if Marvin knew or whether this was her own private patch of pleasure. As I eyed the plants with quiet admiration—for Mary Jane, presumably—I heard the raised laughter of women from the vicinity of the picnic table and realized one of the secret ingredients of the potato salad was looking up at me. It sounded as if the twin-like mother and daughter had been unknowingly celebrating the nation's special day in an herbal way. By the time I returned to them, I had no doubt about it. One of them was twirling the other to music only they seemed capable of hearing. Bill and Lucille were unchanged by whatever they had eaten, and I doubt it would have had much impact anyway; they were so in their own altered state to begin with.

§

My departure from the picnic was almost unnoticed, except by Bill who came partway down the road to remind me of the model train extravaganza in his basement. I thanked him as he clasped both of my hands and assured him I was finding this to be a far more interesting neighborhood than anyone might have guessed at first glance. I asked him if he knew anything about the Underground Railroad going through here. While he wasn't certain, he did know the Railroad had little to do with actual railroads. He had slightly known the father and son who had been the last occupants of my house, though he thought it was more like twenty years ago than ten. They were, he said, a little eccentric, often dressed in what Bill called "Boy Scout uniforms" as they tended to the yard. He thought that such a length of abandonment for a house was a sure way to make a place hungry for meaning. "You seem about right for the task," he concluded softly. "You'll be doing your own scouting." It was a little unsettling, but he presented the information to me with the encouraging nod of a man who called his wife Squirrel.

It was nearly sunset, and to my bemusement Michael and Willie came out of the shadows of the yard as I approached the house. The smell of marijuana smoke trailed them, but it came so closely on the heels of my corn-patch discovery that I was driven to an outburst of teary snorts and snickers and a flashcard picture of Marty and Maud having their Amsterdamnable buzz in my father's book of mysteries. I wondered to myself whether getting buzzed at our age was any different from a person Mary Jane's—whether doping was doping regardless. They looked at me like a pair of hand-puppets, but it was Willie who said in her own organ pounder's way, "What the fuck's the matter with you?" The calico cat was moving along at their pace but a few feet behind them.

"Willie and Mikey," I spluttered, "how very nice to see you. And, Michael, what brings your lady fair to this place of forgotten dreams? I thought you had renounced us, my dear." Something had speckled my brain, whether it was the potato salad, Marvin's concoction, the discovery of Mary Jane's plants, a combination of ingredients or the mere sight of Willie Furman questioning my existence. The release felt pleasant after trying to shape myself to the afternoon picnic.

"We just wanted a place to hang out," she said, "but if this is giving you the shakes, we can split."

It was an occasion too good to waste, and I led them to the house with an arm around each of their shoulders. She tried at first to shake off the contact, but by the time we got to the front door, she turned and put both arms around me and drew me to her. "You're a ridiculous human being," she said, "but I have to admit—and I hope I never do it again—that there are times I can miss you as much as I feel sorry for you."

Michael looked on with the pleased expression of having achieved something worthwhile—the first slight smile I'd seen from him in some time—but when I tried to create a group hug, he scooted into the living room, turning on its solitary lamp. It had been a week or more since he had been there, and he looked at the room with grateful nods—finally aiming his phone to click a picture of the Morris chair and rocker, which were still facing each other from Eleanor Jewett's visit. He looked at the woodstove as if he had lost and recovered it again. "Let's fire up," he said quietly. I didn't know if he was talking about the stove or marijuana.

It was Willie who read him. "It's eighty fucking degrees," she scolded. "The fuckin' Fourth. And you want a fire?"

"What better, Will?" he replied calmly. Since I moved in, I had looked at the stove with my own kind of longing, knowing that, in a matter of weeks, it would become necessary to my way of living. More than once I had been tempted to have a small trial fire but had talked myself out of it, remembering my poor attempts at learning to play the fireplace in my apartment—and the person from the registrar's office I'd smoked out of my life. I suppose now I had been waiting for someone to teach me how to keep from incinerating the house.

And here he was—the multitalented Michael Feller. He had read my thoughts, was out the door, intoning "Hang on, Will" with the simple faith of a country curate, and back in a minute carrying a double handful of small sticks and pine cones. Before turning out the light, he instructed me on how to open the damper—a springy-looking handle on the stovepipe—and laid a few pieces of his gatherings inside the stove, on top of a wad of tissue he had in his back pocket: used or unused I didn't check to see. He had a lighter, of course, and handed it to me, saying "You do the honors." I felt an urge to kiss him, but he had already moved several steps backward to take in what was feeling like a ritual lighting.

The small fire came to life easily and cheerily, pulling almost immediately at the dampness of the room. He fed several pine cones into the flame, warning me that if I made it a habit I'd gunk up my chimney. I nodded gratefully, and the three of us sat on the floor to watch, and, in fact, to share an occasion. Michael talked about chickens. He thought it was what the place needed—that they would look great eating bugs from the ground—they would be free-rangers just like me, but they'd probably get eaten by dogs or foxes or weasels, which was one of the problems about living on at the edge of the wilderness. He murmured about how much people get worked up over things they can't do much about, but was that any reason not to let a bunch of chickens have the chance to walk on real ground like the rest of us—and even if they did get nailed, they would at least have had a chance to do what they were supposed to do—namely, be chickens. Of course, we could build a big pen, but we'd always be wanting to let them out anyhow—and that would cause a lot of stress.

And on he went, the ideas rolling easily from him as if he had finally gotten the stopper out of a bottle. Willie herself was calmed by the process and snuggled up against him in an apparent gesture of apology and gratitude. They were still there as I crawled to the couch and half-rolled my body onto it.

The next sound I heard was Nancy's voice.

THIRTEEN

"Michael?"

"No. His former teacher."

"Jeremiah?"

I swung my feet to the floor, trying to get a sense of the time. The trial fire was out, and the only light was coming from the hallway. Nancy was grasping the partially opened door to the room and holding her keys in the air like a small lantern. There was a sound from elsewhere in the house, a rhythmic one I couldn't identify at first, before it came to me clearly. "I think Michael and Willie are upstairs."

"I saw her car."

"We made a fire and I then proceeded to conk out. National holidays have that effect on me."

"You gave them your bed?"

"Not that I was aware of. Apparently they shanghaied it while I was nodding here." There was the sound of quiet moaning from above. "I assume you don't want me to get him?"

She looked upward. "No. Most certainly not. And it was you I was looking for."

"What time is it?" I asked as she came toward me, detouring briefly to turn on the lamp.

"Late. Eleven."

"You told me you don't normally have a pulse after ten."

"I have a pulse," she said, extending her arm. "Care to check?"

I stood and reached for her hands. The keys pressed with determination against one of my palms. "Then this must be an event of some importance."

"I'm not sure." There was another long, low moan and an attempt at muffling as it was choked off suddenly. "But *that* would seem to be. Jeremiah, is that Michael?"

"One of them, I hope. Though I've always thought I was a person who would take poltergeists at face value—perhaps share a glass of amontillado."

"Do you think men and women moan differently?" she asked with clinical suddenness, pulling her hands from me with casual concern: the mother in her at odds with the woman. A single short moan punctuated her look. "I'm not sure I can do this."

"I must remind you that you make such sounds with rich beauty."

"Never mind that, please." She took a deep breath. "I'm not sure I can talk seriously with you while my son is..."

"You can say it."

The note from upstairs was sounded again. "There's no need. So stop it."

"Apparently he saves up his verbal energy for more useful activities, although he was on a roll earlier about chickens and life."

"Jeremiah, let's both stop this. Let's try pretending. You're very good at that."

"Pretending not to hear?"

"Yes. Although how sad it sounds. It's not a sound to be listened to by outsiders."

"It's beautiful. It's like pigeons." I walked to the door and pushed it most of the way shut. The sound of bedsprings was beginning to underscore their crooning.

"Like carnival music, I think."

I tried to divert her attention by recounting a few of the picnic highlights at Mary Jane's, leaving out the corn patch and downplaying Marvin's drunkenness. Nancy looked uninterested and finally parked herself in the misplaced rocker, facing away from me. "After the so-called picnic, the two of them were waiting for me, like happy goblins actually. I thought they did want to have a little fire and visit with me, but it would seem they were primarily in search of a bed."

"I completely doubt that," she finally replied with fixed protectiveness.

I came around her and sat on the Morris chair, facing her. "Did you come to have a serious talk?"

"I came because I wanted to be with you."

"For what?"

"For crawling between your sheets and lying next to you and holding you." Her mouth shaped into a small pout. "But someone beat me to your bed."

"Well Christ, if I'd known you were going to be in the neighborhood, I would have made a reservation."

"I had this immodest vision of slipping in beside you and being there when you woke up." Her voice had freshened, like a late-evening breeze.

"We've still got the couch. We're good on a couch."

"I haven't forgotten." She smiled. "But I also came to ask you a question." She waited until she found her moment. "Jeremiah, were you imagining proposing marriage to me at a future date?"

"I thought that was the last thing you wanted."

"It is. And I want you never to forget that. You don't want that, do you?"

"I have no idea."

She leaned toward me. "I don't believe you. You always have an idea. You have too many ideas. This house is an idea."

"Whose time has come." A burst of sustained moaning from upstairs sounded as if it were working its way down the uninsulated wall cavities. I considered what effect it might have on honey bees. "That was unfortunate wording, I guess."

She broke into laughter. "Yes. Yes it is. What should we do?"

"It turns out to be a house with interesting acoustics, but we should ride it out, I think." It was a reasonable proposal—better than running into the night with our ears covered. Perhaps we would have passed the time listening to the midnight noises outside but they seemed no match for the sounds from upstairs. There were no real screens on the windows yet, only old-fashioned sliding inserts I had found in the side attic off my bedroom. The four living room windows now had trashy-looking ones of various sizes, so *they* might have been a topic of conversation. I might have told her about Rachel VanNoys getting demoted for being perceptive and clever. None of that was necessary, however, as the crash from above cut the night with a new suddenness followed by poppings of laughter.

"They just broke the bed, didn't they?" Nancy wondered aloud.

"See? If you and I had given it a test-drive, we might have saved them serious complications." Then, I called out in a voice that reminded me in its tone of Marvin's first visit to the house. "Everybody okay up there?"

Nancy was too late in trying to cover my mouth and stood with embarrassed exasperation. "Good, Jeremiah. Now they know we know,"

"They know *I* know. They may have missed your arrival."

"That's true. Where are my keys?"

"I believe you're holding them. And stop being silly." I walked to the living room door and opened it wider. "Mrs. Feller wants to know if anyone was hurt." I turned to her, saying quietly, "I never know how to refer to you around the young people."

She turned me back to her. "Dammit, Jeremiah, you *do* use people for your own amusement, don't you? That was cheap, even for you, and I'm sorry to have to say it."

Michael came down the stairs, bouncing several steps at a time. He had a sheet wrapped around him from the waist down. His face was lost in the eddying moment, but his voice was more decisive than normal. "Hey, Mom. We crashed."

Nancy was flustered. "Are you all right? I mean, you haven't hurt yourself, have you?"

"No. It was easy."

"Easy?" she asked.

"Easy, Mom."

"That's Michaelspeak," I interrupted, "for easy as falling out of bed."

"Well good for you," she said. "And I'll be leaving."

"You're going?" he questioned with disbelief. "Did I scare you?"

"Of course you scare me." She gazed at him. "My God—you're still so skinny." He responded with a shrug. "Is Willie all right?" she asked uncertainly.

"She's great!" he informed her with enthusiasm.

"I didn't mean...I...have to go." Nancy's befuddlement was precious to watch, and I experienced the inappropriate desire to put my arms around her to assure we were all going to get through this.

"No she doesn't, Michael," I told him. "She needs to stay."

"Mom," he said with a further upping of his resolve. "Don't go. Hang out."

"No, thank you. And you, my darling son, are the one in danger of hanging out."

He loved her for it, discovering a mother, apparently, that he hadn't known he had. "Oh, wow," he exclaimed, gazing downward at the sheet. "Good one, Mom."

"Michael, let me say something to you." He gazed at her uncertainly while he adjusted the sheet. "Come in here," she said, pulling him into the living room by one of his bare arms. "I know I say things all the time. *That*, as you've learned, is one of the uncontrollable things about being a mother. But one of these days it will all stop—especially if you keep destroying beds in front of me."

"I t-think it just fell apart," he corrected. "Not broke. We just gave it too much juice."

"Fine," she said nodding. "Too much juice it is. That's what your friend Jeremiah and I have, now that I think of it."

"Cool." He was more than interested, and I shared his fixity, watching the two of them working out boundaries of the spoken and unspoken.

"No. It isn't exactly cool. For you and Willie it can be cool...and no doubt it is...when it is." She made an effort to calm her voice. "I just want you to know that if I don't come here very often, it has nothing to do with your...juices. You have a very good friend in Jeremiah, and I know you know that. Now, Michael, go upstairs."

"Mom," he lamented. Something had twisted too quickly for him.

"I didn't mean it the way it sounded. Stay if you want. You'll hear it anyhow."

He looked at her, at me, at the door of the woodstove that was still open from earlier, and then announced "I'm leaving" before moving quickly up the stairs.

Nancy turned to me once more and hit me on the shoulder with an unladylike punch. My "ow" seemed to give her added energy. "You big dope," she began, "you've sent me back to being Nancy and Marvin again, shooing Michael upstairs so we don't have to communicate with him about how rotten we can be at communicating with each other. That part of my life is over, Jeremiah. I don't want to do it again. You haven't even begun what I've already finished. Don't you see how awkward that is?"

"No," I tried to interject.

"And not because of how we'll look to the rest of the world—I don't care about that, trust me—I'm more than ready to be looked at askance. I welcome it. It's not *that*, believe me, but how we'll look to ourselves. You'll want a child...children—that's bound to happen—if only so you can show them how not to waste their lives."

There were heavier footsteps on the stairs. Willie appeared briefly in the doorway, wearing a flannel shirt and her untied hiking boots. The shirt had been a birthday gift from Nancy, along with the promised Dvorak CD and a plum sapling that I had added to the line of fruit trees along the back. "Have to whiz," she informed us and then nodded at me. "I had to borrow one of your shirts. Hope you don't mind." She disappeared as quickly as she had appeared.

I tried to ease the moment with another unsuccessful one-liner. "You have to wonder if there's a future for anyone who wears boots on these floors."

Nancy remained motionless, staring at the doorway, then moved to the woodstove where she closed and latched the door just as the toilet flushed. "I wish it hadn't been that shirt. I really do. I know it's ridiculous."

Willie moved past the door and put one foot on the steps before turning into the room. "Your john still wobbles."

"No kidding." I had been told by PQ that the entire bathroom floor would have to be replaced before I could properly anchor the toilet. That project was nearing the top of my list but had not quite arrived there.

"It might make you dizzy, Professor. I'd hate to see you fall off your throne." She turned to Nancy with a softer voice than normal. "Hi."

"Hello, Willie."

"It's late," she said for no apparent reason.

"Yes—a little."

"The bed sucks," she announced.

"I heard," Nancy replied calmly.

Willie looked intently at me. "Nothing personal."

"Sounded personal to me. Maybe you should have taken your boots off."

She folded her arms. "Maybe I did."

"Maybe I put it together wrong. My apologies."

"I thought you knew your way around a bed."

"Don't you have some unfinished business upstairs?" I asked.

"You're the ones with the unfinished business." She turned to Nancy. "Am I wrong?"

"You're wrong," she replied.

"Do you want me to leave?" She unconsciously fingered the top button of the shirt before pulling the collar forward with a tight tug.

"Why would I want you to leave?" Nancy asked her, standing by the woodstove with the palm of her hand flat to the top.

"I break beds. I'm bad luck."

"You probably are," I said. "So what?"

"Because I want to be a good fairy," she said resentfully or regretfully—I couldn't tell. "I can't believe I broke the fucking bed." Then she looked directly at Nancy. "I'm sorry."

"What are you sorry about, Willie?" she asked.

"Bad words. Bad beds. Banging your son while you're in pleasant conversation with your boyfriend."

The last word hit Nancy with sudden force, driving a release of laughter from her. "You aren't a good fairy yet, are you?"

"I'm bad. I'm just as bad as can be." It was the same phrase she had used in my office the previous fall. Though so many months had passed, what she said now—and the way she said it—sounded like an echo that had shrunken time.

"How bad is that?" Nancy wondered.

"I don't know exactly. Maybe not bad at all. But as bad as can be. No more...no...never mind."

How long we would have stood there, three still figures creating a triangle in my first draft of a living room, I can't be sure. We seemed to be having a game of catch, like I had outside The Professor's study with Ellen, but we were tossing ideas, and we were a chamber group making the most tentative connections rather than a quiet twosome tending the flight of a ball without an idea in sight. There was, however, a shrill call of "Yoo-hoo" from outside, an unmistakable sound that spun the three of us in the direction of the doorway.

"Hello, neighbor," Mary Jane's siren-like voice pitched out of the night. "Bet you're still up. Your light switch is on."

"Jesus God almighty," I said to the other two, feeling like their protector. "The stack deepens."

Marvin's call of "Jerry"—divided into a succession of several syllables—was dripping with a day of drinking. He repeated the sound, adding, "We've come to play with you."

I went onto the porch and asked stupidly, "Why are you here?"

"To McMurray," Marvin informed. He had two game boxes and tried to show them before dropping them on the ground.

"To make merry," Mary Jane translated. She held up an open champagne bottle.

Marvin was stepping on the boxes as he attempted to gather them up. "Molopoly," he informed, "and...something else. Good neighborly games." He finally saw Nancy standing behind me and straightened up with a pulsing shriek that drove us both backward. "Why, it's my little cheerleader. Did you know, Jerry, she cheerleaded? Great legs. Did splits and all the rest."

"Go back to your nest, Marvin," Nancy said icily. She tried to move around me toward him but was cut off by Willie Furman shoving past both of us.

"I *do* know you—and not through this old sot," she told Mary Jane accusingly. "You used to teach."

"Damn right."

"I had you."

"Oh, God," I heard myself muttering. "I don't want this."

"Did you? How I'm de-lighted."

"You'd just changed your name back to Otto. You made a big deal about it."

"That's what I always did," Mary Jane confirmed pleasantly. "Convenience, you know."

"Tell me you were the paste-for-brains brat," I blurted to Willie. She had unbuttoned the shirt collar again and looked like she couldn't decide whether to go after me or Mary Jane.

"Is that what she called me?"

"Of course she was," Marvin chimed in cordially, his moustache arching over the breadth of an inebriate's grin.

"Whoa," said a voice from behind us. Michael had cast aside his sheet for shorts but no shirt. Nancy was right; he was almost alarmingly thin. I couldn't be sure of what he heard, but he had sized up the situation and realized a pleasant, moanful evening was about to rip apart.

Willie ignored him and took a step closer to Mary Jane. "I thought that sucked."

"See?" Marvin fluted with calm irrelevance.

"Divorce sucks," Willie continued.

Marvin continued with interjections to no one in particular. "I told you."

"Except yours," she corrected.

Mary Jane gazed with drunken or stoned bewilderment at the girl in front of her before summoning up a coolness that was close to supernatural. "You were instructive, my dear."

"And so were you, Miss Otto."

Marvin suddenly saw himself as peacemaker, dropping the game boxes to the ground again and trying to put an arm around Willie's shoulders. "Come on, Wilhelm, sit down and play with...us. With us. We'll bury the hatchet."

"Yeah, in my back, Marvin." She ducked under his arm. "And stop making me into a fucking jack-in-the-box."

He was undeterred. "She called me Marvin. I could kiss her."

It was Michael who dragged her back to the porch. "Come on, Will. They're unglued."

"And, Mike," his father asked, "you're half butt-naked. Except your butt. Need a loan?"

I could hear Willie saying to Michael, "I've seen her four frigging times. This time I couldn't hold back. The bitch." She seemed ready to move toward Mary Jane again, but Michael bear-hugged her until she fell back against him with the weariness of contention. The calico cat moved through us again, comfortable with the ways of humans and looking again for a leg to rub against. The choice was Marvin who seemed not to notice, and the animal finally sat atop the Monopoly box, wetting whiskers with a serenely closed paw. A flash of Eleanor Jewett stroked past me, and I had to think one of the luxuries of being a cat is you don't kick doors.

Regardless, here, in my very first front yard, before my place of retreat, was another slack-webbed configuration standing as if there was no retreat—except this grouping had doubled the size of the one in the living room. Independence Day had probably ended by this time—I doubted anyone of us knew what time it was—and if so, the day of celebration checked out, leaving the six of us, and possibly even the cat, strung together with this muggy negative dependency. We were such a snarly mess of badly coached actors that, whatever the role of coincidence in thumbing fantasies about individual will, it had left off its laughing mask and hovered about us in frowning contempt. Jeremiah, Nancy, Willie, Michael, Mary Jane and Marvin—lover and lover, parent and child, former and current, teacher and pupil, escapist and confronter—a team of graceless, unsorted emotions and inside-out convictions trying to believe in themselves while making do with only far-off whiffs of intuition. I tumbled once again through the images of the day: white hots, farting dog, "A Mideast Proposal," untied boots and sheets and toilets that rocked, Monopoly money spilling outward, the noise of "Yoo-hoo" and metal on the floors and "Jerry," the taunting newness of a flannel shirt, and beds crashing in the night. There was heat lightning in the distance or fireworks whose sound was unable to reach us; the air itself had taken on a stillness that matched our own as we stood without the benefit of a plausible next step—until, finally, Michael said:

"What the hell." He spoke with a voice of increasing steadiness and volume. He was still standing behind his apparently exhausted lover with his arms linked under her breasts. "Am I the smartest idiot here? I was having a pretty good night until you all started messing with each other. I was about as happy as I'm probably going to be. I mean, there's stuff that sucks and stuff that doesn't. I know we are what we are...and things, I guess, are what they are, but do we have to make a bad film out of everything? I guess I just want to get my things and go home, although a guy can have more than one home and more than one person who makes him feel good if he has the right picture in his head."

He let go of Willie, and when Nancy attempted to touch his head, he moved to avoid her. I could hear him leading Willie quietly up the stairs to the second floor. Even her boots had become noiseless. Marvin and Mary Jane moved in a sidling way to the hamlet's narrow roadway, leaving the two games on the lawn. Nancy hesitated and then moved into the living room, where I could hear the noise of the Boston rocker pulling faint cries from the floorboards. It was, to finish Michael's film metaphor, a slow dissolve. Only the cat was unmoved.

PART THREE:

Settlement

ONE

In the days following the Fourth, I began to notice the familiar tug of August. It wasn't quite what Jefferson had said. After all, I wasn't going back to school for the first time in more than two decades. I was breaking from a primary rhythm of my life. But there was, nonetheless, a pull that felt like an unbranded inevitability, cousin to what I felt all those years leading up to this one. August, and then autumn, would bring untried challenges. The weather would change, and the warmth that had made homesteading feel like a camp-out in its early stages would give way to the challenge of heating a house the way it had been over the century and more of its existence. The practical Nancy Feller had told me I could install a workable version of central heat for ten or fifteen-thousand dollars, and she was unimpressed by what she called my "pioneering pecker-headedness." I admired her cleverness, but there are those things you know you will give into at some point that are all the more resistible because of it. I knew it would be only a year or two. I was twenty-seven. I needed, for whatever reason, to see how adaptable I was to this new transition, this new demand of the calendar. I would need to work out a settlement with the call of the obvious.

Late on the night of the Fourth, Nancy had sat silently on the rocker after her son and Willie dropped onto the mattress that now kissed the floorboards of my room. Five or ten minutes later she had risen, saying "Your additional problem, Jeremiah, is you're too hungry to take part in not being part of anything." I couldn't recall what the other problems were. She kissed me with a deep, probing kiss that was scolding in part. While I lay on the couch later, I thought sadly of how her having come to curl beside me turned into frames of Michael's bad film. She had promised, though, with steely assurance that she would find her way to trying it again when and if her blood pressure normalized. I missed her more that night than I had at any time since...whenever—since ever, most probably.

Michael, Willie, and I put the bed back together the next morning, and the three of us gave it a bounce-test. Nothing had broken. Their enthusiastic love-making had apparently knocked it out of its grooves, and Willie commented with real satisfaction, "I bet I was conceived in a bed like this. In a less fucked-up world, people would tell you those things." Downstairs, we poured three bowls of Cheerios and sat on P.Q.'s back porch, where Willie told us she thought she had recognized Mary Jane when she and Michael dropped by Marvin's apartment in February.

"But I didn't catch her last name," she explained. "And I think, what are the frigging odds that the bitch is getting it on with Mike's gelding of an old man? Then," she continued with a rising voice and removing the last of the cereal from the bowl with the tip of a finger, "the first time we came out here to see what kind of mess you were getting into, she's down the road, in your wreck of a store—right?—arguing with some guy about the crap they put in dog food. She looked at me and I looked at her, and I swear we almost linked our nightmare memory of each other—but she started sneezing and leaking snot and looking for anything to blow into and I headed back here. I mean, what's that all about? She's all of sudden like this new smell in my life, the kind you can't get off your shoe after you step in it. It's crazy. And then last night—sorry if I wrecked your neighborhood. But her and Marvin and the whole thing?" She stood. "What are we all doing here, you know?" With that, they gathered their things and left.

For most of next three days, I puttered and watched. It was the part of the season where daily changes in growing things had stark visibility. Fruit trees were putting out secondary bursts of growth. Even Nancy's pint-sized plum tree extended its slight branches six inches at a time. I thought of the line from Eudora Welty about how nature "pervades"—a word I had loved her for giving to me but now saw and understood more fully. Michael's garden was showing the pods of snow peas and spinach large enough to take bites from. His plum tomatoes had toe-sized fruits, and I looked ahead to standing gratefully before them and pulling them into my mouth. Clumps of what I would learn to know as coral bells and astilbes and dianthus and hostas were gifts from hands of the past—from men dressed as Boy Scouts perhaps—that grew near foundation stones and in shady places along the boundaries of the property. My yard continued to look more and more like *lawn*, and I had grown to love the odor of gas going from its can into the mower and the smell of the clippings themselves and how robins would hop about the mowings with a measure of trust and gratitude after I had finished. My fingers gradually became better at removing weeds without injuring the plants around them, and I would drop the pulled weeds like a careful banker onto a starter compost pile I had begun at the far end of the sheds. I began removing the collapsing tops of daffodils, learning to feel the proper pull of separation that kept the bulbs from coming with them. Those, too, I added to the pile. It all seemed good.

I considered, at the same time, words that had been spoken on the night of the Fourth. In the low-thought zone of chores, I found myself rereading scraps of what we had told one another. Nancy had brought so many ideas with her that night—about marriage, parenting, and the kinds of things normal couples eventually come to feel the need for, even if *normal* was a concept of monkish origins, I imagined. But she had experienced what I had not—the desire to exchange permanent vows with another and the nonbiological complexities of creating a child. She had disavowed the vows, of course, but not the long contrail of birth she had shown in the presence of her rather grown-up son that evening. Did I want a child? I didn't think so. Would I? It was a question she was right to ask, and I was without an answer, even to myself. She had reminded me again that I had too many ideas, but whether I had any idea of being a parent...I didn't know. Many my age *were*, and Nancy had had Michael when she was twenty-five. She was probably correct in charging that I tended to use people for my amusement, but did that mean I was a *user*? Was it the same thing? Did it imply a kind of cruelty as opposed to floating in the intricacies of others? Would I use a child—my child—as a thing of amusement? Or would I be wrong not to? And could my child, if I wished to have one, come from a woman who felt herself to be beyond all that? Would we need to be bound by, not biology, but the rhythms of need felt and need surrendered to time? Even adoption, she seemed to be saying, was a choice she could not imagine making. The parenting part of her had been fine—and fine was enough. Then, too, there she was, proclaiming not only her willingness but her desire to be looked at—what was her word?—that the world look at her "askance." The word had so much resonance it had the pull of two decades ringing from it. It was a word for a schoolmarm who could mold worlds. Would that be our offspring—that calmly defiant view of those who viewed us?

In her absence, she sounded throughout me, and I ached.

§

After more than a week, I had heard nothing back from Ellen. I had launched a taut possibility into space, but for now there was no way to track its trajectory. As I waited, I thought of the divided picture I had created over the course of so many years. I had come to envision her as both a moving and a stationary object. The conception of her traveling from place to place as an itinerant spirit, like a medieval troubadour, satisfied my hope that she was free, if nothing else—that she was not bound to another, perhaps, any more than she was to me—which meant she had the freedom to return. Alternately, though, I had pictured her as cloistered in some manner, planted within a dimension of purpose that was both less and more than my own—rooted in constancy and free in a different sense from the dissatisfaction of wavering. When she had suggested our meeting, she was clearly in motion, at least for that interval of time. It was Nancy who had given me careful instructions about transplanting the plum tree to keep it from experiencing root-shock. Had Ellen, had my one-time mother, so situated herself that she could choose when and if to attempt our reunion again or was she replanted where that might never happen?

Or was I, as another alternative, so committed to constructing either-or patterns that whole other scenarios were just as likely? I thought of the time she had spent with my father's parents, absorbing the fretful ways of theater before suppressing them under the skin of a community college instructor. How she had wrenched herself free at such an early age from the Italian enclave in the Bronx was a detail she had never wished to explain, though it never sounded as if she had been estranged from them. I did wonder what she might have told them had become of me after she vacated The Professor's world. In *Reconsiderations*, Maud, noting a leak in the ceiling above them, says, "*Family* is scored to resound with trumpets...until the notes are seized by kazoos." Maud was, after all, a guru of the kitchen table, meaning it was something to consider.

§

For the first time since I moved to Quaker Falls, I experienced the need to get out of the house. That is, get out of the house, out of the property, out of the hamlet. I had worked steadily for most of six weeks and had liked what I was doing. Mostly. I had loved creating each day as a sequence of tasks, some of which only provoked unimagined new ones and some of which signified a step taken that would not need to be taken again for a foreseeable time or forever. I had read nothing besides instruction manuals during that period, joking to Michael at one point that I was dumbing myself into a new form of enlightenment. He was pleased to hear it, and I believed it most of the time. But ownership does own one back, to paraphrase what Thoreau had said in *Walden* as he mooched off of Emerson to conduct his pond-side experiment in dropping out. I wondered whether freeloading was, finally, the purest form of possession since it can only expect disapproval at some point.

Driving with no goal was immediately freeing. I had made any number of trips to hardware stores and lumber centers, and I had brought Miss Jewett for her curious visit. Now, I hoped to accomplish nothing, although I provided structure by going slowly past my childhood home where a handsome leather-brown sign on the front lawn confirmed its reinvention as a visitors' center for his university—as Louisa had told me. I fought the snide idea that it was continuing to be what it always had been, but I was secretly pleased that it looked better tended than it had in the recent past, freshly painted and with the landscaping trimmed and modified. It looked more collegiate than it ever had. I also drove through my former campus, and I was gladdened to see several dozen Canadian geese on one of the prominent quadrangles, signaling the president must be at his vacation retreat in the Hamptons.

I drove down the Old Post Road to where a variety of fast food outlets were strung along the outside edges of shopping centers. I had, during my weeks of homesteading, been eating simply but healthily and even going for an occasional run on the back roads that fed into Quaker Falls. On this day, however, I wanted crap. I wanted artery-clogging juices to run down my fingers; and I chose a place with burritos the size of a folded *New York Times* and ate two with all the pleasure of perversity. I washed it down with a fully sugared Coke and celebrated the play of ice cubes as I refilled. It was the meal of a condemned man, though at least he would be spared the repentance of it—something I hoped not to do on this day of unlimbering counter-purposes.

It wasn't until the end of the second burrito that I felt the familiarity of a boxy structure across the street—as blandly colored as an antacid tablet. It was the building containing the office of Joanna Wexler, Esq., and I knew that my journey to nowhere in particular was over—if, in fact, that hadn't been my intended goal the entire time. I crossed Route 9 on foot, leaving the Dakota under the shadow of the restaurant's oversized, two-dimensional cactus.

I was greeted solemnly by the same male secretary whom I had briefly met the last time I visited the lawyer. I couldn't remember his name, but I remembered his pony-tail, which had grown noticeably longer in the months since I was there. He seemed to recognize me and announced brusquely that she wasn't there before dropping his fingers to his computer keyboard in a gesture of dismissal. I stood still, hoping the lack of movement would cause him to look at me again. I studied his face in profile, the scattering of pockmarks in his hollowed cheeks, the sharp angle of his chin, and the feeling he too reminded me of someone. He was trying to give his fingers instructions that would get them working again, but they remained paralyzed above the keys.

"Is it something personal?" I asked at last.

"Pardon me?" His head turned deliberately toward me. His eyes had gray haloes around them, but the pupils themselves were a keenly focused shade of bluish-green, not unlike my own.

"Your poorly executed dismissiveness. Is it something about me personally?"

His chair spun in my direction, his disapproving face now looking directly at me. "I sense things about people that make me behave badly if I don't watch myself." I wondered whether people associated with Joanna Wexler have such a thing about behaving badly that it makes them want to share it outwardly with others.

"And are you behaving badly right now?"

"*You* might think so."

"And you've heard things about me...such as?"

"I sense things," he re-emphasized.

"And these *sensations* have presumably come via your boss?"

He pushed on the chair arms as if he were about to stand, then eased himself back down again. "Where else would I get it?" He paused, considering. "For the last few months, she seems to be...fixated on you."

"Oh?"

"Like you're a new toy in her life."

"Did you just say toy?"

He snorted slightly. "She talks about your luncheon like it was a sacred holiday, and she keeps asking if you've called or e-mailed—like a dumb-struck teenager."

"I assure you I'm not her anything. So if you've got your own thing with her, it won't be me who's going to be cutting in."

"Then what is it?"

"What is it with her? I wish I knew. She does have a way of making me feel like I'm part of a scheme. Does she do that to you?"

"At times." He shook his head wearily, and I thought I saw in him a person detached from the day-to-day, a kind of Bartleby who spent most of his waking hours in this office. Yet, he had disappeared during my first visit there, supposedly because he didn't like the sound of argumentation. Where had he gone to that time?

"Why do you work for her?" I asked. He was clearly unsure of the purpose of the question, and I realized it could imply any number of things. "Why did she hire you? You're not most people's idea of a legal secretary." He said nothing. "You were in prison."

"She told you?'

"Where else would I get it?" It occurred to me that I not only might be acting like a damn fool but I might also be generating enough annoyance to cause him to come after me. Confrontation had never been my A-game, but a charm offensive was obviously out of the question here. Hamilton Graham had already made it clear that—as far as he was concerned—I had lost whatever schooled advantages I might have thought I had. I had never charmed Willie Furman, as much as others might have thought so and for whatever reason, as much as I wished to. Even people like Eleanor Jewett, who seemed to find me worth engaging, saw past my defenses with disarming ease. Hausfrau: an interesting term for a homesteader.

"She was proud to be saying it...about prison," I told him. "She may have been trying to see how I would react, but she wasn't giving up any dark secrets. She must value you."

"She hired me out of prison. I got a paralegal degree while I was in." He spoke crisply with an air of justification that was both candid and defiant. "We've been together a respectable length of time, and I'm good at what I do."

"Yes, he is."

Joanna Wexler had apparently entered her inner office through a private door. She stood viewing us with her Navaho bag tucked under one arm. She looked tired and thinner in an attractive way, her silken blouse wrinkled but exposing the tanning her cleavage had received from the summer sun. Willie had told me that her mother lived in a condo with a large community pool where Joanna unwound by "baking" on a chaise. Willie herself spent little time at her mother's, crashing wherever she could, referring to the condo as her has-been home. "I hired Bartlett because he's talented and because he got screwed by our legal system—not necessarily in that order." That's right—*Bartlett*. "He did serious time in Greenhaven for low-level dealing and possession when the Rockefeller Laws were still at their horrid worst. Did you think I got him out to be my fancy man?"

"Pot?" I asked him.

"Mostly." He was still sitting, looking from one to the other of us with clinical appraisal.

"And, Jeremiah, did you come to see Bartlett or me? Or both? Have you missed us?"

"Must be," I told her. "I was across the street doing a Mexican food romance to an embarrassing degree and I got this silent summons."

"What is it that you want?" Her voice had the same edge of anger Bartlett's had earlier.

"It's good I came. Your...assistant...has been hearing charges of rampant misconduct on my part, and I do need to protect my virtue." I turned to him abruptly. "Did you really think I was shagging your boss?"

Bartlett blanked and Joanna moved to stand next to him. "My daughter's right," she said between firmly locked lips. "You can be alarmingly silly."

"Regardless," I said. "Let me assure you, Bartlett, that whatever your worries might be, they are groundless, bedless, and whatever else. I used to teach stories. While I learned you can never be sure where they come from, you can be even *more* unsure of what they're intended to do."

Joanna had deposited her bag on his desk by this point and went to stand protectively behind him, her hands on the back of his chair. "And would you care, Jeremiah, to ask Bartlett if he's your other lost brother? He believes, Bartlett, that there are missing siblings scattered about the area and a mother trying to make her way back to him. But as you can see, Bartlett is a little old for the role." He didn't take that well, giving the same spot on the keyboard several staccato taps.

It was quite a performance on her part, and I didn't know if she was simply an unpleasant person whose difficulties in being close to others added to the unpleasantness—or whether a need to hide from some inner truth had made her devastatingly brittle. "You see, Jeremiah, not every aha moment comes with the ratings we were hoping for. I'm sorry to see you go through the twists and turns you've been wearing yourself out with since I got to know you this spring. It's good you have an abandoned house to play with. It's a fancy you can at least sit within and lock the door when you want."

"As you wish," I replied.

Joanna looked at me with a searchlight fixedness. "I'm sure Alban Curtin would be pleased to know we've been busy helping you to learn that not everyone in the world will think you're perfect just the way you are."

"Why thank you for invoking his spirit." It was obvious once again that even an unplanned session with Joanna Wexler was apt to go nowhere. Whatever it was that she was protecting—a person, a reputation, a needed payback, or positioning—she had the determination and skills to hold her ground.

"And have you figured out the meaning of March twenty-second yet?"

"I haven't," I responded. "It might mean nothing actually. He had the wiring of an existentialist. In his mind, coming face to face with nothing could be the ultimate act of self-discovery. But screw it, I don't know. Do you? You're the one who spent so much time with him doing whatever you were doing. Wouldn't a meaningless clue be just the cherry on his cupcake?"

"I doubt he ate cupcakes. If he did, I never saw it." She picked up the cloth bag. "Would you like Bartlett to set up an appointment so you and I can delve deeper?"

Bartlett looked at me with the icy anticipation of one who was daring me to do just that. "Thanks to both of you," I said. "I am a hopeful person—in spite of what you may have suggested just before—but I hope we all won't have to be that necessary to each other."

The orange Dakota waited for me like a gaudy steed, in a way my Toyota never had. On the day of purchase, Woo told me the color was some guy doing lipstick with a paint gun—that there had never been an orange Dakota in its history. That was enough for me: I was not only buying a truck but also conducting a rescue mission. On this day, it was still new enough to my life to feel it had been anxious for my return and would reward me with the prompt feeling of partnership. It had taken me several days to become comfortable with the stick shift rising from a hump in the middle of the floor. I had to be thankful to Sara Sampson during our time together for shaming me into confronting a standard transmission. She had warned me that if I ever came with her to Wyoming and it became known I couldn't drive stick, I would be run out of the state as a probable pedophile, but she did promise that she, like any girl from her part of the world, had enough testosterone get me out of there alive.

I drove to one of the parking areas for the Walkway Over the Hudson. It was full, which normally would have sent me on my way. On this day, I was willing to wait, idling until a group of Sikh men and women—turbaned and scarfed and sandaled—approached a car and signaled me to wait for their spot. The Walkway, in its few years of existence, had become a melting strip—a little over a mile on top of what had initially been the world's longest railroad trestle and still called an architectural wonder in publicity blurbs. The span was no wider than a double driveway, and on days like this a thousand or more hikers, joggers, bikers, skateboarders, dog-walkers, little ones in strollers, and wheelchair riders would flow in and out of each other's' paths as they crossed and re-crossed the Walkway from the Poughkeepsie or the Highland side. Ages, races, nationalities, breeds, and anything else mixed and remixed into what Michael Feller had called a "soul-braid" the one time he and I had attempted a roundtrip run together. He had stopped frequently to take pictures, interruptions that normally would have annoyed me, but not on that day. I ran in place while people flowed around the photographer, more of his growing passion to put movement into the glass jar of his imagination in the form of sealed images.

Part of the atmosphere of the Walkway was seeing the brief encounters of people recognizing each other, pausing for a minute or floating words and signals back and forth without stopping. On this day, I saw two couples from the neighborhood I grew up in and the woman from the registrar's office whom I had smoked out of my life. The couples, about The Professor's age, were doing a shared outing in a personally defined assortment of shoes, shorts, hats, and accessories. There was no prescribed form of being cool for people a couple of hundred feet above the surface of the Hudson. The Walkway was a club whose only dress code was built upon mutual acceptance. Pam from the registrar was with a gentleman wearing a pith helmet and other elements of what looked like a safari outfit. They were holding hands, and if she saw me, she didn't show it.

About mid-bridge on my return journey from the Highland side, I came face to face with two-thirds of The Triumvirate: Chuck Gillis and Phyllis Friel. They were seated near a sign displaying a variety of fish found in the river. As I was about to loop out of their line of vision, they waved me over with synchronized hand gestures. There was nothing clandestine about their being together. They were two longtime colleagues out for exercise and a chance to catch up on things. There was no reason to think otherwise.

"Greetings," Phyllis said. Her legs were crossed with one knee over the other and her ankles locked in a position that looked painful. "Come pass a restful minute with us." Gillis patted the section of bench next to him, but I remained standing. He was dressed pretty much as he had been the last time I saw him, in shorts and a Notre Dame jersey, showing, however, the fitter look of a person who has received a medical wake-up. He asked how the process of renewal was coming with his skill at showing an interest in something whether it was a true interest or not. I admired him for it.

My former chair was less interested in my home and more in getting my reactions to events on campus. "You've heard Richard Woo is now chair?" I hadn't and said so. She unlocked her ankles slightly, creating a quiet clicking sound in one of her joints. "Just yesterday, actually," she went on, "so I doubt much of anybody knows."

"He may turn out to be a worthy choice," Chuck suggested. "I doubt anyone else wanted it, and he, of course, can be counted on to keep a low profile and quiet demeanor."

"What," I asked them, probing but trying to sound a note of detachment at the same time, "is anyone to make of all that's been happening?"

Phyllis seemed pleased with the question. "Rachel, of course, should have known better." She looked briefly at Gillis. "He knows?" Chuck nodded, and she went on. "Of course, he does. You're a creature of the academy, Jeremiah. There will come a time again when you will need to understand these lapses in judgment. Rachel is an exact demonstration of how sins can become crimes if we're not careful to guard them. And she, to speak the obvious, was outré enough to broadcast hers to the world."

"The proverbial hand that feeds her," Chuck offered in shorthand.

"You mean she owes her soul to the company store?" I said, referring to a lyric on a country CD I'd recently purchased as a present for the Dakota.

"'Sixteen Tons,'" Chuck said and started singing the phrase in a surprisingly strong baritone voice.

Phyllis turned to him with a look of surprise, one lacking in approval. "There are people like Rachel," she instructed, "who believe they should be thanked for going public about what is, after all, internal business. I can see you making the same mistake, Jeremiah. You have that quality about you. Save it until you retire."

"I've already retired."

"I doubt it. Don't you, Charles?" He nodded.

Inevitably, I thought of The Professor and shifted the subject. "You told me, Phyllis, that you talked with my father last fall."

"Did I?"

"Did you?"

Gillis straightened himself as if we were about to take him into a private garden. Phyllis generated the studied look of one who would have stroked her beard if she had one. Whether she was hedging or trying to recall having spoken to me or whether she'd made it up if she had, she was not quite prepared to satisfy either my or Chuck Gillis's interest. While she combed her thoughts, I looked out over the railing behind them at the river moving toward us from the north. It was a hazy day, July hammock weather, the rounded shape of Overlook Mountain visible in the far distance. I had heard stories of the train engineers in the final days of the trestle before it caught fire in the early 1970s—how they received a type of combat pay to locomotive across the structure but also, hopefully, took the view as enough of a bonus to justify any risk.

Phyllis finally got her bearings. "Well, yes, I did talk to Alban Curtin, but I don't remember saying that to you."

"Were you sworn to secrecy?" I asked her.

"No, certainly not. I can't imagine such a thing. He merely called me as a long-time acquaintance to see how his son was doing in his first semester of teaching."

"A nice gesture," Gillis commented. I had learned over the year that for Chuck anything with the word "nice" attached to it meant it would have drawn the approval of his Samuel Johnson.

"And how did he sound?" I asked Phyllis Friel.

"Sound?"

"Was he worried that I was going to disgrace the family name?"

She locked her ankles again. "He thought, in fact, that you were too insecure to screw up—although I don't know if he used that term or another, but that was the gist. However, he added that as far as he was concerned, it was best for all of us."

"My insecurity? And you two never feel insecure?"

"After all this time?" Gillis wondered.

"It goes away?" I asked him.

"Wouldn't you imagine?" His voice bubbled with pleasure, a verbal cocktail tilted in my direction.

"Too bad," I responded.

Phyllis batted at what I had said, waving a hand at an imagined insect. "We all have days. But we also know that *we* know more than *they* know. It keeps us well grounded."

"And does what you don't know do that as well?" It was a question either of my parents might have asked.

"My young friend," she scolded, "are you trying to conduct a department meeting, even in your position as fugitive emeritus?"

Gillis liked the question, snorting with benevolent satisfaction. "You two will miss each other, won't you?"

I looked at her. "Will we? And why are you no longer chair?" It was bad of me to ask it, but the opportunity kept trying to present itself—our narrowing dialogue becoming a walkway of its own. I had come to realize over recent months that I actually liked Phyllis. I didn't trust or respect her, which made it a queer form of liking, but I had begun to feel sympathy for her nonetheless. Her insecurities were clearly greater than mine and she had so little time to come to terms with them—if that is what we were expected to do.

"I thought it time to bow to the audience and leave one of my many stages. It was a form of rehearsal."

"It was just so sudden," Gillis told her, repeating what he had said to me on-campus a month earlier. He still hadn't digested it and seemed pleased to have this unexpected chance to revisit it. "It took my breath away—that and my visit to the cardiologist."

She shook her head. "There's no need for either of you to be put off by my simple decision—sudden or not." She stood abruptly and turned to face the river, looking like she was trying to hear a sound reaching up from it. With her back to us still, she repeated one word three times: "Sins, sins, sins." She finally turned back with a puckered smile on her lips. "Your father did say one odd thing, Jeremiah."

"Only one?"

She had no further desire to equivocate. "He said you came into the world a changeling and you would no doubt leave as an un-changeling. I imagine that's close to how he said it."

"Imagine that. The good Professor Curtin," I told them, "was occasionally so clever he squeaked."

"Do you think," Gillis asked with the satisfaction of one with insider knowledge, "you were swapped for a goatherd's child and that's why you've taken to country matters?"

"I don't think it works that way, Chuck. But it's a captivating idea." I wished them well and completed my crossing, trying not to think about my father's latest clue. Whether his statement to Phyllis was ever intended to reach me, her delivery system had made it worth a listen.

TWO

One day, I found in the handle of my screen door a note from Bill down the road informing me there was news he thought would be of interest. He didn't indicate the nature of that news, but I did learn his last name from the note when he signed it "William 'Bill' Gaussmann." It was a rock solid name for a guy whose wife called him "Bobo." That he had left a note was odd since I had been at the house almost constantly since my visit to Joanna Wexler's and The Walkway. Nancy and Michael were at the Jersey Shore, maintaining a family tradition as a twosome rather than a family of three. Willie and I had both been invited, but my growing sense of urgency about the coming of fall kept me rooted in place. Willie had a summer job at the area's largest mall selling tickets at a Cineplex—where, presumably, she wouldn't have to change her storm-boots to sit behind a counter.

The newlyweds stopped by briefly to check on my progress. Barbara Lynn had cleaned out her office on the evening of June 30, as close to her evacuation deadline as she could cut it. She had asked for an adjunct position in her old department, but was told by someone—whom she had simply named "Asshole"—that the school didn't think it would be a good thing to offer part-time work to a faculty member who had basically been told to shove off. It would, as she explained, pollute the pure waters of the institution. So she complained about having nothing to do while Emily noted that she had to work year-round with occasional days off and that the adjustment issues of those she worked with didn't take summer breaks. Still, their love, if anything, seemed to have deepened, and they promised to play Meals on Wheels soon to keep me from eating twigs and acorns.

I called Richard Woo, trying to lure him and his wife and daughter to share a pizza in my backyard. He asked for a raincheck, wondering where I would find a decent pie in "God's country," but mostly he was beginning to freak out about agreeing to be chair.

"I can't believe it, Jeremiah. I can't believe I'm doing it. I just today realized I'm going to have to put my sketchpad away during meetings unless I want to draw ridiculous caricatures of myself." How did it happen? "I was just enough drunk—only two shots of tequila, mind you—when His Eminence the dean called. It was after dinner, and no one with anything serious to propose should be allowed to do such a deed after the belly is satisfied. On top of that, Christina, my daughter who still owes you a huge hug for the dog and cat book, was watching the same film for the thirtieth time at least, which had me feeling frenzied as well as tipsy. But you do these things, you know? You don't want to tell her that she's going to permanently frost her brain when she's enjoying herself, and you could leave the room, but I was contributing a couple of minutes to family time when the dean made his thoughtless intrusion." And what did Richard tell him? "I said, naturally, that I would think about it, but it was clear he'd marked that on his board of good deeds as a booming acceptance on my part. Before he clicked off, he was already talking about the extra pennies that would go into my pension. Do you know how much extra a chair makes?" I assured him I really didn't—that I'd never thought about it. "Enough to buy a few of your frozen pizzas and not much else. They were to be of the freezer variety, I assume?" I assured him they would be the real deal. Then, he paused after the flat-picking of his narrative—a banjo term I owed fondly to him. "Do you know what really feels bad about this whole thing as if sitting like a sucky toad in the Dean's Council isn't enough?" Rachel, I ventured. "Precisely. Our Rachel. Your partner in crime. After she gets sent to The Principal's Office"—his voice capitalized the three words—"for doing what any of the rest of us with balls should have been doing right along with her, I come loping onto campus like an old nag." Had he talked to her? "Of course. I couldn't apologize enough. She wanted to throttle me—not for being the Successor Stooge"—he capitalized again—"but for apologizing at all. She said she's never felt as good as she has since she got the ax. She loves that her thing went viral and that His Excrescence looked to be frightened of her when he did his deed." I told him to convey a tasteful hooray to her when he saw her again. "I will. I most humbly will. She also said I would most likely be good at the chair thing, and I could serve as the champion of quiet people and doodlers. That's pretty heady stuff, I suppose."

I had the feeling that Richard would be a thoughtful and interesting chair once he got over the sensation of coming into the position butt first. My interest would be at a distance and would, of course, fade over time, but, like driving past The Professor's house, I hoped my feeling of one-time residency would actually grow to be a better one. I popped an e-mail to Rachel VanNoys, urging her to keep the new chair forever hopeful and congratulating her again for giving conviction CPR. Her response was brief: "I hear the beat."

§

As I walked to Bill Gaussmann's house, I saw Mary Jane Otto standing like a ship's figurehead on the step leading from her front porch. I didn't remember having seen her motionless before; she was one of those who projected movement even while standing still. She was a snow globe of a person for whom the flakes seemed never to settle completely. On this day, though, she was rooted to the spot and could have been standing that way on that spot for hours or days. Steverino was in the enclosed porch behind her, scratching daintily at the aluminum of the screen door, making it sound like the snares of a collapsed and discarded drum. If she heard him, there was no indication in her stare toward the rear side of The Emporium across the way. It seemed I could pass by without her noticing or caring, but her pained woodenness drew me toward her.

"Mary Jane?" She blinked at me but looked unable to decide whether to speak or not. "Has something happened?" The dog began staccato yips, sad in their own right.

"Nobody's died if that's what you're wondering." She said it dismissively before finally looking at me. "Oh, Jerry. It's you. Our little village has grown forlorn on this day. That's all."

It was actually one of those exceptional July days when a fair-weather breeze brought small but shapely clouds from the north and made tree leaves flutter their undersides upward. It was a day you wanted to pin in place. "Marvin's all right?"

"He wouldn't understand—and I wouldn't tell him!" she said with a look of alarm. She turned and let the dog out but ignored him as he stretched a forepaw up one of her legs.

"And?"

"Violation. Simple violation. It is a world of violators, as I am once again to discover."

In that moment, I was genuinely frightened for her, thinking of the worst. "Someone...did something to you?"

She straightened to her full height. "To me? Certainly not. Why would you even suggest such a thing? Not to me, Jerry, not to the me you see." She finally came down off the step and gazed dreamily at where the yard extended to the side and back. "There is a me beyond me," she said like an enchantress. "There is each little flower and every piece of grass and there might even be more, you see?" I didn't see. "Our pure little Quaker Falls," she continued, "has the taint of the slums. And you should know it. You should be aware."

I still didn't see. "Should I?"

"Yes," she exclaimed. "You should be aware of...predators!"

It was a chilling performance, and I was impelled by it to venture a guess. "Something has been taken?"

"Yes, of course it has!"

"Namely?"

Her voice softened to a funneled whisper. "Oh Jerry, I can't tell you that."

I began to see, wishing I could walk to the rear of her corn patch to find out for myself. It was a dreadful moment. How does a proper lady tell anyone that her illegal plants have been relieved of their place in her garden. And how, at the same time, does one console that lady without admitting he knows through snooping what has most likely happened to her: a peaceful violation, the work of neighborhood kids with a lot of summer left to fill and a keen eye for cannabis? I doubt they had mussed one tassel of one corn plant but violation nonetheless. Devastation. A person as disconnected as Mary Jane Otto probably had no place she could buy a bag of the stuff—not like a college student. This was her way of sustaining a reasonably pleasant habit: cleaning the seed from each year's ladylike harvest to plant the following season and carefully meting out her stash through the winter months.

I wondered how many years she had been comforting herself with this sure cycle, confident in nature's way of returning good treatment. And now it had been broken. As I'd assumed, Marvin hadn't been invited fully into her toker's boudoir, only into her bed. To tell the new man in her life that she was a pot grower must have tested even her powers of inclusion. Besides, I could well believe this woman of so many men over so many years may have come to cherish a secret she could hold in her lungs or hide in her potato salad.

I felt badly for her, honestly. But what to say? I promised myself I would at some point bivouac through the back meadow to inspect the garden to make sure I had identified the violation correctly. Undoubtedly that was the point of attack for the marauders. I owed each of us that much. What to do about her depleted harvest from last year—her little weed-bank—was another question to be worked out or let die. It was a conundrum The Professor would have relished, and it was like Marty and Maud had arranged things so I could negotiate one of those slippery gray areas that made learning an adventure launched upon banana peels.

Suddenly, as if it all didn't matter—and as if I was completely off the mark–she brought up Willie Furman. "That girl who aligns herself with Marvin's son—what's her name?" I told her. "Yes. That one. Did I understand her to say that I had been her teacher? I was a little...tired... that night, mind you, so I didn't hear her right. But I do remember her coming toward me and Marv like a wild boar. And I think she was wearing shoes far too big for her."

"Hiking boots."

"Laces flying in every direction. Isn't it interesting the things you remember?"

"I still have a couple of games you brought over. You left them."

"We did? Games?"

"Games."

She was losing the focus she had gotten from the shoelaces. "What kind of games?"

"*Neighborly* games, you called them."

"Well, I'm sure they were. And what exactly was her problem?"

I was hoping her focus would keep loosening and even considered consoling her on the pillaging of her garden to avoid going in this new and unmarked direction. With Willie Furman at the hub of any situation, it was unlikely to go well. "What do you recall?" I asked as tactfully as I was able.

"Teacher," Mary Jane reminded. "She said teacher."

"She might have."

"Might have and did. She said I taught her, didn't she? Since I only taught for three months the last time I tried it, she was tied up in my leaving." She challenged her memory. "I called her a name, didn't I?" She became fully alive to the recollection, nearly stepping on Steverino who was lying in the grass near her feet. "She's the brat who got me fired, isn't she?" I held back. "Her father came in. Some jock with a crew cut. He tried to work things out with the principal. Then her mother came. She wanted my ass out of there or she was going to sue the school district. Unbelievable, wouldn't you say? Jerry?"

"I'm sure you were a good teacher," I suggested weakly, wishing I could move on to Bill Gaussmann and his model trains.

"I was. I was good. I didn't just teach them the boring stuff. I brought in paintings. I played them music. Classical music. Brahms and Bach and that other B guy."

"Beethoven."

"Berlioz! Beethoven was too pompous," she reflected. "Berlioz told stories. Ah, such stories."

"Organ music?" I asked tentatively.

"Of course. Soaring music. But not Berlioz. The other one."

"Bach."

She took a deep breath. "Don't you think that was progressive of me? The other times I taught, I did the same thing. No problems. Not a one." She explained having had four or five different stints as a teacher—moving with various husbands from one place to another, without a chance to ever establish her career. Her experience with Willie Furman and Joanna Wexler was the end of it all for her. She would jeopardize herself no more. "But why, after all these years, did she come after me that night at your house. I do remember the games now. Monopoly and...something else."

"Things get stored up," I suggested to her. "And then...you know."

"Do me a favor, Jerry. Tell this person to get over it. I did. Tell her it's bad for her."

"Bad," I echoed.

"Very bad. Bad for all of you. You should know better." With that, she opened the door to the porch, nodded at the dog to follow her, and went inside.

My attempt at becoming a genial semi-hermit was not unfolding as the saga of a man fingering a knotted beard in a cave—realizing, at the same time, that the concept of a plan consisted mostly of making compost and preventing my toilet bowl from rocking. It wasn't that I had come to the country to write a book or do watercolors or be particularly green. I was there primarily because I had presumed I didn't like where I was. Quaker Falls would be, I hoped, a destination for people who passed peaceful hours doing as little as they wished. And when they were gone, I would have opportunities to step inside myself and read what was written there—a cloudy idea that might lead to discoveries I had yet to know existed. Still, discoveries could be out there, a couple of houses down the curve of a road that had tried bending away from better traveled routes for two centuries or more. Possibly Mary Jane Otto, accompanied by the highly inconvenient Marvin, was there to provide her own lesson in convenience: that people are a difficulty only when we expect little from them.

Lucille Gaussmann beat Bill to the front entrance when I pulled on a doorknocker just beneath the porch light. The sound was made by a carved woodpecker, brightly painted and attached to the half-cylinder of a tree branch. A brass chain extended below the mounting piece, and pulling it made the bird peck out a sharply resonant signal. It was not the kind of device that would normally have gotten my attention, but my session next door had made me hyper-focused and searching for anything unusual in a pleasing way. Lucille was telling her husband that she had gotten to the door first even before she welcomed me. It was like a longstanding competition apparently, and Lucille was gently energized by it. She was in the kind of housedress I didn't know American women wore any more, one that could have stepped out of the *American Gothic* painting of the grim and desiccated farm couple. Lucille, however, was anything but desiccated. Well into her seventies, she had a softer and prettier face than I remembered from the Fourth of July happening, where she might have been as out of her element as I was.

"You found Woody," she said cheerily. "I don't believe he's had his chain pulled for ever so long."

Bill shushed her. "Be careful, Squirrel. Our guest will think you have naughty thoughts." He reached around her to open the door. "Greetings, neighbor. I see you got my invitation. Welcome aboard."

The interior greeted me with bakery smells. Its layout was similar to mine with the kitchen straight ahead down a hallway of distinctly proper floorboards. I remarked on the odor of cooking, and Lucille told me how fortunate it was I had come on baking day—their once-a-week routine, she told me, that produced a single apple pie, intended to last her Bobo for the next seven days. He clarified, with a degree of pride, that he was one of those second-rate diabetics who didn't have to stick needles into themselves and could still enjoy Lucille's baking skills if he behaved himself: "One nice slice a day—no more, but never less." She looked at him with pleasure and added, "Always French apple—the kind with raisins." We were in the kitchen by now, a beautifully modernized version of a traditional country workplace and a promise of what my sad space could become eventually. With the skill of a conjurer, Lucille had me seated at a harvest table and was cutting into the pie.

"But your husband?" I asked. "What about the rest of his week?"

"He'll have a slice with you and be good a couple of days. It won't hurt him."

Bill had slipped briefly into another part of the house and returned carrying a large envelope and moving with a noticeable bounce. "Lucille could bake for the angels," he said, "who I've always imagined would wolf down a hunk of pie when they finally put their harps down. They have to take a break at some point, wouldn't you imagine?" I pictured Nancy's seated ghosts.

"Think of the boredom," Lucille added instructively. She had placed Bill's slice in front of the chair next to mine along with a cup of coffee. She held up an empty cup, and when I shook my head she slid it behind her onto a counter. Everything she did seemed so effortless, so fluid, I was growing to see Bill as one of those blessed creatures under the spell of a personal fairy godmother. "I'm going to leave you boys alone because I know my Bill wants to share his surprise without interference."

She kissed him on the forehead, and, as if kissing her back, he said, "Actually, I imagine they would prefer lemon meringue to apple." She nodded thoughtfully, pleased by the suggestion, and moved noiselessly from the room.

He watched her with the eyes of a young suitor. "I knew a minister who would say 'Perfection is for the next life' when people complained about their setbacks. He never knew Lucille. Eat," he said, pointing at my plate with his fork.

It seemed all too purely constituted, this half-century marriage.

The brown envelope sat before us, but Bill wanted to share more of his life with Lucille first: that they had wanted children, but when it became clear that was not to be, they agreed that a long and good life with each other would be the offspring of their love. They had spent as much of their time together as they could, he selling insurance from his home office and she serving as his Girl Friday—as he termed it—though adding with gustatory pleasure between bites of pie that she was more correctly his "Girl Everyday." They had talked often about serious traveling but had not quite gotten around to it except for an occasional off-season week on Cape Cod when the crowds were gone and they could continue to have each other to themselves. She created needlepoints of stunning intricacy, two of which were on walls of the room we were in, and she had already told him she would create one for me as a welcoming present. He, of course, had his model train empire in the basement, something he had begun when they moved to this house twenty years earlier. When he learned from his realtor that this had been the station master's house for decades during train times, the passion began and had continued until now. But I would have to wait a few more minutes before he would bring me to it. He had the contents of the envelope to show me first.

He extracted several pages of material that had been produced with the uneven keystrokes of a typewriter. I had come across the same look in archival searches: the strikeovers of one letter by another, the varying shades of black and gray generated by a person whose fingers were not those of a typist.

"You got me thinking," he said, "when we talked at the end of the picnic. You asked if there was any truth to the Underground Railroad going through this settlement. I like that expression, don't you—settlement? It sounds like both a beginning and an end." He had pointed out what I had not realized before: another of those intersections of a single word that can go whichever way it wishes—a self-contained crossroad.

"It's a word with versatility," I told him, and he patted my hand like I was a grandchild.

"So I went to the town historian, a woman I know through church. Very nice. She has a sign in front of her house, like a notary. I should put up one as station master—don't you think—except Lucille would say I was carrying the train business a little too far. Or maybe not. She's usually fine with my quirks so long as I don't injure myself. My friendly historian made a copy of this for us—for you and me, that is." He held the manuscript aloft as if it were a translation of the Rosetta Stone. "Done at some point during the Depression, she thought. There's no date, but it was the kind of activity people did to keep themselves busy and feel better times were coming."

The title was all capitals at the top of the first page—given the look of bold print, I had learned, by typing over the original once or twice: **THE HISTORY OF THE UNDERGROUND RAILROAD IN QUAKER FALLS.** My pulse sped up, and I took a deep swallow, the kind of response I'd had at other times, during more scholarly researches. More, it was the way I had felt when Nancy brought the railroad book to my office, coming face to face with an effort that had ended up meaning so little to all but those few with an original desire to know what no one else cared about. Here was another filed away task, drawn back into immediacy by a simple question, and breathing again. It pulled at me like a different kind of homecoming, and Bill must have read my face.

"See what you think," he said simply.

It turned out to be the kind of investigation, years after the possibility, which offered no proof. It was based upon oral history with no clear documentation to support its suggestions. But that made it better, in spite of the way oral narratives can get twisted. In this case, voice-to-voice felt appropriate to a search looking as much for a feeling as a factual recounting.

The "History," by means of a hand-drawn map, did connect the now-Gaussmann house and my own house to several said to have been temporary hideaways for those fleeing the South. Like the others, mine, The Elmendorff house, had a small star next to it, where the sheds would be now, and the text itself offered the following:

The Elmendorffs who built the house, undoubtedly did so with the cheerful hearts of any who settle new ground. According to descendants, they first built a three-room cabin, which they added to many years later, the new, larger addition bringing them closer to the road. He ran a small print shop that underwent various changes after his death. It became a barbershop with the coming of the railroad and was said to have been a favorite gathering place for citizens of the hamlet. Well before that, however, his work as a printer not only brought a steady means of livelihood to his growing family but is said to have aided in the Abolitionist Movement. Not only had he published leaflets for the cause but is said to have provided a haven for the destitute and desperate. How many spent a day or two there we cannot be certain, but one hopes they were many. A single incident of sadness was the recapturing of a single male slave on his property and his presumed transport back to the land of degradation. Alas, the Dred Scott desecration! People assumed there was betrayal on the part of some abhorrent soul, a sad succumbing to the reward offered by cruel Paddyrollers. In memory of the freedom seeker, who may have been a freeman, the family is said to have planted a fruit tree, reputed to be a variety of the quince at a corner of the property, next to the cabin. The tree survived until recent years, when it grew diseased and was taken down.

I turned to Bill and said, "I believe it."

"Why would there be a need to doubt it?"

"Yes. There is no need."

There were about eight pages to this small manuscript in all, and he slid them carefully into the envelope again. "I made a copy for myself. This is for you. I feel awkward—a little—playing with my toy trains when I think of what these people did. What would I have done?" He considered the question briefly, rubbing a patch of dry skin under one of his eyes. "But let me show you."

He led me into his basement, an actual basement. Mine still had a dirt floor with a sump-pump at its midsection, and I had to bend my head when I moved around in it. His had masonry tiles and a sheet-rocked ceiling and walls, and I was able to walk without stooping. The train set took up at least a third of the area with the tracks themselves looping around a group of houses recognizable as Quaker Falls. Bill apologized that it was only partly accurate and that the real train had, of course, run past the village rather than looping around it.

"But what could I do?" he asked. "My train had to go someplace. I couldn't have it go back and forth on a tabletop." He smiled confidingly.

I located my house easily within his village—its front parallel to the painted road and its back to his attempted hillside, the one I had gone to with Nancy. It felt commemorative, like a model of Gettysburg. The rails themselves were halfway between the house and the hill. As he started the train in motion—the smokestack puffing with nineteenth century enthusiasm—he commented that he hadn't put the little shop on my property but he would now get his X-ACTO knife working on it as soon as he was able. "What I've tried to know throughout my life is what's important and what's not," he told me. "Who could know a small structure like that could offer so much? We can only make stories that we want to hear, but I think my ears have been ringing since I read what you've got in your hand there."

"Who do you suppose...? "

"Wrote it? Wish I knew. I feel like it was a woman—a person like my Squirrel, my Lucille: quiet to the eardrums but able to hold big thoughts as soft as you'd want to imagine."

"There is a quince tree in my yard—although a friend had to point it out to me. Whoever planted it knew the story of the original one—if that's what it was. They knew, and they kept the memory of it going—hoping, I imagine, that someone else would do the same."

"And here we are." He looked triumphant and added to the train's speed after it had stopped at his depot. I thought of the woman in the postcard picture from the 1880s and wanted to suggest he put people on the platform, but it would have been presumptuous, I think, to have invaded his constructed world.

"Next spring," I said, "you need to come and smell its flowers. You'll know why they might have chosen the tree they did."

"I'd like that."

At the end of his model excursion, as we reached the top of the cellar steps, Lucille was waiting for us with an uncut pie in her hands and a smile of gratitude, as if I had done something for them.

"I always keep one frozen," she said, "in case your friend Bill can't restrain himself. A pie is such a simple thing to create, but I find it nice to hold. It feels comfortable in my hands." She extended it toward me. "It won't take long to thaw in weather like this. I'll do another tomorrow. It gives the day a relaxed way to breathe out, don't you think?"

I was yoo-hooed by Mary Jane after I left the Gaussmanns'—but it was evident from the constriction of the sound that her heart hadn't returned to its normal seat of comfort. She carried the borrowed copy of *Riff and Raggles*, hoped I'd had a pleasant visit with the "turtle doves" next door, and placed the book on top of the pie, where it rested like a missing part.

"We need to be scrupulous about our borrowings," she intoned with preacher-like seriousness before adding wistfully, "I appreciate a book when it rings like church bells." I gathered the dog and cat and cream on the milk still rang for her.

I walked slowly past the house of the mother and daughter I'd met at Mary Jane's, partly because of what I was carrying and partly because of the way walking magnifies what we barely notice when we're driving. The house, until now, had been part of the stage scenery of Quaker Falls, but on this afternoon it became the home of two persons I had met and watched taking part in their own potato salad dance on the Fourth of July. They were people whom I had never seen in their own yard, one of narrow pathways that, at least now, seemed to pin heavy shrubbery like packing blankets against the house. The structure itself was smaller than I'd realized, more vertical than horizontal, like the old constructions in the valley referred to as mill-hand houses. It was buttoned up tightly, all of its windows closed and shades pulled, although I could hear the noise of what sounded like an air conditioner in the back. How many ways people chose to live—how many configurations: husband-wife, lady and lovers, mother-daughter, father-son, and a seemingly endless menu of combinations. And how many faces they make. On this day, the mother-daughter house presented itself like a sheeted secret. A similar house stood between theirs and mine—for sale since before I moved in. At some future date, it would hold actual next-door neighbors.

When I returned home, I opened the unlocked door to the shop and peered inside. I heard the scurrying of small feet, but in the fading light, I couldn't see more than the rectangle of grayness I had just let in. I would find the right chair for it—or have Nancy find one. It would become a place to wonder in when wondering was necessary. It could become a retreat from my retreat, a place to do nothing in particular, a refinement of what brought me to Quaker Falls. I moved next to it to spend a minute with the quince, letting its reach settle about me. There were hundreds of small, knobby fruits on it now, looking like food for farm animals and, right then, especially inviting because of it. I pulled one from its branch and bit into it; the flesh was as I had expected, grainy and sour and difficult to chew. But it was an instant satisfaction with an unforgotten will of its own and without apologies.

The light was steadily softening. As I looked at the meadow in front of me, I knew it was already time to make my circuit to the rear of Mary Jane's property. The prospect of it *did* have the stigma of something a so-called grown-up should be talking himself out of; but a spot of certainty—however earned—felt like a necessary goal. If in some remote way I was to be a benefactor of Mary Jane, I would need to confirm her pain. I put Lucille Gaussmann's pie and the children's book on the kitchen table, noticing the way they tugged the room into a greater feeling of order than it had known since I came there.

Walking through the meadow grass, I could feel it already losing its earlier greenness as it scratched against my legs. I realized, too, that I was not alone. The calico cat was accompanying me, hopping through the grass at my pace but, as usual, remaining several feet behind. Birds flew up from spots near us, and I recognized this as one of the cat's hunting spots. For now, though, there was more of an interest in companionship. There were signs of earlier humans along the way: a deflated football, a paperback virtually melted into unreadability, a glass bottle with the word *Moxie* raised on the surface, and other things from the careless and forgetful past. I promised my companion I would try to pick them up at some point—I would become a one-man meadow patrol, and the cat seemed pleased with the idea, gazing at me with the suggestion of a Cheshire grin. For now I carried the bottle with me, one less object to remove and an amulet for what I was about to undertake.

The back of Mary Jane's yard was defined by a line of bushes and small trees tangled with a rusted fence, the kind with rectangles the size of subway tiles. The fence was beaten down in several places, and one spot in particular had a half-body-sized opening through the shrubbery that would have been an obvious entry point for marauders. The calico was ahead of me, seemingly aware of the mission and for the first time taking the lead. I tucked my way through the opening with an awkward rolling of my shoulders and looked toward the owner's house before coming fully into the yard. I could see her in her lighted kitchen, standing as still as she had on her front step earlier, wrapped in a thought or the absence of thought—producing in me the feelings of a voyeur but without the satisfaction. I turned my attention instead to the corn patch. The stalks themselves had grown a foot or more since The Fourth of July, and I not only admired their explosiveness but was grateful for the extra coverage they provided a person doing a deed as quixotic as mine. I looked at last at the area where I had seen Mary Jane's private plants, and there was the deconsecrated ground, shapely craters where the cannabis had been yanked upward and carried off to a new place of secrecy. I could, as I looked at the emptiness, feel the grower's sense of the depredation committed against her, the unimagined emptiness she must have experienced when she came to gaze upon her vegetative friends. I knew I was giving more importance to the event than it deserved, but despite its comic possibilities, I was surprisingly glad to feel a tighter connection to this person than would have happened otherwise. Two settlers in an unsettled land.

When I got back to the house, I found a three-word message from Michael Feller on my cell: Mom misses u.

THREE

And I had been missing her with the totality of ardency, fondness, and wistfulness, along with a hunger for words and gestures. It felt like absence was honing the sum of us—the growth of months as well as the years I still could not discount. We had agreed before she and Michael left to give ourselves exactly that—absence. We agreed to communicate without voice or text to find out what it was we might hear from each other. It was she who had suggested it, while admitting it was more the kind of field test I was likely to propose. According to her, she was becoming loopier in her way of viewing things—an evolution, she assumed, that should make me happy—and she felt it would be interesting to find out how it worked without my cluttering up her antennae for a few days. "Antennae" was how she put it, and I *did* wonder about having damaged her in some way.

Even through the weeks of June and early July, our progression had become clearer and more surprising to experience. We rarely talked now about the fancies of a first grader, but it was a part of who we were—whatever else might have wound itself around us. It was neither a loss nor a gain, yet it also seemed, at times, that she still wasn't speaking about a few of her own details from that period.

But there was something in particular I wanted to say to her.

The day after she and Michael returned, Nancy called to say she was coming to Quaker Falls. She, too, had things to say. I suggested neutral ground—in this case Poets' Walk, although I did admit to myself that it wouldn't be completely neutral. But that was one of the things I wanted to share with her—the awkward attempt of a lost mother to reappear. Nancy at first sounded puzzled by the suggestion, but as our voices reconnected to each other, she warmed to the idea and told me she had not been there in years and it would be a good place to talk—a word, experience has taught me, that can be stuffed with implications. There was nothing in her voice to suggest a shift in who we were. But it was the word she chose.

We drove there separately, after agreeing on a midday rendezvous. I was the first to arrive and took the time to see what I remembered of my other visit at age eight. At first glance, it seemed a place of little promise. From the circular parking area, the nearby landscaping was cluttered with overgrown, hassock-like patches squeezed onto humps of ground. Sumac and other scrub plants grew as announcements of neglect, and damaged trees around the fringes looked exhausted on this warm day. Split-rail fencing leaned wearily backward from the parking slots. I walked a hundred feet or so down the gravel trail to a pavilion that seemed to serve no purpose. It was structured out of weathered logs but had no benches and its roof was open to the sky, providing little shade. It was like a woodsy monument to disappointment, and I was relieved to hear the sound of tires behind me.

When Nancy got out of her car, the first thing I noticed was the depth of her tan and the way it gave her eyes an even stronger intensity than normal. That or something else. She walked toward me with her Vanderbilt garden stride. It was a walk both sexy and intimidating. When she reached me, she put her hands on my shoulders as if she was about to point out a needed correction.

"You were hardly ever out of my thoughts," she said. "Why is that?" That sounded encouraging, and I was about to kiss her when she stepped back. "No, I mean it. Why is that?"

"Why is it that you think about me? Is that what you're asking?"

"Of course it's natural that I should think about you, but this last week has been ridiculous. It's not what women of a certain age are supposed to do, Jeremiah. It's adolescent. I couldn't even lose myself in beach books, and I'm not sure right now that I'm happy about it. Did you plant a bug in me before I left?"

"Maybe, Nancy, it's because I have things to tell you."

"Good. Let's tell things today. We don't do enough telling. And let's walk."

We entered the path that went directly through the skeletal pavilion, and we proceeded with the silence of interlocked arms until a gentle rise brought us to a field, mowed recently, the cuttings lying on their sides in even rows and smelling like the yard at Quaker Falls.

"That's better," I told her. "I was afraid my memory was betraying me while I was waiting for you. I came here a long time ago."

She laughed and moved her head a half-turn toward me. "So did I. Also a long time ago—with someone I almost did a naughtiness with."

That, of course, brought our side-by-side saunter to a halt. "Ah," I said, as lightly as I could, "so you almost made headlines. And this was during the reign of Marvin, I assume?"

"Was there ever any other time—until last year, that is?" I waited. "I think it was five years into our marriage—a neat number, I would think—quite a while after Michael was born. He, by the way, is going to apply to art school. Michael, that is. He finds it to be obvious and predictable—but, as he puts it, what are you going to do?"

"Obvious follows realization. You may already have known that. I would write a recommendation for him, but one coming from a dropout professor would probably not do him much good. You think?"

"Probably so."

"But I'm excited for him. And I will miss him."

"Oh, you'll never be rid of him entirely, I'm sure. It turns out he haphazardly chose you last fall as a path to enlightenment. I think that's how he put it. He didn't know he was doing it at the time, but he trusted you enough to empty himself."

"I will grow to be flattered, I'm sure."

"He put it that way on the boardwalk—the emptying—while he was eating blue cotton candy, although I'm not sure you can call it eating."

"You sound like two Zen masters."

"He's the master. I'm the Zen mistress."

She broke into gentle laughter.

We were walking again before she returned to the earlier item, clasping her hands together in front of her. "He was a person I knew from those embarrassing cheerleading days, although we were referred to as a pep squad. He was a male member of the squad until he hurt his back. He was one of those obsessively fit people who lifted us into the air and twirled us. And it wasn't me he was lifting at the time he hurt himself, in case you were wondering."

"I'm still working on male member."

"Yes, you would, wouldn't you?"

"And?"

"He was at a reunion—that's right, our fifth. He told me, as men apparently tend to, that he had been wondering about me and all that. But he looked handsome, as he always had, and he wished this and that had happened to us when we were still in school, and he had a soft voice that cut right into my dissatisfactions at the time. A hot knife, I guess you could have called it." She looked at me, waiting for a response, and when I could think of none, she went on. "He lived and worked across the river in Saugerties. He had a wife, but he admitted he'd already cheated on her once, and I imagine that was his way of saying the sheets were already dirty, so why not? It wouldn't make me the other woman. Only the 'other other' I would guess. I have to admit *that* had a certain horrible appeal, and the idea of betraying Marvin didn't seem so bad. In my mind at the time, he deserved it."

"And?"

"We agreed to meet here. It was a halfway point, and he thought I'd enjoy the view."

"Of him?"

"That, too, most certainly. And I did."

"All right."

She ran her hand over one of the pods of a trailside plant she later identified as milkweed. "And yet...as much as the thought of violating my shrunken marriage had its fascination, the idea of betraying myself didn't. I thanked him and went on my weary way."

"You *thanked* him?"

"Yes, Jeremiah, I thanked him. It was enough to keep me faithful to my marriage for another fifteen years. I'd thank him again if I saw him."

"How was his back?" I asked inconsequentially.

"I imagine it was everything a repressed housewife could have wished for. I didn't ask."

I tried to place this brief semi-episode into the life package of the woman I still knew so little about. It was the kind of thing I had experienced with writings that reached deeply into me, that ode or monologue or scenic description that spoke openly and personally to me while at the same time I would wonder, as an exercise in demystification, what had been going on in a writer's life the day he or she penned perfect lines. Had there been a toothache to deal with or problems with the plumbing or the forever loss of another phrase crowded out by the pure insistence of this one? Had the writer spent the night searching for a family animal or stumbling about to find a candle during a power outage? Had the food of the morning been disagreeable? Had global disaster been talked about in the streets? Had the day-after-day of annoyance and malfunction and stupidity been pushed out of its way by the inner sense of rightness within a grouping of words? Did people come to love one another in much the same way, and were the textual magnetics any less forceful for not knowing all there was to know? Even on a day of telling things, how much needed to be known at last?

"I came here with my mother around the same time. Maybe you and I passed each other on the trail," I commented. It was time to talk about Ellen, especially since it was she who had brought us to this place on this day.

"Maybe we did. It might be nice to think so." She smiled in a way that brought her forward in time.

I told her about the childhood poem that caused me to be here long ago, and my gratitude for the maternal fuss my rhymes had caused at the time. I could only remember one couplet:

> When I talk myself to sleep,
> I'll make my wishes short and deep.

The lines had no meaning to me now, and I doubt they meant much when I committed them to paper. More than likely, there was a sound to them that I charmed myself with. And, once again, who knew what was going on in my life then? I wasn't John Keats contemplating consumption and the brevity of existence. I was me in the elevated discovery that one word could make another word ring itself—a product of the *Riff and Raggles* school.

But Nancy liked it and kissed me fondly on my hand. "It's you in two breaths," she exclaimed, "all fluffed up and ready to baffle."

"I told you I was a prodigy."

"And so you might have been."

I spoke at last of the note from Ellen, the reunion she had suggested at the place we were exploring now, my e-mail to her, and my inability to stop wondering after years of keeping conjectures about her as hermetic as possible.

"Do you think it's another of my oedipal foibles, Nancy, inviting you to rendezvous where the absent mother claimed she was willing to present herself?" I didn't wait for her to answer. "It was only a matter of curiosity on my part, to see what memory might roll out of the woods. And look what I learned about you from bringing you here."

"Are you going to wait for another dozen years if you don't hear back from her? And, by the way, I've stopped applying Freudian readings to what you find so irresistible in me. It's simply too tiring to think about. If this is a mess, I'll take it for what it is, though I'm never completely sure about you."

"It's a mess only if we decide it is."

"Wouldn't that make it convenient, at least?"

"Never mind. This is a day of telling rather than weighing feathers—which, by the way, is an expression my father used more than once when I was trying to be clever—the feather thing, that is. We didn't do much telling."

"You seem freer to talk about him. Yes?"

"Yes, I suppose so. Probably because he won't leave me alone. And I *will* tell you about it, but not yet. First things first—like the Underground Railroad." I told her of Bill Gaussmann and Lucille and French apple pie and his model train and village, the clumsily-typed story of the print shop and the possibility of the quince tree and my deepening belief that a curious force had brought me to Quaker Falls—a force I could no longer dismiss as random acts of coincidence. "I'm convinced, Nancy Feller, that I bought the house not as a means of justifying my flight from a profession full of corridors that don't intersect but for a reason I know is there and simply hasn't chosen to reveal itself to me, except in little notes tacked to parts of the landscape. In some bizarre way, even your Marvin's Mary Jane might be more than a yoo-hoo running up my spine. *That*, I'm sure, will take some serious decoding. But it's you, more than anything, who makes it all so obvious when it's all *trying* to be obvious. How's that for weighing feathers?"

"I'm listening." We had arrived at the point of the trail that passed through Overlook Pavilion, a structure assembled like the outline of a Swiss chalet as we neared it. It was an inviting place to sit with the mountains rising before us, but we remained standing, claiming the view much as we had exiting the stone chapel after the wedding of Barbara Lynn and Emily two months earlier. I could, as we stood there, imagine Washington Irving discovering the visual impulses he would use to open "Rip Van Winkle" and the words he penned about "The Kaatskills...swelling to a noble height and lording it over the surrounding country." They *were* lording, fully indifferent to the two of us in our unsteady droplet of existence; they were prepared to outlast words, paintings, and the people who crafted them. The thought flashed briefly of Lucia Solis and her young daughter in their Bronx apartment with the copy of Irving's *Sketch Book* I had given her as an act of contrition. Would she ever open it to the descriptions of these mountains and would she feed the hunger for a larger reach she had shown in the classroom and in my office? I was about to speak of her to Nancy when she sensed my thoughts. "But I gather you're listening to someone else. You look like a confused professor."

"Do you ever get over it?"

"Teaching?"

"The classroom, at least."

She stared directly at Overlook Mountain. "I don't think I ever did. And I gave up trying a long time ago."

A floating shadow passed in front of us, and the length of wing-span caused a catch within me. "Eagle?" I wondered aloud.

"Without a doubt."

"Something to share."

The trail became a grass lane as we left the pavilion behind and eventually broadened into what could have been a par-four golf hole moving downhill and opening to our sight the length of the Kingston-Rhinecliff bridge, a flat span with the traffic upon it moving soundlessly in the distance.

"Why didn't you ever go back—because of Michael?"

"No. Not Michael. I'm sure I grew frightened of the idea."

"Why?"

"The emptiness kept growing, I think. I became more convinced I couldn't fill even a part of it. I think I was right about that. For many years." She subsided behind another look into the distance. The Catskills were shaped by the open spaces they themselves created, and were, for several seconds, the outline of feelings she had never expressed to me before. Then her tone shifted. "I'm glad about your new friend Bill. He sounds like a good and necessary person."

"They're a good couple. They've made a life out of what they couldn't have."

She looked at me suspiciously. "Tell me more. Tell me about your father."

"And a tangle of characters that grows more confusing each day. His lawyer, the mother of our Willie, who both seem to hate me—not all the time, mind you, but when their burners are on, they can be real scorchers. Then there's Hamilton Graham, Willie's half-brother, who lived upstairs from me and across the hall from the ninety-something woman who I'd swear admitted he'd lied to her and got her so angry she tried to break her toe kicking a door or something she shouldn't have attempted. I told you I brought her to Quaker Falls and how she loved a limekiln we drove by but made comments about my tea. I keep getting the feeling she's wired in, too—that I'll find out she's The Professor's real mother or Joanna Wexler's or both of them, even though I only know she made films in England and lived on a farm devoted to the pleasures of free love. It can get pretty hairy when I give these thoughts too much play."

"So I see."

"I'm in danger of making her into the wise woman. Lord, lord. Then there's the ex-con male secretary to Wexler Esquire who constructed an edgy disliking of me the last time I came to her office and accused me of immoral intentions he didn't care to elaborate on. For a dropout, I seem to be generating the vibrations of close-quarter combat."

"Apparently."

"Want to try this trail?" A sign pointed to a final destination called Summerhouse, but she insisted on going back the way we'd come.

"I remember that trail," she instructed. "It was rocky, tangly, and grabby."

"Are you referring to pep man, the gifted lifter?"

"I might be." She didn't elaborate.

As we started back, I told her about the will, filling in the borders of the money she only knew as a dollar amount. I summarized his verbal admonition to me, the question mark for the woman he was still married to, his generosity to Louisa, his bequests to each of our campuses—one direct and one indirect—,and about March 22 and the way he had wanted the room arranged and lighted. While she had no doubt wondered about the details, she had never asked, waiting for me to decide when and what to tell her—particularly after my waiting nearly a month to tell her anything at all. I told her of *Reconsiderations*, how it opened an alternate vision of Alban Curtin's mind to me, one initially bordered in the neon lights of absurdity and how it then drove me into a tumbling search for who I was and whether or not I had a missing brother who might be connected to a missing mother—or whether I was, finally, my own missing brother.

"And you think he intended for you to read a book delivered by the woman who prepared his suppers?"

"But that's the thing, Nancy. Was anything about him ever accidental, or am I too obsessed with finding a plot to suit the characters? Louisa called him 'the Elf-king.' It seems to fit. But I don't know."

"And you think Willie's half-brother might be *your* half-brother? And the secretary with the ponytail fits in somehow?"

"It's like the quince tree. It might be a compelling story standing in my yard or it might be a tree that smells good in the spring. And the original might have been a plain old maple tree, you know? I ate one of the quince fruits, by the way." She looked at me with warm approval. "It had the texture of a towel and the taste of a long-neglected grapefruit. But, damn, it was happy to have been chosen. I could tell that in one bite."

"I'm glad to hear it."

"And, by the way, if Willie and I are half siblings to the same guy, does that make her and me quarter somethings? And more to the point, does her schizophrenic attitude about me have anything to do with our being related?"

"Jeremiah, I think it has to do with a complicated and passionate young woman slowly coming to terms with her own sexuality."

"She seemed to do that quite effectively when she and your son tried to drop my bed into the kitchen."

"I think she finds Michael sexy in his own way because he puts no direct demands on her."

"He did that to me last fall, and I don't remember finding him to be particularly sexy—although he was alluring."

"You know what I mean."

"And is that why you find *me* so sexy?"

"Oh? Because you put no demands on me?"

"I'm the chiffon headpiece in your life, my dearest Nancy."

"Yes, you are a headpiece. I'll ask again. What will you do about your mother? Can't you put an end to at least one part of your speculations?"

"How? How do I find her? Her family moved back to Italy decades ago, under vague circumstances. She left the area thirteen years ago—at least I assume she left the area."

"See? You know so little. It's all scenarios in your mind. Perhaps this whole time she's lived nearby—a block away from me or your father."

I recalled the story by Hawthorne where a man leaves his family to move a few doors from them so he could spend his years watching their comings and goings and growing. I couldn't remember the title or the logistics of his survival, but it didn't matter. The germ of the tale stayed with me. "And that they were never divorced, you know—my parents? Or so I was told by the vixen lawyer, Willie's reluctant mom. What do I make of that?"

I filled in the story of Willie's childhood, her ballplayer father, her return to Joanna in her early teens, and the series of trust exercises she and her mother put each other through.

"And does her mother have feelings for you?"

It was a playful question but one I couldn't answer with any certainty. "She has feelings, all right. Predatory ones. If she's guarding a secret, it's a mission that makes her nasty—even in her more congenial moments."

Nancy appraised what I had said, before suggesting we start back along the trail. In spite of the tawny glow of her skin, she looked tired. The fine lines around her eyes had deepened in the time she was away, and she walked now without her normal strolling motion, as if the afternoon had wearied her. I had begun, in recent months, to face up to the way I could be like a weight gain for others, even if there were no added pounds that would show up on any scale. Sara Sampson had repeatedly told me I took too many things too *ponderously* (a word she had seemed to enjoy saying); but that was Sara, whose tumbleweed personality could make most anything seem ponderous. After I said what I needed to say to Nancy, I would try to work on the ponderous stuff.

When we reached Overlook Pavilion again, she was glad to stop—and, this time, grateful for the bench just outside the structure itself. It was next to an old hand pump, no longer serviceable but a sign of antique encouragement to those making the upward climb. I stood behind her, as I had in the campus chapel when we listened to the rumblings of organ playing. I started to put my hands on her shoulders and then pulled back. The sides of the mountains were dappled now by the shadows of clouds moving quickly across them. The air about us was softened by textured puffs off the river. I watched the way the circular breezes fingered her hair, lifting it away from her head and revealing the specks of gray underneath. She had told me more than once how she'd made up her mind to do no more tampering with the natural look of her hair, particularly since I had come into her life. She wasn't going to let me forget any number of essential things about her, and my feelings for her had only deepened when she said it.

I finally said to her what I had wanted to when I invited her to meet me here on this day. "I want to propose to you, Nancy." Her head jerked upward slightly. "But I don't know what it is I can propose. You've ruled out marriage. A never-ending engagement sounds ridiculous. It sounds like a jail cell for minor offenses that can never be corrected. Can you see me kneeling, slipping a ring on your finger, and asking you to please, please, please *never* be my bride?"

She turned partway and looked up at me. "And what is it you would like to propose?"

"See? That's the problem. You've gotten me fancying a life you will always be a part of, that we will always make each other the best thought of every day, that we will always know ourselves to be better because of each other, and that touching each other will always be a culmination of reaching out to each other."

She stood and came around the bench. "And why is it that you're not touching me now, Jeremiah?"

"Because, Nancy, the culmination of what I'm trying to say hasn't quite gotten its sea legs yet—namely because I don't know what it is I want to say."

"I understand. Put your arms around me, and we'll see if that helps." I did, and it did, at least for Nancy, whose eyes took on a reflective depth I'd not seen in them before. "I know I haven't made it easy for you. And I know in your heart of hearts you want it all to be as easy as my coming into your office and having your thoughts about me float up out of a past whose only complication was a little boy missing teeth. And out of that, out of your beautiful fixation, would be the wisdom to know what it is we are to each other and what is it we *are to be*. I don't think we're all that different, my sweet Jeremiah. I hope not, at least. We want to be both old and new. Most of the time. Being both. Your quince tree is like that, don't you think? Isn't it a special thing to know that there's so much for it to teach you? And that it lends so much to the belief that dominance of others is a horrible thing for any human being to do? I've been thinking about it since you told me. There was a slave, maybe many, who walked down the steps of your little dollhouse. One didn't get away. But others did, I'm sure. And the one who *didn't* let himself be caught by you, so many years later. He—or *she*, Jeremiah—left you a challenging little fruit to pucker your lips for. Maybe you should propose emancipation. What could be more sacred?"

"Jesus God Almighty, Nancy Feller, I love and want you so much my toes are numb. Instead of a ring, I could give you a broken shackle while being on both knees."

"We might be making progress, Professor, in spite of everything. But there is one thing I have to tell you."

"Is it bad?"

"I don't know. Let's walk again." It was nearly a half-mile back to the parking lot, and we walked slowly, taking the pulse of the telling that had happened and the telling yet to come. "I trust you know what a hysterectomy is," she said when we were part way along.

The word vibrated within me like a thin branch. "You're having...?"

"Maybe," she said decisively. "I have to see the horrible person who examines me again. But my plumbing is quite noticeably out of whack. Female issues, my mother would call it. I'd still like to believe it's the recent bursts of enthusiasm in my most intimate regions—thanks to you—but it's just as likely a midlife malfunction that will have to be corrected."

"Surgery?"

"No, voodoo." She looked at me maternally. "Yes, surgery...but it's all gotten fairly uncomplicated in recent years. I've been doing research. You'd be proud of me."

"The idea of someone cutting into you...

"That's not how it goes—they're not going to split me open—so let it be for now." Her face darkened. "The point is, Jeremiah, can you imagine yourself guiding a lover into her senior years while you're still young and lusty? Not that I'm talking about infidelity necessarily. Those things will take care of themselves. It's only reasonable that you'll want to do other things besides tending to my declining years. Even if my insides turn out to be a false alarm, it's going to happen: you and the woman in her decline."

"And you picture me sitting next to your bed for the rest of your life, dabbing at your forehead with a damp cloth and staring out the window at the world going on without me? *You* are a very healthy woman. I can testify to that."

She offered a weak smile. "Yes, my darling, you've caused me to do surprisingly acrobatic feats. The Sleeping Cheerleader has had quite an awakening. But I have this not-very-mystical understanding that I will, at some point, be falling further and further behind you—and feeling guilty that I'm dragging my man with the broken shackle into places I won't want to take him. Do you understand me?"

"A not-very-mystical understanding, no less? And if our situations were reversed?"

"They're not, so you don't need to approach it that way. I'm talking about *us* as we are—which is what we've been talking about all afternoon. Jeremiah, I meant pretty much every word I said before when I did my lecture at the overlook: slaves and quinces and who we are. I amaze myself by finding growing comfort in what we are becoming, even though we should congratulate each other for our attempts at staying away when we need to. But I have this idea that it's going to become more difficult—decidedly more difficult. I might even find myself not wanting to be away from you. There's that possibility, Jeremiah."

"Yes. I think there is."

"It's one of the reasons I thought of you so often at the shore. I was, believe me, never going to let it happen. It was too deliciously ridiculous. It was probably insane. Still..." She ran her hands up and down my forearms, generating what it was she was trying to qualify. "But I was also thinking about this other thing—this medical thing—and all that we need to think about." She looked at me with affection that was immediate with weariness. "I hate to keep giving you these assignments, but I do want you to think about it. I want you to think about everything that's happened here."

"You tell me I think too much."

"Just a little more then. After that, you can stop if you want to."

We were near the edge of the parking area, and I noticed a small sign next to the pavilion that had puzzled me earlier. It said simply ARBOR, giving it redefinition. It *had* had a purpose, one of providing floral beauty to those beginning or concluding their poet's walk. Shrinking budgets had no doubt put a finish to that, but I did wonder if there had been flowering vines when Ellen and I had passed through there.

There were half a dozen vehicles now, and one older woman was just getting out of a car the size of Nancy's—small and efficient. She looked about the same age as the Gaussmanns but swung her legs toward the gravel with difficulty, pulling on the door handle with one hand and guiding her knees with the other. I sucked my breath into an inflated pouch of concern, thinking of all the things that could go wrong with her. The Professor had told Louisa that one of the most difficult things in his last months was getting out of his car on his own—that getting in was still a relatively comfortable process, but exiting demanded painful contortions of the body and spirit. Nevertheless, he did, according to Louisa, keep driving himself until shortly after our Christmas together. Then he stopped.

The woman before us completed her method of extraction without mishap, and once her sneakered feet were planted on the ground and she had closed the door with some effort, she moved ahead with a stiff but steady stride, smiling at each of us.

"It is too fine a day to let pass without a good walk," she said as she came abreast of us, showing no inclination to stop now that she was underway. She carried a cane, but held it above the ground, as if she was dowsing with it. She started down the same pathway we had come back upon, she with the fixity of a person who had done this many times over many years—concerned less about watching and listening than with the pleasure of known motion.

As Nancy watched the woman's departure, she commented vaguely, "A punctuation mark."

FOUR

Then, what happened to Emily instantly idled any further discovery fantasies—though before long it would generate a new tangle of events. It was Mikhail who called to tell of the stabbing that left her hospitalized in guarded condition. His voice was laced with anxiety that tore through his usual modulations of ironic control. That, as much as the act of violence itself, caused my own immediate inability to focus on anything but the image of a knife piercing with shining self-satisfaction the skin of a human being. One of the boys she counseled. Emily.

In a twisted way, as Jefferson shared what details he knew, I found myself wishing it had been a bullet, that there had been no hand guiding the blade inward, only the force of a finger locked around a simple and indifferent mechanism. I had always had a fear of knives based on nothing that had ever threatened me in any way. The edge, the simple width dominated by length, honed to violate—that was enough. Even as a child, I had made sure the business sides of kitchen knives were facing downward in sink drainers and facing backward in pullout drawers. If I'd had my way, I would have put all but butter knives into leather sheathes. In spite of special effects, most violence on TV or in film had struck me from an early age as artificial and boring unless it involved an edge or pointed object of almost any sort: switchblade, guillotine, hypodermic needle, scalpel—it didn't much matter. I would leave the room, switch the channel, take long looks at popcorn or a ceiling—

anything to keep from having a falling out with it. I had this fanciful but utilitarian theory that in a past life—or many—I had been executed by the severing force of a blade—for acts against the state, against the church, or for any assertion of common sense. On this day, as Mikhail spoke, I was unable to look away: the picture was internal this time, with no switch to protect me. Emily.

Mikhail said she had been trying to deal with two of those charged to her for a summer of attitude adjustment and a hoped-for acceptance by them that succeeding in school could be of greater benefit than reactive anger. The two boys had scrapped with each other repeatedly and were usually assigned to activities that kept them apart, but each had a special fondness for Emily and each saw her as his own spirit guide, chosen by unspecified forces to favor one over the other. For a month, she had juggled their mutual dislike with their individual need for her approval, but on this day, she had stepped between them to prevent their impending knife fight.

"And stop it she did," Jefferson lamented. "One little fucker apparently claimed he was trying to protect her from the other. How does the fact that he put a blade into her to protect her make any fucking sense, even to his back-alley brain? He plain lost it—if he ever had it to begin with."

"And Barbara Lynn?"

"She swings between saying nothing and ranting about having told Emily to give up working with those who can't make sense out of their own shrunken little pricks with both hands on them. If I feel angry, you can imagine how she must feel. She sits next to her in Critical Care, takes an occasional break, and calls me, describing what Emily looks like." His voice dropped suddenly. "What are we to make of humans? That's what I keep thinking. My whole life I've done it—turned over slimy rocks to try to understand humans—but not like this. To see gentleness sliced up is grossly beyond all understanding. But Barbara's sure she'll make it through this. Thankfully we've become civilized enough in this state that a woman can sit next to her beloved spouse, even though they happen to share the same biology."

“Can we go?”

“There are waiting rooms. But we can do one better—we can donate.”

“Donate?”

“Blood, brother. Stop by here and we’ll go together.”

“I’ll be there.”

Among those things I had never done that I *should* have done, giving blood was listed high among them. I had not even had a blood test since, presumably, I was on the delivery table. It undoubtedly went together with my difficulties about other sharp objects. While I hated the circumstances that were bringing this about, I was heartened by the fact that I would at last be forced to do the right and necessary thing without equivocation. I called Nancy before I left, and her insistence on doing what she could for Emily was part of a growing confluence of purpose that would bring several of us to the hospital. Nancy called back to tell me she had told Michael who told Willie who told two other former students of Barbara Lynn’s.

Jefferson had admitted to me at one time that he was not the Hudson Valley’s best driver. Now, as he drove distractedly to the hospital in Ulster County, I was sorry I hadn’t driven him. He started at one point to enter an exit ramp until the sound of horns pushed him slowly out of the mistake, leaving him swearing repeatedly at the stupidity of what he had done. “As you would imagine, I have gone this same pisshole way hundreds of times, and here some fucking little terrorist pulls the plug on my brain. God, I hate to be the last to see how crude it all is, even though I think I’ve studied the subject backward and forward. What a piece of work is man. What a piece.” His jaw muscles rippled with the power of what was ultimately inexpressible.

I tried to tell him about the Underground Railroad, believing it would take him into a place of positivity. It wasn’t a successful attempt.

“I imagine I should offer up a hosanna and give half of it to you for tracking down some freedom-seeking slave folk. But I don’t want you getting all up-righteous about having runaway narratives hatching on your own property. It had nothing to do with you.”

We rode in silence for several minutes. I tried not to weigh what he had said, given the purpose of our journey. His sourness was his business for now, just as well-deep sadness was mine. The recapture of a slave had hardly been small talk, but it had been a diversion, perhaps too obviously so.

"Sorry." He offered the word out of our growing silence. As part of the day, I guess, it stabbed the air with a brief thrust of exasperation.

"No need."

"There's always need, my friend. I give you your discovery with a contrite heart. May it serve you well. But now that that's out of the way, I find myself needing to tell you a thing or two about Emily." I waited, feeling a cold cord of fear being pulled up from my belly. "In case I don't make it through the afternoon with my dignity intact, I want you to understand why. And you said your woman friend will be there to drive you home?"

"Nancy. Yes."

"This must never go beyond you and me."

"I hate that. It's always an unfair condition."

"Unfair or not, you will keep it to yourself." He paused and then pulled onto a bump-out from Route 9W. "She was a brief, glorious miracle not that long ago."

"How long?"

"It doesn't matter. Call it a one-time memory."

"You had a...?"

"I'd like to stay with the word 'miracle,' if you don't mind. Except it's difficult to label an event that possibly should not have happened a miracle. If there *are* such things, they are things that *should* happen—hocus-pocus or not. So let's assume it was." He leaned toward me, "If you're expecting details, you won't get any."

"Good, because I don't want to hear any of this, Mikhail. And why you're putting me into this famously disappointing position makes no sense. So I can hold your hand if you misbehave?"

He smiled weakly at me. "Because you handle disappointment so well. Take it as a compliment."

"I'd rather not take it at all."

"Too late for that. The Father Confessor must keep his insides dry. I see you as capable of that."

"I'm not sure I particularly believe that or like it."

"You're about to find out."

"I see, Jefferson. More partial puzzles. I'm tired of them."

"Too many?"

"Far too many. And here you are adding another."

"No puzzle at all. There's nothing to figure out. It was what it was and now it isn't. And the 'it' is self-evident. Free yourself of additional curiosity. And I have told you what I have to alert you to a certain strangeness you may detect in me. And I may finish off the day by driving into the mountains and doing something profoundly escapist. I just didn't want you to be left without a ride."

He put the car into gear and edged back onto the highway. He drove the rest of the way to the hospital at a slower pace than he had earlier, as though his brief unburdening had encumbered the car somehow. He said nothing more, and I worked unsuccessfully at not thinking.

§

The entire collection of donors was on parallel tables, and the insertion of the needle into my arm had finally been accomplished after a missed first attempt. There was, I discovered, nothing much of pain, only the slightly disorienting feeling of intrusion for the first moments. Once I was assured by a large, sable-bearded technician that the blood was leaving me, I found myself relaxing into a state of protective detachment, until a voice coming sideways pulled me back to the reason for being there.

"She better fucking make it. I hate this blood thing." It was Willie Furman, of course, her head tilted toward me in a way that showed fretful shadows crossing her eyes. Michael was on the other side of me, with earbuds sealing him out from the rest of us. Nancy was just beyond him, and beyond her were Jefferson and two of Barbara Lynn's students I remembered from the wedding. We had met near the information desk like a team reassembling after a long off-season, offering the embraces of absence and renewed commitment, heartening in its own way until the first tears were offered by Nancy Feller. For her, the tears were noiseless until they were joined by the gulping sounds of Patty Desmond, who had a name and looks from the 1950s—something about her bangs and decisively applied blusher. Her sobs projected a sense of bewilderment, like a child's sudden discovery of a horrid truth, and we became a knotted group until a nurse came to lead us to the room of the parallel tables. It was the use of the patient's full name—Emily Acampora—that finally ended one of my mysteries.

"Are you all right?" I asked Willie.

"I've had better days." She was chewing on the edges of a hard candy, using it more for its texture than its taste. The action had a delicacy I rarely associated with her. Finally, she looked directly at me. "You probably like this kind of thing, don't you?"

"I like nothing about it except to help a very special friend while having this quiet conversation with you."

"Hunh. The first part I might believe."

"Believe what you wish."

"I've never given blood before."

"Then we have one thing in common. How does it feel?"

"You're old, dude. How come this is your first time?"

"I don't know."

"You were chicken, too?"

"Probably. When they had blood drives on campus, I would be doing other things. Intentionally."

"Me, too."

"I would, Willie, have expected to see you at the head of the line with both sleeves rolled up."

"I'm not as tough as I try to be."

"Except when you are."

"Except when I am." She paused. "I'm rotten to you when I don't mean to be. I haven't totally figured it out, but I'm getting closer."

"I haven't figured out much of anything lately, even though there are times when I feel like I don't know too much—yet."

"That sounds like a pain in the ass."

"But I may have figured out one thing about you."

She stirred slightly, raising the arm with the tube coming from it and dropping it again. "This better not be family stuff."

"Not exactly. More like music stuff. A simple question: why do you like it so much—the organ?"

"Because it can make my butt vibrate."

"You don't want to study it seriously."

"No. Why should I? Why should I want to be serious?"

"You're always serious—about most things. Why not this?"

"I'm afraid if I get much more serious, I might have to start believing in something."

"What a burden that would be," I replied. "And where do you think it came from—the music thing?"

"From a hole in the ground. How should I know? I started taking lessons when I finally went to live with my mother. Probably, I was hoping to find a way to make louder noises than she did."

"Interesting tidbit. And do you remember the first time you were turned on to it?"

"No."

"I think I may have figured that out."

"Oh, great. Einstein strikes again."

"Do you remember hearing it in school?"

"In school? Not likely."

The attendant came by, a darkly looming presence outside the normal outlines of a helper angel, but he moved softly with the footwork of a Vaudevillian. After checking the seven of us, he announced that I for some reason was leading the uncontested race to fill the bag. Willie was pleased by the idea, noting to our new friend with the Bluto-beard that I was a known overachiever when I was in a horizontal position. I noticed the name-tag reading "Stephen" on his hospital blues, and it jiggled slightly in response to her comment. “Steve,” she asked, “does my blood go right to Emily?”

“Possibly to her,” he said. “Or to replace what’s already has been given to her.”

“Make sure mine goes straight to her.” He promised to try and moved on. “Wouldn’t that be the best thing,” Willie said to me, “my stuff going right into her to make everything work again? And that will happen. Everything about her is going to work again, right?

“Yes.”

“Do you pray?”

“No. Not exactly.”

“Good,” she replied. “I pray to her. Not some Tinkerbell god. Why not go straight to the person who needs it? And what’s this about school?”

At that moment, Barbara Lynn Hynes came into the room, saying in one of her softest and drawliest voices, “I love y’all.” She looked as unslept as one would imagine, her lids drawn back from her pupils, creating a gothic stare. Her usually explosive hair was pulled back into a single, untidy braid, and as she moved into the room she scratched the back of her neck with both hands, as if she had exposed a newly sensitized area of skin. The seven heads on the tables rose with synchronized precision, the buds popping from Michael’s ears, and she was momentarily paralyzed, uncertain where to move. It was Jefferson who finally voiced the simple question “News?”

“No,” she exhaled. “No news. The words *guarded condition* are still hanging over my baby’s body,” she said with dramatic resignation. “There is still bleeding inside her, and they may have to go in again.” It was the first any of us knew, presumably, that Emily had already undergone surgery. The heads of the listeners fell back onto the tables. There was, in fact, little any of us knew, except for the event that brought us to this place. Presumably Jefferson knew more through phone conversations, but he was becoming, to my mind, an excluded member of the group. He had cast a shadow between us, one I was trying to tack into place. If he had done something improper, the nature of that impropriety may have been too wound up in my own pristine fantasies about Emily as a being who hooked normal desire to small, transparent parachutes. It would take time to work out, I supposed, for the slow downward drift of my own conflicted feelings about her to complete their journey. And how inconsequential it all seemed just then—this preservation of a fantasy.

Barbara Lynn moved into the space between Willie and myself after she had talked to the others. Close-up, her eyes looked even drier than they had from a distance, the look of staring that was unable to reflect even faint images. "It's surely nice to see the two of you acting like you actually like each other—even though it took an awful thing for the lion and lamb to lie down together."

"Which one's the lion?" Willie asked with a sniffle.

"Why, which do *you* think, darlin'?" She took Willie's freckled hand with one of her own and kissed it with chapped lips.

"Stupid question."

"No, my sweet. Ah've seen the lamb in you when you weren't pretending she didn't exist. Ah've seen the lamb," she repeated with a muted revival cadence.

"Probably," Willie murmured.

"No doubt about it." Barbara Lynn patted the hand. "Ah wish there was another table right there next to you. They won't let me give even a thimbleful of blood. They think ah'm too shaky. But it would be fine to lie down with the rest of you. It would be lahk summer camp. We could tell stories and make up di'logue for the crickets. I used to do that. One cricket says this. The other says that. A third makes fun of the other two. You just have to fill in the blank spaces." There was a suddenness of tears in her eyes and her knees started to give out, pitching her against me. "Sorry, Jeremiah. Thought you was a bullfrog."

Stephen appeared by her side and led her to a wheelchair across the room. She sank onto it with an almost grateful collapse, sharing with the room a version of "I love you all" and what sounded like "I'm going back to the Smokeys where my true love waits." Jefferson sat upright and motioned to Stephen with his free arm. He asked to have his needle taken out. Though the attendant assured him he would be done in a few minutes, Mikhail insisted he was done and a few more drops of half-breed blood wouldn't matter and he would take care of getting Barbara Lynn back to where she was supposed to be. His feet were on the floor as soon as he was freed from the bag, and while Stephen was a head taller than him, the intensity of Jefferson's voice and physicality persuaded the other to see what he could do. Jefferson urged him to talk to those in charge and to give them his name. When the attendant came back with an upraised thumb, Jefferson crossed briefly next to me, to say with a look of dour realization, "You can never be sure where your actions will take you until you get there. In this case, they're trying to take me to a waiting room and I don't believe that's where it's at right now. See you later, my friend."

FIVE

I did ride home with the others in Willie's SUV—filled with an extreme number of empty water bottles that set up a rhythm of plastic chattering, and she prattled as accompaniment with the buoyancy of one who has met a dreaded test successfully. Michael was in the passenger seat, his head bobbing at meanings along the way that weren't apparent to the rest of us. Nancy and I were in the back, our hands joined and her thumb stroking my knuckles with steady pressure. The driver looked at our hands by way of the rearview, puckering her lips slightly between the slippages of an unraveling monologue.

"So at least I managed to get off the table without falling on my boobs or cracking my brain open in front of that guy Steve. What a nice moose of a character. But I was a little dizzy. I think I forgot to eat anything this morning, and the hotshots that do this sort of thing to impress the world are always saying, 'Make sure you eat an ample breakfast.'" She raised her voice to curl the quote and repeated "ample." "I'm fine now, though, in case you think we're going to end up in the ditch with our shoes in the air. Quite a picture that would be, right Mike? But you and Nancy look cute, Prof." In my memory, she still had never used my first name. "Two kids coming home from the prom. Although I never did a prom—probably because I never got invited. Who wants to ask a chick who might eat them? But Mike said he'd take me to one here before I graduate. Although now he's going to get tucked away with his cameras in Boston or LA, I have no idea how he's going to pull that off. No big deal. I probably dance like an ostrich, although it's been so long, who the hell knows. But what's that about Jefferson and the waiting room—and what's this to-the-rescue bit with Professor Hynes? Like he's her father or her boyfriend—though that would be a surprise to the folks back South, wouldn't it? Maybe if you stuck with teaching"—her eyes locked with mine in the mirror—"you'd make friends like that who'd come to your rescue when you're laid up. I still think you're an idiot, by the way, for giving it up. Idiot, of course, is my way of saying I like and probably respect you but still think you dropped the ball as far as your students are concerned. I might have taken you again, but I doubt you would have let me because you'd be a stickler about—whatever. Even Mother Esquire said I shouldn't take you a second time—and she was the one who steered me your way in the first place. Clever lady." She paused, her reflected eyes on my face. "I wouldn't have met Mike, right?" She jabbed at his shoulder with an index finger, and he looked at her with muddled affection. "Did I say you two look cute? It took getting used to, but so does going to MOMA. Now I like it. A white dot on the wall is almost beginning to make sense to me. It's like spit on the sidewalk, which somebody must think is pretty cool."

Nancy had been mostly silent during the afternoon, the adult, maybe, trying to keep her emotions as much in check as she was able. "Are you comparing us to saliva?" she asked Willie with restrained impatience.

"Saliva? Nah, I can see where you'd think that, but I was only trying to say that things stop being wacky if you give them time. People my age have a hard time looking any ways but sideways. It's like our heads are still flat from bumping up against you older types." She waited for a response, but there was none. "Do you think Emily will go back to doing what she was doing? I mean, when she's better. And she will be better. There can't be any other way. Half the world loves her, if you ask me, and that by itself should bring her through all this mess. But she's the kind of person who will put goo on her scar and go back there because that's who she is. She could be one of those Seals who stand up to evil.

But I guess pledging your life to a bomb-thrower like Hynes takes strong insides. Amazing."

She took a breather as we approached the Mid-Hudson Bridge, a respectably sized suspension-type span, a smaller Golden Gate painted silver. Heading across it eastward, the church spires of Poughkeepsie thrust above a broad canopy of leaves. Locals call theirs "The Queen City," and on this day, no one in Willie Furman's SUV would have argued. The softness of the treetops and the parallel span of the Walkway Bridge created the vision of altitude held securely in place. The fixed idea of Chuck and Phyllis still talking away there freshened my mind for an instant, and I wondered if Richard Woo had settled into the machine of what they called governance. An odd word, since clearly he was part of "the governed." I wondered, too, if he knew about Emily, and what, if anything, he knew about Emily Acampora and Mikhail Jefferson.

Willie had apparently talked herself out and drummed with the fingers of both hands on the steering wheel until Michael told her she was creating what he called rat-scratch vibes. She looked at him with dark puzzlement but said nothing as she fixed her fingers in place and finished the drive to the Feller house. She remained in the car as the rest of us got out, her hands still clenching the wheel. When we were partway to the front door, Nancy turned back, gestured for her to put the window down, and said a few words to her. Willie opened her door and stepped gingerly onto the driveway, leaving Nancy to close the door. By the time she reached Michael and me, Willie said with succinct articulation to Michael, "Your mother said you weren't being a dick, and we should think about more important things. I assume she meant Emily."

"The word was not 'dick,'" Nancy corrected. "But, yes, let's try to keep ourselves together before the horror of all that has happened makes us into a bunch of thugs." The word was chosen with cool and weary precision. "Let's go in and I'll make dinner."

In the composed familiarity of the living room, Michael offered up the suggestion that what we'd experienced that afternoon was a crisis of beauty. He seemed to be on the verge of an extended rollout of his unique form of thought but seemed grateful to leave it at that until Nancy asked him to explain himself. He was still inclining toward letting it pass when Willie added, "Come on, Mike. You owe me one. We'll get to the rat business later, but you can't keep your audience hanging. You've got mothers and girlfriends and former teachers crazy with waiting."

"Look, Will, rats are cool until they start tap dancing. Then it gets edgy. We're all edgy. And you're a little messy about the whole business. We want Emily to be a whole part of us again. The times she and Dr. Hynes came out to the country to paint windows, I watched the way her hand held a brush. It was the coolest picture I'd ever seen—or almost one of the most. She had fingers that were so happy doing what they were doing, I wanted to stop doing what I was doing and watch *her* doing what *she* was doing. You know? She told me I would become one of the great appreciators about how things work. I don't know about that. It sounds like a pretty special idea." He stood, rubbing his nose and looking on the edge of tears, a place I'd not seen him go before. "What if her hands don't work like that anymore? What the fuck?"

"'A crisis of beauty?'" his mother asked, trying to pull him back.

He looked at me. "*You* said that—one day in class when I was paying attention." His voice had become grainy with the effort to control it.

"They weren't my words," I told him. "They came from another person in this room."

"Will," he whispered, nodding toward her. "You read them out loud."

"He did?" Willie challenged.

"From an essay you wrote," I reminded her. "I was quoting you for a discussion we were having."

"And I was there?" she asked.

"Parked in your usual place, with Michael looking over your shoulder."

She shrugged. "No wonder they sound familiar. I wonder where *I* got them?"

"From inside. You were writing about people and the planet. You honestly don't remember?"

"I don't know. Maybe I do. It's a long time ago. It could have been me. I hate how grubby it all is—this mess people make trying to pretend being here and then leaving doesn't matter. Yeah, I might have said that."

"Trust me," I assured her. "You did."

She looked at me with some satisfaction. "And what was this at the hospital about me and music?"

"I may have discovered who turned you on—but I'm not sure you're ready to hear it."

Her face clicked into focus. "It was that bitch, wasn't it?" I saw Willie once again coming off the porch toward Mary Jane, her breasts ready to burst out of the borrowed shirt and Michael's arms pulling her back to him. The anger had been raw and dangerous in its own way but unlikely to be repeated once she had vented as much as she did—and for reasons she might soon understand were unjustifiable. I also saw the figure of Mary Jane standing on her front step, the day she discovered the skillful attack on her garden. In her case, it had been personal violation with no intent to harm her—but harm her it did, her and where she lived and the rhythms of her life as different from Willie's as they were similar. In some way, the two were connected by more than a schoolroom confrontation and the music of a Baroque master. It was contrapuntal in a way they would have to figure out, if they had the stomach for it.

"Willie?" Nancy asked.

"The crazy lady that's doing the deed with your ex."

"Mary Jane?"

"It's her, isn't it?" she asked me. "She played music all the time, didn't she? She didn't teach us anything else except how to bust up marriages—but she played records and CDs. I remember the records now, and the clunky machine she played them on. It looked like a box for carrying horseshoes. You should set up horseshoe pits in your backyard when you get the chance," she advised me. "I used to pitch the ridiculous things in the park with my father. Poor bastard was a wounded jock. He could do things underhanded he couldn't do over the top. Like horseshoes. Like his ex-wife." It was the only time she'd mentioned him, ever, and the expressed contradiction showed briefly how her process of defining feelings was never that easy. "But records. I'd never seen them. I thought they were cool. Why do you think I just got this really clear picture? Mikey, that's your department. Why am I getting this video of her and her records right this minute?" He shrugged. "Come on, man. You're supposed to know this stuff." Then, she turned to Nancy, who had given up trying to go into the kitchen to find food and had settled on the arm of the couch next to me. "And you," she said to her. "You taught for what...a year?"

"Yes. A year."

"You and this guy do have a lot in common," she commented, gesturing at me with a shoulder.

"Perhaps we do," Nancy responded with a half-smile.

"Even so, you must know *something* about how these things get into kids' heads."

"I don't know much."

"Nancy has convinced me," I said, "that she doesn't remember much of anything from back then."

Willie shrugged. "That's right. You were sitting there in love with her, according to Mike. What a story."

"Yes," I told her. "Not every story is fiction. Like your Miss Otto, maybe?"

"Not the same at all. I don't have dreams about my teachers, and here you are now having your way with Mary Poppins."

"Mary Poppins?" Nancy's weariness had begun to lift, and we as a group seemed determined for the moment to forget what had brought us together on this day. She got up to pour a glass of wine from an open bottle on the pass-through to the kitchen and then held the bottle aloft. "Anyone?" No one accepted. As she walked toward us again, she commented as coyly as I'd ever heard her, "I like Mary Poppins. I think she was probably splendid in bed...once she got free of her wires. And, Willie, are you preparing to be bad again?"

"No doubt."

"Is it your music that makes you bad? Is that why you've blotted May Jane out of your mind?"

"Not me. Not her. I knew her the minute I saw her in that run-down store. Not at Marvin's, I guess. I just didn't remember everything."

"We all do that. Or we pretend to. But your music—it's one of the things you've told me that I don't forget: how you feel old, old tunes come to your fingertips—like 'friendly demons,' you told me. It must be what makes you pretend you're bad, don't you think?"

"Sure. Why not? I'm a wild child."

"Yes, you are. You and Jeremiah. He goes to his wilderness to plant his beans and you push your wild things out of ancient music. You're both looking for a long-ago sound I understand a little. The few people I taught are that way for me. They are...such...little demons. Because I can't remember them. I can only feel them. Sad, wild music they are. Except for a few." Even with only a few small sips of the wine, she began to sound more tuneful herself, but as she turned to Willie, she addressed her with her eyes tightly focused. "There was, though, a little boy I taught back then. He had a face like a small gray moon and walked like he was still in diapers—like you, sometimes, Willie...like you're marching against orders."

"Hah!" her listener exclaimed.

"He was an actor. He would make himself up in class with pieces of paper he'd stick on parts of his face: He would make beards, mustaches, eyebrows, beauty marks, scars. He'd be there during arithmetic drills sticking bits to himself with paste or saliva. Yes, saliva, Willie. Better there than on the sidewalks. He didn't ever seem to know he was doing it. His hands had lives of their own—like Michael's fascination with Emily's. His addition and subtraction were usually excellent. Very precise." She took a deep breath, continuing to look at Willie, before turning to Michael. "I cared about him so much, I got pregnant. I shouldn't have—but that's the way it was. Friendly demons."

Willie gestured in my direction. "You're talking about him, aren't you.?

"Of course, I am."

"Me? I stuck paper on my face?"

"Yes, Jeremiah, you stuck paper on your face."

"It's not something I would have done."

Willie was fully engaged with the disclosure. "You're such an asshole, Jeremiah," she trumpeted at me, acknowledging my name for the first time. "She just told you she had Mike because of you, and you're thinking about paper!?"

Nancy looked at me with intense affection, as if she was breaking a type of bad news to me, while I tried to understand my own feelings. "When I came to see you last fall, I knew exactly who you were once I saw your face up close. There wasn't that much of a change."

"I have a face like a gray moon?"

She was well-prepared to ignore my questions. "I'd been trying to place your name ever since Michael mentioned it. But I hadn't gotten it until I saw you. You looked perfectly ridiculous and ridiculously perfect in your professor pose, which you seemed so uncertain about. I had this naughty urge to stick Post-its on your face."

"And you didn't tell me because..."

"Because, for one thing, I didn't want to believe it. Believing it would open me up to an extra assortment of vulnerabilities, which, as you've discovered, it may have done." She set her glass down, turned to Michael for a moment, and put her hands on his cheeks. "I hope you're following all this, my darling son. After all is said and done, I wanted you because I wanted you. And while I believe much of what I've been saying—with the help of your Willie—I love you as you."

"The fruit of her loins," Willie said.

Nancy was undeterred. "Yes, put it that way, if you wish."

Michael reacted with his usual succinctness. "What's better? You saw a little boy who made music in you. You wanted to make your own. Now we've all gotten back together. Nothing better." His face reflected his pleasure in what he had been hearing, and he dropped from the couch onto the floor, lying on his back and looking at the ceiling as if finding a place to project what he was visualizing

"Nancy," I finally suggested, "so you dragged me away from the

Vanderbilt gardens for making startling revelations that weren't news at all to you."

"My dear Jeremiah, it was startling to hear you say the things you were saying."

"Such as?" Willie asked.

"Such as loving me from the age of six. That didn't square up at all, in my mind at least, with my adoring a moon-faced child from my single year of teaching and giving up teaching because of it. I couldn't balance one with the other—a difficulty you seem to be having at this moment, if I'm not mistaken."

"But you *did* lie," I suggested to her.

"Point one, Jeremiah: I covered up. And point two: you wanted to make too much of things I still think we would have been better off without."

"Better with," Michael spoke from the floor. "The day we went to his office, Mom, I got tingles in my ears. It was crinkly, and I didn't know what it was. Now, I do."

Willie had begun pacing, a detective applying the finishing touches to a case—one hand behind her back. The distant sound of a siren underscored the moment. "So, are you two getting married?"

"No," Nancy and I replied simultaneously.

"You're just going to...?"

"No," we repeated.

"Whatever that means," Willie concluded.

"Yes," Nancy laughed, "whatever that means."

For the first time, Nancy and I slept together in *her* bed that night, leaving Michael and Willie to have a smoke and scavenge for food and hopefully find a calmness within their own shared space. For Nancy, it needed to be a time of celibacy until she knew what was happening within her. I suppose we were both glad not to have to worry about sending the stifled sounds of lovemaking to those elsewhere in the house. But it was more—it was something we had not done before, experiencing the simple blessing of holding each other in a way that had its own sufficiency and made us partners of the silence. A light rain had begun, and our joined breathing became a lighter layer of its descent. She disliked air conditioning, so the windows were open, bringing the pattering into us along with the scent of the surrounding night. Our arms and legs interlinked and caressed with the peaceful rhythms of being neither foreplay nor climax. Simplicity. Our feet had been mere acquaintances to this point. But on this night they developed a relationship of their own, doing a new dance of tracing and familiarizing. They got along well. My fingers learned the way in which touching her neck or forehead or hair could change the texture of her sleeper's sounds.

There was a part of me that wished to talk, but we had come to the bedroom with the understanding that the day had spoken enough after the unspeakability of what had brought us to the hospital. Emily. Emily Acampora. Acts of violence—against many or against one—kept us grinding the finish from the ancient human yearning to believe we are made of divine substance. We can produce the music of Bach and Lennon and the paintings of Vermeer and Botticelli, but days like this produce deep pangs for the way we can astonish each other with the exquisite and then shred it apart...reminded of how easily we are able to hate one another. If, as the woman lying next to me had seemed to suggest, I went to plant beans in a movie set wilderness, at times it promised little more peace than the asphalt playgrounds of the ghetto. The past jabs at us with lessons that can be learned and relearned and unlearned through the swift and sudden animosities that eradicate what should be the greater memories of our making a collective world. It is, sadly, not always enough to nest gratefully together.

SIX

As I waited to hear that Emily was growing stronger and we would be allowed to see her, I devoted my energies to the print shop that had become a barbershop before becoming a home for mice and an otherwise empty dollhouse waiting whatever renewal I could contrive. I had made good progress on the main house in this first of many rounds of bringing it into the present. The living room was done except for a new floor—no small item, I realized, but I began to think it was the kind of project I could do myself with advice from P.Q. and help from Michael. I had bought triple-track screen and storm combinations for the four windows, the kind I had grown up with in The Professor's house. The dining room was usable after being a staging area for the first two months. The clutter was gone, and the walls were painted. The table and sideboard that had come with the house had been cleaned and polished with a concoction of turpentine, linseed, and lemon oil Nancy had prescribed, and she promised she would do the same with the piano. So far there were two rush-bottom chairs at the table, an inexpensive purchase from Bill and Lucille who had conducted their version of an argument with me about making them a belated housewarming present. We actually did a form of reverse bargaining. I gradually lowered the price I had insisted on giving them and they raising the acceptance price step-by-step from a few dollars. One with arms was at the head of the table and the other was positioned at the side that faced the kitchen. No one had yet sat in them with any conviction or purpose, but the time would come. The kitchen was not yet Louisa-ready, but it too had been partially decluttered, and I had cleaned and repainted the windows of its large bay and given them blinds to replace the ragged shades that came with the house. The old screen inserts had been moved to these windows from the living room so more air came into the house without a blanket of bugs riding upon it. Honeybees, however, were still within the rearmost wall of the kitchen. While they had treated me with hospitality, I realized the time was coming when I would have to assert an owner's rights. I'd been hearing more and more that mankind's survival was bee-dependent, so I would need to find a safe and respectful way to move them elsewhere.

It was nearly August, the witching month that would bring me gradually up against the change of seasons and my own new version of normalcy. I would need to order firewood, create a place to stack it, and gather kindling. I would soon have to treat new cycles as reality. I would need to put insulation into the small attic and crawl spaces and find a way to protect any unprotected windows from the coming of fall and winter. If I had come to play an effete Thoreau, I would need to plant a whole lot more in the way of ideas and solutions. I would need to keep improving on the wisdom of my move to Quaker Falls.

I needed time, however, to do something that didn't matter in the way of wood cords and insulation, and that would be the cabin. I had told Nancy about it when she drove me to get my truck at Jefferson's the morning after our night together. We had woken to the sound of Michael's harmonica and the smell of bacon and the wispy rediscovery that we were in her bed together—our first full night—the sexless legitimization of ourselves to those who were doing the business of the house without us. Willie served bacon and pancakes with the cool polish of a person who does catering to the puzzles of others day by day. I told her she had a surprising flair for the domestic and she told me to keep it to myself. For her, it was a degree of aplomb.

"It's like she's given up on trying to make sense of things—for one day, at least," I told Nancy in the car. "A whole new composition to learn." Nancy nodded and referred to it as Willie's domestic dervish. She asked how I liked waking up in her bed, and I assured her it was a luxurious sensation. She agreed.

We talked of Emily and evil and the emotional battering Barbara Lynn was taking. Like Willie, Nancy asked what I made of Jefferson's sudden command of the moment, his rescue routine, and she offered her belief that there was more to it than good friendship. I conceded there is often more than we know, and she looked at me with the clear understanding that I was hedging. She left it at that.

She told me she hadn't seen the house in more than two weeks and needed to see how badly I was messing things up. I gave her a rundown of what I had done recently and my plan to step away from it for a time to work on the shop. She liked the idea as another of my whims but one that fed her own feelings about the property: "I know you and I are still trying to understand what you're doing there," she suggested supportively. "And taking another step away from what you're supposed to be doing might actually make sense. If that makes sense." I thought it did, and I was heartened she felt that way since I didn't know where, if anywhere, this diversion was leading.

As she dropped me in Jefferson's parking area, she added instructively, "Possibly you need to find if there's more meaning in a print shop or barbershop." I watched her drive away, thankful for a reason to build on. It felt like a friendly handshake.

I was glad to be in the orange Dakota again and stopped at the country hardware store that had become my safe haven during periods of practical puzzlement. It was my newest reference tool, my anthology put together by wise hands and minds understanding the ways of dividing, joining, uncovering, surfacing, supporting, reducing, enlarging, shaping, and skills beyond. The store was called Crispin and Sons, and I did ask during one stop whether the name still applied. It partially did. The elder Crispin had died a half-century before, but two brothers, most likely in their seventies, still ran the store, bobbing about from shelf to shelf, from backroom to backroom, from porch to outbuilding—reminding me of the two gentlemen who tended the bookshop in

Rhinebeck. They had quickly sized me up as new to the game of being handy, took pleasure in worming from me my previous and only occupation, called me the headmaster, and treated each of my questions as an affirmation of their ability to continue in a business the box stores would have devoured for breakfast.

I came in on this day with the word "whitewash" playing in my mind like two half-notes. I had known the word primarily as it spoke about the tendency of humans to make the faults of themselves or others look like virtues, the manufactured mirages of the irresponsible. But what I wanted was applied to wood—in this case on the walls of my mutable shop. The Crispins cooed like fraternal pigeons when I presented my question to them, and each brought a different one-gallon can to place on their counter, pointing out the advantages of each brand and introducing the word "pickling" to my life. It was a way, they told me, of adding white color to wood while letting the grain show through—a way of making the present a ghost of the past. They had a brotherly disagreement about which of the two gallons I should finally choose, so I let them work it out through what seemed a practiced routine for them, and they did it lyrically. They armed me with a small vibrating sander—different from any in Michael's inventory—along with a packet of paper to fit it, and sent me on my way with the wishes of the venerable. I was ready to pickle.

After sweeping out the shop, I brought a small stepladder from the house to reach the tops of the walls, and ran a power cord out one of the living room windows, up the two steps and through the door of the shop. I sat on the ladder for several minutes looking at the project before me, as the sun came in over my shoulder and through the window beside the door. The ceiling I would leave untouched. Its faded boards would contrast with the walls and serve, for a time, as a remnant of the past. It would have the beauty of being what it was. The floors I would think about later, floors being what they are: where the feet of humans have sounded the emotions of days and nights, pacing to discover, scuffling to forget, moving to greet or dismiss. But now, here, in particular—in this generations-old place of work and escape and whatever else brought people inside—I thought of the printer and the barber and those who came to them to have their needs met, who gossiped and were gladdened or left with their disappointments. I looked at the marks on the floor, where barber's chair or desk or printing press or cabinet had left their indentations, their scuff marks, and scratches. It was too soon to cover this up, like sealing an unread book in a layer of wax. For now, I would cover it in drop cloths to read and reread before deciding what to do. I would read, even before the drop cloth. I would lean, for a time, on the ladder and do a first few paragraphs.

As I looked at a rear corner of the floor where a piece of apparatus had perhaps been bolted down, I read what I had not before. The sun threw its light on two large and empty screw holes not far from where I was standing, the ones I had noticed the first time I inspected the outbuildings. Three feet behind and parallel to them, however, were two rusted, flat-headed screws. The four markers together—two screws and two empty holes, created a relatively perfect square, and it became clear in the flutter of seconds what I might be looking at. One of the hiding places on The Underground Railroad could be staring up at me, at rest for perhaps a century-and-a-half, a silent outline of harsh necessity and hope. Had this door never been lifted from its opening in all that time? Surely someone, the printer who constructed it or the barber or the father and son who owned the house before me would have been moved to peer within, particularly with the legends of rescue and loss that existed in the hamlet. It couldn't have lain like this—a sealed memory—without someone taking it into his or her hands and coming to a realization of what it meant. On the other hand, it didn't matter. If it was the top cover of forgotten actions, I would, at this instant, allow myself the fiction of being the first to peer within.

I brought a screwdriver and work light from the house. I had developed some skill with a power drill and its attachments, but this wanted to be done by a plain, hand-guided screwdriver. I hung the light from one of several vestigial hooks in the wall above the square of wood. The heads of the two screws were rusted, but their slots had kept enough of their edges for the screwdriver to bite in without slippage.

Each screw groaned patiently as I began the process of loosening, each turn a little easier than the last, and the shafts of the screws retained much of the original shine from where they had bitten into the joists beneath them. I finally put the screws into a pocket of my shorts, feeling the pointed end of each jabbing against my thigh in the way of live things with the power of earlier hands still encased in them. I pried the square of wood upward with the screwdriver, making use of a small indentation along the front side—where, it was easy to believe, the same process had taken place for vastly different purposes in hidden times. The odor of sealed space was as I had expected: the damp compaction of dirt, the rancid tang of framing lumber—a smell I'd come to know from the basement of my house. But there were more presumably old, old smells I couldn't put a name to.

Before I directed artificial light into the space, I noticed a narrow path of daylight coming into it, like the tight glimmer of a miniature searchlight. I inserted my head into the darkness and saw the light coming from a small opening in what was the rear of the building. I had never inspected the backsides of the outbuildings and went to look, skirting the quince tree with its dozens of fist-sized fruits. The opening itself was facing northward, letting in what light it could. It was a rectangle, about a foot long and six inches high, covered with a heavily rusted piece of metal mesh, textured to let in air and the strangled light but to keep out animals. Its purpose was obvious, and I thought of the small hole in a side attic where slave woman Harriet Jacobs had hidden within her grandmother's house for seven years. I had taught her narrative in the same course as *Huckleberry Finn*, and my students and I recoiled under the weight of her description. I had wondered to myself at the time whether I would ever have the guts to teach it again. There is claustrophobia of space but also one of the imagination unable to project itself properly. I was freed now from that particular wondering, even as its reality moved from a page to a hole in the earth.

Returning to the shop, I entered the square opening in the floor with work light in hand, shining it below me to see how deep the drop would be and how I would lower myself. It seemed about four feet, and the problem of entering was solved by a makeshift set of wooden steps supported by a piece of fieldstone serving as their threshold. My breath caught as I went backward down the steps and onto the dirt floor, brushing at spider webs as they attached to me.

Only half the area beneath the floor had been dug to a depth where a person could move about by crouching and could sit, listening, with a degree of comfort. The other half was less than a crawl space, six to eight inches between the dirt and the floor joists above. The person who constructed the shop had done so in part with the configuration of the area below the floor clearly in mind. In fact, the shop may have been built for a greater purpose than making a living. How I needed to know more about the person or persons who built this structure.

There were only a few discoveries in this four-by-eight space that could rightfully be called artifacts. If there had been furniture—a cot, a stool, a small table, perhaps—it had been removed by those who may have placed them there. With emancipation proclaimed, with the Civil War finally given to the future to sort out its meaning, had these liberators considered their work done? Had they given themselves permission to unassumingly erase what they had done and move anonymously onward as though the entire episode had never happened? And why would that be? The creative writing teacher I had as an undergraduate—when I was generating poetry to a muse carrying another man's baby—one time said that stories come into our heads the way stories come into our lives: like lost buttons found again. It made some sense.

And here, in the underworld of a print shop, I did find an actual button made of bone perhaps, along with what looked like the chewed remnants of a dress or shirt. The latter had most likely provided nesting material for generations of field mice, but outlines of its stitchery remained, like a cloth skeleton. More compelling were the leather covers of what might have been a pocket-sized notebook or small volume of readings on the edge of the crawlspace. Whatever it had contained had been gnawed away by time or teeth.

I brought these relics through the opening, clutching them in one hand and the work light in the other, and I inhaled the air of the shop with a hunger for freshness that was both satisfying and enervating; I wobbled for a time between the two, while my eyes were slowly adjusted to the sunlight coming in the doorway. I had the pedantic thought of Plato's Cave, where we face realizations too blinding to look at directly. In this case, however, someone was standing rigidly within the sunburst, and as my eyes returned partway to normal, I could see the shape of a woman.

"Nancy?"

"Jeremiah," the figure said. "It's Ellen. I hope that's all right."

I believe I said "Oh fuck"—but if I did she let it pass unnoticed.

"I followed this extension cord from the house." She held a slack section of it with one hand. "It led me here."

My eyes had partially readjusted, and I could see a face that had not changed in any meaningful way, although the hair was longer and lighter than it had been. She was wearing a multicolored top and a khaki-colored skirt that reached to her ankles. "How did you find the house?" I asked.

"Through a nice older woman in Rhinebeck named Eleanor, who seemed a great fan of yours."

"And how did you find Eleanor?"

"In good spirits." She intended it as a joke, the type of wordplay that had been a source of amusement to my child ears and then corrected herself apologetically. "I was given your old address by Phyllis Friel."

"You know Phyllis?"

She dropped the electrical cord to the ground. "I've known Phyllis a good many years. She thought you had moved, but she gave me your last address." She looked at me with the calm compression of her lips I found stored in my memory. "Jeremiah, are we going to talk about Phyllis? That wasn't what I came to do."

"And what did you come to do?"

Her head bobbed slightly. "That sounds peevish but to be expected. You did inform me, however, that you were sorry we missed each other for your birthday and you had this idea we might wish to try again. Am I correct?"

"Quite. Words to that effect. It did seem there was a reaching out to each other—after all of those oblique e-mailings during the last year, the ones telling me I would be better off to not think about them. That was your motherly prescription for being better off as our years apart went forward." She peered at me with the look of a mechanic adjusting a critical setting. "And it was through Phyllis you knew where I was teaching—or even *that* I was teaching—and, I gather, that I was no longer teaching?"

"Partly through Phyllis, yes—though I can't imagine why you have this preoccupation with her."

"It's no preoccupation. But she has been, and possibly continues to be, a burr in my brain, and she was my chair—a leader into the battle."

"A preoccupation," Ellen insisted with a slight frown. "Could we move into the shade and could you possibly offer me a chair and a refreshment? Today has been difficult." She looked at the shop. "Then, perhaps, you can tell me what this cabin is about, what brought you out here, and other things of that sort. You look well in cobwebs, by the way." She started to extend a hand toward me before pulling it back.

"Perhaps," I suggested, "we could catch up on you before catching up on me."

"Very well." She looked about the yard.

"But, yes, let's move. There are chairs out back. And I'll find a bottle of water." I stared at her before moving, picking at the cobwebbing on my shoulders. "Do you suppose we should clasp hands or embrace or whatever is appropriate in these situations? We used to high-five with the very best."

"Let's see how things work out. We're in still waters." It was a phrase I had heard her use any number of times during my childhood to describe a situation whose outcome was in doubt. I liked hearing it now, though it continued to be, as it always had been, a saying whose appropriateness was sketchy.

"Well enough." We had just started across the lawn when I saw

Nancy Feller's car taking the curve of the road and stopping behind the Jeep that had brought Ellen. Nancy honked, two quick toots signaling a happy arrival. She got out of the car aiming a small wood-framed mirror at me. She raised it briefly to shoulder height, and I could see how dirty I had gotten during my explorations. I could also see Ellen watching over my right shoulder. As she approached, Nancy lowered the mirror and asked if she was interrupting something important.

"That hasn't been decided yet," I told her. "This is my mother, whom you've met before, a long time ago."

Nancy was undeterred, relieved, it seemed. "Yes," she said affectionately to the woman behind me. "I remember you, though I doubt you would remember me. I was Jeremiah's teacher in the first grade. You came to see me."

"I remember," Ellen said in a parched voice, reminding me I had promised her water. "You had a classroom that looked like a clearing in the forest. There were plants and pictures of various trees."

"I'm grateful you remember that."

"It is no wonder Jeremiah has come at last to Walden Pond, though I don't see a pond."

"Only the most enchanted millstream—over there." She indicated the direction with her head. "If you listen—"

"Yes. I hear it. It cleans the air. And you are what now?" Ellen asked her.

"Pardon me?"

"I think she wants to know," I suggested, "whether you are still guiding me in the fundamentals of learning or whether you are something else." I turned to Ellen, whose look had softened in the moments since Nancy's arrival. "To which my answer is 'both.'"

"I see. Jeremiah, were we just about to sit down in a shady location?"

"Yes. I'm sorry." The three of us walked to the chairs that still faced the meadow and hillside beyond the yard. Ellen was mostly silent but observant of the details of the property, pausing to peer into the vegetable garden and looking up into the bird-pecked and misshapen apples of that nearest tree. She asked if she could pick one and, removing it with a practiced twist, polished it on the side of her skirt. "It looks," she commented on its knotty shape, "like it's attempting to inhale but can't quite do it." She took a careful bite from one of the few normal spots on the fruit and nodded her approval. "It tastes of McIntosh. Sharp and decisive. No mixed-up tastes. You're to be congratulated. Next time, though, you will need to spray." Her voice modulated between a tone I knew from her mothering days to cadences and inflections she had acquired during our years apart—or, for as much as I knew, from the suddenness of this day. It was difficult to know whether to view hers as the act of a conjurer or a vagabond. I thought of her dead husband before setting the idea aside.

Nancy read my indecision and offered to bring another chair from the back porch. She showed no indication that she should leave Ellen and me to sort things out on our own. She acted, in fact, as if committed to hosting this event that had been so long in coming. If others might see her as intruding, she was tuned to doing the best for everyone. And she was right. She was right to be there at that moment, triangulated as it was and needed to be. I told Nancy I had already promised to bring water and I would bring another chair, causing her to nod me on my way.

By the time I reached the house, the two women had settled into place with the apparent naturalness of those who had been having backyard chats for years. Their heads bobbed companionably, nearly erasing me across the short distance—allowing me to adjust to the sequence of what had just happened. My discovery in the cabin was so clear in its initial meaning I could not yet question its actuality; the sun-ringed figure of the woman who had left me a dozen years ago, like Joanna Wexler at the reading of the will, each of them haloed by a trick of nature that proclaimed the right of annunciation; Nancy entering smoothly into this unbalanced moment and rediscovering an old friend who was never her friend.

When I brought the three bottles of water, the women were communicating with the quiet flourishes of practiced gossipers. And as I returned with the chair, I heard Ellen saying something that produced light laughter in her listener. Nancy—who so often during our months together had felt like the keeper of laughter, parceling it out as scoops of light and reassurance, even when it was calling me into question—made it sound now like it was already softening the off-pitch tones of unexplainable separation. Hopefully.

When I returned with the chair, Nancy once again held up the mirror she had brought with her, forgotten in the minutes since she had been introduced to Ellen.

"Your mother thinks," she announced, "that it will be useful on days like this to get your hair back into place. You *do* look like a barberry." The mirror itself was somewhere around nine by twelve inches, with a frame of striped wood, recently oiled, and what gazed back at me matched her description pretty well. I patted the top of my head with the palm of one hand before positioning the third chair facing them. Over Ellen's right shoulder, the open doorway to the cabin had become a darkened rectangle. "I have been doing yard sales since you readjusted my life. I never thought they were worth my attention, everyone pawing through each other's junk. But I've wobbled once again, thanks to you, no doubt. And, yes, I have informed Ellen that you and I are an item in our own yard sale. She seems to have taken it fairly well." She turned to Ellen, clipping the words to sound like her listener. "Is that correct?"

Ellen drank from her bottle before saying, "It's unexpected but refreshing, I would guess. It is an event to wonder about. And I shall."

I looked at them. "You two have covered an impressive amount of territory in a short amount of time," I commented.

"I remembered this woman as a person with unusual gifts," Ellen said, looking at her. "She assured me long ago that you were a special part of her work. And so it appears to have turned out."

I watched Nancy take a long sip from her bottle. She had set the mirror on the ground, leaning it against the side of her chair where it reflected the woman next to her. "And has she also told you where she's been for the last dozen or so years?"

"That hasn't come up, until now," Nancy said. "Possibly she would like to choose her own time to tell you."

"Yes, yes I would," Ellen agreed. "I've made a treaty with time in recent years. I will demand as much from it as it does from me. I've sworn off merely accommodating it, if you must know. It has its own responsibilities for the way things are, but I won't forget myself in the process. It takes practice, but it's worth the effort, as grasping as that may sound. So it won't be today—the sharing of my hidden history. I had only intended, Jeremiah, to see how you and I would look at each other—to each other. So far, we have possibilities as far as what we need to learn about ourselves." She stood. "In this case, brevity will be the refinement of curiosity. And I still don't entirely disagree with what I said to you by e-mail: that you might well be better served by my being out of your life completely. We'll see." She held the bottle aloft. "May I take this with me?"

"You're going?" I exclaimed.

"Yes."

I rose to join her. "Not that I should be surprised, Ellen. You're an accomplished goer." Nancy spoke my name with cautionary firmness, and I looked at her before turning back to Ellen. "I realize you made the first move—twice now. Does this mean I might see you again, or is there the equal possibility I might not?"

"How would you feel about that?"

"I spent half my life pretending not to feel betrayed. I would be sorry to lose that ability."

Ellen looked at me with lonely eyes and puckered her lips. "I hope to be back. In August. I should like to see you in August."

"That's only a week away."

"And other weeks to follow. The first doesn't make the month."

There was so much to say, so many questions darting into the moment. She was moving toward the front of the house, bottle in hand. I followed while Nancy stayed in her chair. "You and my father never divorced."

"Yes, I know that."

"Why is that?"

"It never seemed a necessary action."

"But he left you out of his will. That seems unfair."

"It was entirely justifiable. I didn't want anything. I'm glad it's given you opportunities you might not have had. Your Nancy can bring things for your adventure. It's good for her. She's good for you, though I assume there are occasional difficulties—for you and those who watch you."

"Yes, occasional." We had reached her car when I thought of the overblown question mark still tucked inside *Reconsiderations*. "If you could wait a minute, he did leave one thing for you. It's a piece of paper he included with his will."

"I'll see it another time. Not now." She smiled thinly. "You've become a nearly handsome man, Jeremiah, and I believe there will be more of that to come. Now, I would like to give you a quick hug and then start on my way."

"And, once again, that's it!?"

"Yes. For today."

"We are strange people, Ellen."

"I suppose."

I looked toward the shop. "I'd like to tell you about my place of cobwebs."

"Next time."

"So many delays."

"Yes, a good many."

"What about your family?"

"Family?"

"In Italy."

"*I* am my family," she replied in a conjurer's voice. "Though there might still be a quiet place for you."

She put her arms around me, and while it was as she promised, quickly done, the strength of her arms was unexpected and they left an impression I could feel for the next several minutes. I tried hugging her back, but she had pivoted away and opened the door to the car. "Jeep," she said simply and as if by way of explanation. What I was to take from that I didn't know.

As I returned to Nancy, I heard my phone buzzing on the window sill of the workshop, where I had left it before beginning my exploration beneath the floor. The text was from Jefferson, announcing that Emily was out of danger but there were new dangers ahead. He didn't elaborate.

SEVEN

As if she could feel the air heavy with things near but unseen, Nancy asked to spend the night. It was unpremeditated. She had brought nothing with her except the wall mirror but promised she was ready to rough it in the name of solidarity. She would even do the unthinkable and share my toothbrush. We sat for a time in the lawn chairs after I had returned the third chair to the porch. The late-day noise of katydids was that of a machine honing the edges of the midsummer heat, and the leaves of the tree Ellen had pulled her apple from were fluttering in a self-soothing way. Our trysting-hill looked down to us with mindful secrecy. It would have been a time to be satisfied with silence if there hadn't been so much to speak about. I held the cell to her so she could read the message from Jefferson and asked what she thought the last part might mean.

"More news," she guessed. "But I get the feeling it's not bad news or he wouldn't connect it to what is so important to hear. Why don't you just call him? I know you have a thing about phoning, but this might be a time to give in."

"He'll tell me when he wants to. And this was no broadcast message. It was to me. He's preparing me for something. I can wait."

"We can go see Emily, at least."

"Yes, that will be good. We'll see how well our blood colors her cheeks. I wish we could devote ourselves to thoughts of nothing else." I paused. "And what did you decide about my mother?"

"Your *mother* is it? And what was it I was supposed to decide?"

I picked up the mirror and finger-combed my hair before setting it on my lap and tucking it against myself. "Who is she? *What* is she? Did she come here to explain herself or is she trying to establish a final version of why no explanation will be forthcoming—and none is necessary?"

"Another of you and your either-ors. In those few minutes I talked with her, I found her quirky in a graceful way. She's not unlike someone else I know."

"I never thought of myself *or* her as particularly graceful."

"You can be. She's a mother, I think, who's not in love with being a mother. That's obvious, I suppose. But she asked me if I had children, and when I told her I had one son, she wondered whether that made me feel isolated. I think that's what she said."

"Isolated?"

"Yes," she said, touching one of her hands to the other. "It's interesting, isn't it? You and I are both only children, and I'm the mother of an only child. Does that mark us in some way?"

"It may mark *her*, but..." I had no idea what I wanted to say. Then, I asked her, "Does she think we'd all feel *less* isolated if we had *no* children?"

"I don't know. You'll have to ask her. She'll be back. I'm quite sure of that. I think she wants you to have something, but I'm not sure even she knows what that might be." Nancy stood. "Come show me what you've accomplished in your cabin."

The whitewash, the square in the floor, the space beneath had been pushed to a waiting place by Ellen's sudden appearance. Though both she and the cabin carried secrets of the past, the living presence who had stared in at me through the glare of one very particular moment, had muted the reverberations of what I had found inside: the found news retiring patiently, waiting just moments longer. Foster child of silence.

"You know, don't you?" I said to Nancy.

"Know what, Jeremiah?"

"That I've found something—in the cabin."

"How would I know?"

"Sometimes women just do."

She smiled. "Yes, that. I recall someone saying that. And what is it that you've found?"

"Come." I took her hand and led her to the cabin. She smiled at the extension cord trailing along the ground and the way it gave the lawn a crooked smile. I could feel the objects in my pocket pressing against my thigh, most especially the tips of the screws. I removed them to show her.

She read them off in her practiced show-and-tell voice: "A pair of rusty screws, a button, and a hunk of cloth. You've started a collection?"

"Yes. A collection. Along with collecting puzzling older women, I've branched out. And there's much, much more. Come look."

The work light was still on, hanging from one of the metal braces of the stepladder, and Nancy was immediately drawn to the hole in the floor.

"Jeremiah?" She bent to peer into the darkness, and I brought the light, holding it over the opening. "It's not just a cellar, is it? It's something more?"

"Yes."

She sighed and swallowed. "It's where they hid, isn't it?"

"Yes."

"There are steps. What else?"

"Nothing more. Not now."

"Could I go down?"

"Do you want to?"

"Yes, I think I do." I held one of her hands as she went backward down the set of steps, and I handed her the light when her feet touched the dirt floor. For several seconds, her head disappeared beneath where I was standing, before reappearing fully above the opening. Her eyes were wet with tears. "Oh, Jeremiah, you can feel them breathing here. They went on, but they left the feeling of their breath behind. Do you think there were many? Did they make it?"

"At least one probably didn't," I reminded her. "But there could have been many who did."

"Yes—yes, there must have been." She snuffled. "Silly of me, but I can't believe how powerful it is. Please help me up before I lose total control." After drawing her through the opening, I brushed her eyes with a finger and kissed them lightly. "Oh glory," she said, "coming from down below, it's like being born. It must have felt that way to them, don't you think—when they were told by others it was safe to move on? And those dear people who risked their own selves to be in a position to tell them. I can only begin to imagine." She paused. "I think I'd like to cry again—just a little one."

"There's one other thing," I said while I held her. "The remnants of a book." My cell rang. The caller's number read "Unavailable," and my normal inclination would have been to ignore it, but on a day such as this one, unavailability had its own attraction.

"Am I speaking to Jeremiah?" the voice asked. It lacked the tones of one trying to sell me anything, and while the sound was familiar, I couldn't place it. "I have called to see if you got to speak with your mother today." It was Eleanor Jewett, briskly without preliminary, the person who had sent Ellen on her way to find me. Her voice conveyed both curiosity and pleasure. "I've never called you before, but this seemed such a special occasion. She did find you, I trust?"

"It's my other girlfriend," I told Nancy, before answering the caller. "Yes, Eleanor. She came by. For a few minutes."

"I see. Only a few, was it? Were you nice to her?"

"Reasonably."

"She seemed a nice person, easy to be nice to."

"I'm glad you think so."

"I would appreciate your telling me more when you have more to tell. I've had this feeling that there is much going on in your life as a... what was it I called it?"

"*Hausfrau.*"

"That's good. It's kind of you to remember."

"Happy to. You are not a person I would want to disappoint. And I believe you are correct about things going on."

"Well, of course. That's all I wanted to know. It's been very nice talking to you, and I'm sure we'll talk again."

"That's pretty much what she said."

"Your mother? I have certainly never been a mother, but I think that's fine." And she hung up—neither a hello nor a good-bye; the heart of the matter was her cup of tea, as usual.

"How I wish I could be that succinct," I said to Nancy. I explained the purpose of her mini-investigation, realizing I'd not told her about Eleanor's role in directing my mother to the doorstep of the cabin. A male cardinal in the quince was offering what sounded like words of encouragement to his mate. His scarlet feathering was right for the occasion, a little pompous but instructive. He, too, was voicing the heart of his own matter. "It must have been a vitalizing thing for her, being the trusty guide. I'm surprised she didn't jump into the Jeep with her. And why a Jeep?"

"Why anything?" Nancy scolded.

"You, my lady, are getting more wicked as the weeks go by. I couldn't have said a more exasperating thing myself."

"I'll keep practicing."

"Do."

"You were telling me about a book."

I pulled the leather covers from my back pocket, looking at them in full sunlight for the first time. They were still somewhat attached with a few remaining strips of the thin leather binding linking them. Whether it had been book or journal was no more evident in this light than it had been by the work light, but whatever importance it had once possessed had not fully disappeared, left as it was for our imaginations to acknowledge. Nancy took it from me and held each cover in the palm of a hand, hymnal-like, trying to draw from it a clue to its identity. She was still teary from earlier and sniffled again.

"It doesn't really matter, does it?" she said. "It doesn't really matter what it was because it was something good. It must have been.

It was a source of comfort for what it contained." She brought her hands together, closing the two pieces gently. "They could have been punished—or worse—for knowing how to read, couldn't they?"

"Yes."

She looked at it with stern conviction. "I'd like to imagine it was a diary and it held the thoughts of a person who was dreaming how new the world would be." She considered. "But then I wouldn't like to think of that person when he or maybe she realized it had been left behind and there was no way to retrieve it—and all those feelings left underground. I may have to change my mind, Jeremiah, and make it into a book—inspirational writings that were known by heart, anyhow. Do you think that's possible?"

How beautiful she was, weighing her reactions, negotiating through her imagination with the puzzles of lost meaning. There were still those fluctuations in time when I could be astonished by the expressiveness of her face in a way not terribly different from how it had been in my childhood. The precocious young teacher was still wired into her, the person who had and did bring to discovery an air of quivering refinement. I asked her impulsively if she ever thought about being in the classroom again.

"What," she laughed, "and give up yard sales after making them my great new discovery? They're everywhere. And you're the one who should be rethinking your reasons for leaving. But I've told myself I won't talk about that anymore."

"It wasn't reasons. It was feelings. Reasons would make it more defensible."

"Willie says you enjoy not doing what you're good at—although I could probably think of exceptions to that." She placed the soiled and tattered book cover into my hands like a promise returned. "Are you going to tell others? You have to, you know. You can't just use it as your wishing and dreaming place, can you?"

"Nancy, I have to get to know it first. It's selfish of me, but I don't want others digging into it yet. It's important to us—you and me, that is—in a way I need to get to know. And you, too. When it's time to tell others, we will."

"You won't tell the man down the road?"

"Bill? Not yet."

"You *are* your mother's son, Jeremiah."

"Perhaps *that*, Nancy, is part of what I need to find out in there."

The mail carrier stopped his mirror-encrusted box-vehicle near us rather than the mailbox. He was a chatty character a little older than myself who had been among the first to welcome me to the neighborhood, though admitting his "neighborhood" was much larger than Quaker Falls. He was my first carrier who drove rather than delivered on foot, giving me another measure of my becoming a country boy.

"Your place is starting to sparkle, so to speak" he said to me, while nodding at Nancy. "Your mom?" I shook my head. "Well, not sparkle exactly. That will take a couple of coats of paint. Even your roof. I'll look forward to seeing you up *there* when the time comes. Fun job. But it's coming. Been a long time." He reached behind him. "Oh, yeah, your mail. It would have been dandy for me to just drive off, wouldn't it?" He handed his delivery to me—a few windowed envelopes, some circulars, and a small US Postal Service mailer box. "Later, gator." He nodded at Nancy. "Ma'am." I could see Mary Jane Otto standing beside her mailbox along with Steverino, fingering each piece the postman had left her. She waved at us tepidly as the dog peed briefly on the post.

"What a big deal we make about mail we can still hold in our hands," I said as we went toward the front door. "Every day a new rush of excitement. She waits curbside for him, though there aren't any curbs. Then, more crap to throw out until the next day."

"Such a brusque boy you can be," Nancy suggested. "I like mail, too. Why don't you handwrite something nice, put it in an envelope, and put a stamp on it. You know how to do that, I assume?"

"Would you like it on green stationery?"

"As you wish." She held the screen door for me, guiding me inside with a slight flourish of her free arm.

The return address on the mailer was clear enough. The Office of Joanna Wexler. I dropped it onto the kitchen table and stared at it. Nancy, meanwhile, had discovered the Moxie bottle I'd picked up from the meadow on my scouting expedition to Mary Jane's garden. I had placed it on a battered shelf over the sink, along with dishwashing liquid, soaps of various sorts—including a yellow one said to prevent poison ivy—Brillo pads, a box of stick matches, and Band-Aids. Louisa would not have approved, I was sure, whereas Nancy had taken the bottle with notable enthusiasm.

"Moxie!" she exclaimed as if casting a spell. "Where did you find this?" I told her, and she began washing it. "Did you ever taste one?" One what, I wondered. "A Moxie. It's the worst-tasting soft drink in the world. Something only a mother could love. I'm one of them. You can only get this in a few backwater parts of the country—Chautauqua County being a particular example." I thought of Mary Jane's regionally limited white hots. "It's been around longer than Coke, I think, and it's made of nasty roots, but it's supposed to give you moxie. That's where the word comes from, for your information." She waved the bottle at me. "We'll go on a road trip one fine day, for you to meet my family and buy Moxie."

"Fine." And then, "Do they know about me?"

She poured out the water she had run inside the bottle, bringing with it globs of field debris. "They know I am 'seeing' one of Michael's college teachers. That will have to satisfy them for now."

"Will I have to wear makeup to be presented to them?"

"I'll prepare them when the time comes."

"And?"

She laughed naughtily. "Probably, they will shoot you. These are hill folks."

"We have much to go through. And when we tell them we are firmly committed to never making honest partners of each other?"

"They will be greatly relieved, I'm sure—if they haven't begun the shooting yet." She wiped off the bottle with a paper towel and held it out for me to admire. "Moxie. That's what we'll need. But I'd like to think that's what we'll be giving to each other without having to drink this stuff. You really would hate it, I'm sure."

"Moxie."

"Yes. But possibly not. There are a few souls brave enough to permit its deep pleasures. You might be one of them, my dearest." She set the bottle on the table and picked up the package. "And what is this from your lawyer?"

"A small bomb. Or ricin."

"You trust her that much, do you?"

"She has a hidden supply of secrets that should eventually burn out her insides. Did you ever eat a tabasco pepper—a whole one, not the spicy goo you shake over your scrambled eggs?" She shook her head. "I did, once—the night after I defended my dissertation—after several shots of mescal provided by well-meaning friends. It blew the stars out of my eyes for the next month. That's how she looks—like there's an entire galaxy she's scorched out of herself. Her eyes make me think of the insides of two sealed closets. I can see why Willie tiptoes around her."

She gestured with the package. "Shall I?" I told her to be my guest. She unzipped the box and opened a flap, before shaking out a book. "All right," she commented. "This doesn't look too dangerous." She held it out to me, and I recognized it immediately: a copy of *Reconsiderations*.

"I told you it was a bomb. You've held its twin. In my apartment. You temporarily defused it." I opened the front cover and removed a piece of paper, the lawyerly letterhead folded into quarters, with the simple phrase: "A work of your father's I thought you might be interested in. JW." I handed it to Nancy. "The bitch."

"It seems innocent enough."

"The wicked women of the west are ganging up on me today. They're dropping by in every way imaginable. It's like you all got together this morning with a game plan to get the dropout to drop his teeth and his shorts."

She sighed warily. "Are you including me in your blanket statement, Jeremiah?"

"No, ma'am, not in any way—unless you're about to leave without telling me something I would need to know."

"You'd like me to leave?" Her voice had become icily insinuating, and she began rolling the piece of letterhead into a tight tube.

"Of course not."

She inserted the tube of paper halfway into the neck of the bottle she had just washed out. "And why is this book so important you want to rid the world of women?"

"And men. Women and men—leaving just you and me and a few close acquaintances to sit on our own beloved butts and remember." I showed her the front flyleaf of the book. "Look—a tiny little tease of an inscription: "Spare change—from A.C.," printed in small ink strokes in the upper right-hand corner. Otherwise the book looked unmarked and unread. "Just 'A.C.'—like a courtesy gift from a kilowatt. But what the hell...*Spare change*? What is *that* supposed to mean? When did he write it?—if he wrote it?—unless she wrote herself before entrusting it to the caring hands of the US Postal people. Her little game. And why send it to me at all? She knew it would cause me to act the way I've just done. Did I *fulminate*, Nancy—is that the right word? Did she try to pull my cork?"

"You don't see this as a goodwill gesture? Perhaps she's not a—what you called her."

"She may or may not know that I've seen this book already, that I spent a lonely evening beating myself up over his last piece of dialogue about little lost boys and their indifferent parents, thinking, of course, that it was about me. Not that *that* makes me a narcissist as much as an offspring who seemed to fit the part. And if she phoneyed it up for my benefit, she still wants me to know something or to at least *think* I know something. It's a planned situation on her part. That she thought I might be interested in this odd volume of The Professor's own subversions for their entertainment value or as a nice memento is crazy. Crazy. And you're right: I generally hate phones when faces are usually so much kinder. But it's time to make an exception."

"You're calling her?"

"If I can find my stupid cell." It wasn't in the house, and I realized I had left it in the shop after talking with Eleanor Jewett. "Sometimes landlines are better. You know where to find them." I stood momentarily in the doorway to the shop, recalling the feelings of the earlier discovery, the rush of pure purpose and empowerment arising from a hole in the earth not much larger than a burial site—the breath of it, held in place throughout the decades and finally released to touch us now. The cell was on a middle rung of the stepladder, an artifact of now, calm in its compaction. I scrolled to the contact list until I found WEXLER and then tapped. When I heard the answerer's voice, I was surprisingly gladdened. "Bartlett, if you can get over whatever grumpy feelings you might still have, could you tell your boss I would like to speak with her? It's urgent and possibly of no real importance except to her, but I wouldn't like to piss this moment away."

As I looked out, I could see Nancy watching me from the front porch, holding the bottle with the note half-way down its throat. Moxie.

EIGHT

The call to Wexler did, in fact, have more than a little importance, but it would be two days before all of that would come to pass. Bartlett informed me with no apparent animosity that his boss and Willie had gone on a mother-daughter retreat and were not reachable during that period. They had entered, as he put it, into a shared zone of silence, or "solitary confinement for two." He laughed at that, promising he would convey the message, and advising me to "chill." I asked Nancy if she knew of the mother-daughter thing, and she said only that Willie had told Michael something about dancing with her mother's demons and she would leave him to his harmonica and a new video camera for a bit.

"Michael," his mother said, "is not one to pry unless it's in the form of pictures." She suggested I follow Bartlett's advice and use quiet hours to sand walls, stop thinking, and pay a hospital visit.

Emily Acampora was sitting in bed trying to give motion to a cube of Jell-O on the tray in front of her. She manipulated a spoon with the attention of a person developing a new form of artistic expression but showed little interest in feeding herself. Barbara Lynn and Mikhail Jefferson were both in chairs, each reading from an electronic device. Emily looked pale still, but seemed serenely pleased with her Jell-O experiment. It was she who finally saw Nancy and me in the doorway and said with an immediately quiet insistence, "You two look beautiful, standing in my threshold. I've been wanting to see you so much, and here you are. We have wonderful things to tell you, and you two are the first who will understand." We crossed along either side of the bed to lay cumbersome kisses on Emily's forehead and cheek, dodging the tubing that was still a part of her recovery, before looking at each other across the top of her head. Barbara Lynn had stood to join Nancy by the bedside, putting her arm around Nancy's waist and tipping her head onto her shoulder. It was another trick of time that they had only known each other for two months since the day of the wedding. They made it seem so much longer.

Jefferson remained in his chair but reached over to tap me on the butt with his reader and asked if I was ready. "We are going," he said, "to conduct an initiation."

"But first," Emily corrected, "we want to thank you for placing your blood and love inside me and lifting me out of a bad place. When Barbara told me who was donating, I knew I was going to be ready for anything again. You can't imagine my thoughts of those boys who were being so ridiculous. I didn't think in my bad moments that I could ever get up and make my way back." Jefferson groaned softly behind me. "The worst thing now would be for them to think there's nobody who will believe in them again. So I thank you for strength and clarity. Probably they go together—and they come from the mixing of blood from a troop of loving people." She coughed and took a sip from an insulated tumbler in front of her. Then, with a quick wavering glance about the room, she smiled. "So the other thing that needs to be said is ...we're going to be a family. The three of us."

"You're pregnant?" Nancy asked excitedly and then reconsidered. "Or Barbara?"

Barbara Lynn slipped an arm through Nancy's. "Not that, y'all. Not yet. Here, sit." She led Nancy to the chair she had been in. "It's all so simple. Mind, it might seem complicated. Jeremiah, sit on the edge there." She gestured toward the foot of the bed. "Keep Emily's toes warm, would you?"

As if on cue, a nurse came in to check the patient's temperature with a device she held to Emily's neck. She was a roundish person with silver hair and a face strikingly younger than she must have been in actuality. We joked about how the positioning of thermometers had changed over time, and she said something about once having to go places to check a temperature you hardly ever came back from unchanged. She clearly loved her work, and I envied the warmth she brought to it.

Barbara Lynn waited until the nurse had left before continuing: "So here's how it is, you two. When Jefferson here talked his way into taking me back upstairs the other day—and I'm still not sure how he pulled *that* one off—"

"Oratorical flourish and persuasive purpose."

"Fine, darlin'," she said. "Ah like the sound of that. Bullshit in a candy wrapper." She went on. "So we—he and I—get talkin', once I'd slept in that wheelchair for a while." She looked at him. "You see, Mikhail and I had what we thought was a low-grade series of indiscretions shortly after ah came to the college. His wife—"

"Number two."

"...had decided she was going the gay trail. When he came to me for some gay girl reflection on the event, I decided I wouldn't mind a sample of heterosexual heat—being as I wasn't involved with anyone else at the moment—ah do have *some* scruples, mind you—and we...you know." She sighed and exhaled a whew. "So the other night—he also convinced someone in this place that it was okay for a non-whatever to stay over—"

"I do know people who have *positions* here at this place of healing," he interrupted again. "And I write a monthly column on the Bible for the local paper—nothing too religious, as you might expect," he added, looking directly at me, "and those were my tickets to ride."

"Ah-hah," Barbara Lynn exclaimed, "so it was more than charm and good looks."

"As you wish," he conceded with a slight nod.

"So, when I thanked him for being here at the same time as I asked him what the hell he was *doing* here, he admitted to me that he and Emily had also had a joining of the ways a couple of years ago." She looked at Nancy, who had cupped her chin in one hand. "You can see why I offered you the chair." Barbara Lynn smiled wistfully. "Emily it seems was more conscious of what we were talking about than we had reason to believe—that the three of us had done the triangle over time and without ever being unfaithful to each other—if you're following."

Emily had been listening now with restful concentration, underscoring the narrative with nods of affirmation. "Realization instead of recrimination," she said quietly. "I knew about their short time together. No problem finding *that* out. You put a campus of students together and add them up and they know everything about everything except what they're studying. I'm surprised teachers never know that. We decided to sleep on the possibility of becoming a family of three."

"And...? "Nancy prodded.

Barbara Lynn pressed her lips together. "The next day, it felt good. It seemed all right."

"More than that," Emily corrected. "It felt we had found something natural."

"Though," Jefferson offered, "it isn't going to feel that way for anybody else. Except you two, on a good day. People are going to be psychoanalyzing the two of you up one leg and down the other, if they haven't already."

"They have," I assured him. "Including ourselves."

He laughed, the tightly cynical but supportive laugh I had first heard in the campus coffee shop. "Well, I should hope so. I certainly do. Think of the job we have ahead of us, if we decide to do what we've talked about doing if it continues to feel...was natural the suggestion?" he asked Emily.

"Until I come up with something better," she said. "People won't like it."

Leaning against the wall by the head of the bed, classroom-style, Barbara Lynn shook her head, "They most assuredly won't."

"And what is it you've decided to do?" I asked no one of them in particular.

"Why, to become a unit of some sort, Jeremiah," Emily said. "Isn't that right?" she asked the other two. I had a flash-thought of Eleanor Jewett and her communal house in Surrey, but that seemed almost quaint compared to what I was hearing now. Spread before me was a frontal attack on a host of conventions.

Jefferson clearly read my thoughts. "Can you see the great analytical machines grinding away with this one—a black man joining together with two white women who have previously pledged their lives to each other, pushing a shopping cart together—*the three of them*—in the local A&P, or, better yet, pushing a baby carriage." He started offering up different voices. "'Whose brat is it, Hortensia?' 'I don't know, Mother. Can you get a peek?' 'How dark would you guess it is?' 'Well, Jessie, I heard the women were going to do it on their own with outside sources.' 'But which one, Frances? Which one actually did it?' 'Do they all do it together—and where?' 'Do you suppose they share a room?'"

Barbara Lynn was enjoying the performance and added her own snippet of dialogue: "'Ah heard, Beauregard, he was married many times and his last wife ran off with a dyke. Now *that* must tell you something!'"

"But it feels...natural?" I asked tentatively.

"So far," Emily said to me and then turned to Nancy. "There's so much room for doubt, you see. Here I am, still wearing off the drugs in my system, not exactly full of energy. And these two, after stressing themselves for these past days and reading too much junk on their Kindles, are in full crash mode, which makes it like nobody should pay attention to anything." She coughed and reached for a tissue to cover her mouth, but her eyes remained clear with conviction. "I mean, I guess we're all pretty messed up now. But our defenses are down and our thoughts have no way to go but to the truth. Don't you think?"

Nancy took her hand. "I think, Emily, as someone who's known you only a little bit, you are one of the exceptional people I've met. I can see why Jeremiah gets palpitations around you."

"Oh, that," she said, drifting toward sleep. "He's imagined me his fairy queen. Isn't that it?" she asked me. "Well, maybe I am. But I hope this all isn't too confusing. In a little time, we'll know whether we've imagined the whole thing or not."

Her falling asleep was our signal to leave. The shadows of fatigue and discovery did show on the faces of Barbara Lynn and Mikhail, and she took back the chair she had given to Nancy, curling her legs under her.

He walked partway down the corridor with us. "Not your ordinary hospital visit," he commented. "I tried to give you a little advance warning."

"The three of you are serious about this," Nancy said. "How brave and insane of you."

"We'll have to see. Like any new love—and that's what this is and isn't—it makes you feel giddy at first, and you wish the giddiness never wears off, even though you ultimately want it to. Because once it does, then you know what you have. But that is what matters, folks—when the giddiness is done." His voice was losing resonance, but he clutched my upper arm. "And won't they love this on campus, bro. Our scrawny adulterer of a dean will need an extra blue-pill. At least I've never done his adultery thing. Like Barbara, I do have a *few* scruples—and what others see will be for them to decide. You, for example." We reached a set of double doors. "Wait until I tell Brother Woo."

"Should you wait?" I asked.

"I don't know."

He left us.

Nancy seemed to have digested the scene in Emily's room better than I had. "How fortunate it was a private," she joked as we left the building. "You think of all they might have in store when they tell colleagues and family. If you think *my* family will be a challenge for us, imagine theirs."

"Do you believe them?" I asked her.

"You of all people."

"I know. There will be many who think they're only setting out on an antisocial lark."

"You've told me the condemners are only lacking in imagination."

"I did?"

"Or I did."

"And this is going to cure them?"

"I don't know," she said, putting her hand into mine as we entered the hospital's parking garage.

As we drove to Quaker Falls, Nancy speculated on what it was that made the three back at the hospital trust us enough to be used as sounding boards. While they had not in fact asked us our opinions, they were able to hear their voiced words communicated beyond their own private circle. They were, as Nancy suggested, able to see how it sounded, like reading aloud a piece of writing of one's own, keeping the words on the page from fooling the reader.

"Voicing," she said. "It was an idea I found for myself in college. You've never done it?" I told her I hadn't, but what she was suggesting made sense, and I would try it if I ever wrote anything that seemed too good to be true. She conceded the possibility, though, that there was something about us so out-of-kilter we might find ourselves inspiring crazy moments of trust in others. I told her I thought that was a good thing if it was true and asked whether it might apply to her people in Chautauqua County. She thought it might if we *didn't* act like we were just trying out an idea—bringing our thoughts back to our friends at the hospital. And on we drove to Quaker Falls.

We found Willie's car parked in front of the house and assumed at first the retreat had turned into a rout. But we found Michael on the steps of the cabin and realized he had borrowed her car while she was away. He was holding his new camcorder, not much bigger than his hand. He looked somewhere between dazed and amazed—so much so that he didn't respond to us until we were a few paces away and Nancy said his name.

"Oh, wow, Mom. I have something to show both of you." He gestured with the camera.

"What, my son?"

"A hawk. What makes it so hard to believe they're real?" Nancy didn't think she knew the answer. "Because they are. But they're more than real, too. Look."

We huddled to see what he had recorded. At first the close-up of a bird with a fiercely square head, a cap of dark feathers on top, orange eyes, and a yellow beak curled into a chillingly predatory hook. He had landed on something unstable, since his brownish wings flapped to hold him in place. The bird's intensity was as Michael had put it, fixed somewhere beyond the real.

"I was just sitting here," Michael said, "and he was there—or she." He pointed to the Andromeda bush, where a pair of cardinals had been nesting, and the story became apparent. After his initial close-up, he had adjusted the setting, pulling back to show hawk, bush, and the raptor's ballet—focused and efficient, coolly ruthless but without malice. A day's work.

"Oh, Jeremiah," Nancy said sympathetically but without sorrow, "your family of cardinals. But most likely it was one of the babies."

"I figured," Michael said.

"You just sat and watched—photographed?"

"Sure," he replied, unsusceptible to whatever I might have been accusing him of. "It was there and it was done. I can't believe it happened in front of me."

"Jeremiah," Nancy asked, "did you want him to throw rocks?"

"No, of course not. You did what your instincts told you to do, I guess. There's beauty in rawness. It's part of becoming what you're going to become. I just wish... "I had no idea what I wished, so I sat next to him on the step. "I've heard it's tough to punch a hawk."

"I'm sure Michael will remember that," his mother said with just a slice of conviction. He gave up his seat to her and parked himself on the grass. The extension cord was next to him, still on its way into the shop. "Are you going to tell him what you found inside?" she asked me.

He set the camera on the grass, and we told him. He listened the way he used to in class with the look of one who intended to absorb everything without committing himself too obviously. He did eventually go inside for a minute, squeezing between us, turning on the work light, and peering down the opening in the floor. After he had turned off the light and come back outside, he said simply, "I want to help you paint."

The three of us would spend the rest of the day and the following morning sanding and whitewashing the interior of the shop. Michael was taken by the concept of a pickling project and approached it with both a fascination for the term and a solemn dedication to the process. He would say the word "pickle" from time to time, like a mantra or personal incantation. It was he who put the piece of square flooring back into place with his sure hands, using the two screws I gave him and turning them with the delicate hands of a reconstructive surgeon. Protectively, he covered that piece of the floor with a double-layer of drop-cloth and set an empty cardboard box over it before placing two discarded bricks from behind the shop inside the box.

We stained the walls with brushes, though according to the Crispin brothers a roller would have worked as well. The stroking of paintbrushes seemed proper to the occasion, and we went forward with little discussion. I missed my window team of Barbara Lynn and Emily and approached the multi-paned mullions with a can of goo called glazing compound—which they had used like a pair cosmeticians removing lines and wrinkles. Emily's words ran on a loop through my brain as I smoothed the compound in place, particularly the phrase "realization rather than recrimination"—repeating itself and re-repeating. Could she, I wondered, actually be that evolved or that defiant of reality that she was without the instincts for self-protection? Could she, as she had indicated, go back to doing what she had been doing before she was injured? And was she so without the sinews of self-protection that she would be the guiding spirit of a new and implusive domestic arrangement that would be without the recriminations of ownership and control? It was all so problematic in spite of how simple the three had made it sound in that room of healing.

On the second day of restoring the shop, Michael assigned himself the responsibility of creating a screen door and a screen for the window. He built it from scratch with materials and tools obtained from the Crispin brothers, including a chop saw and a staple gun. He took the Dakota and rummaged up a small potbelly stove at a salvage yard, a slab of bluestone to set it on, insulated stovepipe to run through an existing wall opening that had been covered by a square of sheet metal when the shop was shut down, and pieces of fireproofing material to keep the belly of the stove from setting the wall behind it on fire. It was a masterful performance, nearly outdoing his construction of the garden.

Michael seemed to know things about the future of the structure that I didn't, and I asked him at one point what he imagined was likely to happen here. "Plenty," he replied with emphasis, positioning the piece of bluestone without measurement in a way that made sense to him. "The learning place is right here. You'll dope it out."

"It sounds," his mother said, "like he's made contact with his whisker friends."

"Mom," he protested.

She ignored him. "When Michael was about six or seven, he had this group of pretend beings he would have long discussions with. Though you wouldn't tell me much about them," she said to him, "except they were very good at predicting things, and they had whiskers."

"Whiskers like a cat or whiskers like old geezers?" I asked him.

"Just whiskers," he replied.

"You used to say the fireplace was the best spot for your discussions, as I recall." He was aligning the bluestone with the toe of his running shoe, still ignoring her. "He would sit in there in perfect contentment. I tried not to listen, but I doubt it would have made sense to me. It did cause me to have one of the cleanest fireplaces in the valley—until the whisker friends went away. Or did they go away?" she asked him, reconsidering.

He gave her one of his dopey and endearing smiles—his version of an answer.

We were done with our renovations by early afternoon, although Michael was already talking about running an underground electric line from the house to the shop but was fretting suddenly about bringing Willie's car back to her. The mother-daughter thing was supposed to have broken up by then. Willie Furman, after being locked away for two days with Joanna Wexler, was a fearsome thing to contemplate.

And so it would be but in ways far beyond what we expected.

NINE

I remembered Joanna Wexler's car from the reading of the will. It had been a side-note then, given the events of that day. Her cloth carrying bag had made more of an impression. Now, as part of a stationary convoy at the front of my house, it stood with dark assurance. All four vehicles were facing the wrong way for that side of the road, against traffic if any came. Michael Feller rubbed his head as the two doors opened. Joanna was in jeans and pink deck shoes that looked too small and too outdated for her feet. The narrow straps of her top displayed upper arm and shoulder muscles also looking young for her age. She sent a rounded, forceful "Good afternoon, everyone" across the yard to where the three of us now stood. Willie, however, after leaving the passenger seat, closed the door with noticeable impact and began walking down the road. Joanna explained to us that "My daughter has a deed to do." She approached with uneven strides, fanning a few afternoon flies with both hands, working them like a set of windshield wipers.

"Well," she exhaled when she reached us, as if it had been a long journey across the lawn, "Jeremiah, Michael, and this must be Michael's mother. It's quite odd that we've not actually met until this moment."

Nancy was running her tongue along her lips. "And yet I feel we've been meeting constantly. But here we are."

"Yes," Joanna confirmed, almost singing it, "we are. Michael, you're suddenly looking well-tanned and...well *brawny* wouldn't be quite the word, would it? Your lady friend had business with that peculiar woman down the road, the teacher person—although that would apply to most of you, wouldn't it? Am I right," she asked Nancy, "that she is involved with your former husband?"

"Yes—or they have sex, at least. Would you consider that *involved*?"

"Sex, yes. I would think so." Still, she seemed puzzled by the idea. "Nonetheless, my daughter and I have had an interesting two days. We ate little besides trail mix, although she kept referring to it as 'trial mix.' Clever, don't you think?" she asked none of us directly and then turned to me. "I think you might find that a clever twist on her part—you who has been said to value her talents as a writer."

"Yes, I do."

"We spent most of our waking hours sitting on the floor with our legs crossed, facing each other, and trying not to speak—for the first day at least. I expected they would hand us a peace pipe at any time, but my impression was we were supposed to make one up in our heads." It did seem like she hadn't talked nearly enough for the two days or had talked with constraints she was unused to, and the words were coming from her now with an irresistible energy that made it difficult but oddly pleasurable for her to shape what she was saying. And difficult to stop now that she had begun. "Which, of course, is not what they expected at all—the peace pipe. I made that up. They expected our spirits to make themselves known to each other, if only we would learn to listen—even when there was little or nothing being said. These people were highly recommended to me. At first, I thought we were being guided by quacks. My tailbone began to complain even though we were on cushions, and we could *only* stand from time to time, and go pee, and eat our *trial* mix, and drink large bottles of water."

She offered a brief, fluttery smile as the four of us stood frozen in place. "And the next day, Jeremiah, Michael, and Michael's mother, the next day—today, actually—we were permitted to talk—or forced to talk, I might almost say. And talk we did. They gave us commands about what it was we were supposed to address—items, presumably, of mother-daughter-centeredness—though some made no sense. Things about chewing gum and subways, for example. We were both so worn out by the end of it that we started bawling, which probably was the idea—and it wasn't until we got into the car that Wilhelmina suggested we come here and I come clean with you, Jeremiah. And now she's down the road clearing her conscience or who knows what with that eccentric neighbor who has sexual proclivities—or so I'm being informed."

She stopped, and we all took shivery inhalations. She seemed on the verge of dropping to the ground, but before she did, I asked what she meant about "coming clean." Apparently, she didn't remember having said it. Instead she commented on the "nice little cabin" behind us.

"It used to be a shop," I told her, trying to establish a degree of connection between us. "A print shop. A barber shop. A shop for wayward sons."

"A shop," she repeated. "Show me."

Nancy and Michael fell back as I followed her up the steps and into a space more notably brightened than I had realized. It was now, as Nancy might have said, "voicing itself" visually. Joanna looked immediately charmed by it in a way I could not have understood and placed her hand, palm-down, on the top of the potbelly—blessing it, one might have thought. Then she turned to me with her eyes clearing from the monologue on the lawn. "It's charming," she said. "Could we talk here?"

"Talk?"

"There are things I need to say, Jeremiah, and this seems like the place to say them. We need chairs. I need to sit to do this."

"And what is it you're going to do?"

"Get me a chair and I'll tell you," she said with insistence. "Two would be better."

I asked Michael to help me bring the pair of chairs from the dining room, my housewarming gift from the Gaussmanns. On our way, Nancy whispered, "What's going on?"

"I'm about to find out."

"Is she having a breakdown?"

"I'm about to find *that* out, too. If she's going to, she would apparently prefer to have it in the shop."

Joanna was conducting an inspection of the interior when Michael and I returned with the chairs. She was running her hand over the surface of the front wall and testing the amount of give to the new window screen—poking at it with the tip of her index finger. She took a sip of an invisible something as she turned to us. We set the chairs near the stove, and Michael was about to leave when she said to him, "Your lady friend tells me you're going to be a famous photographer in a few years. That's nice." Michael said nothing, and she added, "Will you use this cabin for one of your settings? It has mystique." He nodded. "That's fine," she concluded. "You may go now."

When he had gone, she angled the two chairs toward the potbelly with their backs to the doorway. It *did* feel like she was constructing a set for *someone's* eventual shoot—as she had in The Professor's study. She stood for a moment, looking to see the chairs were positioned correctly, slightly adjusting the one with the arms. She chose it to sit in and gestured toward the other.

"First," she said, "we'll talk about Bartlett, and then we'll talk about Alban." Her voice had firmed noticeably since unloading itself outside, and she was reminding me now of the woman who had ordered the calamari salad with efficient command. "Would you like anything before we start?"

"Such as?"

"I don't know...anything?"

"Is this to be an execution?"

"Hardly. *My* head may roll, but that should be of little concern to you. Or possibly not." She looked at me again and said "Nothing?" I assumed she had reverted to her offer of anything I might need. I thought of getting the book, but I felt settled in for whatever was coming. "I met Bartlett in prison where he was serving a ridiculous sentence for possession and harmless dealing."

"I believe I knew that."

"Probably so. Probably I told you that much. I became his advocate while he was teaching himself law in the prison library. Many inmates tend to do that, looking for loopholes to send them back to the outside world they still think they can game, so they can make the same stupid errors and make their way back into prison again. But that's their business—and the State of New York's, which takes officious enjoyment in the uselessness of a corrections system that doesn't correct." She paused, squaring her sneakered feet in front of her, like a child sorting out ideas. "Bartlett was not one of those. He was a prison philosopher, whose use of soft drugs had given him the ability to see close up from afar. I, of course, fell temporarily in love with him."

"No doubt."

"Yes, no doubt."

"And when was this?"

"Ah, yes—your investigations. I may tell you or I may not. We shall see." She stared fixedly at me. "Did you receive the book I sent you?"

I stood and looked at the cardboard box and carefully folded work-cloths Michael had put over the door to the hiding place below. I micro-wished I could drop her and her pink sneakers into the hole and leave her just enough air to talk herself to death. The thought was embarrassing and from embarrassment comes anger. "You knew," I said, bending toward her, "that the book was no goodwill gesture on your part, which is why I was once again snippy with your receptionist—with Bartlett."

"He didn't find you snippy. This time." She paused. "I thought it *could* be viewed as a positive gesture. That, like most things, would depend upon you."

"But this one had a peculiar inscription on the flyleaf and his initials."

"Did it? And by 'his' you mean the author's."

"By his I mean The Professor's."

"Yes, certainly."

"And how did you obtain this?"

"He gave it to me, of course."

"When?"

"At some point during the last year of his life."

"Did he say when he wrote it? Or why?"

"No, he did not."

"You didn't ask?"

"No—and here you are again, Jeremiah, playing at cross-examination. I haven't come to talk about the book. It's a dodge."

"It looks like it's never been opened."

"It hasn't—not by me at least."

"And why is that, Joanna?"

"I was afraid it might be about me, and I chose not to find out."

"Oh, and was the inscription for you?"

"I don't know, and he didn't say. He simply wanted me to have it. And that's all, Jerimiah. That's all either of us—you and I—have been allowed to know. So leave it." She stood with a gesture of exasperation and circled behind the stove before moving toward me. "I actually came to tell you the meaning of March twenty-second."

"Of this year?"

"Many years ago. Very many."

"You and he, I suppose?"

"In fact, it was the date we came to an agreement."

"Which was?"

"He would help me through law school, and I would provide a uterus when I was done."

She put it so calmly—with such a measured willingness to make her statement feel like a family recipe—I gave up my position by Michael's protected corner of the shop. I sat in the other chair and angled it as nearly face-to-face with hers as the stove would allow. I waited for her to sit again, and she did, grasping the chair arms unsteadily. It had begun to rain softly—creating a scrim of droplets wrapping the shop. I heard the sound of wet tires on the main highway, oblivious to this small, square structure on the elbow of what I now knew had been a section of the primary route through the area in milk train days. I could feel the two people in the house or on the porch trying to imagine what was happening here. I thought briefly of this woman's daughter three houses away trying to make peace or finally having it out with the teacher she claimed she had never forgiven. I continued to wait, until finally Joanna Wexler tilted toward me.

"You do, as I say, have an obsessive investigator's need to get to the bottom of things. I could spare you going forward with this, but you would never allow yourself that luxury."

"Correct. And the word was *uterus*, I believe."

"Yes, it was. The man I've heard you coolly refer to as The Professor wanted a child. The woman you know as Ellen—as your mother—was unable to provide it for him. I assume you see where this is going?"

As simple as that, I was looking at my actual mother, a woman who had never been tempted to run off because she had never been tempted to stay. She had provided a service for her former professor and his infertile wife and then gotten on with her life of lawyering, marrying, and producing children by other men.

She went on. "He and I had been partners in dalliance in my student days—but you seem to have smelled that out a few months back."

"And you couldn't admit to it?"

"It might have led to this moment before I was ready." She stared at me. "You're taking this all quite well so far."

"Do you want me to put on white gloves and sing 'Mammy' to you? Did you go away with him for a conception weekend when your ovaries were playing the right tune? Was it a cabin like this one, with the rain coming down? Did you shout out 'Alban' when he shot me into existence?"

As if to caricature what I had just said, the calico cat mewed in the doorway, the sound like the choking rasp of a sore throat. Joanna rose and opened Michael's screen door to let it in. The animal's fur was napped down from the rain, and it entered a few feet to clean itself. I had not seen the cat in more than a week and had begun to assume any attempt by it to become a permanent part of my life had been abandoned. It sat now, as cats do, with the self-possession of having never been away.

"You have a cat?" Joanna asked with some surprise.

"A stray—like me," I said.

"Yes." She took her seat again, adjusting herself to the exact center of it and wrapping one hand around the end of each wooden arm.

"Could we please get on with this? I've just seen you stick your head through the plywood cutout of 'MY MOM,' and I need you to finish so I can go buy you a card."

"This could be easier, Jeremiah, if you didn't need to be quite so clever." She gestured to the calico, rubbing her thumb and fingers together, inviting it to move closer. The animal blinked twice and continued washing. "And, yes, it was a setting like this—a place, if you must know, where we had gone while I was his student, up near his parents' place in Maine. Once or twice," she clarified. "I wouldn't call it torrid, in case you wish to know."

"What would you call it?"

"Academic. As sexy as chalk. We mostly talked—experimented some—and slept together. *Slept*," she emphasized. "That was enough. Technically sexless."

"But I gather I was not a technicality."

"That was several years later. We had made a pledge that if we were ever to become lovers, it would be the result of an irresistibility we didn't feel at the time. Having a child would become the irresistibility factor, and the March Twenty-Second Compact—that was how we referred to it—that our compact was an admission of being able to imagine it."

"Let me try to make sense out of this...you sat down one day, on a March twenty-second, and agreed that in few years you might carry a child for him? It was that simple?"

"No, Jeremiah, things are never that simple. I did care a great deal about Alban. He was everything people said about him. He was brilliant, and he was charming and warm in his own way. He made groups of people feel his presence—like a great judge walking into his courtroom. He made me want to be a lawyer, even though he had little but contempt for the whole profession. But he wanted two things as far as the agreement was concerned. First, he wanted it to be a consummation for us, one he had deferred during our retreats to his cabin. And, second, he wanted it to be totally agreeable to your mother...to Ellen."

"Pardon me," I said and stood again. "I can't, as they say, take some things sitting down. You'll excuse me if I stick my head out in the rain for a minute." She nodded. I went down the steps and stopped on the slab of stone that fronted them. The raindrops were finely sized, prickling the hands I reached out toward them and tapping out dots and dashes of memory. I pictured an afternoon with The Professor, walking along the sidewalk to his campus office, admiring the geometrics of other walkways intersecting it and wanting to dash off along them into a child's game world. Why I was there was pointless to remember, and my age was a guess—maybe seven or eight. But it was a personal event of some sort. My visits to his austere building—with sculpted owls over the entrance—were highly infrequent. It was raining then, and I could, at this moment, still picture his manner of walking, his precise, wooden-legged stride, the thinness of the legs themselves, the shine of his shoes as they punctuated the wet concrete. Their inexorability. He paid little attention to me until he reached the building...before turning slightly to put an arm around me for the purpose, it seemed, of guiding me inside a place of mystery. In my recollection, I was startled but pleased that he had done it. He rarely touched me, and it must have been a sacrifice on his part to acknowledge me quite so directly. Was he, then, for the moment, thinking about a child crafted out of the body of a woman who was not his wife and, until minutes ago, was not my mother?

There was much more to know, and I could see Nancy Feller across the yard just disappearing into the house, as if trying to slip out of my sight and the structure behind me. Or to alert Michael that Willie was approaching the yard with the empowered gait of something resolved. My sister. That piece had finally slipped into place—and I wondered what her mother had told her on her way to *coming clean* with me on this afternoon. Willie hesitated momentarily at the end of the lawn, looking first at the house, and then, seeing me, veering toward where I was standing.

"I offered to bring her a bag of dope," she told me without preliminary or context. I could feel myself breaking into a needed smile. "She's a loopy old bat, but with me being a loopy younger bat, it worked out just peachy."

"She told you about the raid on her garden?"

"Can you believe that? She's a low-level grower. For years. How we got to that point it will take me a year to figure out—but there we were. She even yanked me out into the rain with that stupid little dog to show me. She's been growing her personal entertainment for...ever, I guess. Marvin doesn't have a clue. She's sure he'd have her committed. That's typical Marvin—a sex-addict he can put up with, but a pothead? I told her I took up the organ because of her, since I probably did—so what the hell? She cried a little. I hate when old people do that. But what the hell again. And what the hell are you doing standing by yourself in the rain? You look as batty as the rest of us."

"I'm not alone." I glanced behind me. "Your mother's inside the cabin."

"Aha! The moment has arrived! She told you."

"She told me."

She put her arms around me. "Now I can hug you. I don't have to wonder about screwing you anymore." She stepped back partway and didn't elaborate. Finally she smiled, a new shape forming on her mouth before fading. "I've known awhile now. A couple of months, I guess. I poked it out of her the day of the wedding."

"Emily and Barbara's?"

"I was off my game. Weddings do that to me—even gay ones, I guess. And when I saw her that night, she started saying weird things about you. It was like you were the devil's own brat."

"We have had our moments."

"I got so pissed off, I shook it out if her—though it was like she had been waiting for a shaking." She brushed some rain from her face. "Then I nailed her this morning at the mother-daughter funfest, when the Gestapo ladies finally let us talk. I told her I wouldn't stop being pissed at her until she told you." She dropped her arms. Inside, as Joanna talked, I had thought about wanting to look into a mirror—like the one Nancy had found—to see who and what I looked like. Did I look anything like the woman who had just slid into the position of birth mother? I never thought I resembled The Professor in any noticeable way: I was taller, a little more filled out, with different-colored eyes and a different texture to my hair. But Joanna? There didn't seem to be much there either. So I looked at Willie, my new sibling—meaning I now had a pair of siblings—using her as my mirror; but I couldn't find myself there either. She was, after all, the freckled dynamo with her unrelieved intensity of mouth and eyes. Except for the moment. She had nearly let herself subside into a swoon of acceptance.

"And that's that," she added.

"But I'm pretty sure she hasn't told me everything."

"She never does. It's how she gets on. Then again, she might. On the way over here, she sounded ready to tear off her clothes and be the angel of truth."

"At least *that* hasn't happened."

"Yet. Go back in. See what happens. Maybe she'll swaddle you." She started toward the house. "I missed Mike."

"Does he know?"

"Not yet. That's your job, buddy. You need a few more real responsibilities."

When I reentered the shop, it was as if no time had passed. Joanna was sitting so nearly identical to the way she was when I stepped outside, I thought at first she had fallen asleep. However, her crisply delivered "You're back" cleared away the idea. The only outward change was the presence of the cat in the chair I had vacated, curled into a closed comma of acceptance. Whatever was going on in this room had met the bounds of feline accommodation.

"I saw your daughter outside," I told Joanna, adding, "She is your daughter, isn't she?"

"Yes, yes she is. And she is the primary reason this conversation is taking place. She's been hounding me for weeks to finally have a candid revelation. She finished it off in grand style this morning when we were leaving the retreat—insisting that disclosure would be good for both of us—her and me, that is."

"Why?"

"What does it matter?" she asked wearily, seeming like she was about to abandon this conversation as she had our earlier ones, but she went on. "I told her in the spring. I don't recall when exactly. Something made her alert to the possibility, but I don't remember that either. You'll have to ask her. She remembers everything. She's a sponge. I envy her. I used to be that way."

"She's made peace with the lady down the road. You should be proud of her."

"I'm always proud of her. This time I'm pleased as well. That isn't always the case. It does remove an instance of excessive parenting from my record, hopefully. I was very unkind to that woman many years ago. I had delusions about out-teaching the teacher."

"I see. Very neat. Quite a day." I watched her re-gather herself. "She hugged me, just before."

"Why shouldn't she? You're free to care for each other now. You can love each other if you're not too choosy."

I looked from the doorway, noticing that the convoy out front had shrunken by one. Nancy's car was no longer there, though I hadn't heard it leave. I felt a small tug in my stomach, but this scene needed to be played out. I turned back to Joanna. "You said Ellen was in agreement with his plan?"

"She knew me when I was his student. She thought me special in some way. She thought I would be right for the part."

"You talked with her...at the time?"

"We talked with her, yes."

"She knew you'd been slipping off to the woods with him?"

"No, she knew nothing about that." Joanna shifted in the chair slightly. "You're actually very good at examining a witness. Who knows where you get that from?"

"And who knows what else, Joanna?"

"We could go on like this—if you want details. But there is one other thing you should know, and this would most certainly be where *you* decide. What I've already told you is what I had firmly decided on after my daughter harangued me all the way here. The rest she knows nothing about—and, as such, it is optional."

"Let's not stop now. This is too much fun."

She narrowed her eyes, seeming to focus on the tip of my nose.

"Fine. Ellen gave her consent. No artificial insemination. She insisted. She said *that* would be an empty conception—chaste but hollow. And she was convinced no one would be better with the legalities than yours truly. I was thrice-blessed: candor, trust, and genuine skill with paperwork. It was all ridiculously correct. I had monitored my body for several months, making him privy for a time to my ovulation charts. Theoretically, as I told him, the timing was as certain as such things can be. The week before Labor Day, we went back to our cabin while your mother spent time with a friend. *That* hardly seemed fair. Not fair at all. But Alban was so alive to what was about to happen that he did make it feel like a precious gift we were giving to his marriage. That's what he called it: 'a sacred revision to his vows.' Charming in its own way. They had chosen your name if you were a boy. They assumed you would be. In their minds, there seemed no other possibility. Alban was like a meditative Casanova during our week—watching us, watching himself watching us, watching the tick-tock of passion like a young teenager. It was very nice, all things taken together. He called it a thin volume of coupling, rich but brief. There was, however, a significant problem."

"Yes?"

She took a long and considered pause. "I was already pregnant."

TEN

There is a scene in *Uncle Tom's Cabin* when the slave girl Topsy is catechized by her new master's pietistic cousin about her origins. Miss Ophelia asks the girl where she was born, and Topsy tells her "Never was born." The cousin is dumbstruck.

As I stood in the whitewashed workshop where the floorboards had just days before revealed the probability of a long-forgotten hiding pit for those fleeing their past, I felt myself being drawn downward, into a never born place that pre-existed me not only in time but in purpose as well. To say I was unplanned was too dismissive. Writers have contrived such devices forever, revelations to justify the existence of a character within a plot: being freed from the hiding places of history by the fresh air of truth and deservedness. How often I had anticipated those moments in my reading, no matter how loudly the wheels of fairness were churning within the text, or how long it took to happen. The longer the delay, the greater the satisfaction.

Joanna's last words were the most unexpected and unsatisfying reversal I could have imagined. Ellen had been dematerialized a few minutes earlier, and now Alban Curtin had joined company with her—he dead, she living, but the two of them wedded to the fanciful error of my existence. Ellen had spoken to Nancy about the feeling of isolation in one mothering a single child. How much more for one who's mothering the single child produced by another woman?

And The Professor? I had just been biologically erased from him, but it too was a betrayal on my part, since it quite likely changed nothing, except my perception of plotlines. What would the theoretician in him have had to say about it?

The rain shower had ended, and I needed to leave the shop. I needed to acknowledge my sense that things were changing around me, not just in my genetic printout. In the living room, I found Michael and Willie in the Morris chair, he sitting on her lap, she cradling him awkwardly.

"Michael," I told him, "I love you, but you look like a moron. Where's your mother?"

His perplexity could have come from any or all of the things I'd just jammed together, and he rubbed the back of his head before saying "She's going to my grandmother's."

"Meaning?"

"She was acting boogedy-boogedy."

"And *that* means?"

"It means 'get moving,' asshole." That, of course, was Willie directing her cold spray of words at me, while trying to shove Michael into a standing position.

"Do you think they'll eat me?" I asked him. "Your mother's family?"

"Great Uncle Teddy might."

"Nobody named 'Teddy' can be *that* dangerous now, can they?"

Michael shrugged, stumbling at last to his feet, and uttered an ambiguous "Unnh."

"I need the keys to the Dakota and a bag. Do we have a bag someplace?" He moved quickly into the kitchen while I ran upstairs to get something. He was waiting for me holding a Crispin and Sons brown bag with paper handles. "Perfect. And the keys?" He reached awkwardly into the pocket of his shorts and dropped them into my hand. I kissed him on the cheek. "Okay. If she's staging a runaway, she doesn't have a chance." He nodded gratefully, rubbing the spot on his cheek with the back of his hand. "I promise to bring our Nancy back alive."

They watched me from the front porch as I crossed the yard, showing no inclination to follow. I was heading toward the quince tree when I noticed Joanna and the cat standing side by side in the doorway of the shop, like they had shared a life there for decades. Joanna looked pumped out, the disclosures apparently causing her to sag noticeably.

"Bartlett?" I asked as briskly as I was able.

"Bartlett." The response was simple and grateful, seeming to restore her posture.

"Shit," I said.

I moved toward the quince, and began looking for the least misshapen of the fruits at picking height. Joanna followed me.

"Does he know?" I said without turning from the tree.

"Nobody knows." She paused. "I take that back. One person knows."

I plucked the seventh or eighth fruit, giving the paper bag a heft of purpose. "Ellen."

"Correct."

"I'll add that to my to-do list. But I have to go. It's been interesting so far." She was crossing toward Willie and Michael as I dropped the bag of fruit and a book behind the truck's seat back. I realized that was all, that I was heading west with no change of clothes, nothing for hair or teeth, and no phone. The last almost caused me to dart toward the house, but the three on the porch were a convincing barrier to unnecessary necessities. It was, after all, time for a face-to-face.

As I was closing the passenger door, Marvin pulled alongside. It felt like weeks since I'd seen him, and he looked pale for the last week of July. He asked how I'd been, in a cordially interested way, before telling me the obvious, that he was on his way to see Mary Jane. "I don't want to suggest that women are a strange species, but she's been distant for a while, and minutes ago she calls me up to say she's pining away and if I was in the neighborhood I should stop by for a little smooching. I happened to be reasonably nearby, and here I am, Jerry. But I don't know if I'm ready for smooching. Those things need a little revving up." He started to pull away. "I'm not a machine, after all." Mary Jane was obviously happy to know where her next ounce was coming from.

Nancy was in her kitchen when I came through her front door, sipping from a bottle of Guinness. "Is that what you normally do before a long drive?"

"It was only the bottom third. Michael never finishes. It's flat, but why waste it? Meanwhile, what are you doing here?"

"You're going to your mother's?"

She set the empty bottle on the counter. "Jeremiah, I want you to let me go."

"Go where? To the Alleghenies or out of my life?"

"Both, actually. I can't take care of you, and you can't take care of me."

"I beg your pardon?"

"Jeremiah, it was nice of you to follow me here. It's downright manly of you," she said sarcastically, "especially with all the things going on at your house lately. I hardly think I'm up to it, and I am going to my mother's."

"Well, of course you are, Nancy. And it's nice of you to invite me along." That froze her in place, and she gave me one of those contemplative looks where her eyes became both deeper and flatter-looking. "We are, in fact, going in the truck. It will make me seem less like a Hudson Valley snob. I've also got a freshly picked bag of quinces to bring to your mother. And, as a mutual friend would say, if that's not a ticket to ride, I don't know what is."

She frowned slightly. "We won't get there until midnight, Jeremiah

"So?"

"Will that give you enough time to generate wrinkles?" Her level of intrigue seemed to have risen a bit.

"Quite possibly. Today has given me just the tools."

We took the fabled Route 17, joining it at Monticello. I was about to learn that we would be threading through the Southern Tier, past Binghamton, Elmira, Olean, and Salamanca, old transportation hubs where goods of the forests and mines had been sent eastward and northward.

Nancy had gotten into the Dakota without real objection—tucking a small knapsack between us—but for the first fifty miles, there was the impression she was waiting for me to turn back. Her hands remained interlocked in her lap, and she asked about the details of my impulsive decision, testing it for its genuineness. I told her that while all kinds of strange things *had* been going on in Quaker Falls, they were secondary to my riding off into the sunset with her, and my lack of clean clothes should assure her this was no idle gesture: it was the sign of a man willing to risk the most basic of improprieties and her fearsome Uncle Teddy to be with the woman he honored above all others. That brought the first balloon of laughter from her. Her hands unclasped and she began to act as my tour guide for Route 17, pointing to the legendary Roscoe Diner, a groaningly flat-topped highway stop in Sullivan County. She crooned briefly about French toast before shifting to Michael's mention of Uncle Teddy. He was, she confessed, as gentle as his name—usually—but he had developed a fearsome dislike of Marvin that caused him to exceed his normal two-shot allotment of Blanton's bourbon and threaten to drop him down a mineshaft if he couldn't make himself more worthy of the woman he had married. Uncle Teddy had apparently developed an immediate distaste for Marvin at the wedding, telling Nancy's father the groom reminded him of a pencil without a point. I asked if Teddy was apt to be drunk at midnight, and Nancy assured his worst moments came during daylight—but we would see.

I told her of Marvin's roadside lament about women that afternoon, about Willie's rapprochement with Mary Jane, and the promise of a bag of pot that had caused her knees to begin to quiver for him. Nancy was in better spirits by this point and confessed that in her time with him, Marvin was partial to setting up sex-dates, and the quirky impulses of Mary Jane must have been frightening for him to the point where even Uncle Teddy would have helped pull Marvin from the mineshaft of his contempt.

I had never driven beyond Binghamton, and it was my passenger who alerted me to the fact that the old route was being modernized, gradually transforming itself into Interstate 86. The midsummer sun squeezed around the visors of the Dakota until finally settling behind the hills near Endicott, and we went on with a single stop for gas into the darkening landscape. We didn't talk about Joanna Wexler until we saw signs for a place named Horseheads. Nancy had known the name most of her life; for me it was the first time, and she was pleased with my interest. "When I was younger," she said, "it was a sign I wanted to steal."

"A gift from the past. I wish all of them could be this uplifting—and I wish certain signs could include a footnote."

"It has something to do with the Revolutionary War, and you should treat yourself to a Google." She stared ahead into the darkness. The number of cars was thinning out, and there was the increasingly eerie feeling of exploring a back road with no clear sense of outcome.

"Here, Nancy, is what you probably need to know about this afternoon." I told her most of what had happened, in a disjointed order: about the readjustment of my family tree, the sudden removal of The Professor from the list of those I had cool respect for to those for whom I felt a deep sadness. He wasn't, I told her, the type of person to *not* know things, but he was presumably left out of one of the great secrets of his life, as much as he was a key player.

"And your mother?"

"Ellen? I haven't known what to call her for years, but that might now become easier."

"Why should you want it to? She's no less your mother now than she ever was."

"That's the point, and what do I do with it?"

"And you said she knew...who the father was?"

"Apparently, but I was too busy picking quinces and coming after you." I said. "It was Joanna herself who told Ellen. She said only one other person knew. Do the math, if she's not lying. I don't think she was, in this case. But when, and why?"

"Sisterhood?"

"Announcement of the perfect crime?"

"No. Something better." She grabbed the handgrip above her window, stretching her back slightly. "The quinces are a nice touch. I'm still not certain about the rest."

"Because?"

"Because, Jeremiah, as I told you before, there's a real part of me that wants you to let me go."

"And which part is that?"

"The practical part—the part that doesn't want to fall apart in front of you—and I don't mean emotionally. That's all well enough by itself. That I think I can handle. You've given me excellent practice. I just don't accept the idea of being your decrepit lover—or decrepit former lover—after we began at such a good place."

"You're talking about your health issue?"

"That we'll find out soon enough. But it's not that. That's only the signal going off. But there's more, my darling. This afternoon I watched you and the lawyer. While I didn't know quite what was happening, I knew *something* was. Something was up. And there was this very real idea that said, 'Nancy dear, how you are going to take care of *him*?'"

"Me?"

"You. Time didn't do a very good job with us. While there seems to be something rich in what we feel, it has to end up with both of us feeling we haven't been able to do what we needed to do for each other. Do you understand? It's like the hole in your cabin floor. Even if it is what you think it is, what real difference will it make—except for your need to construct stories? Or that crazy idea of your three friends. For a day, I was charmed by their creating a 'unit' of their own and living happily ever after. Lately—or just this afternoon—the idea of their doing any such thing no longer makes sense. Not a ticket to ride. Almost none—even though they're people I find likeable. But your Emily..."

"*Mine*?"

"As much as I want her to be everything she seems—a perfect earth angel—I'm afraid she's a drug that has to wear off at some point."

"But we can't know that."

"Until we do?" She considered. "I think it's another reason I ran away today."

"Ran away?"

"Started on this journey to gain perspective," she corrected firmly.

"And here you are clouding that up." After several seconds, she asked, "Jeremiah, don't you find their idea too *something*?"

"Perhaps it will go away. As Emily says, they'll come out of their spell and drop the whole thing."

"I hope so."

"Do you really?"

"I think I do." She waited before continuing. "Impurities. Even perfectly wholesome grade school teachers have them. Don't doubt it."

"I see. And she's not my Emily. She's everyone's."

"Perhaps." Nancy stared at the windshield, either looking through it or puzzling at her own unsatisfied reflection.

"I brought one other thing with me that might help us understand ourselves better."

"What?"

"You'll see. And meanwhile your family will applaud your wisdom."

"Which wisdom is that?"

"That you've brought a man armed with good surprises."

"That's what I'm also afraid of, my friend. There *are* going to be surprises. I come from pleasantly predictable people—and pleasantly predictable people don't take to being surprised. It's an unpleasantness."

"Normally, I don't like to be surprised either. Surprise parties are too aggressive and mean-spirited. However, in this case, I'm ready to see what happens. Plenty of recent surprises have toughened me up."

"I truly hope so," she said again.

We drove on for another two hours. She called her mother to tell her she would indeed be reaching her by midnight, adding that she was bringing somebody with her, assuring the voice on the other end that it was not Michael. I could hear an insistent, "Fine, but don't drive while you're talking on the phone. It's against the law, you know." She smiled to herself and turned on the truck's radio, searching for a local station she had known growing up, and reacting with pleasure as it finally came into clear listening range.

With each mile, she represented to me how going home can make a person appear and act younger, something I could less and less visualize myself doing. The music was a mixture of soft country and 'seventies and 'eighties pop, and she nodded along or sang phrases to the night beyond her half-open window. Her hair spread outward with girlish indifference.

At Jamestown, we turned north on Route 62, before heading east on a country road where all traffic disappeared and I felt I was driving into the foothills of forgetfulness. After several minutes of silence she told me matter-of-factly, "If we'd stayed on 62 for another half-hour, we'd have ended up in Eden." It was, she explained, a place on the way to Buffalo, and her offering this piece of information prompted me to tell her I was toying with the idea of writing an Adam and Eve play in which Eve was considerably older than Adam, once I solved its logistical problems. "Sounds interesting," she said. "Do I get to perform naked?"

"It's not about us, and no, Nancy, you don't."

§

A long, rutted driveway led into the family homestead, where her parents, she told me, had built summer cabins around a small lake they had shaped into existence. The main house was brightly lit, and from what I could tell, it looked to be of the same time period as the house in Quaker Falls. Her mother appeared upon the front porch and waved in a way that looked decisively welcoming. She was joined by a large man I assumed was Uncle Teddy. He didn't wave.

They both started down a walkway to the pull-off where Nancy directed me but remained on the driveway until we got out, and Nancy went to put her arms around them in a family hug. I hung back, extracting the bag of fruit from behind the seat, and, I suppose, giving them time to process my appearance and for me to do the same. It was quite evident that Uncle Teddy was no stuffed animal. He had instead the tall, wiry look of a Lincoln, a kind of vertical battering-ram with bristling eyebrows distinctly visible even in the mottled light of the driveway, twenty feet away. His sister, on the other hand, was someone from the front cover of a cookbook, exuding a capable sweetness and an ease of motion. Another Lucille. She came toward me with a hand outstretched.

"I'm Katrina Jensen. Michael tells me you've brought a gift I will appreciate."

"Michael?"

"He called an hour ago. He's my moon boy, so I try to do everything he tells me."

Her hand was warm in mine, and she left it there during this initial exchange. It was a clasp of acceptance and I could have held it indefinitely. Her face was indelibly pretty and relatively unlined. As I looked into eyes that were the color of her daughter's, she said with cordial assurance, "This is the way Nancy will look in a few years. What do you think?"

"Your grandson apparently told you a good deal," I suggested to her.

"He usually does. His mother just doesn't know how much and how often." She winked softly.

Nancy had moved behind her, her arm through that of her uncle. He had yet to speak to me. "He's been telling you things?"

"Lately," she told her daughter. "Since last fall. We haven't talked so much since—ever. No, not for...ever." She turned to look at Nancy. "He's been afraid you're going to turn your head into a cinderblock. That was his way of putting it tonight. I haven't seen him since Christmas, but, my, he's growing. He talks in complete sentences now. Meanwhile," she said to me, "let me introduce my brother, Theodore. And then it will be time for bed. We'll have a real visit tomorrow."

Teddy's handshake was convincing without being overpowering. His taciturn greeting was "Pleased," and, happily, he seemed to be. Michael had prepared the way for us with alchemical skill.

Nancy and I were to spend the night in one of the lakeside cabins that was unoccupied for two days. It was Uncle Teddy who guided us by flashlight and carried his niece's small pack. Nancy's mother had carried the bag of quinces into her house, after announcing to the still night what they were. An almost full moon showed the compact size of the lake and the outlines of the structures that surrounded it with random spacing.

One was lighted, but the rest seemed to have acknowledged that finest of summer luxuries: early bedtime. Our cabin was unlocked, and Teddy reached one of his long arms through the door to turn on a light, before setting the bag inside without entering. He pinched Nancy's cheek and patted me on the shoulder, before explaining, "Katrina doesn't start a visit without exactly two cups a' coffee. Then, she will teach you how to fish, young man, if you would like to learn."

I thanked him as he left, his work shoes sounding like Willie's crunching the gravel path.

"You fish?" I asked Nancy.

"With the best of them, except my mother. For her, it's religion."

We were in the kitchen part of the cabin's main living area with a counter she dropped her bag onto before leading me into an area of couches, rockers, a game table, and an imposing fieldstone fireplace at the far end. Doors to two bedrooms and a bathroom stood in an open line along the rear wall. Another door on the wall facing the lake opened onto a screened-in porch. Nancy guided us onto it and pointed me to one of a grouping of wicker chairs.

We would talk our way for the next several hours through a scattered agenda, while the moon crossed the lake and we could hear the smallest of waves breaking against the shoreline a few yards beneath us. She was most interested in Michael's phone call to his grandmother, after months of similar calls.

"They've been conspiring," she said. "It's interesting to think about, but I'm not sure it pleases me. After all, it comes at a time when I'm trying to be led by nobody's thoughts but my own. And here's my son informing on us to his grandmother, who until recently thought of him as a dodo—or maybe I'm wrong about that. What do you suppose he told her exactly?"

"Don't you imagine she will tell us?"

"Not if he swore her to a secret conspirator's pledge. Do you think it's too late to call him?"

"Your mother—who is certifiably too perfect, by the way—your mother has made it abundantly clear that whatever he told her was intended to make our arrival a smooth one, and it was not intended to be known to us."

She looked unsatisfied and went inside. In a minute, I could hear her talking with the cadences of a person not at all concerned about the time of night. She gradually moved back toward the porch, allowing me to hear more of the specifics. "She's where?...On the couch?...Why would she be on the couch—or, better yet, why would she be there at all?...She said she's what?...Bless us all. It's quite, quite amazing...the Apocalypse." She was by the door to the porch by now. "Normally, I would apologize to people I've woken up at two a.m.—in fact, my son, I don't think I've ever called anybody at two a.m., not even when I was about to deliver you. I'll apologize at a later date, if necessary. Meanwhile, I love you, don't call your grandmother for at least twenty-four hours, brush your teeth, and go back to sleep." She looked puzzled as she set her phone on one of the wicker tables. "I should have let you call since you've become his hero."

"I didn't bring my phone."

"You left without it?"

"I was on urgent business. Of course, I could have used yours."

"Never mind. *She's* there."

"Willie?"

"Willie's mother. *Your* mother. Everybody's mother." She paused. "I wish we had some wine."

"Sorry. I hadn't planned on seducing you—only to convince you that you couldn't live meaningfully without us paired together."

She crossed to look at the lake, rubbing her nose against the screening. "Why do I feel like everything changed when she came into the yard in her ridiculous little sneakers?"

"They bothered you, too?"

She ignored the question. "I could feel my heart shift its location, Jeremiah. It went off someplace. And what's really upsetting is I don't know why. She obviously stood everything you know on its head. That I get, and yet you seem as unaffected as ever. Which is certainly part of it. But even before I knew *anything*—just you and her heading into your emancipation cabin—there was a change going on in me. And I wanted to get away. So I left. And you came and insisted *you* would drive me to the place where I wanted to get away from you and I was so taken by your surprising boldness that I let you. And here we are in one of Jensen's Cabins, on the edge of Jensen's Lake, and I learn my son has been doing his moon man's version of sweet-talking his grandmother into overlooking whatever others might find peculiar about us as a couple. He, of course, thinks you and I are just spiffy—feelings I've known myself at times. And *she's* sleeping on your couch because she told them she was afraid she might feel lonely and frightened after all that had happened during the course of her day. And I want to hate her for no good reason. Most likely for making me unreasonable. That's the problem. I adore you when you're unreasonable. I hate it when I am. Goddammit, Jeremiah."

I'd heard sound travels well across water, and I wondered how many in other cabins would remember a woman swearing at a person with an Old Testament name when they awoke in the morning. More, it reminded of the first of her monologues I was privileged to hear: in my apartment, on the night she brought cake and free-associated her feelings about how the lovemaking we had just engaged in came to be. As if her thoughts had linked with mine, she turned to me. "Here we are in this cabin on a moony July night and we can't even have sex." She sniffled. "How's that for a rough day?"

I rose and stood behind her, holding her. "Is that what this is about?"

"It most certainly is not—but you have to admit it would make sense to throw ourselves into a parked car rapture. Just a small one."

"With your mother just up the trail."

"She, apparently, would applaud it. She'll put it in the church bulletin. It's all quite unusual, don't you think?"

"You did say Eden is just nearby?"

"I didn't make that up."

"Eden's always just a few trees away, if I know my geography. And when did you say your next doctor's appointment is?"

"Day after tomorrow." She calculated. "Good god, we have to leave tomorrow—today being tonight."

"I almost followed that."

§

We spent our remaining time at Jensen's Lake experiencing what felt like well-earned amnesia. So much had happened, and there was so much to both assimilate and evaluate, a day's delay seemed as proper as any vacation should feel proper—just that ours was very short. When I awoke, Nancy had already left the cabin. As I looked from the porch, I could see her and her mother on the small strip of beach in front of the cabin. The lake was already busy with rowboats and swimmers, and I could hear the squeals of children off to one side. I would find out later that five of the seven cabins had been rented for a week by one extended family: grandparents, siblings, cousins. It had been a many year custom for them each July, virtually owning the lake for seven days. I would come to know them as a morphing family photo on this one day with them.

Katrina Jensen was whipping a fishing pole with graceful sideways strokes as I approached them. She was wearing shorts that revealed legs as fit as Nancy's, who stood with her arms folded and her head tilted back in laughter. The group of children in a small field on the lake's only point of land was engaged in relay races: self-regulated, no adults in sight.

In a ghostly way, I was joined by Uncle Teddy as I walked down to the fisherwoman and her daughter. He nodded at me and seemed a little shorter than he had in the darkness. He finally spoke, talking about his bygone fishing days, but held up hands that were gnarling. "Can't slip on a night crawler if I wanted to. It's strange watching hands and fingers grow old. Hard as you try not looking at them. Just try it when you're my age." I nodded, thinking of Chuck Gillis, before Teddy added calmly, "You're not thinking of marrying my niece, are you?" When I told him I didn't think so, it was he who nodded and said, "Just as well." And that was that, apparently.

The two women turned slightly to welcome us, just as Katrina began reeling in her catch. A half-filled bucket of water next to her already held three box-shaped fish, and as she pulled in this new one of the same variety, she pronounced it "a keeper and enough for lunch." She and Nancy, I learned, had been early to the local village to buy bait and other "necessaries." They looked at me like the sleeping-in tenderfoot that I was. Time waited a little longer as the four of us stood on the beach, and I asked Katrina if it was true she talked to the water. "Of course." She was undeterred by the question. "But only when you are sure it's paying attention."

The rest of the day moved more quickly, as much as we tried to rein it in. The fish were bass, I learned, and the four of us lunched on them with a summer slaw and potato salad that was in pure opposition to Mary Jane Otto's. No special additives. Katrina talked of how she and her husband—and eventually Uncle Teddy—had actually created the lake by damming up a stream, beginning with a shared vision of a place where families they didn't know could pass peaceful days or weeks. "Oh, there has been an occasional scrap, people who are upset by the quiet. Two divorces that I know of." Most, however, came back year after year, like the family there this week, building a ritual around the grandparents' anniversary. "It's nice," she said simply. "I've only had Nancy and my Sunday puzzle of a grandson, but the kids and grandkids and all the rest I've seen grow up here, one year's leap at a time." Her face was lighted with satisfaction.

She tried to teach me a little about fishing that afternoon, doing me the favor of baiting my hook at first, and guiding my fingers through later attempts. Inwardly, I hoped I would hook nothing, the guilt of an amazingly enjoyable lunch hanging over me, I suppose. I was unsuccessful, catching two but knowing it would soon be over—until Nancy arrived with a handful of small frogs she had gotten poking along the banks of a small cove. Worms, I tried to tell her, were one thing, but frogs were a few steps up the evolutionary ladder and a matter to consider. The women laughed with appreciation, but Nancy nonetheless baited my hook, the barbed end going in under the chin and out through whatever an amphibian's nose is called. I thought of Kermit as I cast the poor bastard into the lake and, as fate would have it, I landed what Katrina judged to be the largest fish of the summer. Kids in one of the rowboats cheered as Nancy held it in the air. It was embarrassing and fulfilling, and she took me on our own boat ride around the boundaries of the lake to get my ego back in place.

That evening, we carried two beach chairs to the edge of Jensen's Lake. Nancy had brought a freezer bag from the house and set it between us. Mallard ducks were feeding near the far shore, tipping their behinds upward and eating invisibly. That, in its simple way, could have made an evening by itself, but the multiple family was gathered en masse at the cabin to the left of us, and the children were involved in constructing things too small to identify. Nancy opened the freezer bag, taking out two bottles with the orange label I already knew as Moxie. "You've passed every test so far. My mother loves you, though as my partner or another grandson I can't tell and I'm not asking. Teddy wants to hear more about your house and hopes you'll invite him to bring a hammer. They hurt themselves, almost, remembering Marvin in Bermuda shorts and dark shoes and socks. You even stomached my torturing a frog and then catching a bass who's probably as old as you are." She twisted the cap from one of the bottles and handed it to me. "But it may all depend on this. Drink."

I took a deep swallow and waited for the worst. It never came. I'd never liked root beer, but this was root beer with a shot of engine oil. And that, apparently, made all the difference. "I like it."

"Then you may kiss me—but nothing more."

"Agreed." It was a kiss longingly shared, the crankcase taste of Moxie rolling from tongue to tongue. If any from the gang down the lake were watching, it didn't seem to matter. And they were well-engaged in other things.

"Whew," she exclaimed before reaching into the bag one more time. "I believe books don't freeze; it's one of their many good qualities." She held up *Riff and Raggles.* "My mother was charmed to find this in with the quinces, which are now being boiled into an elixir on her stove. She wondered if you brought it to *her,* since it was one of her favorite things to read to me on those unusual days when I was good. She wonders if you have wizard powers."

"That, I can now assure you, is something I did not inherit." I reached for the book. "I brought it as the final way of cracking through to you if your defenses held up. Moxie seemed to have done the trick instead."

"'Trick' is it?"

"I've never held a book this cold. It's how the libraries of monasteries must have felt."

By the time it was nearly dark, the object of the children's activity was made clear to us. A girl about seven or eight with freckles like my new sister's came to us with a waxy paper bag, partially filled with sand, topped by a votive candle. "We're going to float them tonight," she told us, breathing quickly. "Would you like to do one?"

"Yes, we would," Nancy told her in an *Oh, my* voice. "And tell your family I think you're very beautiful."

She blushed. "Did you have a boy with you last year?"

"Yes. Michael. My son."

She blushed again. "I liked him."

"And I'm sure he liked you."

The girl darted off as if she had caught a lightning bug, and I went into the cabin to where I remembered seeing stick matches over the fireplace. As I came back, the lighted bags were beginning to drift across the lake, moving with the current that led to the small dam, a wistful flotilla that had the entire family leaning forward in unison on their beach. I lighted ours and we pushed it into the water, where it hesitated for a time before catching its own current. Nancy had the unfinished bottle of Moxie in her hand and raised it in the direction of our fellow launch crews—although it turned out to be intended for just one of them. "Here's to her first crush and to all first crushes. Michael would be so thunderstruck he'd have no comment to make."

"Possibly. But I wouldn't be so sure."

"Yes, there is that. The Apocalypse."

"And when did you have your first crush?"

She considered, watching the floating flame move away from us. "Today, actually." And she linked an arm into mine.

ELEVEN

And then, lo, it was August—that month of strangulating suddenness. I came back to Quaker Falls with three jars of quince conserves to find a job offer awaiting me on August 1 exactly, a reminder of cycles from which I thought I had extracted myself. I also returned to a hubbub of communal practicalities unfolding like a medieval festival, setting the tone for events to follow.

By the time we got to Nancy's in the early evening, we had been well-fed and well-hugged by mother and uncle, had learned that the name of the girl fascinated with Michael was Rosemary, had driven through the center of Horseheads, judging it disappointingly clean and up-to-date, and heard my passenger discover Flatt and Scruggs with the gusty inebriation I had seen before. I told her as I walked her into her house how surprised I was a mountain girl hadn't experienced much bluegrass before, and she reminded me, as I had discovered, that she was a girl of hills rather than mountains and she had grown up as a fairly typical teenager with dreams and imagined romances and the wish to leave the perceived backwardness of Chautauqua. She confessed to having been typically wrong about that, and that with age comes the occasional pleasure of acknowledging such realizations. I asked if she thought us in danger of "unsettling down" together. She shooed me off to my place and insisted on staying at her own house for the night. It was just as well.

The road in front of my whimsical homestead had seemed to turn into a permanent parking lot, containing more vehicles than when I left. I recognized P.Q.'s van, and I could see him and Michael engaged in collective doings by the shop. Joanna's car was still there, along with Louisa's, and one only teasingly familiar to me. I was about to discover that the two woman, along with Willie, were working at civilizing my kitchen, though how this enterprise came about was another in an ongoing string of peculiarities. I would be drawn toward the male activities before finding out for certain.

Michael greeted me with unusual bravado, and it seemed likely he had talked to his grandmother once the twenty-four-hour moratorium passed. P.Q. was also outside the boundaries of his usually understated handyman self. In his case, the can of beer he offered from a cooler on the steps would serve as his explanation. They were trenching from the house to the shop, fulfilling Michael's vision of bringing electricity to a building that had never known it. They were nearly done and were threading wire through tubing that would protect it underground, and the hole where it would enter the shop had been drilled and surrounded with fittings. I peeked inside and discovered Hamilton Graham securing a small breaker box to a wall. Thus the other car. I could have imagined dozens of others before placing him there.

"Ham," I said as more of a statement than a greeting, and he smiled halfheartedly. He was still in his IBM success clothes, having apparently come from work. His necktie was loosened and thrown backward over a shoulder, and the top of his shirt was unbuttoned. "Did Joanna send out a general summons?"

"Consider it my goodwill offering. I give to you my electrical knowledge." His smile was now more fully at ease with itself. "Things were a bit chippy the last time we saw each other."

"So they were."

"Miss Ellie accused me of making you into a movie villain."

"A dashing one, I hope."

"As much as I tried not to." He chuckled briefly, while securing strands of wire to a bar inside the box. "We are, as you can see, electrifying your shack of dreams. Michael here says you have magic plans for this little hut. Is that so?"

"Yes?"

"Pretty easy," Michael assured me from the doorway. "I set up an account at Crispin's. They trusted me. They told me it was my good looks. One of them came by this afternoon to see how it was coming along. You still have to sign a paper."

"Pretty amazing. Progress through absence. Quite a trick. And dare I ask what's going on in the house?"

"Scary stuff," P.Q. intoned. "Women's stuff. I'm glad we can piss outside."

Michael explained it as Joanna's idea to bring the kitchen to at least an equivalence with the rest of the house: to clean, paint, sort through things—whatever that meant—and make the room overall less like a hapless bachelor's dumpster (Joanna's words apparently). She had not only remembered Louisa from the reading of the will but had used her as caterer for a recent function of area lawyers. They had talked briefly about my house then, making today's attack as much Louisa's idea as Joanna's. The electricity was Michael's initiative, of course, but when Joanna got the gist of it, she summoned Hamilton to do the interior wiring. A linkage of house to shop: my own Great Cable.

When I stepped timidly to the kitchen door, my welcome came from Willie. "Hey, big shot, how come you never said you got a piano?"

"And hello to you. I didn't get it. It got me. If you had gone into the dining room with a clean head, you might have seen it."

"I never *did* go there. It's always looked like bugs and werewolves from what I could see."

I remained in the doorway looking at a transformation that might have been part of a television program. Without the help of new appliances, the room had achieved a rough quaintness I couldn't have envisioned without gutting it. Spices and cleansers sat in orderly groupings. The sink and refrigerator had had their surfaces scrubbed. The walls were a calming shade of light tan, and there was a leafiness of organized female energy in the room.

Louisa waved a stubby brush in my direction. "You find it pleases you, yah?"

"You threatened me a month ago. You've more than made good on it."

"It was Yoanna's idea, since you weren't going to be here."

Joanna had the serenity of a successful impresario, and the exhausted woman I'd seen little more than a day before had been replaced by the smoothly confident manipulator I was more familiar with. It was primarily a relief, but, still, there were questions I needed to ask her. I invited her to step outside, hearing myself sound like a street thug ready to pick a fight. She seemed well-prepared and followed me into the back yard, removing the apron she had been wearing and holding it in one hand.

"How is your friend?" she asked.

"Nancy is fine. We had a pleasant dash across the state and back."

"That's good," she replied with a degree of sincerity. "I get the feeling she's not well."

I bypassed her feeler. "Question one: Why are you acting as if you want me to like you? It's out of character, and I can't believe you think it's a good idea."

"People change."

"Under duress."

"Well, there you go."

I waited for several seconds. "Question two: you asked Hamilton to come here, like you're throwing a family reunion and laying the groundwork for taking over my life."

"Hardly."

"I won't be taken over."

"I'm sure. No need to worry, Jeremiah."

"Question three..."

"The inquisitor again."

"What does he know?"

"Michael is going to get you chickens," she said, evading.

"Yes, at some point."

"Soon."

"I'll talk to him, but first you talk to me. You're not the dodger type."

"On the contrary, I obviously am. Yes, he knows you're half-brothers. I talked to him on the phone last night. He took it rather well since he had apparently developed a disliking for you over the months. That's as much as he knows. I would assume it's unnecessary to tell him Alban—"

"Question four: When and why did you tell my...*Ellen*...what the facts of my conception were?"

"I'd prefer she tell you, if she wishes." Joanna was coolly grounded now.

"And, finally, how did you know my father wasn't my father?"

"Interesting you should put it that way. Let's just say a little subterfuge and the wonders of modern science."

I looked at the chairs where Ellen and Nancy had sat a week or so earlier, when it had been the now-discarded month of July. Louisa called from the porch to tell me she was leaving and to bring me what she called my *lilla*—or small—phone, which had been ringing its bit of Mozart. She was flushed with satisfaction the way Nancy's mother had been that morning, and I informed her that there were Swedes in Jamestown. She nodded. I asked Joanna to have a seat, and she shrugged in compliance.

When Louisa and I reached the road, I leaned into the truck and pulled out one of the sealed Ball jars from Nancy's mother, explaining how it had come into being: the domestic witchery of changing spotted and misshapen fruit into what people into Chautauqua County conserves. She held the jar between both hands, staring at it with a sudden loss of expression, followed by a growing look of sadness.

"What?" I asked.

She placed the base of the jar in the palm of one hand and laid her other on the lid. It was as if she were examining an arrival to a laboratory. "It is my husband's favorite."

"And?"

"He's not here."

"He's gone?"

"He left many weeks ago." I waited, feeling the stupidity of the unaware. "He needed time alone."

"Why didn't you tell me?"

"It is not easy to do. It is a silly business."

I studied her face, now unprotected by her usual spirit of command and good cheer. "Did it have something to do with the inheritance?"

"Yah, but you must not blame your father. Men can be very silly when they t'ink too much."

"Yes, Louisa. I do realize that."

"Not you. I could never feel that vay about you." She gave the jar a slight shake. "But I take this, yah? It might be good for the end of vait-and-see." She placed the conserves in her car, and when we hugged, she said something about the book.

"The Professor's?"

"Yah. He thought money vas funny business, I t'ink?"

"Not in your case, Louisa. I don't think he could thank you enough, and he wasn't very good at thanking. He would be sorry to know this has happened. What can I do?"

"Vait and see, that's all. Your father will see to it." A monarch butterfly floated by in agreement. "I go now."

I watched her drive away, like I had after the will-reading. How she trusted him still with her array of soft-voiced convictions that had been so important during his final months. Clearly so. I could picture her serving as a daily tutorial for him to the point where he had the pleasure of becoming a student of her quiet presence. As he approached death, she must have cared about him to the point where he finally had learned the beginnings of listening. Perhaps I had seen it but had not recognized it.

I skimmed my messages as I walked reluctantly to the back yard, reaching the last three—all from Richard Woo—as I came to Joanna again. Chuck Gillis had decided to leave teaching for health reasons, and Richard had convinced "Captain Fuzzy," the Dean, to consider me as a temporary replacement. With that, my continued interrogation of Joanna was put on hold.

"The school may want to give me a job," I told her. "I have to talk to this guy."

"Don't do it." She was adamant and then pulled back. "I'm sorry."

"Yes, please be." I was quietly moved by watching her dealing with conflicting emotions. "You're most likely right, Joanna. But I owe him a call." I walked toward the shop. The work crew had packed it in and were finishing their beers by P.Q.'s van. Hamilton crossed to me, one hand wrapped in a handkerchief, explaining he'd given himself a "boo-boo" with a power drill. But he was in congenial spirits and told me, "Getting my hands dirty—and damaged—is a forgotten pleasure. Welcome to our dysfunctional family, by the way. I didn't want to believe it, but probably you'll work out." I thanked him for his mild vote of acceptance. As he was turning, he added, "By the way, the wild woman from Wyoming is headed back this way."

"So much for her marriage plans."

"Marriage?" And I recalled I had been mistakenly designated to pass on her temporary good news.

"Some guy in Arizona. A professor of whatever."

He looked understandably puzzled. "Add another to the scrap heap."

"But she gave you the honor of announcing her return?"

"Her bronco-buster's way of appointing. And with it, Jeremiah, the reminder that you and I have already had a shared experience."

"So we have."

"Be careful."

"*Me*?"

"We'll talk more." He put the blood-stained and dirt-soiled handkerchief into his pocket and left with a wave to the others. "By the way, my father was an arborist who electrocuted himself. Pretty ridiculous."

"I'm sorry."

"At least Mother Wexler has shown a wide variety of interests in her men. I might have been a little more forthcoming, I suppose, but at the time, I thought it was none of your business. I'm not even sure why. It even got Miss Ellie hopping." He frowned narrowly. "See you."

I needed a thinking and phoning spot. The inside of the cabin wanted sweeping, with snippings of wire and staples scattered about the floor, but it had the gratifying smells of recent work. The chairs were much as they had been when Joanna delivered my new back-story to me.

Richard was Richard. "Where the hell have you been?"

"Away for a day. No phone."

"My God, isn't that dangerous? Separation from a device is supposed to raise blood pressure and cause strokes."

"Cut the crap. Chuck has quit?"

"He says his ticker is bad. It may be, but more stuff has come out on Phyllis's misdeeds. I don't think he could handle it."

We talked for a time, and he assured me I could do Gillis's eighteenth century courses for a year along with assorted others, and I might be able to work my way into a vested position again, given my satisfactory first year and my "pedigree." He added, "Besides, you're at the age when people think you still know everything you learned in grad school, when, of course you *did know* everything." I asked how long I had to consider it. He granted me two days before he'd have to resort to adjuncts.

"Did Phyllis quit, too?"

"Or course not. She's doing what we all do, pretending to be what she wasn't—only she did it on paper, a long time ago, so who really cares is the attitude around here—except for Gillis, apparently. Whether she confessed to him or he heard it from somebody else or he had a senior intuition, I don't know. But there you have it. So, think it over."

As I thanked him, Joanna and Willie came to the shop to announce they were pulling out; they had both had enough of domestic duties. Michael was going with them but would be back tomorrow or the day after. P.Q. was gone, and the soundlessness of the yard and its structures came upon me like the discovery of what you know is there but have forgotten. My place of singular purposelessness had been strung together like the seams of a baseball by the desires and needs of others. The ability to be alone, I had intuited from brief periods of my life, was a process difficult to attain and most likely even more difficult to maintain. I assumed it was like the loss of any skill: a challenge to believe in once the feel of it is taken away.

I sat in the armchair by the stove, angling it toward the doorway. I had entered through Michael's screen door earlier without being aware of it, focusing instead on Hamilton as yet another permutation in my life. Now, the door was there in a way it hadn't been. It had assumed its door self, a work of careful and committed hands that now kept out the micro-static of animal nature; it was both connection and barrier to the rest of everything. It was the barely visible, but it was defining.

A cool breeze had arisen, forestalling the drawer-swelling humidity of the new month. The air was at play, and as I felt it come inside the shop, I yawned a doggy yawn, like a canine check to impatience that stretched and startled my jaw muscles. I had slept little in recent days; I had had the story of Jeremiah Curtin chopped at the knees; I had gone on unanticipated journeys and stood inspection by people who fished for lunch; I had been invaded by mostly well-meaning and temporary caretakers of this small piece of property who had pulled me forward in time more quickly than I had wanted; I had been offered the temptation of teaching again.

The thought of a college campus felt almost idyllic at that moment, in spite of the wrongheadedness and self-directed energies of many who were in positions of belittlement. But it was a place of textured lawns and geometrical, neat certitudes, and ceremonial comforts. And classrooms: the places of opportunities to reach and awaken and perform unanticipated magic another time. It was clean to imagine. And the eighteenth century: a time of splendidly horrifying contrasts between Gin Lane and neo-classical estates, between idiotic dandies and those who would lay down ideas for democracies and modern science. The Age of Satire. The Age of Reason. Voltaire. Mozart. But with it all, a time of definition and edges. My mind was propelling itself into thoughts of syllabi and assignments and strategies for breaking down the resistance of even those who took such courses voluntarily. I was being fed the catnip of empty seats and fresh hopes. However, as Chuck Gillis had taught me, there was nothing like the shine of a new semester to fool an academic into believing this time it would matter. Education: there had to be a way to truly re-imagine it and awaken its slumbering possiblities.

But why had Joanna wanted me to turn it down? She was so immediately adamant at first until, perhaps, she caught herself acting like a mother or an administrator. Not that she more than likely hadn't done so for many years, seeding The Professor with suggestions about how to bring up his manufactured son, actively coscripting the will. It was not at all difficult to envision. I could picture them clucking over the amount to leave me, and she approving the final decision for reasons of her own. And how she must have enjoyed beckoning to me with her March 22 casualness. How well-placed she looked sitting in his chair that day as she played to the house of university bigwigs, The Professor's cook and companion, and the son she had brought into being by way of a guy in prison. How *that* had happened was another thing I would need to ask at some point. Was I conceived in a closet and would I remain in one? If Bartlett was what she said he was, did I simply ignore it as a fact that *he*, in her wisdom, didn't need to know?

In fact, *nobody* needed to know except for the woman I *thought* was my mother—and how *that* transfer of information came about was a further decision. Would I get it out of Ellen when or if I saw her again? Nobody needed to know, evidently, except my one-time mother and me? And why would that be? Joanna could have remained in supreme possession of that knowledge, keeping it from me while I went on waiting for the cold breath of The Professor to work its way into my own future self. Did she wish to spare me that by substituting a disgruntled victim of the Rockefeller Laws? Could I grow a ponytail? Would it improve my teaching? Could I launch a periodic attack on stupidity while I was unable to tell myself how the text of me had been drafted? How to parse an ode when I could not parse my own creation? Or would the latter be an excuse for not doing the former?

And her coordination of all that had been going on in house, shop, and yard while I was gone for a mere day? Opportunity seized? And opportunity for what? *Did* she in fact wish for me to find my way to liking her? Or was she scripting a melodrama that would flatten out the prominent characters like saltines? And Hamilton? Was she trying to construct a patchwork family after the segmented years of her marrying and childbearing—not necessarily in that order? Then, too, how on earth did she get her truculent daughter serving as a scrubwoman for a day?

Would Joanna and I ever need to acknowledge more than the most fickle of connections?

And why did it feel that while everything had changed, nothing had? Truth should be a more compelling teacher, but in this case it didn't seem up to it—wilting as it was under the dome of August's arrival.

TWELVE

After two days of the house being empty of people, the filling-up came quickly, if mostly from a distance. Nancy called to tell me the now-less-gruesome doctor wasn't going to cut into her quite yet, preferring to try things that came in pill form first. She also announced that she had written her vows, but would not be revealing them to me until a proper time—and she was unclear about when that might be. When I asked her to define *vows*, she indicated it was a word I and everyone should know the meaning of.

Mikhail Jefferson texted that he would be needing my yard soon, and a call from Barbara Lynn on the following day announced that since she and Emily and Jefferson could not get married, they would like to perform a ceremony of their own devising in Quaker Falls. It was, she explained, the perfect place for deflecting the thumbing of noses into an act of faith and trust. Their feelings had become even more defined than they had been in the hospital: they had pounded each other with a barrage of obvious and not-so-obvious objections—testing them, rolling them along the edge of probability—and their desires had grown stronger. Emily was nearly ready to go back to work, Jefferson was feeling an unusually early and potent desire to be in the classroom, and Barbara Lynn was writing for both a radical and a Southern Baptist blog-site, the latter under an assumed name. She liked the balance and the subversive hypocrisy of it. The "Ceremony of Transgression," as she put it, would be best if it happened in the dog days. If it could bear up under that, it could stand up to anything. Whether I could bear up under it—this open commitment to subversion—was a separate issue, but their affirmation of purpose made it difficult to withstand.

Sara Sampson called to tell me what I had already anticipated, that she was back in the area, anxious to tell me about a low-level administrative job she was seeking at The Professor's school, and no doubt wanting me to put in a friendly word for her. She said nothing about the anthropologist, and I gathered she was staying with Hamilton, the strands of indecision working their way into and through themselves. Even Eleanor Jewett provided me with one of her cracker-edged inquiries into Ellen's well-being and seemed to be hinting she would appreciate another ride into the country and would be pleased to provide me with merry company for the effort.

As for Ellen, there had been no communication.

It felt like August had turned in on itself, trying to expel its own inner demons with fingers of artful originality. There was time to absorb it, helped by the delivery of three cords of seasoned firewood, dumped like a small mountain near the quince tree, and moved with a Crispin wheelbarrow to the second-last in the line of outbuildings—now the woodshed. It was a gratifying process, the arranging of necessity, row by row, layer by layer, and it attracted Bill Gaussmann. He was wearing a Yankee cap and sunglasses, looking very much like a senior bleacher-person, and he lamented his own abandonment of wood heat years before as if it were a World Series loss. He sniffed the pile, banged a couple of pieces together, and judged them good through their making the special tap of two Louisville Sluggers kissing each other. He and Lucille were on their way to a game that evening, but he admitted he couldn't resist the lure of so much neatly split hardwood. "They do it with hydraulic contraptions now. It's fast and efficient, but it doesn't have the inner life of splitting by hand. It's a feeling difficult to describe." His eyes grew younger with the recollection.

It was time to tell him what I had discovered in the shop. "Come, see," I said as if to a child.

I switched on the new, unadorned overhead light and led him to the corner where the opening had been made. I had swept the room, and its whitewashed walls rose like new packaging above the floor, defining it in the way of containment. Michael's protective covering had been removed, like peeling away a dressing. Bill instantly grasped the meaning of the square cutout: but when I offered to open it for him, he waved off the idea and backed toward the doorway, protesting, "I think it would break my heart." Outside again, his focus turned back to firewood. "That potbelly in there, it will need smaller pieces. I've got an old stump that will work as a chopping block, and you'll need a maul, and you'll need to find a way to get air into your shed. Probably it would have been better to stack it outside." He said it with grave decisiveness, before adding, "It's a responsibility—that, in there," meaning the opening in the floor. "It's a terrible treasure. Use it wisely." His words reminded me of The Professor's will.

Lucille came to find him then. She was wearing her own Yankee cap, making her look about seventeen, and I could have converted to a fan right then.

Grudgingly, I began to think about my invitations even as I moved load after load of wood. The ache in my shoulders was, in fact, an incentive to act on several things. I would give Woo my thanks and regrets, but I could not accept his offer to teach. I thought instead of Barbara Lynn Hynes doing the blog thing because a place of higher learning had refused to accommodate her unorthodoxies and could not adapt to the way she spoke and looked. The school had refused, even, to award her the Teacher of the Year honor voted upon by students, but even her award had been sponged out of the commencement routine not by snow but by an unexplained technicality. It sickened me to think about. The students: what could I do for them? Teach them the mechanics of heroic couplets? Make fun of Chuck's adorably grand Samuel Johnson, hoping there were one or two who might respond to him? The eager-minded like Lucia Solis would call my decision cowardly if they had the chance, but there it was. It all seemed too unaccomplished, compared to the bites I was taking from a hill of wood.

I could ignore Sara Sampson, having had several years of practice. She would find her way to Quaker Falls, I had no doubt—probably in the presence of my newly hatched half sibling who might or might not risk one of her shrieks by telling her of our kinship. It hardly mattered. She and Hamilton would both receive an invitation, the wording of which simplified with every few loads of wood: "Please join me in Quaker Falls for a housewarming and Celebration of Transgression on the afternoon of August 17."

I cleared the wording and date with the three celebrants, who found both perfectly to their liking. Emily called it "a shot across the bow of indecency," her voice alive with fifteenth century brushstrokes again. The list was to include as disparate an assortment of people as I could come up with: Rachel and Richard and Edwina from my former department; Michael and Willie and any peers they could lure to the event; Bill and Lucille; Marvin and Mary Jane; P.Q. and Mrs. P.Q. (whose name I had not yet learned); Joanna and Bartlett (definitely Bartlett); Hamilton and Sara, whether or not they were in each other's thrall once more; and, of course, Eleanor Jewett, who I saw presiding like an aged essence over the celebration. I wasn't sure about Louisa; it seemed an indignity to ask her to bring her personal wounds to such an occasion. I invited the postman on a whim as he handed my mail to me. He accepted, assuring me that transgression was fine with him so long as it wasn't too "flummox-y"—whatever that was intended to mean.

And Nancy. What was *she* up to? We had talked a number of times during my two days of squirreling away firewood. While she sounded softly serene about having brokered a large real estate deal, she still had not worked her way through her doubts about the ceremony. She would say nothing more about her "vows" but did indicate that if she showed up on the fateful Saturday, it might be an appropriate time for her to share them. Nonetheless, "The three of them are," she said, "plain-as-day out of their minds, and I can't wonder about them enough."

I did the inviting in the shop. I called Eleanor to explain what was about to transpire in my back yard, and she was devilishly charmed. She had often thought, she said, that if adults lived in "threes" they might hold up better, like an easel. She was pleased with the analogy and offered to bring an "inebriate" to the celebration, since she recalled my liquor supply as being good for nothing. I talked to the Gaussmanns, wanting them to know how much their presence would mean to me, but at the same time to be candid about what they would be coming to witness. It was Lucille who assured me (sounding like Riff or Raggles), "Wherever there is love, it will be my happiness." Bill looked less certain, rubbed the top of his forehead, and told me his wife was light-years ahead of him in such things. Mary Jane was delighted by the prospect of what she called such an unusual "theme party," and she was certain Marvin would enjoy detesting it. It was a worthwhile insight. P.Q., who was making repairs to the top of my chimney, thought it might be better than most weddings he'd seen, but he couldn't speak for his "Mrs." yet. He promised, in any event, to stabilize my hyperactive toilet before the seventeenth.

For the rest, I set up a weak-jointed card table in front of the window and trusted my laptop to it until I could find something better. It was a place where I planned to work in the fall, though work at what was another of those phantom inducements to myself. Then, it would be writing of a sort, but for now it would be brief messages of invitation to an event I was growing more impassioned to see done properly. When I only heard back from Michael, Willie, and Sara Sampson ("charmed to my toes," she said; at what, I didn't know), I followed up with a note of explanation.

The responses came like an assortment of sneezes, properly apologetic but head-clearing. Woo said, of course he would come, but his wife was having nothing to do with more of what she called Jefferson's shenanigans. Edwina Sharpe would be on Cape Cod, but she was tempted to change her plans. A housewarming she could ignore (nothing personal, she added), but the other was almost as appealing as full-belly clams. She was uncertain, on the other hand, how she would explain it to her husband and children. Rachel VanNoys was apparently unaffected by the follow-up message and did not respond directly except to say she hoped I was well. Bartlett himself phoned on behalf of Joanna and called me addled-brained for coming up with the idea, but his boss had nonetheless insisted he be her escort—and what could he say? The voice of my pop-up father was deeper than it had sounded during our other conversations, and it did have a paternal ring that could have been nothing more than his being dragged inexplicably to the country against his will. Still, it was good to think of Joanna having *him* place the call, and I passed some pleasant time imagining the reasons she might have given him. I didn't hear from Hamilton, but I assumed Eleanor or Sara would take care of making him available. That would be about fifteen guests—including Nancy (presumably) and the mailman—and the three guests of honor: a respectably-sized Celebration of Transgression.

THIRTEEN

First, though, there came the call from Phyllis Friel, whose transgressions would be difficult to elevate to a ceremonial status. She was delivering her own invitation, one impossible to turn down. Ellen, she said, had requested to meet with me in Phyllis's office, at a time of my choosing, so long as it was within the next two days. When I suggested we meet that afternoon, Phyllis's response was "Why wait?" She said it with the circumspect laugh of one envisioning an enhanced powwow.

As I approached campus, I realized my attitude about being there had gone into a sharp decline over the weeks. I was no longer driving onto a place of negotiated acceptance where the reason for my presence was everybody's business, including my own. Now, such feelings had peeled away, and the parking lot where I had shared a tailgate with Emily Acampora had come to feel like a visitor's area. The building I was about to enter—at one time *my* building—was lighted by a different sun, one that hyper-sharpened its lines and pulled at its angles. It had been re-erected without a tool touching it--and I believe it would have looked that way were I not going to this particular meeting.

Suitable to the occasion, I was carrying a manila envelope with a question mark inside.

It was by some irrational whim that I walked past my old office, though it was a floor out of my way. The small room was still unoccupied, its shelves empty and desktop clear. In a school where office space for faculty was at a premium, it was a silent disturbance, a disappointment, and a goad.

One floor down, Mary Milligan was outside the main office, removing items from a bulletin board, and she greeted me with a look of confusion before organizing a recognition. "What brings you to these parts?" she asked.

"Phyllis."

She nodded a tired acknowledgment. "That one." It was a declaration. No doubt they had baggage, but I'd not seen it this openly before.

"Yes, that one. How are you?"

"I wish I could tell you."

"Meaning?"

"Meaning if I knew, I would be glad to tell you. I'm not as smart as the people around here. Go to your meeting." She looked relieved to be pushing me along. "And let me know if you're ever in town again," she added with some flippancy.

Phyllis' door was open, and I could hear the pair of voices as I approached. Each sounded subdued but companionable—two old acquaintances sharing a sensible moment.

I used my encounter down the hallway to avoid directly greeting either one: "Mary Milligan seems depressed."

Phyllis looked pleased with the opening I had provided. "Wouldn't you be if you were her?"

"And why is that?" I asked.

"Nothing in particular: just doing what she's doing and being what she is." Her mouth puckered as it had at times during her graceless handling of the department meeting with Jefferson six months earlier, and she turned partway toward Ellen as if seeking a degree of understanding.

"You disdain with notable effect," I commented sloppily, wishing right away to retract it in the face of Ellen's brief scowl. I *did* notice the office was even more disorganized than my last visit to it with the look of having been thoroughly searched without success. Ransacked might have been a better word, and I could picture Phyllis on the prowl for something that would eradicate her recent difficulties—whatever that something could possibly be. Both women were dressed casually, each wearing shorts and sneakers and looking like a senior center's beach volleyball team.

I finally put the obvious question to Ellen. "Why did you ask me to come here—if that doesn't sound too much like getting down to business?" Phyllis laughed slightly, and I continued to look at Ellen. "Question two: why are we being chaperoned?"

"This isn't a date, Jeremiah, and hello again," Ellen responded. "But if you're troubled by the number of people in this room, either Phyllis or I can excuse ourselves."

"Certainly," my former chair affirmed. The pair of responses sounded so finely rehearsed I could picture them huddling earlier with pen and pad. At the same time, there was also the sense of longtime connectivity of which I had recently gotten hints but no clear picture. Phyllis had been in contact with The Professor during the fall of my single teaching year. She had collected his misgivings about me. She had facilitated Ellen's July visit to Quaker Falls, in Phyllis's Jeep, it turned out. The three of them—Ellen, Phyllis, and Alban Curtin—had been long-time acquaintances. And while I assumed I wouldn't be facing more genealogical detonations, I could feel the springs of history coiling again. It had become my waiting place, not sinister but prickly as ever with lessons to be learned.

"No, no. You're clearly both in this together, whatever it is that you're in."

"Very well," Ellen said. Her eyes grew reflective. "One of the reasons for asking you to come here is that I was not the most polished visitor when I came to you last month. Seeing you grown and in your own place had much to do with it. I have tried to adjust my picture of you as the years went along. I tried in my mind to grow you. I don't think I was successful. I *did* like your yard, however. A country hamlet wasn't where I'd imagined you'd be, but I'm growing to believe it suited you."

"I'm growing to believe it, too."

"You know, your father, for all his urban ways, used to have musings about owning a farm and planting an orchard. You have eclipsed him to a degree."

"Did you know," I told her, "he informed Phyllis last year that he thought of me as a...?" I glanced at Phyllis, who was once again monitoring this initial dialogue with the look of having written it, tilting back in her desk chair, her fingers interlocked across her ribcage. "What was the expression?"

"I'm sure I don't remember," she countered.

"Don't be telling stories," I scolded. "It only causes people to question your honesty." She scowled. "You remembered it last month—with a little prodding. Something to do with changelings."

"An apt metaphor, wouldn't you say, for a person as prone to transformation as you appear to be. I believe, too, that it was a father worrying about his son."

Ellen was standing by one of the office's crank-open windows. "And I worry as well." She didn't look at either of us but was evidently speaking to me.

"How long have you known Phyllis?" I asked her.

It was Phyllis who spoke first, sounding pleased with the new direction. "What an interesting question, Jeremiah."

"I thought it might help me to understand better why the three of us are bundled together in this office."

Phyllis nodded her approval. "We've known each other since our youthful theater days."

"In Maine," I said.

"In Maine, yes," Ellen confirmed. "Where youth had its day. I can still see Phyllis as Joan of Arc. Her characterization was so good I couldn't even be jealous of her." The other nodded her appreciation. "Your grandfather called her the toast of summer stock that year. Your father agreed."

I looked at Phyllis. "And?" It seemed an undeserving follow-up.

"I was never as good again." She said it simply, without

embellishment, as if she had long ago accepted that once was enough. I thought of my wooden-cross dream and the way it now intersected with this piece of unknown information—unless I had heard it spoken of in those childhood days at the dining room table when I was allowed to be seen but not heard by a mingling of academics. Including Phyllis. I left it to coincidence as I looked at the woman who had been my one and only chair, who had sat in judgment of never-known colleagues who came and left, who had gotten caught with her hand in the plagiarism pot—but who had also once given summer audiences the very best of her, and who, possibly, had no experience come close to it since. She seemed on the verge of cracking open, a figurine teetering from a tremor felt within but soundless to anyone else.

"I'm sorry," I heard myself telling her.

"No need." She stood and looked around the office as if she were about to begin searching for a lost object again. "Now, it's a beautiful day." She glanced out the window. "Or it was. Why don't you and your mother go for a walk? I don't mean to break up this gathering, but I have things to do. Your Mary the secretary being one of them," she added icily.

As we walked down the stairwell to the ground floor, I tried to gauge Ellen's mood by suggesting "She just tossed us out of her office, didn't she?"

She looked at me noncommittally. "She had obligations."

"But she seemed to be enjoying it."

"*Us*, do you mean? I'm not sure I would put it that way. But please yourself."

We left the building and walked in silence until we came near the library. "A good many of his books are in there," I noted.

"Phyllis told me. There were so many. Too many for you?"

"I'm afraid so. Too much obligation. And I suspect she's been sharing the recent changes in my life to a variety of people. Little bulletins about me kept finding new ears this spring, when they had no business being there."

"It's possible. She has her weaknesses—like any of us."

"And what is it she's going to inflict on Mary?"

"They had an altercation, but Phyllis is not going to inflict *anything.* They're going to work it out with the dean. They are two long-time players here. There are bound to be clashes."

"And that's her excuse—too many years together?"

"Why do you dislike her so? Because she sees gossip as intimacy."

"I don't know that I *do* dislike her, in fact. When I've come close to writing her off, I can't. It would be so much more definite if I did. "

"She's had her share of bumps—especially a very bad marriage very early that kept her from trying it again." I didn't know if she was steering the discussion to her own marriage, but something in her manner held me back. "She sticks to her work instead—or has. She tells me she's grown tired of it. She partly blames you."

"Did I snuff the flame of her idealism?"

She looked at me. "Was it disdain you accused *her* of?"

"All right. Well-taken."

"I think she feels she failed you to a degree—or failed me, or your father. She wasn't very explicit about her disappointment. She is, it is clear, struggling with a loss she will not identify. "

"And you've maintained your friendship throughout the years?"

"Oh, yes." She stopped walking. "We competed for him when we were young—nothing with extended claws, just enough to give Phyllis and me a closeness it would be difficult to explain. And, to an extent, with your father too, whom she grew to see as a mentor rather than the man she couldn't capture. It's how I knew things. And before we get to all of that, she tells me you're having an unusual gathering later in the month."

"It's amazing how people come to know things."

"She heard it from your friend Eleanor, who actually contacted her to see if she might be going."

"Amazing."

"And is this something you've thought through carefully? It is, as I understand, the joining together of two women and a man?"

"Two married white lesbians, to be precise, and a twice-divorced

African-American male who's had a brief involvement with each of them. At different times."

"Oh good, Jeremiah" she replied with a slight wince. "And is this youthful grandstanding on your part? Are you proclaiming your right to be unorthodox? It looks like a gesture to me."

"And are these questions a way of claiming your right to be my mother again?"

She laughed briefly. "My god. Call me an interested spectator who has no rights in the matter. Only a degree of human curiosity. I might have given the same appraisal to anyone doing an unconvincing thing convincingly. Would you compare it to leaving teaching?"

"No, I wouldn't."

"They're not part of a pattern?"

"I have this looming idea we're finally reaching the end of higher education's feudal period. Beyond that, I don't know anything—although I feel like the new era is going to be wrapped in plastic. I wish for something else."

She considered. "I wouldn't disagree with that, although I've been out of the classroom for what feels like a considerably long time. Even your father might have found a truth in what you're saying. He had begun to grow tired of academic pomposity."

I blanked. "Seriously?"

"He once asked me how I would feel about changing our positions. It was unlike him to suggest such a thing. And, of course, it was impossible. He might have gotten hired at a community college, but I was in no way qualified for the halls of ivy."

It had begun to sprinkle softly, casting droplets onto the hot sidewalk that were at first pulled back into the air. "Ellen," I said, "I think we're at the moment where we both know an additional truth, but one of us has to speak it."

"Ah," she sighed. "That may well be. Why don't you speak first?"

The nearest building was the chapel, and while I resisted the idea of overlaying my meeting there with Nancy, the rain increased to the point where we finally retreated under the modernistic porte cochere that covered the semicircular drive fronting it.

I still held the envelope I had carried to Phyllis's office, and Ellen chose this moment to remark on it. "Have you brought me a certificate of merit or an award?"

"I've brought you your inheritance."

"I see—something you mentioned when I came out to see you."

I held the envelope out to her. "From a person who never lost his feelings for you. Or would you doubt it?"

Her face took on a waxen cast as she fingered the envelope and opened it without comment. The multicolored question mark slid out easily and looked at us with its peephole power of observation—an eye of fixed certainty formed around the thick punctuation of unknowing. She spoke to it as if we had been offered a shared metaphor. "Printed nonsense." Then, she spoke to him directly, having in her own way pulled him from the envelope with the sheet of paper. "You would look at me, Alban, in just this manner when you could not make sense of what I was trying to tell you—but with two eyes—with double the intensity. Or when you were unable to believe my refusal to question you. The power of inability. You had it, didn't you, my foolish friend?" Her lips had drawn tightly together, and I could imagine them staying that way indefinitely

"Are you thinking of a specific time?" I tried to shape the words as softly as possible.

Her look unfroze, and she turned to me. "We're coming to that, aren't we? But don't you wonder about his casting this monster eye, even with a computer? He had many gifts, but visual artistry was not one of them." She stared at the image again with increasing fascination. "Look at it, Jeremiah. Look straight at it. On second thought, the gaze of a single eye is more terrifying than that of two. It is vision without perception. Without periphery. It is ugly and graceless! A question should have at least a hint of grace. This has none!" The words came from her throat with searing exactitude. "None."

"There is something on the envelope," I told her and ran my finger under the line of writing.

She read it without comment, virtually ignoring it. "Was *she* the one to tell you? But, of course. She's the only one who would or could have."

The rain had started to angle inward to where we stood, and I suggested we go inside the chapel. She refused, saying she might wish to raise her voice and outdoors would be a better location. Water began to puddle around our feet as one of the chapel doors opened behind us, and we divided to let a maintenance person pass between. I knew him as one who had tidied up my office corridor and emptied wastebaskets during much of my year there. We had developed a friendly relationship as he finished his early morning duties and I was one of the first in the building. He called me "Sir" now, as he had throughout the year, a sign of respect I'd not known how to break him of without seeming ungrateful. He held onto the door, urging us to go inside, before leaving with a sharp nod.

The chapel was empty of people and sounds, no Nancy in the front pew and no insistency of organ music. We stood by a blond table with a vase of gladiolas and a sign-in book, though I couldn't imagine why one would need to indicate having been there.

"As empty places go," Ellen commented, "this is fine."

"Yes," I said quietly. "And, yes, of course it was Joanna."

"How was her delivery? Graceful? Bombastic? Contrite?"

"*Vintage*, I would say, though I've only known her a few months. But aren't you at least relieved to be done with it?"

"Why *done*? Is that ever possible? Does our biology free me of what I've done or not done to you?"

"Isn't it a step to our understanding each other—you and I, who once shared a meaning?"

"Possibly. Possibly there are things that persist, and not all of them need be bad." She considered. "But there will be more. A person like her will have more to tell you. She will." Her voice dropped. "She will": sounding the words to herself before going onward. "She will feel justified."

I took her hands, like a gesture of proposal were anyone watching. "Ellen, she already has."

She spun away from me. "That disgraceful woman! That completely despicable manipulator! She stripped you of that as well?"

"She stripped me of my father, yes." I had tried to say it as gently as possible. "But he was a father I never had. She did me that favor, at least."

"Favor?"

I looked at her. The interior shadows of the chapel intensified facial lines whose depth I'd not noticed until now. She gazed back at me with an expression of abject puzzlement, before I asked, "You and he *did* care about each other, didn't you?"

"We had our own version of being a united couple, Jeremiah. It wouldn't have shaken the fruit from your trees, but it was not unreal."

"Then why did you leave him? It feels like leaving me was secondary to leaving *him*. Am I wrong?"

"Because you weren't *my* child would never have driven me away—because you were. The agreement to have you the way we did was not that far from ordinary. Compare it to adoption, and it was as much a product of desire—and more so, I think."

"Yes...and?"

"Jeremiah, do you know who your father is?"

"Yes, I believe I do."

"I don't, and I would beg you to never tell me. But that was not your *real* father. Alban Curtin was your real father. The real one." she persisted. "And there grew in me the dread that he might come to know you as an untruth. And you too would know the same untruth. Worst of all, that it was never an untruth until it came from the mouth of that woman. His knowing was more than I could anticipate. And anticipate again. And continue to anticipate." It was another cadenced repetition, the sound of an idling engine.

"So you took your bicycle—"

"The bicycle. Yes. I had forgotten." She gazed toward the distant altar area. "But, yes, I left you both."

"Why did she ever tell you?"

"Simple enough. I asked her to." She reached a hand out to me, more comfortably than she had during her brief time in my yard. "After you came to us, she would pay an infrequent visit during your early years. You wouldn't remember. The three of us behaved ourselves with reasonable finesse. We would butter our bread with dabs of gratitude. We were grateful to be so civilized and so skillfully enacting it. Will those who are joining themselves in your yard feel the same as we did?"

"Don't ask me,"

She sighed and appeared to drift. "And how is anyone to know? I only remember. Prediction is useful only when it is right." She gathered herself to her narrative once again, speaking with confidence. "But there was always this sense of her withholding. Which made no sense, Jeremiah. What would she have to withhold? We—the three of us—we were a partnership of withholders. But from each other? Why would *that* be necessary? And then she married, had a son, married again, had a daughter, and we saw almost nothing of her—as far as I know." She was walking along the rear aisle, running fingers along the back of a pew, stroking its smooth roundings. "But that's not what I needed to know. I was not cut out to be the jealous virago. And it didn't *feel* like that. It felt like a whole other piece was not what it was intended to be."

"And he felt it, too?"

"What do you mean?" She seemed struck by the possibility, apparently having never considered it before.

"I'm just trying to understand his disconnection from us—from you and me."

"I left."

"Well before that. It's a memory I haven't made up."

"You can be so sure?"

"You don't wish to be?"

She looked weary and sat suddenly in the last pew. "What can be gained from it?" She spoke to herself or some unseen presence before her.

"Should I teach myself to hate her?"

Ellen looked at the floor. "Do that and you've failed."

"At what?"

She stared up at me. "At learning your lessons. And then... making sense of them."

I slid in next to her. "Ellen, are you finally ready to tell me what you've been doing while you've been...gone?"

"Nothing, really. I've been writing."

"Writing *nothing*?"

"And making quite a good living at it. I assume you will need to try it at some point?"

"Why do you say that?"

"Won't you need an income?"

"Not yet."

"He was that kind to you? The man who was no kind of father?"

"Perhaps he did it for you. Perhaps it is actually yours, left to me for safekeeping."

"It is in no way mine. And I don't need it. More than likely, if it's as much as you suggest, he left it to you as a benefit to resist. How you do that will be an interesting undertaking for you."

"I don't doubt it."

She reconsidered, speaking less speculatively. "He was your father, after all, or he supposed he was. And I'm not sure it would be any different if he knew he was not."

"There's a nice piece of plotting." I gazed at her. "And what is it that you write?"

"Trash." She stared before her as if the word had just been imprinted in midair. "Who would have thought, Jeremiah? I'm quite adept at it."

"Trash?"

"Pitiful romances—of the necessary sort. It's quite remarkable, actually. Once you spin out the first sheepish chapter with your own enjoyable fascination and then type the words Chapter Two, how easy it is to follow it to its logical end. Logic. Trash has startling logic. The logic of hunger. There are pangs and you feed them." She looked at me with pleased relief. "You won't find my name on any book. I've given myself a new one, mine for the making and the keeping. When I die, I'll tell you what it is."

"And how will you do that?"

"In a conspicuously non-trashy way. Leave it to me." She stood. "I've yet to write a trashy piece about a widow. I shall need to do that, don't you think?"

"Will you tell me where you live?"

"Why?"

"So I can at least picture you somewhere."

"Why do you need to?"

"To make you real again."

"I see. I suppose I might grow to accept that. I have never lost interest in you. Nor will I." She smiled at me. "I live in Maine. I do my writing in an old cabin, a little like the one that has come into your life. You might see how yours suits you."

"Would you care to elaborate? Maine is a big state."

"Yes, yes it is. But, no, there's no need to elaborate. If you wish to see me, I will come for a visit—if the lady in your life doesn't mind."

"I have several."

"Probably you do. I was referring to the woman who sat with me—who taught you your ABCs."

"And still does."

"I commend her for her dedication."

"As do I."

"She says you've done a fair job of convincing yourself that she is not a stand-in for...me."

"You did talk, didn't you?"

"We worked quickly. Out of necessity. She is wisely not as convinced as you are."

"I see."

"Though I could be wishful."

"Try." We stood and paused briefly by the vase of gladiolas. "Did you actually go to Poets' Walk on my birthday?"

She gazed as if she were trying to relocate a lost idea. "Yes. In fact I did."

"Did you think I would come?"

"I had no way of knowing. And I was just as glad you didn't. It was nowhere as attractive as I remembered it."

"No?"

"I thought of taking a short walk, but it looked so apologetic, I simply left when I knew I wasn't to see you that day."

We came out of the chapel lighter than we had entered it—the weight of the unfamiliar partly lifted from us. It was still raining, but more softly, and vertically rather than horizontally—as if it would soon end. We paused by a litter basket while Ellen tore the sheet of paper and its envelope into pieces. She dropped in each fragment as a separate item, unconnected to the others, and said at the end, "Probably she did it. I doubt he had the gift."

"And Phyllis," I said.

"Yes?"

"I'm told you went away with a friend when..."

"Yes, with Phyllis. We did a week of Broadway. And you can say the other person's name."

"Joanna."

"Yes."

"And Phyllis knew *why*?"

"Would that be a discomfort to you?"

"Only more to digest."

"She was not happy. That's all I remember. Perhaps she wished it was her. I never asked."

"Phyllis?"

"Yes. Phyllis. And I assume she knew the will from Alban—well before he died. She would have needed that."

We stood side by side, looking at the empty campus sidewalks. "Jeremiah?" she asked. "Why have you abandoned teaching?"

"I'd rather not answer, not until I know for certain. I can only say that this place and what it is supposed to be all about feels like it's abandoned itself. And it doesn't seem it knows how to fix that. It's so damn sad, Ellen."

As we walked down the inclined driveway, I asked her if she had ever seen or heard of *Reconsiderations*. She hadn't and asked me to describe it. When I did, she said simply, "Joanna Wexler had something to do with *that*, I'm quite sure. He may have had it in him. But I never saw it. I never saw a good many things, I would guess. That's probably what gives the world its delectable strangeness. I wish I could produce books about it, but trash suits me—and it—just as well at this point."

When I told her I had brought a copy of the book, she walked quietly to the truck with me and nodded at the slender volume when I reached for it. She took it without comment and then told me she was leaving by bus the next day, a journey she looked forward to. "I like the loneliness of buses, and loneliness gives me as much room to breathe as a new month." She spoke the words with an affectionate but cautious smile and turned toward my former building. The blue book dangled from her hand like a disappointing exam.

FOURTEEN

Three days before the Transgression Ceremony, Nancy Feller finally made her decision, after continuing to question the collective enthusiasm of three people who, as far as she could tell, had demanded rather than requested my services. As she suggested at one point, it looked oddly intolerant on the part of those who were seeking a public display of tolerance. When I asked her what had turned her against a concept she had fielded so gracefully at the hospital, she reminded me that she had first voiced her doubts on the way to her mother's.

"In the middle of being abducted by you," she told me, "it seemed only right to wonder whether you were being taken hostage by them. I brushed it aside during the rest of our time at the lake, but it kept coming back. Keep in mind, though, my feelings about them as individuals hadn't changed—haven't changed. I'm still fond of them."

"Some abduction. It ended up with you teaching me to torture baby frogs."

"It was good for you." We were in her home office, and I was leaning awkwardly against the curved side rail of the rolltop. It was a pop-in visit, one I hoped would finally shake a declaration out of her. She looked from the window at the swimming pool, which had been left covered for the summer. "I want to know how you really feel about this plan. You talk about the preparations you are making—such as they are—but not about how you're feeling." She faced me again. "Tell me."

"Telling-time again?"

"Yes."

"All right...I feel awkward."

"Okay." She was waiting for more.

"As you say, we weren't given much of a choice."

"We?"

"You were there. The original announcement was delivered to both of us. They assumed, for their own reasons, that you and I would be up to it. Apparently, they were wrong." She studied me fixedly. "And just how would you explain not attending?"

"Family matters."

"Nancy, this isn't like you."

"It's *very* like me up until last year. You only know this year's model."

"Not true."

"My apologies. You remember me from when I was making my classroom into a clearing in the forest."

"I do."

"Maybe you *are* the right person to be hosting this event."

"Possibly so." I saw sad shadows crossing her eyes. "My...Ellen thought I might be doing this as a gesture."

"And?"

"I'm not. For *them* it may be. It's for them to know, now or later. But as much as it was an edict presented by three calmly crazed people, I'm not gesturing. I'm not waving at anybody's passing scene—not even my own. I'm glad she forced me to confront it—Ellen, that is. I think, in fact, I'm being schooled in what sent me to Quaker Falls—one lesson at a time. It could be a screw-up, but The Professor would undoubtedly find value in that, since it was *me* screwing up."

"Well," she said, "we shall have to see, won't we?"

"You said *we*?"

She sighed. "Jeremiah, we don't have to be together to see."

"You're not coming." I spoke as declaratively as I could.

"That's my intent."

"What will you do?'

"Do you mean how will I fill my Saturday afternoon?"

"Or more, if you wish."

I saw on her face the look in the Rhinebeck coffee shop eight months earlier—a look of clarity and purpose. Missing, though, was the dance of play in her voice. "Do you know what I've realized, as much as it was right there to see?"

"Should I know?"

"You should. A year ago, or however long, I had barely taken a step into my future. And then, there you were. A whisper from the past. All grown up, too. Or nearly. No bits of paper on your face, but still precious."

"And?"

"Precious is dangerous, Jeremiah. Or it can be. It can fool us. Like this weekend's ceremony. And you. Here you are patching yourself back together. Patch by patch. A mother here. A father there. Add a sister and a brother for good measure. And Ellen. She is such a weary soul. From carting too much avoidance and too much fantasy, I would guess. Her own patches. And yet I don't see you embracing any of it. Why is that?"

"I don't know."

Her shoulders sagged. "I can see how it might feel like too much all at once."

"Or not enough." She turned away. I tried changing focus. "Nancy, you were talking about vows not that long ago."

"Those! They were an exercise. Better...I think they were a lesson plan. But my teachings days are..."

"Please don't say that. What is it you want right now?"

"From?"

"Me."

She looked at me again and moved closer. "I want you to go make ready for this weekend's events. I want you to be fully there and fully aware. And take good notes. In spite of it all, I may wish to know parts of it. Go," she repeated with insistence, the back of her hand brushing briefly against my mouth, sealing it.

FIFTEEN

August 17 was as it should be, steamy with threats of thundershowers. People started arriving early afternoon, bringing various offerings to a host they undoubtedly suspected wouldn't be that accomplished at throwing a party of any sort, let alone one of challenging overtones. Michael engineered a sound system and used the shop as his command center and he helped me erect a canopy from a rental center. Willie had helped me buy liquors and mixers, showing artful sophistication in her advisement. I set aside qualms about Louisa, who served as emergency caterer and brought a frosted cake with a configuration of three shooting stars iced in the center. She stored it magically in an already full refrigerator.

For several hours, the guests consumed and drank, and most of those who hadn't known each other before became comfortably acquainted—"convivially" so, I heard at one point from Mrs. P.Q., whose actual name turned out to be Lorelei. (It was a nice-sounding word, and I felt rewarded when she said it.) Mary Jane, in her own high spirits, went trolling for other neighbors, people I had primarily waved to during my time in Quaker Falls. She had hopes, apparently of turning this into a semicircular block party, but she managed only to collect the mother-daughter (Moms and Allegra) from the house next to her and a pair of middle-aged women who lived near the Emporium. Given Mary

Jane's seemingly haphazard way of approaching things, they came not knowing what it was they were getting into.

Joanna Wexler, Bartlett, Hamilton Graham, and Eleanor Jewett were later arrivals. Sara Sampson was there, however, at the dot of one, the first arrival, covering Willie and Michael with wet kisses, greeting me more modestly. She had not been staying with Hamilton, but she soon found willing companionship in Taylor the mailman, still in his postal shorts and packing a silver-colored bottle of tequila and a pair of shot glasses. It was like he had a presentiment about Sara's thirsty desert ways, and she obliged by concluding he indeed *had*. They spent much of their time in the Adirondack chairs, a gathering at the edge of the gathering. Richard came with Edwina, who had, in fact, cut her vacation short by a day, leaving her husband and children on the Cape. It was difficult to imagine how she had accomplished that, one of those demonstrations of family physics outside my realm of experience. But she came to party, drinking many glasses of merlot and being so companionable with Woo, I speculated about their having done this kind of thing before. Bill and Lucille arrived carrying their own lawn chairs, and he went back to bring an apple pie cooked in a rectangular dish—because, as Lucille proclaimed, "Square corners make for extra bites." Marvin wandered down from Mary Jane's an hour after she had, acting like a reluctant pursuer. He kept looking unsteadily from guest to guest, trying, perhaps, to imagine who the transgressors might be, and Michael assured him they hadn't come yet. With that, he seemed to relax and cajoled Willie into making him a gin and ginger and to make it hearty. She was decidedly happy to oblige, and he was on his way to his July Fourth state of being.

Eight students, the blood donors and others from the May wedding, appeared in two cars, and filled in gaps of age and energy. They were, to me, a needed omen—the hoped-for emissaries that would help loosen the strappings of a worried and worrisome society. They were all women, and I thought not of Chuck Gillis's memorable pronouncement about female stature but rather of the ways in which young women were becoming the impresarios of learning and risking.

How emotionally rumpled the majority of young men in my courses had appeared to be, like they had surrendered the field to a superior, and clearly feminine, force. Appropriately, one of the eight, on that afternoon, told me succinctly that it was a good thing to be hosting this ceremony but that I was nonetheless a wimp for leaving teaching to what she called "machine-made marionettes." It was as impressive a judgment as Willie Furman could have delivered, and I noticed, too, the young blond woman addressing me was at least three inches taller than I was.

There had been questions about Nancy's absence. She had evidently explained the decision to her son and Willie, who left her name out of conversations. Marvin and Mary Jane wondered in their own cheeky way whether I had finally worn her out. Sara thought my lady could be at a Social Security office except for its being a Saturday. When the marital trio asked and I mentioned family issues, they clearly didn't buy it, but let it go. Others didn't know her or didn't ask.

The featured guests had arrived by midafternoon, each in a white outfit, similar to the wedding in May. Each carried two bottles of champagne, which they deposited in a tub of ice under the canopy. Most, of course, knew them and knew why they were there, but in case anyone wasn't sure, it was Marvin who announced, "That's them, isn't it?"

Over the ten days since I had been commissioned to put this event together, I'd thought obsessively about the timing of the afternoon, certainly more than I had about feeding people. As I mowed and trimmed and removed fallen fruit from beneath the trees, I calculated. Like a set-designer, I had planned the ceremony for four o'clock, when shadows would have moved across the yard and a breeze might begin to stir smaller branches. I wanted textures.

It was difficult not to think of The Professor's atmospheric calculations for the reading of his will.

Repeatedly, I also heard Ellen's questioning voice coming at me like a slow, erratic pulse I tried to ignore. I was aware, too, of the things that could misfire: those who would suddenly find it within themselves to believe what we were undertaking *was* transgressive, particularly as the August heat and the prodding of alcohol blurred whatever resolve they had brought with them.

Nonetheless, it needed to go on, and Willie was delegated to reach Hamilton, to find out whether we should wait for them. I didn't really care about Joanna Wexler and her Bartlett—so I told myself—but I wanted Eleanor Jewett to be there. In a considered way, I wanted her to add legitimacy to the afternoon, and I was becoming increasingly regretful I hadn't gone to get her myself.

As the latecomers were in fact on the road, we agreed to wait, and their arrival at 4:30 helped to revive those sagging from an afternoon of eating and drinking and fanning themselves. Hamilton assisted Eleanor from the car, and with the sixth sense of a fellow transgressor or recognition of the only man of color present, Eleanor moved nimbly to the trio now standing near the quince. She took each of their hands in succession, and, for a moment, the four of them formed a wheel of clasped figures. For the first time, I heard Mikhail Jefferson's throaty laugh.

Joanna Wexler, wearing a slight, coral-colored dress, worked her way through the guests, introducing herself to the unfamiliar as a friend of mine and Malcolm Bartlett as her law partner. She continued to be the bringer of news: that Bartlett was his last name and she had given him a phantom promotion for the occasion. His hair was not pulled into a ponytail on this day, and with its expansiveness seemed a copy of Nancy's. He nodded to me, with little to say at that point, preferring an eggroll and a glass of vodka instead. It was Edwina who whispered, "He's good-looking, isn't he? They make a handsome power couple." He *was* a presence on this occasion of my seeing him standing for the first time—handsomer than me, certainly. As I looked at the two of them, like figures from a sports car advertisement, I thought it interesting that nature hadn't crafted me to remind anyone of anyone. And, of course, I had just seen how easily Joanna could fabricate and had heard Ellen jab repeatedly at the idea during our truth session in the chapel.

Eleanor came to me on the arm of Hamilton Graham, who was carrying a bottle of brandy and a single small glass. She smiled and pulled me down so she could kiss me. "I like to travel prepared, but it looks like you've outdone yourself this time. You make me happy. Thank you, Hamilton," she said, nodding to an empty place on one of the tables. He set the bottle down and gave her the glass to slip into one of two deep pockets of her dress, from which she would remove it when her thirst called. "He has to be good today. The last time I came here, I had given his door an unladylike kick because he was being so stubborn about things. I hurt my toe." I told her I remembered quite clearly. "But that's all over now. Brother and brother." She gave a satisfied sigh. So *she* knew, and I wondered for how long and whether it was a secret she would preserve—and whether it wanted or deserved preservation. It had so felt like a disclosure without branches, the idea that anyone could wish to share it with another seemed ludicrous. With the exception of Willie.

"Now let's get on with the show," Miss Ellie finally insisted.

She was right. It was approaching five o'clock, and I sent Willie and her friends to gather the guests together, everyone but Sara and the mailman, who had wandered off, after she asked me, in her succinct way, whether I had been needing younger lady friends recently. I assured her I hadn't been. The weather was holding and providing the breezes I had hoped for.

I tried acting as master of the occasion, giving an official greeting, explaining how I wanted to make a housewarming into an event that would stand up to time, that the fruit of the quince tree (which I gestured to) had old associations with Aphrodite and Eve and phantom boundaries, that restoring an abandoned house had given me hope for making sense of the very difficult and puzzling things we do—before I heard myself lapsing into a classroom voice, and faltered.

Jefferson took over, looking at me. "You done good." He turned to the rest. "What we would like you to do shortly is form a circle around us. Any of you who have misgivings about what the three of us are about to do—to live as married as any couple and to declare that openly right here in the sight of you and the firmaments—we ask you not to violate your own consciences, but to feel free to go back to the food table or go home, if you are capable of getting yourselves there." There was mild laughter, edgy and uncertain. In the face of what none of us had ever experienced, the absence of real levity was understandable. "The State of New York, or any other state, for that matter, will undoubtedly need a long journey to endorsing what we are doing here this afternoon, though a number of cultures throughout history have embraced the concept with sacred devotion. We may not see it here in any of our lifetimes, but you can never know such things absolutely. So much else is changing. Except the need by some to play dumb. That never changes. So we're asking you, the good-hearted and open-minded, to be our state of the moment. At the same time—"

Barbara Lynn put a sudden hand over his mouth, smiling the wild-smile I had missed during the afternoon. "Mikhail tends to go on at times, though I do like listening to him. But to keep y'all from thinking we're silent and obedient household victims of his wordy ways, ah'd like to say mah own piece—and, no doubt Emily will, too. We've rehearsed the part that's coming shortly, but not this preamble. And I do think it's important that you hear our thoughts as well as our declaration of what we are and will be. We asked Jeremiah and"—she paused and then recovered—"asked him to do the ceremony by the little cabin behind us. Some of you already know it most likely has a sad and beautiful history. There was a time, as far as we can believe, when runaway slaves would stop here as part of what people at the time called the Underground Railroad. While they were here, I want you to know, they were literally underground, waiting beneath the floor of that building. I want you all to know that on this day." She was sounding even more professorial than Jefferson and I had, her words propelled by the rhythm of her own classroom voice. Her hair had been contained by a yellow ribbon for the occasion, but it looked ready to unleash itself.

Some were hearing of the shop for the first time, and there was a quiet flutter of voices. Two of the neighbors brought as part of Mary Jane's roundup—the two women around Nancy's age—looked particularly impacted by the mention of the Underground Railroad. Allegra and her mother had already left during the course of the afternoon for reasons they didn't share.

Barbara went on, "Those slave folk didn't know much, I bet, about the places they hoped to get to, but they had the conviction of their hearts. And that's what the three of us are asking you to believe of us."

One voice filled the pause she offered to those listening. "I'm not sure I get it. I wish you well, I certainly do, but why not live together, at least for a time, without calling attention to it? I worry for you. I truly do. I worry about the lunatics." It was Bill Gaussmann, whom I had seen struggling with his feelings throughout the afternoon. While he had drunk very little, he had made several short trips back to his house. "An old man's bladder," he told me once. "And nerves."

Marvin Feller peered out of his own mistiness to get the gist of Bill's question: "Good advice from my friend. You'll get no argument from this corner."

Eleanor Jewett uttered a brief "Pooh," which was absorbed by a collective pause.

Then, the silence became total for several seconds. I noticed the calico cat had at some point been let into the shop and was sitting placidly in its open window, waiting for whatever was to come next. Finally, the interval was broken by Emily. She was still spectral-thin from her injuries, making her even more beatific than usual. She spoke with the soft articulation of a boy soprano. "It's sweet of you to worry," she said to Bill, before speaking to the onlookers as a whole. "You should all know this was my idea at first, while I was recovering from... an accident. I was in the hospital and still weak when I suggested it to Barbara and Mikhail. They promised they would wait to see if I had lost control of my senses when I proposed it. Some of you, like this dear man, may feel the same way right now, as we propose this to you." She put a hand against one of Bill's cheeks; his eyes closed briefly before she continued. "We don't know who the men and women were who waited in the dirt pit beneath this cabin. We don't know if they made it all the way north from here, although my guess is Jeremiah will try to find out. He's a little obsessive, and we value him for it." She nodded at me, and the tension began to ease. "As far as that goes, we only have such small pieces of evidence to say they or he or she were actually here in Quaker

Falls. Dr. Hynes would call that just fine, though. History isn't always perfect—and it's a process with a lot of commas and question marks."

"They were here," Bill interrupted, his voice less tentative now.

Emily smiled at him, seeming to gaze downward at the man who was a head taller than her. She adjusted her glasses slightly. "That's good to hear. It is, even though we know the bigger story. And you see, we don't want to be guessed about either. We truly don't. We want to say to our children and our grandchildren even..." she paused to let the idea reach out to the others—"that we stood together surrounded by people who trusted in more than what they already knew. There can't be any greater love, can there?"

Eleanor took several steps closer to her. "That was beautiful, every bit as much as you." Emily's gaze lowered toward the ground. "Why don't you three go ahead? I'm sure those who wanted to have gone by now."

The wind had increased earlier, suggesting the approach of a storm, but the skies were brushed only by wisps of clouds. The cat was mewing from the window, and I asked Michael to let it join us and to bring the armchair outside for an obviously tired Miss Jewett. He lowered her upon it with the skill of a head butler, and she sat ceremonially, her hands folded together. Hamilton moved behind her to hold her arms in a grasp so light she seemed not to notice.

The three who were to be united in the sight of earthbound people on this afternoon clustered with their backs to each other and guided arcs of the watchers into a full circle—using hand gestures and the nodding of their heads. A cardinal whistled short blasts of commentary, the only sound of nature then. The wind had stopped. The trees were soundless. Mary Jane had taken Marvin's hand with cautionary comfort. Edwina's head dropped for a moment onto Richard's shoulder before she removed it. On the other side of the circle, the eight students and Willie were passing a box of tissues, which continued on to Joanna, who took several before putting the box under one arm. Bartlett looked at me, his face fixed in puzzlement. Lorelei was quietly combing P.Q.'s disordered hair with her fingers. Lucille and Bill looked into each other's faces, as if they were about to renew their own vows, his reservations put to rest by her and Emily.

It was at that moment I felt Nancy's chin pressed against my back, the distinctive smells of soap and sun and skin reaching around me with the indelibility of shared memory. Then she took a step forward to link an arm into mine. The two remaining neighbors I had met only that afternoon stood closely on either side of us, like rediscovered friends.

At a mutually understood time, the three in the center began to speak, still facing outward, one after another, phrase by phase. Emily spoke first, then Jefferson, then Barbara Lynn.

– *We are here today to be joined*
– *We are here with one purpose and many*
– *We are here to feel your presence as you feel ours*
– *We are grateful*
– *We are at peace*
– *If certainty exists, we are certain*
– *We will be fruitful*
– *We may multiply*
– *We may educate*
– *We will be broken and healed*
– *Misunderstood and found wanting*
– *Taken to task*
– *But our task will grow lighter*
– *Our healing more graceful*
– *The music of our hearts more appealing*
– *We will honor those who have struggled*
– *Who continue to struggle*
– *And those who have forgotten to struggle*
– *And all who come to share our discoveries with us.*

The last line was said in unison by the three of them, who then clasped hands with their backs to each other still. They paused before turning inward, rejoining hands and taking a step backward, as if admiring one another. Those of us around them waited quietly.

I noticed a county sheriff's car moving slowly along the ear-shaped road of the hamlet, the driver pausing briefly to look at the circle within a circle before moving onward. I thought little about it.

The voices of the three resumed in unison with the non-melodic cadences of a chant. The cat was drawn in their direction and sat next to Jefferson, blinking comfortably.

We come this day
From the hidden way,
Three spirits joined as one.

We come to be
A trinity
Of personhood begun.

Once you, now we,
The mystic three
Two daughters and a son

We love this day,
We humbly pray
And trust thy will is done.

They finished with three distinct kisses and an embrace of interlocked arms, the blond, black, and red hair creating a field of contrasts as their foreheads touched. When they turned to the rest of us, Jefferson and Barbara Lynn exhaled in obvious relief and Emily swept her hair with the palms of her hands. They moved outward to clasp the arms of the watchers each by each, until the stillness was finally broken by Barbara exclaiming, "Where's the champagne, y'all? This is a hot and thirsty business."

It was the cue for the rest of us to release our own contained emotions—the unspoken feeling in some of us, at least, that we were part of events bigger than we might know, done with an intimacy of delicate contours that had transgressed transgression. Applause, cheers, and raw clamor grew to the point where it tested itself against the hill across the meadow and returned to us. As it subsided, Michael went to the shop to cue up a play-list he and Willie had assembled with suggestions from Barbara Lynn. It began with a brief version Lennon's "Imagine," devoid of lyrics, the melody itself played on an organ with forceful tenderness by an obvious keyboardist. As the track subsided, I saw Joanna Wexler walk briskly and briefly toward the rear of the yard. Unless I invented it, her shoulders were shaking and she was dabbing at her nose. She returned, however, with her composure restored, as if she'd had a momentary reaction to the air-currents of August.

Jefferson asked Eleanor if she was up to leading a champagne toast, and she assured him she was. She pulled the personal glass out of her deep pocket and filled it with Willie's assistance while others splashed small pourings into paper cups. The woman of so many years was at her ceremonial best, a nonagenarian whose time had come. "Raise yours, all. It's time to be grateful. In my experience, I've noticed many of us live in caves—caves with doors, walls, windows, and all kinds of pretty bunkum. Now, these three beautiful people have made it clear it doesn't have to be that way. I'm tickled. I truly am. I lived to see this. A courageous spirit is at hand. And that's what Spirit is. It's the courage to be trusting of ourselves. And that's a whopper. So...good, yes, very good for you." She emptied her glass in one swallow, as if it were her last.

Louisa, a silent observer through much of the afternoon, presented the cake to the guests of honor, and Barbara thanked her for her good and understanding eye.

At that point, I turned to Nancy. "I took notes."

"No need," she replied, lowering her head slightly.

The reception, for that's what it was, went on for several more hours, until darkness began to fall. Some wandered off earlier, like an exhausted Bill and Lucille. Mary Jane took Marvin back to her place but returned by herself to have a session near the fruit trees with Willie.

They spent parts of the evening with their arms around each other's shoulders, and Willie treated her to some rewired Bach on the piano in the dining room. Barbara was commandeered by her former students for much of the time, and it was difficult not to think *this* was why she was denied tenure in a miscarriage of injustice that would instead have her teaching in backyards and alternative byways. Jefferson and Woo inspected the shop together, asking Michael for a flashlight and screwdriver. I found them at one point standing on the downward steps of the hidden cellar drinking bourbon and throwing curses at the darkness. Edwina was seated on the floor with her back to the potbelly, waiting for them to finish and nodding at the color of their language. It was clear the rest of her evening would involve Woo, and for a moment, I felt an indefinable sadness.

Sara Sampson did, of course, have her moments. She had melted back into the event at some point during the ceremony and later tasked Emily with answering inappropriate logistical questions many of the rest of us were thinking. "I mean, Emily," I could hear her say at one point, "do you mean to say you've worked out sleeping arrangements and bedroom questions? You keep smiling like it's none of this girl's business, but it's a great challenge not to wonder. Should I wonder?" Emily's smile served her as well as ever, but it must have been a relief to her when Sara noticed the presence of Hamilton Graham for the first time. He was standing alone under the canopy with a beer bottle in hand when she called to him from a shattering distance. "Why Hammy, what a surprise to see you—and at an improper occasion like this. Have you decided Jeremiah's not a bad boy after all?" As she crossed to him, I experienced my first real brother-feelings.

The only visible blot on the evening was the return of the sheriff's car, about a half-hour before sundown. I walked over when the vehicle came to a complete stop, realizing someone in the hamlet had been jangled by the goings-on.

"What?" I asked in a voice that didn't reflect my usual discomfort around enforcers.

There were two in the car, a male driving and a lady cop in the passenger seat. The driver spoke first. "We've gotten calls about a black arts ceremony going on here."

"Black arts?"

"You know," the lady cop said past him, "witchcraft."

I didn't realize Joanna had followed me to the road. Her voice came past me: "And what if there were? Do we need a license for such an event? You can see we don't even have a boiling cauldron." One strap was off her shoulder and the slightly exposed breast looked as if she'd had a boob job. Her voice, though, showed no slippage, and when she recognized the lady cop, she exclaimed, "Why hello, Maxine. You're doing squad car duty at last?"

Maxine sorted out the context. "Counselor Wexler? Joanna?"

"The same." Bartlett was standing beside her by now and I had the odd wish for Michael to take a group photo of us, with the sheriff's car in the background. "If you want to know what's going on," Joanna instructed them, "two white lesbians—or bisexuals as the case may be—have just pledged their troth"—a word she had difficulty with—"to a black man. I'm sure whoever called you to look us over thought it was the darkest arts for sure, if you get my point."

I added with extreme politeness, "If the state granted licenses for such events, we would surely have gotten one, officers."

Bartlett snickered near my ear, and for the first time since his arrival, I heard him speak in connected phrases. "And surely the county constabulary is better equipped to deal with murderers and pot smokers than interracial multi-sexual shindigs. My suggestion would be for you to help yourselves to refreshments and then allow yourself the privilege of talking about it and us for the rest of your shift."

The two in the patrol car voiced the strains of unwonted reflection as they said the word "sorry"—Maxine echoing her partner. As they drove away, past Mary Jane's and the Gaussmanns' houses and back to the main highway, I pictured them hectoring each other like any other couple.

It was as we walked back to the house that Bartlett spoke to me directly, letting Joanna move on ahead. "I'll tell you one thing, my young friend, you've got guts." I assured him I merely hosted those with the guts. "My point exactly," he added. "You may be a quirky son of a bitch, but you might stand the test of time. Maybe time and a half. Who knows? We might also talk again, but I wouldn't bet the house on it." I looked at him, attempting to x-ray him with the most noncommittal thoughts I could summon up, but I couldn't find an image.

Bartlett, Joanna, and I went inside to fetch Eleanor Jewett, whom we found asleep in the Morris chair, perfectly erect and without the trace of a snore.

"Do you think she would mind?" Bartlett asked Joanna.

She quickly deciphered his question. "No. I think she might rather like it, if anyone bothers to tell her."

He nodded once and scooped her into arms I noticed were well muscled. He did it with the ease of lifting a sleeping child. He carried her through the front screen door, tapping it open with his foot and moving to the car without waking her. No fireman would have done better.

When Eleanor was wedged securely in the back seat between Joanna and a cardboard carton, Hamilton peered in at the sleeping figure and back at me. "She said she wants to do an event of her own: a brother-warming party. That's what she called it. I hope you won't deprive her or me." I assured him I wouldn't.

Before getting into the passenger seat, he asked if Sara Sampson would ever be out of his life. I told him I doubted it and squeezed his shoulder. He added that the guy in Arizona was already married, before considering the fact: "Who knows? Today might convince her of the total irrelevance of that. How's that for magnificent!"

When they were about to leave, Joanna reached across Eleanor to remove still another manila envelope from the box. "In case you're interested, Jeremiah. Once again." She sounded placidly sober and her shoulder straps were both in place. As they drove off, I waited for an interior message about the tangle of her, Bartlett, Alban, Ellen. None came. I had been granted another day of temporary immunity.

The three celebrants were with Nancy near the shop, embracing her one after the other. They looked played out. As they crossed to their car, I noticed Barbara Lynn carrying a napkin-wrapped something, and she lifted it in my direction, saying only, "The shooting stars." Jefferson called from beyond her in his low-rumbling voice. "We told your woman to share some of our sloppy affection with you. We..." He trailed off before getting into the car.

The only outside survivors were P.Q. and his Lorelei, who had asked if they could hit me up for bug repellant and sit for a time in the Adirondack chairs. I told them I had fogged the yard, but she called the other more personal. Louisa had resisted my orders that she not tidy up the kitchen, telling me "It feels like I finish a good book. Do not vorry." Much of the sadness had seemed to lift from her.

Willie and Michael were in the dining room where she was playing a soft-fingered version of "Greensleeves." They had asked if I'd be needing my bed later, and I thanked them for their newfound courtesy.

"Just don't destroy it," I warned. "I realize your time is short."

Willie's fingers had lifted momentarily from the keyboard as the thought stuck within her before she started playing again. "My mother didn't say good-bye to me," she noted. "Typical." I assured her I had received no good-bye either but I could live with it if she could. She touched the keyboard with a softness I'd not imagined her capable of, her fingers stroking the keys of another time with reflective generosity.

SIXTEEN

Nancy was sitting on the top step to the shop. The cat for all people was asleep next to her, one ear flipping at an invisible annoyance. Moths and other things of the night were fluttering about the exterior light Michael had installed the day before.

"We should name your friend," she said, looking at the calico. "I get the feeling she's ready to be your permanent resident. I'm quite sure she liked today's event."

"It's a she?"

"Yes—a she."

"Did you ask?"

"I counted holes."

It was a simple and startling explanation. "I'm afraid I've been too modest."

"And you should think about spaying her."

"If you say so." Nancy's soft beauty had, if anything, super-focused during the three days since I'd seen her, her eyes as charged with convictions as they had been twenty some years earlier. Whatever misgivings she'd had about the ceremony had disappeared.

"I parked in Mary Jane's driveway. Do you think that was perverse of me?"

"It was perfect."

"Could we go inside?" she asked. "As you know, mosquitoes can only ignore me for so long. They tell me I'm succulent."

"And so you are. Willie and your son have asked for the bed, by the way."

"Not the house...here." Her shoulder pointed partway behind her.

"As you wish."

Eleanor's chair had been returned to the shop and had been joined by another, a blue canvas lawn chair left behind by the Gaussmanns. The only light was that coming from the exterior fixture, but her face was distinctly visible as she pulled me to her.

"I almost asked them if they were going on a honeymoon. Can you imagine? Would it have sounded horribly nosy?"

"I don't think so."

She heard the crinkle of paper between us and asked, "What is that you're carrying?"

I told her it was another of Joanna's mystery packages and flipped it on the table. "It may provide entertainment for a solitary night, but not now. Do you think she's warmed to you at all?"

"She looked pleased when I showed up, but I imagine we have a competition going on—a version of the old mother-daughter-in-law testiness—so out of the bounds of the ordinary that there's no book to cover it. Yet." She considered. "I don't know if she's decided where to channel her energies, or if she should at all."

"She'll find a way. Ellen doesn't trust her."

"Yes, you've told me. Several times." She sighed quietly. "She cried, didn't she—after it was over?"

"I think so."

"That's good. What do you think it was about."

"Name anything you wish. She's a well-bundled person."

Nancy sat at last in the canvas chair and patted the other until I joined her and considered how much had been transacted in the few weeks since I had turned my attention to the shop. It had become a living-place. "The featured players told me they were more nervous today than they expected to be," she said, "but Barbara thought that was most likely a good thing. They also said they couldn't thank you enough for agreeing to this, so they decided not to. Emily, of course, was sure you knew it in your heart. On the right day, I could still eat her."

"Yes. What else? We talked so little today."

"For starters," she said, "Marvin thought at first he was seeing the end of civilization, but he admitted it looked like a better blueprint for the Garden of Eden—although I probably coached him into saying that."

"Most likely."

"He's not a bad guy, you know.

"Yes, Nancy—I know. What else?"

"Bartlett. What do you think of him?"

"I don't know. I think he might have the ability to grow on people. Whether I'm one of them..."

"Do you think he's your father?"

"Do you think I will eventually wonder more?"

"I'm completely sure you will."

"What else?"

"Your Miss Jewett told me she still has all of her own teeth and she thought you were likely *playing* the devil rather than actually *being* one. What do you suppose *that* meant?"

"Interesting. The teeth at least. Anything else?"

"Louisa called her husband."

"When?"

"After the cake. She told me 'marriage without marriage' made her feel lightheaded. And she'd had no champagne. She decided it must mean she has truly missed him—in spite of her Old World stubbornness."

"Did she tell you it had to do with the inheritance?"

"Yes, she did."

"Giving can be dangerous."

"So can receiving."

"What else?" I persisted.

"Catherine and Claire, your two lady neighbors, said they were a little afraid to speak to you, you seemed so caught up in the day's importance. I don't think they said 'self-importance.'"

"I hope not."

"They said they are not lesbians, but two women who live productively together and share many good things without being sexually romantic. One talked about 'Boston marriages'—an interesting term, don't you think? From olden days. They were very forthcoming, and they're happy to have you as a neighbor and look forward to welcoming you properly to the hamlet. But they insisted you include me, although I'm not sure they've figured out how to classify us. Could we be considered a Poughkeepsie marriage?"

"My god. *There's* a label to hide from."

"As for the neighbors who couldn't stand up to today—"

"And called the cops."

"They were frightened, I'm sure. Did you think even a place called Quaker Falls would be free of insecurity?"

"No."

"But the ladies called them good people who will probably decide to like you if you don't hold transgression ceremonies every weekend. She's a mother who's looked after a disabled daughter for most of her adult life."

"Disabled?"

"You can't always see it."

"True," I conceded. "And it may be they were sent by a very selective power to keep me honest."

"Just what does *that* mean?"

"How about, for instance, that my fat stash in the bank—deeded to me under highly false pretenses—might be better off without my bastard hands on it?"

"I see." She looked genuinely unimpressed. "And what do they—your cop-calling neighbors—have to do with *that*?"

"Who knows? Nothing. Static electricity." She waited for me. "That's all."

"Fine," she said, brushing it aside. "Mary Jane was embarrassed she had caused the bad things to happen, but I assured her it wasn't really her doing. I think *she's* begun to like me."

"That's no surprise."

"She asked whether she should consider marrying Marvin."

"He asked her?"

"She thinks he might."

"Dr. Johnson called it the triumph of hope over experience—in those who remarry."

"That's clever. I'll promise to read him if you decide to teach again."

"I might. When people don't know everything. And so...what is it you want, Nancy."

"I'll show you. I told you I wrote my vows—not ours, but mine."

"Oh, the vows."

"With revisions. I'd like to do them now."

"Now?"

She stood. "Actually about five minutes from now. I would like witnesses. I'll get P.Q. and his wife, who I think are still pretending to be young lovers. They told me they do it whenever they get the chance. You retrieve Willie and Michael."

"What if they're already...?"

"They were told to wait."

"I see."

"Unless you don't wish to go through with this."

"With what?"

"Good. That's it exactly. And Louisa. She's been tidying up so she can face her husband later."

"Interesting."

"It makes perfect sense, and I'll meet you back here." She kissed me briskly on the cheek, then went out and toward the back. Michael and Willie and Louisa were waiting on the porch with a brown bag on the floor in front of them.

"Ready?" Willie asked without her usual twist of implication. I moved across the shadowed lawn with my silent escort, arriving at the same time as the others.

Nancy held the door as the rest of us entered, then scooped up the cat to bring along. "We might as well have as many witnesses as we can.

Jeremiah, you sit back in your chair. There's nothing to be afraid of. You're not being roped into anything. A single vow doesn't work that way. Wilhelmina, you do the set-up. Michael, help yourself to wherever you wish. Sit. Stand. Be observant. Listen to the Whisker People. The P.Q.'s—have a spot by the doorway—not like you're trying to keep anyone from escaping, mind you. Louisa, my dear new friend, stand by the version of a writer's table there. I want you to represent yourself, of course, but also the parents Jeremiah knew growing up, and my mother who wishes she could be here but can't."

"She's in on this?"

"Of course. In a sense." There was a low-level meow. "And cat? There's no point telling you anything, but try to stay awake."

Willie placed a single stubby candle—like a votive—on top of the potbelly and handed Nancy a box of kitchen matches before joining Michael near the opening in the floor where Jefferson and Woo had been firing curses at the past earlier.

Nancy lit the candle, waiting for the flame to reach its full height and turned toward me, after asking Lorelei to turn off the outside light. In the darkened halo surrounding the candlelight, the cabin brought other senses into play: the soft fabric of the air, smells of old work and new, of earth and the manufactures of the earth, the presence of unknown hands and the hands of now—hands to be touched, others only to be felt—but reaching toward each other—the printer, the barber, the teacher, the hands of cooking and creating and generating lines of music and lines of brick and board and plant-stuff: a settlement in place and time—Bill Gaussmann's crossroads. I could hear the tips of quince branches fingering the roof above us, intuitive and protective.

And then the voice of Nancy Feller: "My dear friend and lover and fellow learner."

She was looking directly at me, and almost, it seemed, through me. I felt the desire to stand, but the concentration of her eyes and steadiness of her voice kept me in place.

"This has been a day of simple promises made complicated by the doubtful—which included me for a time. I only hope this promise, my promise to you, will be uncomplicated and beyond doubt." She paused. "Not long ago, you and I watched candles floating across a pond with no clear purpose but to find their way to where their beauty would finally extinguish itself. That is my vow to you tonight: to be that floating flame for you, believing that we will find our own way, together somehow, and fulfill our own purpose in knowing each other. I ask for nothing else. I wish for no rules, except the rules of respect and honor. And I ask for nothing in return. My flame is reflected in the water. If need be, it will serve for both, and it will make time into child's play." She paused one last time. "All right?"

I stood and held her and said, "Yes, I do believe it is, but that's the idea, isn't it?"

"Yes, my darling. You make an old teacher proud. And the rest of you?" Lorelei was rubbing her nose on her husband's shirt. Michael was holding Willie, and they rocked together from side to side. Louisa's hand was on the envelope I had dropped on the table, as if she was swearing an oath on it. Her light-blue eyes looked distant but contained inexplicable gratitude. The one comment came from the cat, another shortish mew but not without commitment.

"And, Jeremiah, if you wish to do something practical," Nancy added, "how about naming the cat Quincy, so you're not tempted to call her Raggles. I'm sure P.Q. won't mind."

"Honored," he assured her.

"And if I may," Lorelei added agreeably, "I'd like to say today and tonight have stirred my blood for my handyman. I will be taking him home soon. After the toast."

"Toast," I echoed.

We finally heard the sound of thunder, so far from us it was comforting in the way of a rediscovered blessing. Louisa took Eleanor Jewett's half-full bottle of brandy from the brown bag and handed it to me.

"Yah—a toast?" she asked. The encouragement of Louisa's face and voice, the feelings of the afternoon, the thought of the old woman's deep pockets and her own words after the earlier ceremony, the approach of nighttime rain, all pulled my mind into one of those cushioned moments when expression comes without the clutter of thought.

"Yes, a toast," I agreed, holding the bottle at chin-level between Nancy and myself. "It is the role of the best man to say words about a couple joined. I will be best man without a groom, if Nancy Feller is agreeable." She smiled with pleased encouragement. "I've known this couple, Nancy and Jeremiah, for more than twenty years. I have witnessed the impact they've had on each other in ways they may never fully appreciate—but truly hope they might. They are the children of coincidence—both of them—that turned out to feel like fate, actually. And if anyone tries to tell one from the other, especially this couple themselves, they are doing what is unnecessary and wasting what should be accepted as unexplainable loveliness. So I raise this bottle to Nancy and Jeremiah—her best man—and to whatever awaits them." I took a sip and coughed the cough of inexperience before handing it to her.

"I hope that didn't sound like vows," I told her, my throat a little raspy.

"It was fine," she assured me and took her own sip.

The bottle moved from person to person, ending at Michael, who took a practiced swig before offering his own assessment: "It's way beyond anything else."

Then the scattering: P.Q. and Lorelei to cool their blood, Michael and Willie to my bed, the cat choosing to spend the night with them, Louisa to gather up implements and containers, and elaborating on her decision once we reached her car: that she had been so heartened through witnessing what some would call the wrong kind of love, she wanted to try "the right kind" again with the man who had been asking to come back. She made the quotation marks with two fingers.

Nancy and I spent the night in the shop, bringing cushions and blankets from the house. We sat for a time watching the first candle and then a second one burn themselves out. I became more accomplished at drinking from a brandy bottle. As the storm approached, we cocooned our way into the oneness of shared listening. The small building that had stood almost two centuries of weather threats and the shadowed threats of inexplicable human action, stood as protector of two who engaged in the pleasant task of unsettling down for the night. The intensity of the rain when it finally arrived, caused us to close the door and leave only the narrowest opening at the bottom of the window. We were sealed in, in obedience to the so-called elements but also to our lessoned knowledge of each other. It was certain that night that as much as we had learned of and through one another, being enclosed by the unknown would keep us grateful for who we were. When we left the shop in the morning, we, at the least, knew that much.

POSTLUDE

The envelope from Joanna Wexler contained a notebook with cardboard covers and a typed note from her. In it, she told me the handwritten contents of the notebook was a children's story The Professor had drafted during the days in Maine he mistakenly thought were devoted to my conception. "It is, you'll see, about a boy who searches for what he can never identify. It never went beyond this point, but he thought he would call it 'A Golden Apple.' If you are looking for a small project for your cabin, you might consider bringing this to life." He had included places and ideas for illustrations, which I could see as I flipped through: small boxes with notations like stage directions. She added as a P.S., "If you're looking for an illustrator, Bartlett is a very good watercolorist, and he is good with children." It was too neat to imagine, and I put the notebook back on the card table—where it still rests. During a phone call later that month, she said nothing more about the story; however, without prompting, she told me that I had been conceived in a real bed, in her apartment, during a weekend furlough of the kind finally granted to Bartlett and other nonviolent offenders. It was, she added deftly, a liberalization of the New York penal system Alban Curtin had fought for over many years, writing letters to newspapers, state legislators, clergymen, and others who might help the cause. He was, she added, ebullient when the new policy went into effect.

Michael started art school in Boston during the fourth week of August with Nancy and Willie taking him and what his mother described as his "pitifully few" things. Fortunately, her guilt was offset by her certainty that he had more common sense than the rest of us and that even Marvin would come around to her point of view eventually—a first for him. I have missed Michael since the day he left. While he wasn't an everyday part of my life over those first months in Quaker Falls, it felt that way. He had been there much of the time, and his presence was constant in projects that grew around me like the nod of a genie. The boy who wouldn't write for me had become a young man who, in his own peculiar way, knew he owed me that, as if he had banked it like a memory from the future. Willie thinks it quite possible they will eventually marry and have children—and fears their offspring will be so normal she won't know what to do with them. He had created a coop with six barred rock hens before he left. Willie comes to be sisterly, to check on his chickens, and bring their brown eggs back to her friends. Michael had, however, warned her to watch for copperheads, who have an apparent fondness for coops with eggs. She acted as if this were a fact I had known already. I hadn't.

The three transgressors found a house in Woodstock where they assume people won't think twice about what they are and how they manage things. It is, Jefferson tells me, a place so high on reputation and whatever else, that it is the snootiest patch of indifference ever created by man. According to Richard Woo, grateful to be chair of English rather than Religion, Mikhail's first class of the semester was held on the great lawn where the geese dare not tread and featured a black lamb he borrowed from an area farmer. One can only imagine. Emily continues to believe in the healing force of unrestrained caring and trusts her parents will find their way back soon after what she calls "a vacation away from" her and her new partnership. The less traditional of Barbara Lynn's blog sites has been quoted by commentators of all political persuasions, and she calls herself "the frosted pop-tart of disapproval." Her other site has won praise for articulating attitudes that will keep Americans free and Christian. She admits that, of the two, she enjoys writing the second more than the first, referring to her alter-persona as the Good Girl of Gritsville.

As for others, Sara Sampson evidently found such a special delivery in the mail guy, she's applied to the postal system for employment. According to Taylor, she's temporarily committed to driving one of those "darling little trucks" in the future. Meanwhile, he, too, is providing her a place to stay. So apparently, Hamilton Graham is off the hook for now. Eleanor Jewett suddenly proclaimed she would not continue as a second-floor recluse and persuaded Mrs. Clemmons to give up her spooky fixation on the apartment across from where I lived and let Eleanor be the next to die there—in bed hopefully. Hamilton, Willie, and I helped her make her move downward, and she had me purchase a porch rocker that would sit outside of her living room window and be for her use alone, if she could find a way to enforce her edict. As she sat in it for the first time, she rocked with the pleasure of a small child and asked me once more what that tower thing was she had seen on her initial ride to Quaker Falls. When I told her "limekiln," for smelting, she nodded with thoughtful appreciation and said if she were younger, she'd like to own one for hosting smelting parties of her own—one to make Satan sorry he hasn't been better-mannered. I am told a brother-warming is still in the works.

Louisa Sondstrom and her teenage daughter did welcome husband and father back, and I often wonder if she is able to speak with him of her times at Quaker Falls and what she saw there. I found the *Girl with a Pearl Earring* in my dining room on the morning of the eighteenth, and it was immediately clear who had brought it. Louisa told me when we talked later that she had taken it from Alban Curtin's bedroom when she came to remove the dining room furniture and kitchen things from his house. She had grown to *feel* its presence during his dying weeks and had developed a belief it had something of her own younger self in it. I still wonder how much more she has realized about The Professor than I ever will.

Uncle Teddy made it known he wishes to come to Quaker Falls for a month or so to reconstruct Yankee gutters with skills he learned from his brother-in-law. I apparently passed the down-the-well test as adroitly as I could have wished. Before he does, I will learn to scramble about the roof with a large paintbrush, re-silvering the patched and pitted metal. The house, at least, will have its head on right before winter comes.

I heard from Ellen on the last day of August, an e-mail affirming the end of summer and hoping the event in my yard came off as I had hoped. I thought often about the fact of her living and writing in Maine, of the possibility that she returned to where she had known my no-longer grandparents, had met my no-longer father, who had himself gone there to be too late to conceive me. That Ellen might be writing of improbabilities in the same cabin where Joanna Wexler had brought her prisoner-inseminated egg to him was a good point at which to give up further speculation, but it was all enough to tie my Topsy-world in pigtails. I wrote back to her to say I had found enough newness in August to make me wish to see her again. I meant it. She wrote back later the same day to tell me she had read through *Reconsiderations*, and while she declined to comment on it specifically, she directed me to a piece on Jonathan Swift that Alban Curtin had written several years after I "came into being" (as she put it): "How ludicrous," he had written, "is that which we see all too well, and how monstrous is that which we are forbidden to see at all. Partial wisdom resides in our being entitled never to feel the full realization of both." She guessed that *Reconsiderations* might have been written at about the same time and that, perhaps, he "did know."

Nancy, meanwhile, remains true to her vows. She continues to remind me only to fantasize about what we have, inward-moving fantasies concerning how we have come to be woven together. That we love each other, I continue to learn, is almost coincidental to knowing each other. She talks about teaching again but worries about coming off like Mary Jan Otto (who still hasn't closed the deal with Marvin), eager for new beginnings but past some measure of prime. And, as she reminds me, a first-grade teacher doesn't just say she wants to teach again after a long period of selling condos to those who never seem quite satisfied with who and where they are. She half jokes that college teaching looks like an easier gig anyhow. Probably she's right—making it all the easier to resist its call.

§

It is September, a cool and misty day, allowing me to create my first fire in the potbelly. Bill delivered on his promise of a stump for splitting firewood into smaller pieces, and I purchased a maul from the Crispins, discovering it to be a persuasive-looking wedge on the end of a maple handle. I was awkward with the tool at first, but my aim has improved, and I'm now able to pop pieces apart with every second or third swing. Several dozen chunks are stacked together in one small pile near the cutout square in the floor, screwed back into place for now. It remains an appropriate waiting place. The storied dining room chair has been returned to the house, and I'm sitting in the Gaussmanns' lawn chair, which I will soon return to them. It has, for now, a comfort I'd like to hold onto a short time longer.

There is little else in the room, although so much has happened here it feels there should be more. But, once again, not for now. The card table is in front of the window I've left closed for this day. I jammed a makeshift bookshelf between two vertical joists. On it are four objects: *Riff and Raggles*, an inscribed copy of *Reconsiderations*, a book on area railroads, and the two barely attached covers I brought up from under the floor. The latter is the one I feel most compelled to read, though I don't have the language for it yet. The mirror Nancy brought me is on the wall perpendicular to the door. I will move it to the house when the time is right, but for now it reflects the motion of my leaving or entering the shop. It also reflects an object on the opposite wall: the *Girl with a Pearl Earring*. Louisa brought it to me, she said, so it could keep an eye on me when I needed watching. And she is right: the Girl is a careful but unobtrusive watcher, and I am glad for her company and any hints about departure she might choose to reveal. Next to it is

Lucille's promised needlepoint—also in this space for now. It depicts a mop-haired boy propped against a pumpkin larger than himself, reading an unnamed book. His concentration is complete, the stitching of his eyes showing how lost he is to time, but not to the fingers of the artist.

Today, with the fire popping to itself inside the cast iron, I am doing what I often do out here. Very little. For now, it is a place to be—to learn—and feel grateful that I can wait. I think of beginning to research the stories connected to this small structure—those who built it and worked in it and guided lives through here. But I'm not quite prepared for their narratives yet, as much as I can feel their presence on a day like this, with quince branches stroking the roof once again. As Bill Gaussmann says, it's a big responsibility, this holding of stories in one's heart and mind. I think of finding more about Alban Curtin, since there is still so much to know, and especially since my curiosity seems finally buoyed by compassion for him. Again, though, I find an ever stronger need—that of waiting.

The stove, I discover, tells its own tales: brief cracklings that intermingle and give way to others. Counterpoint. I think of Ellen's telling me in my childhood how the Curtins of two generations ago gave her the idea that acting was connected intimately to the glory of risking one's soul. I hardly think that is what I am doing now—but perhaps one has to know something of it before risking it. And enlightenment, I think I have learned so far, does not come as sudden illumination. As Eleanor might suggest, it comes like a collapse of walls on a fog-encased morning such as this one. It is done in time-lapse and is a gradual adjustment, bringing the realization that proclamations of enlightenment are what blow the Buddha's belly to an unhealthy size. But, at least, within the woman who taught first grade and one of her more precocious pupils, in this enclosed space the walls are down, the air is being renewed, our arms are outstretched, and where we stand gladdens us. If there is more, it is worth waiting for; if not, we will need the strength to teach ourselves what that may mean. In any event, I look forward, and I may, in my day, attempt to tell stories about it, once my summer session has finally concluded. First, though, I have a piece of green stationery and a stamped envelope. I will try sending an emancipation note to Nancy Feller. If that is pleasing to her, who knows what I might attempt next?

ACKNOWLEDGMENT

Currencies of August began its literary life several years ago as a play. It was called *An Elementary Education*, and it brought Nancy and Jeremiah into existence. It also included Michael and Willie in their puppyhood. For the four actors who created those roles—Barbara, Jay, Tom, and Diana—thank you again from well in the future. For Lois Gamlin, who was my actual (and adored) first grade teacher and for seventh grade teacher Barbara Heffernan, whose voice I stole for Nancy, your impact has continued over many decades.

For those who have been my stalwart guides through the totally misnamed world of "independent" publishing, you have been invaluable. Christi Sheehan, a one-time student, has become my mentor. Christine Keleny, of CK Books Publishing, has been exacting in the best sense of the word, as well as unfailingly patient and kind. Thanks, too, for the fresh perspectives of Stephanie and Nick.

A 2011 book by William P. Mc Dermott, *Railroads Dutchess County, NY: 1848-1907* helped spur my imagining of a similar work from earlier times. It was published by Kerleen Press.

I am grateful to Rose, who kept me, as best she could, tethered to reality. To my grandchildren Gianna and Tristan, my next book—a very short one—will be dedicated to you. Colleagues and students (perhaps 10,000 of you), I thank you for what you've taught me, even as we worked to make sense of each other. It is one more form of currency we must learn how to value.

ABOUT THE AUTHOR

I first experienced the pleasant push of story-telling when I was six or seven years old. Most often, the narratives took the form of oral tales told serially to a small group of friends on the front step of my house in Rochester, New York. The episodes were impromptu; and, as I like to imagine, they were spun out at the requests of others looking to liven up a lazy summer afternoon. There were also neighborhood puppet shows and "adventures" along railroad tracks and the Genesee River. A host of ways to create stories.

There were books to be read as well. As I grew into my teens, I believed longer books to be the most satisfying—and most given to adventure. Finding *Gone with the Wind* in my parents' bookcase with its glass doors was a discovery I could say "wow" to. And I did. I moved into Tara. Then came other longish writers like Thomas Wolf, Leon Uris, Herman Wouk, and Boris Pasternak, mostly thanks to a convenience of that time called the Book of the Month Club: chubby novels delivered on a regular basis.

When I began teaching, I had the idealistic belief that my students would also care for long works. I offered for their pleasure selections like Don Quixote, David Copperfield, and Moby Dick. And, yes, once... War and Peace. I knew Cliff Notes and Spark Notes existed, but with my greenish exuberance, I never thought my students would yield to such temptations. Silly me.

And now I've produced a relatively lengthy novel of my own, for your pleasure. I know it's not really the thing to do today, but I would point out that it is a mere one-quarter the length of War and Peace. All things are relative, after all. When I asked the youthful academic Jeremiah Curtin how he would feel about being the narrator of an extended piece of fiction, he felt he had the stamina for it. He did warn, however, that as a devoted reader of eighteenth-century tale-tellers like Henry Fielding, he might at moments wish to speak directly to the reader of *Currencies of August*. Moreover, he might succumb to an occasional digression. He did think such diversions could prove beneficial and might provide a chance to breathe and reflect for all involved.

The fact that you have made it to this point would suggest to me, at least, that you have survived the challenges laid before you. And without Spark Notes. It is my sincere hope, of course, that you are feeling more than a sense of survival right now. I would be very grateful to hear your thoughts. You should feel free to email me at the following: donald.anderson@marist.edu. We can also connect on facebook: Donald-R-Anderson or on my website: drandersonsite.wordpress.com. Or leave a review on a web-site. A sequel is a possibility. But I wouldn't dare go on without a word of encouragement from you.

CPSIA information can be obtained
at www.ICGtesting.com
Printed in the USA
BVOW03s0237190917
495268BV00001B/72/P

9 780983 298458